Hand in Hand Collection

MICHELLE REID and ABBY GREEN

POWER

May 2012

JANE PORTER and CAITLIN CREWS

INFAMOUS

June 2012

PENNY JORDAN and INDIA GREY

SECRETS

July 2012

EMMA DARCY and MELANIE MILBURNE

NOTORIOUS

August 2012

LYNNE GRAHAM and MAISEY YATES

POSSESSION

September 2012

SHARON KENDRICK and JENNIE LUCAS

PRICELESS

October 2012

PENNY JORDAN
and INDIA GREY

SECRETS

MILLS & BOON

Mills & Boon, an imprint of Harlequin (UK) Limited,
Eton House, 18-24 Paradise Road, Richmond, Surrey TW9 1SR

SECRETS © Harlequin Enterprises II B.V./S.à.r.l. 2012

One Night in His Arms © Penny Jordan 1998
Taken for Revenge, Bedded for Pleasure © India Grey 2008

ISBN: 978 0 263 89782 1

011-0712

Harlequin (UK) policy is to use papers that are natural, renewable and recyclable products and made from wood grown in sustainable forests. The logging and manufacturing processes conform to the legal environmental regulations of the country of origin.

Printed and bound in Spain
by Blackprint CPI, Barcelona

ONE NIGHT
IN HIS ARMS

PENNY JORDAN

Penny Jordan is one of Mills & Boon's most popular authors. Sadly, Penny died from cancer on 31st December 2011, aged sixty-five. She leaves an outstanding legacy, having sold over a hundred million books around the world. She wrote a total of one hundred and eight-seven novels for Mills & Boon, including the phenomenally successful *A Perfect Family, To Love, Honour & Betray, The Perfect Sinner* and *Power Play,* which hit the *Sunday Times* and *New York Times* bestseller lists. Loved for her distinctive voice, her success was in part because she continually broke boundaries and evolved her writing to keep up with readers' changing tastes. *Publishers Weekly* said about Jordan: "Women everywhere will find pieces of themselves in Jordan's characters", and this perhaps explains her enduring appeal.

Although Penny was born in Preston, Lancashire, and spent her childhood there, she moved to Cheshire as a teenager and continued to live there for the rest of her life. Following the death of her husband she moved to the small traditional Cheshire market town on which she based her much-loved Crighton books.

Penny was a member and supporter of the Romantic Novelists' Association and the Romance Writers of America—two organisations dedicated to providing support for both published and yet-to-be published authors. Her significant contribution to women's fiction was recognised in 2011, when the Romantic Novelists' Association presented Penny with a Lifetime Achievement Award.

Look out for Penny's last books: *The Price of Royal Duty* launched the new continuity THE SANTINA CROWN and was available in May 2012, and her final original novel, *A Secret Disgrace,* became available in June 2012.

Dear Reader,

It is such a pleasure for me to have one of my books linked to a book—*Taken for Revenge, Bedded for Pleasure*—by fellow author India Grey. I love her books so much for their fresh, zesty approach, and for the special emotional intensity she brings to her writing, and I know that you will enjoy reading this book every bit as much as I did. She has such a wonderful and naturally talented writing voice and such an instinctive sense of what readers look for in Modern™ romance books.

I have to admit, though, that there is another reason for having a very special place on my bookshelves for India Grey's books. She and I were members of the same writing group and, after reading her work I encouraged her, indeed bullied her almost, into sending her manuscript in to Mills & Boon. I should also admit here that when I read those opening pages, I became involved with her characters so immediately that I felt rather envious of her talent. However, happily there is room in the Mills & Boon "stable" for a wide variety of authors, each with their own distinctive voice, and it is both a pleasure and a privilege for me to have my book partnered with hers.

Happy reading to you all.

Penny Jordan

NB

Penny wrote this letter just a few weeks before she passed away.—Ed.

PROLOGUE

'WHAT the hell are you doing, Sylvie? Just what kind of game are you playing now?' Ran demanded angrily as he removed her hands, releasing her fingers from his shirt where she had unconsciously curled them in her attempt to get him to listen to what she wanted to say, to understand that she was no longer a child, that she was now completely and totally a woman…a woman who loved and wanted him.

'Ran, this isn't a *game*,' she protested, her eyes starting to fill with anguished tears as he thrust her away. 'I want—'

'Oh, I know exactly what you want, Sylvie,' he interrupted her savagely. 'You want me to take you to bed. But right now what I feel more like doing—'He broke off, said something she couldn't quite catch under his breath and then turned to look at her so that the light fell sharply across his face, outlining the aristocratic arrogance of his profile.

'Your stepbrother is one of my closest friends and my employer and—'

'This doesn't have anything to do with *Alex*,' Sylvie protested frantically. 'This is just between you and me, Ran.'

'You and me? There is no *you and me*,' he told her cruelly. 'You are just a schoolgirl, Sylvie, whilst I am a fully adult man.'

'But Ran, I love you,' Sylvie pleaded desperately,

throwing everything she had left into one last attempt to make him see how she felt.

'Really?' Ran drawled mockingly. 'How much? As much as the pop star you were ready to die for six months ago, or the pony you wanted three months before that?'

'That was before I was properly grown up,' Sylvie told him.

So very little space separated them—a few feet…that was all. If she let him walk away from her now without at least trying…

Boldly she closed the distance between them, taking him off guard as she placed her body close to his and wrapped her arms possessively around him, possessively and far too tightly for him to remove them as he had done so easily a few moments ago.

'Ran…' She pleaded with him, lifting her face to him, her mouth trembling. 'Ran, please…'

She felt something that could have been a shudder galvanise his body before clumsily and inexpertly she pressed her mouth against his in a closed-lipped, untutored kiss.

His mouth felt hard and hot, his skin where he had shaved thrillingly rough against her own. Fireworks ignited and exploded deep within her body; her heart was beating so fast she thought she might die of the excitement.

'Ran,' she moaned passionately against his mouth as she twisted with innocent provocation against his body.

Suddenly his own arms were around her, not pushing her away as he had done earlier, but holding onto her, his fingers biting hard into her slender arms as he slid one hand into the back of her hair, holding her head still whilst his mouth started to move on hers.

Sylvie felt her head start to spin and her knees go weak.

If she had thought that her heart was beating fast before, that was nothing to the way it was pounding now. Her whole body ached and pulsed with the intoxication of what was happening.

Ran! Ran! Ran!

She loved him so much, *wanted* him so much. Eagerly she pressed her still coltishly youthful body even closer to his. She could feel every nerve-ending in her skin aching with the intensity of her yearning for him.

The tip of his tongue was caressing the softly swollen outline of her mouth.

She wanted him to make love to her so desperately. These last few weeks, whilst they had been working together clearing the overgrown stagnant lake in the woods on her stepbrother's estate, working on a conservation project which Ran, as her stepbrother's estate manager, had been overseeing, she had come to see him in a new light and in doing so had fallen head over heels in love with him, with all the passion and intensity of her seventeen-year-old nature.

And now, after the corrosive hurt of all his recent rebuffs, all his painful rejections of her attempts to make him realise how she felt, here he was holding her, kissing her...wanting her...

A fiercely sharp thrill of feminine excitement spun through her. Her breasts ached for the touch of his hands, to be held and caressed by him as she had read about, seen in films. The thought of their two naked bodies entwined in the sensual privacy of Ran's bed was almost too much for her. Eagerly she opened her mouth, inviting him to probe deeper with his tongue, but then abruptly, to her shock, Ran was suddenly pushing her away as quickly as he had taken hold of her, his face dark with anger.

'Ran, wh-what is it…what's wrong?' she stammered.

'What's wrong? Oh, for God's sake…' she heard him mutter. 'The fact that you even need to ask that kind of question shows just how… You're a child still, Sylvie… Six months from now…'

She bit down hard on her bottom lip when she saw the irritation in his eyes as he ran his hand through his thick dark copper hair.

'I'm sorry… I should never have done that…' he told her tersely.

Sylvie felt her eyes fill with vulnerable tears.

'You kissed me,' she protested shakily. 'You wanted me…'

'No, Sylvie,' she heard Ran telling her grittily. 'What I wanted,' he told her bluntly, 'was not you, but what you offered. I'm a man, and when a woman comes on to me, offering me sex…' He stopped and shook his head. 'You're a child still, Sylvie.'

'I bet if we were in bed together you wouldn't be saying that,' Sylvie challenged him boldly, adding recklessly, 'I'm not a child at all, Ran, and I could prove it to you…'

She heard the savage hiss as he expelled the air from his lungs.

'Dear God,' she heard him rasp, 'have you the first idea of what you're saying…*suggesting*…?'

'I want you, Ran… I love you…'

'Well, I sure as hell don't want or love you,' he told

her ferociously, his face suddenly shockingly pale underneath its weather-beaten tan. 'And let me give you a small warning, Sylvie: if you continue to go around offering yourself to men, sooner or later one of them's going to take you up on your offer and I promise you that the experience won't be a pleasant one. You're far too young to be experimenting with sex, and when you are old enough it should be with someone of your own age and not... I'm a man, not a boy, Sylvie,' he told her brutally, 'and...well, let's just say that the idea of taking some over-excited and inexperienced little virgin to bed and playing touchy-feely games with her is not my idea of a particularly satisfying relationship—not sexually, not mentally and certainly not emotionally...

'Go and find someone your own age to play with, Sylvie,' he told her grimly.

For a moment Sylvie was tempted to protest, to argue and plead, or even more daringly to throw herself back into his arms and prove to him that she could *make* him want her despite her age and her lack of experience. She was not normally so easily defeated or diminished, but something deep down inside, some very new sense of womanliness, shrank from enduring another rejection from him. And so, instead, swallowing back the tears she was aching to cry, she lifted her head and, tilting her chin to him defiantly, said, 'Yes, I think I will...'

There had been one boy in particular in the party of co-workers involved in the conservation campaign who had shown a very marked interest in her. At the time, newly, wildly in love with Ran, she hadn't paid him very much attention, but now...

A militant sparkle illuminated her eyes. She could see Ran beginning to frown.

'Sylvie,' he warned. Angrily she refused to stop and listen to him, he had no jurisdiction over her.

The bright delicacy of her newly emergent tender love was already tarnishing and fading as resentment, pride and enmity took its place.

Ran!

She loved him but now she felt as though she could very easily come to hate him—she certainly *wanted* to hate him.

CHAPTER ONE

'YOU'RE not serious...'

Sylvie frowned as she studied the synopsis pinned to the front of the file her employer had just handed her.

Lloyd Kelmer the fourth was the kind of eccentric billionaire who, by rights, only ought to have existed in fairy stories—as a particularly genial and indulgent godfather, Sylvie thought. She had been introduced to him at a party to which she had been invited by some acquaintances of her stepbrother's. She had only gone to the party because she had been feeling particularly lost and insignificant, having only recently left her American college and moved to New York. They had got chatting and Lloyd had begun to tell her about the trials and traumas he had experienced in running the huge wealthy Trust set up by his grandfather.

'The old man had this thing about stately homes, I guess I kinda feel the same. He owned a fair handful of the things himself, so he kinda had a taste for them, if you know what I mean. There was the plantation down in Carolina and then a couple of châteaux in France and a *palazzo* in Venice, so it just kinda happened naturally that he should have this idea of using his millions to preserve and protect big houses, and now the Trust has a whole skew of them all over the world, and more wanting to have the Trust bankroll them every day.'

Sylvie, with her own admittedly second-hand experience of her stepbrother's problems in running and financing his own large family estate in England, had quite naturally been very interested in what Lloyd had had to say, but it had still surprised her a few days later to receive not just a telephone call from him but the offer of a job as his personal assistant.

Sylvie wasn't seventeen any longer, nor was she the naive and perhaps over-protected girl she had once been. Lloyd might be in his early sixties and might, so far, not have done or said anything to suggest that he had any ulterior motive whatsoever in making contact with her, but nevertheless, having asked him for time to consider his unexpected offer, the first thing Sylvia had done was telephone her stepbrother in England and ask for his advice.

An unscheduled and unfortunately brief visit from Alex and his wife Mollie to vet Lloyd and talk over the situation with Sylvie had resulted in her deciding to take the job, a decision which, twelve months down the line, she regularly paused to congratulate herself on making, or at least she had done until now.

Her work was varied and fascinating, and barely left her with any time to draw breath, never mind for any personal relationships with members of the opposite sex, but that didn't worry Sylvie. So far, what she had learned from her experiences with men was that she was a particularly poor judge of the breed. First there had been her revoltingly humiliating teenage crush on Ran and his rejection of her, then there had been the appalling danger she had put herself and her family in with her foolish involvement with Wayne.

She and Wayne might never have been lovers but she had known, from the first, of his involvement in the drug scene and, as foolishly as she had tried to convince herself that Ran would fall in love with her, she had also tried to convince herself that Wayne was simply a lost soul in need of protecting and saving.

She had been wrong on both counts. Love was the last emotion Ran had ever felt for her. And as for Wayne... Well, thankfully he was now safely out of her life.

Her new job took every minute of her time and every ounce of her energy. Each new property the Trust decided to 'adopt' had to be inspected, vetted and then painstakingly brought up to the same standard as all the other properties the Trust financed and opened to the general public.

Sylvie knew that her employer's highly individualistic and personalised way of deciding which of the multitude of properties he was offered as potential new additions to the Trust's portfolio were worth acquiring caused other organisations to eye him slightly askance. For Lloyd to accept a house it had to have what he described as the 'right feel', but his eccentricities tended to make Sylvie feel almost maternally protective of him.

Or at least they had until now.

To return from a six-week trip to Prague, where she had been supervising the takeover of a particularly beautiful if horrendously run-down eighteenth-century palace they had recently added to their acquisitions, to discover that in her absence Lloyd had made yet another acquisition in the form of Haverton Hall, a huge neoclassical building set in its own parkland in Derbyshire, had caused her heart to sink into her shoes.

'But Sylvie, this place is a gem, a perfect example of English neoclassicism,' she could hear Lloyd protesting as he studied her stubborn expression. 'I promise you,

you'll love it. I've had Gena book you onto the day after tomorrow's Concorde flight for London. I thought you'd be pleased. You were only complaining way back in the spring how much you wanted to spend more time with your stepbrother and his wife and their son…

'This house… Did I tell you, by the way, that the guy who inherited it just happens to know your stepbrother and that's how he'd got to hear about us? It seems that he was telling your stepbrother about the problems he was experiencing, having unexpectedly inherited this place, and Alex suggested that he should get in touch with me… I wasn't too sure at first. After all, we've already got that pretty little Georgian place down near Brighton, but, well, I kinda felt I owed it to Alex, so I flew over to Britain and went to have a look.'

Sylvie closed her eyes as she listened to Lloyd extolling the virtues of Haverton Hall.

How could she admit to him that it wasn't so much the house itself she objected to as its *owner*?

Its owner…

There it was on the front page of the report… Haverton Hall… Owner… Sir Ranulf Carrington. *Sir* Ranulf now, not just Ran any longer… Not that Sylvie was impressed by a title. How could she be when her own stepbrother was an earl?

She had known all about Ran's unexpected inheritance of course. It had been the subject of a good deal of discussion at Christmas, when she had gone home, not least because Ran, with an estate of his own to run, quite naturally could no longer run her stepbrother's.

No one, least of all Ran himself, had expected that he would inherit. After all, his cousin had only been in his early forties and had seemed perfectly fit. The last thing anyone imagined was that he would suffer a fatal heart attack.

Sylvie had smiled politely, but without interest. The last thing, the last *person* she wanted to waste time talking about was Ran.

Her memories of the way he had rejected her might have been carefully and very deeply buried but...but every time she returned to her brother's home she was painfully reminded of her seventeen-year-old self and her vulnerability.

No question about it, she must have annoyed and aggravated Ran with her unwanted adoration, but surely he could have handled the situation and her a little more gently, let her down a bit more caringly instead of...

Sylvie was aware that Lloyd was watching her expectantly. How could she, as her instincts urged her to do, totally and flatly refuse to have anything to do with Ran? She couldn't. She was a woman now, a woman who prided herself on her professionalism, a woman who along with her outward New York shine and gloss had also developed an inner self-worth and determination. She loved her work and she truly believed that what Lloyd and the Trust were doing was extremely worthwhile.

Secretly, there was nothing she enjoyed more than watching the houses that Lloyd rescued from their often pitiful state of decay being restored to their former glory... Perhaps it was idealistic and, yes, even foolishly romantic of her, but there was something about watching the process, of seeing these once grand homes rising phoenix-like from the ashes of their own neglect, that touched a chord within her. She could well understand what motivated Lloyd, and she suspected that, ironically,

it had been that long-ago conservation scheme she had
worked on under Ran's supervision which had awakened
within her the awareness of how very important it was
to preserve and care for—to *protect*—a landscape and
its architecture, which had ultimately led to her sharing
Lloyd's passion for their task.

However, Sylvie's responsibility as an employee of
the Trust included a duty not just to share Lloyd's enthusiasm but to make sure as well that the Trust's acquisitions were funded and run in a businesslike manner,
and that the Trust's money was used shrewdly and
wisely and not wasted or squandered—a responsibility
which Sylvie took very seriously. No project, and certainly no bill, was too small for Sylvie to break down
and scrutinise very carefully indeed, a fact which caused
the Trust's accountants to comment approvingly on her
attention to detail and her excellent bookkeeping.

It had been pointless for Lloyd to protest when they
had been renovating the Venetian *palazzo* that he preferred the red silk to the gold which Sylvie had favoured.

'Red is almost twice as expensive,' she had pointed
out sternly, adding as a clincher, 'And besides, the records we've managed to trace all indicate that this room
was originally decorated in gold and hung with gold
drapes…'

'Then gold it is, then.' Lloyd had given in with a sigh,
but Sylvie had been the one who had been forced to give
in to him a few weeks later when, on their departure
from Venice, Lloyd had presented her with a set of the
most exquisite and expensive leather luggage crafted as
only the Italians could craft leather.

'Lloyd, I can't possibly accept this,' Sylvie had protested with a small gasp.

'Why not? It *is* your birthday, isn't it?' Lloyd had countered, and of course he had been right, and ultimately Sylvie had given in.

Although, as she had told her stepbrother defensively at Christmas when Mollie had marvelled enviously at the luggage, 'I didn't *want* to accept it but Lloyd would have been hurt if I hadn't.' She'd added worriedly, 'Alex, do you think I should have refused...? If you...'

'Sylvie, the luggage is beautiful and you did the right thing to accept it,' Alex had reassured her gently. 'Stop worrying, little one,' he had commanded her.

'Little one'! Only Alex ever called her that, and it made her feel so...so protected and safe.

Protected and safe? She was an adult, a woman, for heaven's sake, and more than capable of protecting herself, of keeping herself safe. Irritably she dragged her attention back to the file she was holding.

'You don't approve, do you?' Lloyd demanded, shaking his head ruefully. 'Just wait until you see it, though, Sylvie. You'll love it. It's a perfect example of...'

'We're already very close to the limit of this year's budget,' Sylvie warned him sternly, 'and—'

'So what? We'll just have to increase this year's funding,' Lloyd told her with typical laid-back geniality.

'Lloyd,' Sylvie protested, 'you're talking about an increase of heaven alone knows how many million dollars... The Trust...'

'I *am* the Trust,' Lloyd reminded her gently, and Sylvie had to acknowledge that he spoke the truth. Even so, she gave him an ironic look to which he responded by informing her loftily, 'I'm just doing what I know the old man would have wanted me to do...'

'By buying a decaying neoclassical pile in the middle of Derbyshire?' Sylvie asked him dryly.

And she was still shaking her head as Lloyd told her winningly, 'You'll love it, Sylvie...I promise you!'

Cravenly Sylvie was tempted to tell him that she was far too busy and that he would have to find someone else to take charge of this particular project, but her pride—the same pride which had kept her going, kept her head held high and her spirit strong through Ran's rejection of her and everything that had followed—refused to allow her to do so.

This time she and Ran would be meeting on equal ground—as adults—and this time...this time...

This time what? This time she wasn't going to let him hurt her. This time her attitude towards him would be cool, distant and totally businesslike.

This time...

Sylvie closed her eyes as she felt the tiny shivers of apprehension icing down her spine. The last time she had seen Ran had been when he had unexpectedly turned up at the airport three years ago when she had been leaving England to finish her degree course in America. She could still remember the shock it had given her to see him there, the shock and the sharply sweet surge of helpless pleasure and longing.

She had still been so vulnerable and naive then, a part of her still hoping that maybe, just maybe, he had changed his mind...his heart... But of course he had not. He had been there simply to assure himself that she was actually leaving the country and his life.

Alex knew, of course, that she had once had a foolish adolescent crush on his friend and employee but, thankfully, that was all he did know; thankfully, he had no

knowledge of that shaming and searingly painful, never
to be thought about, never mind talked about incident
that had taken place when she had still been at university
in England.

No one knew about that. Only she and Ran. But that
was all in the past now, and she was determined that
this time when she and Ran met, as meet they would
surely have to, *she* would be the one who would have
the upper hand and he would be the one who would be
the supplicant; she would have the power to deny and
refuse him what he wanted and he would have to beg
and plead with her.

Immediately Sylvie opened her eyes. What on earth
had got into her? That kind of warped, vengeful thinking
was, to her mind, as foolish and adolescent as her youthful infatuation with Ran had been. She was above all
that kind of thing. She *had* to be; her job demanded it.
No, she would make no distinction between Ran and all
the other clients she had had to deal with. The fact that
Ran had once cruelly and uncaringly turned down her
pleas for his love, for his *lovemaking*, the fact that he
had once rejected and demeaned her, would make no
difference to the way she treated him. She *was* above
all that kind of small-mindedness. Proudly she lifted her
head as she continued to listen to Lloyd enthusiastically
telling her the virtues of his latest 'find'.

Ran stared grimly around the unfurnished, dusty and
cobweb-festooned hallway of Haverton Hall. The smell
of neglect and the much more ominous dry rot hung
malodorously on the still, late afternoon air. The large
room, in common with the rest of the Hall, had a desolate, down-at-heel air of weariness which reminded him

uncomfortably of the elderly great-uncle who had owned
the property when Ran was growing up. Visits to see
him had been something which Ran had always dreaded
and, ironically, he could remember how relieved he had
been to discover that it was not he but an older cousin
who would ultimately inherit the responsibility for the
vast, empty, neglected house.

But now that cousin was dead and he, Ran, was
Haverton's owner, or at least he had been until a week
or so ago, when he had finally and thankfully signed the
papers which would convey legal ownership of Haverton
and all the problems that went with it into the hands of
Lloyd Kelmer.

His initial reaction when he had unexpectedly and un-
wontedly inherited the place had been to make enquiries
to see if any of the British trusts could be persuaded to
take it over, but, as their representatives had quickly and
wryly explained, the trusts were awash with unwanted
properties and deluged with despairing owners wanting
them to take on even more.

Faced with the prospect of having to stand aside and
watch as the house and its lands fell into an even greater
state of decay, Ran hadn't known what on earth he was
going to do—his inheritance had been the house and the
land; there hadn't been any money to leave for its upkeep—and then Alex had happened to mention the existence of an eccentric American billionaire whose main
vocation and purpose in life was the buying up and restoring of old properties which he then opened to the
public, and Ran had lost no time in getting in touch with
him.

To his relief Lloyd had flown over to England to view
the house and promptly declared that he loved it.

That relief had turned to something very different, though, when he had received a fax from Lloyd advising him that his assistant, Ms Sylvie Bennett, would be flying over to Britain to act as his representative over the repair and renovation of the property. He could, of course, have simply chosen to turn his back, walk away, and leave someone else to liaise with Sylvie, but Ran wasn't like that. If he had a job to do he preferred to see it through for himself, no matter how unwanted or potentially problematic that task might be.

Potentially problematic! A bitter half-smile curled his mouth. There was nothing *potential* about the problems that Sylvie was likely to cause him… Nothing potential at all.

He had heard scraps of news about her over the years, of course, mainly from Alex and Mollie. Sylvie had completed her degree course and majored summa cum laude… Sylvie was living in New York and looking for a job… Sylvie had got a job… Sylvie was working in Venice… In Rome… In Prague… Sylvie… Sylvie… Sylvie…

Alex and Mollie weren't his only sources of information, though. Only the previous winter in London, Ran had unexpectedly bumped into Sylvie's mother, Alex's stepmother, predictably just outside Harvey Nichols.

Belinda had gushed enthusiastically over his recent elevation to the peerage. She had always been the most appalling snob and Ran could still remember how bitterly she had opposed Alex's request to her after his father had died that Sylvie be allowed to stay on at Otel Place with him instead of being sent to boarding school.

'Sylvie cannot possibly live with you, Alex,' she had

told him sharply. 'For one thing it simply wouldn't be proper. There is, after all, no blood relationship between you. And for another... Sylvie has been spending far too much time with the wrong sort of people.'

Ran, who had been standing outside Alex's library whilst this conversation had been taking place, had turned round and been about to walk away when, to his disgust, he had suddenly heard his own name mentioned. Alex had demanded of his stepmother, 'What wrong sort of people...?'

'Well, Ran for a start... Oh, I know you count him as one of your friends, but he's still merely an employee and—'

Alex had immediately exploded, informing his stepmother, much to Ran's chagrin, 'Ran *is* a friend and, as for anything else, he happens to be far better born than either you or I.'

'Really?' had come back the acid retort. 'He might be better *born*, Alex, but he still doesn't have any money. Sylvie is very much in danger of developing the sort of crush on him that could totally ruin her reputation if she's to make the right sort of marriage.'

'"The right sort of marriage"?' Alex had retorted angrily. 'For heaven's sake, what century are you living in...?'

'Sylvie is my daughter and there's no way I want her mixing with the estate workers...and that includes Ran... And whilst we're on the subject, Alex, I really do think that as Sylvie's stepbrother you do have a responsibility to her to protect her from unsuitable...friendships...'

Ran could still remember how bitterly, *furiously* angry he had been, how humiliated he had felt... He had made sure that he kept his distance from Sylvie after that, even if Sylvie herself had not made that particularly easy. He had been twenty-seven then, ten years older than Sylvie. A man, whilst she was still only a child.

A child… A child who had told him passionately that she loved and wanted him; a child who had demanded even more passionately that he love her back, that he *make* love to her…with her…that he show her…teach her…*take* her…

He could have wrung her pretty little neck for that…wrung it or— He could still remember how she had defied him, flinging herself into his arms, wrapping them round him, pressing her soft lips against him…

Then, he had managed to resist her…*just*…that time…

She had always been so passionately intense. It was perhaps no wonder that the love she had professed to feel for him had ultimately turned to loathing and hatred.

And now she was coming back. Not just to England but here, to Haverton, into his home…his life…

What would she be like? Beautiful, of course; that went without saying… Her mother had told him as much when he had bumped into her—not that he *needed* telling; it had been blindingly obvious even when she was a child that ultimately she would be an extraordinarily beautiful woman.

'You'll know, of course, that Sylvie is working in New York…for a billionaire…' Belinda had cooed happily at him, smiling with satisfaction.

'He's totally besotted with her of course,' she had added, and though it hadn't been put into as many words Ran had gained the distinct impression from Sylvie's mother that the relationship between Sylvie and Lloyd was rather more than that of merely employer and employee…

It had come as something of a shock to him later, when he met Lloyd, to recognise how much older than Sylvie he actually was, but he had told himself that if Sylvie chose to have as her lover a man who was plainly so much older than her then that was *her* business and no one else's.

Sylvie… In another few hours she would be here, their roles in many ways reversed.

'I despise you, Ran, I hate you,' she had hissed at him between gritted teeth when she had first left for New York, averting her face when he had leaned forward to kiss her cheek.

'I hate you…' She had said it with almost as much passion as she had once cried out to him that she loved him. Almost as much…

CHAPTER TWO

FIVE miles or so before her ultimate destination Sylvie pulled the car she had hired at the airport over to the side of the road and switched off the engine—not because she was unsure of where she was going, not even because she wanted to absorb the beauty of the Derbyshire countryside around her, magnificent though it was as it basked warmly in the mid-afternoon sunshine, devoid of any sign of human occupation apart from her own.

No, the reason she had stopped was that she had been tellingly aware for the last few miles not just of the slight dampness of her hands on the steering wheel but, even more betrayingly, of the increasing turmoil of her thoughts and the nervous butterflies churning her stomach.

When she finally met...*confronted*...Ran, she wanted to be calm and in control of both herself and the situation. She was not, she reminded herself sternly, meeting him as an idealistic teenager who had fallen so disastrously and desperately in love with him, but as a woman, a woman who had a job to do. She would not, *must* not allow her own personal feelings to affect her judgement or her professionalism.

In the eyes of other people, her job might appear to be an enviable sinecure, travelling the world, living and breathing the air of some of its most beautiful buildings, able to afford to commission its very best workmen, but there was far more to it than that.

As Lloyd had remarked admiringly to her the previous year, when he had viewed the finished work on the Venetian *palazzo*, Sylvie didn't just possess the most marvellous and accurate eye for correct period detail, for harmony and colour, for the subtlety that meant she could hold in her mind's eye the entire finished concept of how an original period room must have looked, she also had an extremely shrewd and practical side to her nature which ensured that with every project she had worked on so far she had managed to bring the work to completion on time and under budget.

This was something that didn't just 'happen'. It involved hours and hours spent poring over costings and budgets, more hours and hours tramping around warehouses, inspecting fabrics and furniture, and in many cases, because of the age of the houses, it also meant actually finding and commissioning workmen to make new 'aged' copies of the pieces she required. Italy, as she had quickly discovered, was a treasure house for such craftsmen and so, oddly, was London, but always at a price, and Sylvie had surprised herself a little at her ability to haggle and bargain for days if necessary, until she had got what she wanted and at a price she considered to be fair.

This had, of course, led to her often having to take an extremely firm line, not just with the craftspeople she dealt with but very often with the original owners of their properties as well, who very often retained life tenancy in the houses and quite naturally wanted to have their say in how they were restored and furnished.

Oh, yes, Sylvie was used to dealing with sometimes

difficult ex-owners, and situations where she had to use both patience and tact to ensure that no one's pride was hurt.

It was a very definite skill to be able to walk the tightrope between avoiding hurting a prior owner's often sensitive pride and ensuring that the house was restored as she knew Lloyd would want it to be.

But this time it wasn't just the sensitive feelings of a property's ex-owner she was going to need to consider. No, *this* time the person whose feelings, whose emotions were going to need careful handling was herself.

Closing her eyes, she breathed deeply and calmly several times and then opened them again, wiping her hands on a tissue and then re-starting the Discovery's engine.

She had hired a four-wheel drive, not just because she suspected from the plans and other papers Lloyd had given her to study that it would be useful for travelling over the rugged terrain and the no doubt overgrown driveways that surrounded Haverton Hall, but also because, as she had discovered in the past, a large sturdy off-road vehicle often provided a boon for transporting the odd 'find' she came across when scouting around looking for materials for the restoration work to a property.

The statue she had found for the secluded enclosed garden of the Italian *palazzo* had been one such find, bought and paid for on the spot before the vendor could change his mind, and loaded immediately into her car.

Ten minutes later she was driving through the open gates to Haverton Hall. The twin lodges at either side of the gate, joined by a pretty spanning 'archway', had both looked run-down and in need of repair.

Sylvie knew from her homework that they had been constructed at the same time as the main house—and the house, like them, had been designed by one of the country's foremost architects in the Palladian manner favoured by the likes of Inigo Jones.

Theatrically, the drive to the house curved through flanking trees, several of which were missing, spoiling its original symmetry, although those which remained were so heavily in leaf that they still obscured all her attempts to glimpse the house until she had driven past the final curve in the drive.

Sylvie caught her breath. Used as she was to beautiful properties—after all, Alex's ancestral home was renowned for its elegant grace—this one, despite the shabbiness of its fading elegance, was something very special and she could see instantly why Lloyd had fallen so immediately and completely in love with it.

Set on a small incline, so that it could overlook its surrounding gardens and parklands, it was everything that the neoclassicist architects had decreed their houses should be and then some more, Sylvie acknowledged as she drove slowly towards the gravelled parking area in front of the massive columned portico to the house. Stopping the Discovery, she opened the door and started to get out.

Ran had seen her drive up from an upstairs window. She was just a few seconds short of five minutes early. Remembering a younger Sylvie, and her apparent total inability to arrive anywhere on time, he grimaced ruefully to himself before making his way downstairs.

They met on the paved portico. Ran opened the massive front door just as Sylvie mounted the last step. She stopped the minute she saw him, freezing instinctively like a gazelle scenting the presence of a leopard.

He hadn't changed, but then why should he have? He still looked exactly the same. Tall, broad-shouldered, with the smooth warm skin of a countryman, his jeans clinging softly to the taut muscles of his long legs, his forearms bare and bronzed, the soft checked shirt he was wearing exactly the same kind of shirt she could remember seeing him wearing all the years she had been growing up. His hair was still as thick and darkly rich as ever, his jaw just as chiselled—no signs of soft, rich living there, despite the odd snippets of gossip she had picked up from her mother and from Mollie about the discreet parade of elegant, wealthy women who had passed through his life—Ran had always had a penchant for that type, women in the main who were slightly older than himself, *soignée*, knowing…all the things that an adoring, unknowing seventeen-year-old was not.

Only his eyes had changed, Sylvie noticed, with a sudden sharp flicker of sensation which she immediately suppressed. Oh, they were still the same incredible colour, somewhere between onyx and gold, still flecked with those heart-dizzying little specks of lighter colour and still surrounded by those unfairly long, thick dark lashes.

Yes, all that was still familiar to her, but the lazily sensual way they were studying her, the subtle but very male message she could read in them as Ran's gaze flicked over her T-shirt-covered breasts and her slim waist in the plain blue jeans…that was most certainly not familiar to her, at least not from Ran.

And it was only then, when she countered that look with an instinctive and automatically female one of cool reproval, that Sylvie realised that one of them had closed the distance between them from its original safe several metres to a much, much less secure three or four feet.

One of them… To her chagrin Sylvie recognised that it was not only Ran who had moved so much closer and that she herself was halfway towards the front door now instead of on the perimeter of the portico… *When* had she moved…and how, without knowing what she was doing…? Ran had always had that kind of effect on her… *Had* had… All *that* was in the past now, she reminded herself fiercely. And just to ensure that Ran knew it too she held out her hand to him and, raising her voice slightly, smiled with cool authority as she greeted him.

'Ran, good, I'm glad you're here. We can get straight down to work. I've studied the plans of the house, but I always find that it makes an enormous difference to actually walk over a property, so…'

God, but she was so incredibly sexy, Ran acknowledged. He could feel the heat, the reaction, the response surging through his veins. He had been prepared to find her beautiful. She had always been that. But in the past it had been almost a sexless, childish kind of beauty… Now her sensuality, and his own reaction to it, hit him in the solar plexus like a blow.

As for that cool little voice of authoritative superiority, that distancing little outstretched hand… Later Ran was to ask himself what on earth he had thought he was doing and if he had gone completely mad, but at the time…

Ignoring her outstretched hand, he covered the distance between them and before Sylvie could even begin to guess what he intended doing his hands were resting either side of her waist, his scent, his heat filling her nostrils, his body and his mouth less than inches away from her own.

'Ran!'

Was that really her own voice, that soft, husky, and, yes, somehow invitingly sensual little thread of sound, gasping his name in a slow-drawn-out moan that was more invitation than protest?

But it was too late to correct the erroneous message she knew instinctively she had given; Ran was already acting on what he had obviously interpreted her 'protest' to mean, his hands lifting from her waist to her arms, her shoulders, as he drew her closer, his mouth fastening on hers as he kissed her, not as an old acquaintance or a friend of her brother's, Sylvie recognised, her senses reeling, but in all the ways she had dreamed of him kissing her all those years ago, as a man kissed a woman.

Despairingly she struggled valiantly to resist but it was useless. Her own foolish senses were doing far more to aid Ran than to support her, turning traitor and welcoming his sensual assault of her mouth with the eagerness of parched land greedily soaking up a heavy rainfall.

'Ran...'

She tried weakly to summon her flagging defences, but the objection she tried to make was lost beneath Ran's kiss and all the ineffectual parting of her lips did was to allow Ran's tongue to slip masterfully into the sweet moistness of her mouth.

Briefly she tried to challenge its entry, but what should have been the rejecting thrust of her own tongue against his swiftly became, under Ran's sensually skilful manipulation and expertise, more the intimate sparring of lovers rather than the defensive rejection of adversaries.

'Mmm...' Instinctively Sylvie moved closer, close enough to lean her body fully against Ran's and let his strength support her weakness as delicious tremors of sensation skidded dangerously over her.

'Mmm...'

Beneath her hands Ran's back felt so broad, so firm, so...

Eagerly she tugged his shirt free of his waistband, glorying in the sensation of sliding her hands beneath it and onto the hard heat of his skin.

She felt him shudder responsively as she traced his spine and her own body jolted fiercely in excited reaction.

Beneath her white T-shirt she could feel her suddenly swollen breasts pressing eagerly against her bra. Her nipples ached and even without being able to see them she knew the crests would be hard and erect, the soft flesh around them flooded with aroused dark colour.

Ran could not see what he was doing to her, though...what effect he was having on her as his tongue slid erotically against her own, no longer coaxing but openly, fiercely demanding from her the response his sexuality wanted.

Only one man had seen her body naked and aroused, to only one man had she willingly and, yes, almost wantonly exposed the full femaleness of herself, glorying in her sexuality, in her response to him, her need for him, not fearing...not imagining that he would reject her.

Reject her!

Immediately Sylvie stiffened, her nails momentarily digging into Ran's back as she recognised with shocking abruptness just what she was doing and, even worse, whom she was doing it with.

'Let go of me…' she demanded furiously, fiercely pushing him away, her face bright with mortification and confusion as Ran immediately stepped back from her and then, without taking his eyes off her face, casually unfastened his belt and started to push his shirt back inside his jeans.

If her face had been pink with self-consciousness before, that was nothing to the heat she could feel burning off it now, Sylvie recognised as she refused to give in to the silent visual challenge Ran was giving her and forced herself to keep her gaze locked on his as he slowly and tauntingly completed his task.

Why, oh, why should it be that when a woman disturbed a man's clothing in the heat of passion *he* could make her feel so self-conscious and femininely vulnerable whilst he repaired the dishevelment she had caused, but when it had been a man who had disturbed a woman's clothing *she* was still the one to feel shy and self-conscious when she re-dressed herself?

No wonder the Victorians had considered modesty to be a feminine virtue.

His shirt rearranged to his satisfaction, Ran refastened his belt and then, without taking his eyes off her face, greeted her ironically.

'Welcome to Haverton Hall…'

Sylvie would have given the earth to be able to make a suitably withering response but she could think of none. The shaming fact was that, no matter how she tried to convince herself otherwise, she had done exactly what she had promised herself she would *not* do and allowed him to take the upper hand. And worse than that…far

worse…she had… Quickly she swallowed the frighteningly familiar and painful lump of aching emptiness she
could feel blocking the back of her throat. No way…
She was not going down that road again…not for a
king's ransom. The arrogant, selfish, almost cruel way
Ran had just behaved towards her proved everything she
had ever learned about him. She was under no illusions
about *why* he had kissed her like that… It was his way
of reminding her not just of the past, but also of his
superiority…of telling her that, whilst she might be the
one who was in charge of the project they were going
to be working on together, *he* still had the power to
control her…to control her and to hurt her.

Sylvie turned swiftly on her heel, not waiting for him
to see the emotions she knew were clouding her eyes.

'The lake needs dredging,' she commented crisply as
she shuttered her eyes and stared out towards the large
ornamental lake several hundred yards away from the
house.

It was the wrong thing to say. She could hear the
mocking amusement in Ran's voice as he drawled,
'Well, yes, it does, but let's hope this time you don't
end up head-first in the mud. We'll have to hose you
down out here if you do. There's no way Mrs Elliott is
going to let you into the Rectory smelling of stagnant
lake water and covered in mud and weed…'

Sylvie stiffened, for the moment ignoring his refer-
ence to the ignominious fate which had overtaken her as
an over-eager teenager when she had missed her footing
and fallen head-first into the pond they had been cleaning out on Alex's estate.

'The Rectory?' she questioned him with ominous calm.

She knew from the reports she had read before leaving New York that Ran was presently living in the eighteenth-century Rectory which was part of the estate and which, like the living which had originally gone with it, was in the gift of the owner of the Hall. To judge from the plans and photographs which Sylvie had seen, it was a very, very substantial and handsome property, surrounded by particularly attractive grounds, and she had not been in the least bit surprised to read that it had originally been built for a younger son of the family who had chosen to go into holy orders.

'Mmm...you won't have seen it as you drove in. It's on the other side of the estate. I'm living there at the moment and I've arranged with Mrs Elliott, who used to be my cousin's housekeeper when he lived there, for a room to be prepared for you. Lloyd mentioned that you'd probably be working here for a number of months and he and I agreed that in view of Haverton's distance from the nearest town, and the fact that Lloyd has warned me that you like to keep a very keen eye on the budgets, it makes sense for you to stay at the Rectory rather than waste time and money hunting around for alternative accommodation. Especially since it seems that there could be occasions when you might have to travel abroad to check on work you've set in progress at other Trust properties.'

What he said made sense, but still—she wasn't a child any longer; what she did not need to have was Ran telling her what to do!

'But *you* live at the Rectory,' Sylvie commented quickly.

Immediately Ran's eyebrows rose and he told her laconically, 'It's got ten bedrooms, Sylvie, excluding the upper attics—more than enough space for both of us, I should have thought.'

'Does this Mrs Elliott live in?' Sylvie asked him stiffly.

Ran stared at her for a moment and then burst out laughing.

'No, she doesn't,' he told her coolly, 'although I'm not sure why it should make any difference. You and I have lived under the same roof before, after all, Sylvie, and if it's the thought of any unplanned nocturnal wanderings that's worrying you...' He gave her a wolfish grin and to her fury actually reached out and patted her tauntingly on the arm as he told her, still laughing, 'Don't worry. I'll make sure I get a lock put on my door so that you don't come wandering in...'

Sylvie was too speechless with anger to be able to respond.

'What's wrong now?' Ran challenged her mock-innocently. 'There's no need to be embarrassed at the fact that you occasionally sleepwalk... Of course, it might be an idea to make sure you go to bed wearing something, but I'll warn Mrs Elliott and...'

He stopped as Sylvie made a female growl of frustration deep in her throat.

'That was years ago, when I was a child,' she told him defensively, 'and it only happened once... I don't sleepwalk *now*...'

What was she doing? What was she saying? Why was she letting him do this to her? Sylvie ground her teeth. Yes, once, when she had been initially disoriented and upset at her mother marrying again, she had actually sleepwalked, and might, in fact, have suffered a nasty accident if Ran hadn't happened to see her on his way up to bed. But it had happened *once*, that was all, and, even after she had eventually developed a massive crush on him, surreptitiously creeping into his bedroom had been the last thing on her mind then. She had been far too unworldly, far too naive even to think of such a thing.

'No! Then what are you worrying about?' Ran challenged her, his expression suddenly hardening as he demanded, 'If it's the fact that you'll be living under my roof whilst Lloyd is in New York—'

'*Your* roof?' Sylvie interrupted him quickly, suddenly recognising a way of turning the tables on him and regaining control of the situation, of showing him who was boss. She gave him an acid-sweet smile. 'The Rectory may have *been* yours, Ran, but as part of the estate it is *now* owned by the Trust and—'

'Not so.' Ran stopped her even faster than she had him. 'I have retained ownership of the Rectory and the land. I intend to farm it and to develop the fishing and shooting rights.'

Sylvie was momentarily caught off guard. It was most unusual for Lloyd to allow something like that. He normally insisted on buying whatever land went with a property, if only to ensure that as much of its natural background and surroundings as possible were retained.

'If you'd like to follow me we can drive over to the Rectory now,' Ran offered coolly.

Immediately Sylvie shook her head. 'No... I want to see over the house first,' she told him crisply.

Ran stared at her and then looked at his watch before telling her softly, 'That will take at least two hours, possibly longer; it's now five o'clock in the afternoon.'

Sylvie raised her eyebrows. 'So...?' she challenged.

Ran shrugged.

'I should have thought after a transatlantic flight and the drive here from the airport that you'd have wanted a rest before touring the house, if only so that you can view it with a fresh eye and a clear head.'

'You're out of touch, Ran,' Sylvie told him with a small, superior smile. 'These are the nineties. Crossing the Atlantic for a power breakfast and then re-crossing it for another meeting is nothing,' she boasted.

Ran shrugged again and then waved one hand in the direction of the main doorway as he drawled laconically, 'Very well…after you…'

As he walked towards the door behind her, Ran paused. The sight of her had given him much more of a shock than he liked. He had prepared himself for the fact that he would be meeting her as a woman, and not as the girl he had watched boarding the flight for America, but womanhood came in many different guises and took many different forms. However, none of them could possibly come anywhere near causing the kind of devastating effect on his senses that Sylvie's was creating.

Her hair, long and thick, hung down to her shoulders in an immaculately groomed swathe of molten honey-gold. Just looking at it, at *her*, made him ache to run his fingers through it, to watch its silken weight sliding through his hands…

His stomach muscles tensed. The brilliantly white T-shirt she was wearing hugged the soft shape of her breasts before disappearing into her jeans. The T-shirts he remembered her wearing had been big and baggy and invariably slightly grubby as she happily trotted after him whilst he worked.

Even to his male uneducated eyes, this T-shirt was plainly not the kind one wore to work outdoors in.

And as for her jeans…!

Ran closed his eyes. What was it about the sight of a pair of plain blue jeans lovingly hugging the soft, shapely contours of a woman's behind that had such an evocative, such a provocative effect on a man's male instincts?

Unabashedly he acknowledged that had Sylvie been a complete stranger to him, and had he been walking down the street behind her, he would have instinctively increased his pace to walk past her so that he could see if she looked as good from the front as she did from the rear.

But she wasn't a stranger, she was Sylvie.

'I've told Alex that if you don't keep away from Sylvie he must make you,' Sylvie's mother had once warned him haughtily, shortly after her husband's death.

She had caught Ran at a bad moment and he had reacted instinctively and immediately regretted it as he'd thrown back at her bluntly, 'It's Sylvie you should be warning to keep away from me. She's the one doing the chasing. Teenage girls are like that,' he had added unkindly, watching as Sylvie's mother pursed her lips in shock.

It had been then that he had seen Sylvie slipping past the open doorway of Alex's estate office. Had she overheard them? He'd hoped not. Difficult though her unwanted crush on him sometimes had been, the last thing he'd wanted to do was to hurt her. But now, as he watched her, Ran acknowledged that these days if anyone was going to be hurt it was far more likely to be him! Why had she taken as her lover and her intended partner for life a man more than old enough to be her father? Ran couldn't begin to understand. Unless it was because she had lost her father at such a young and vulnerable age.

Sylvie had pulled open the house's unlocked door and disappeared inside. Sombrely Ran followed her.

CHAPTER THREE

THEY had covered the ground floor of the house, walked
the length of the elegant gallery, with its windows over-
looking the parkland and the distant vista of the
Derbyshire hills, and were just inspecting the enormous
ballroom which opened off it when Sylvie acknowledged
inwardly that Ran might have been right to advise her
to wait until after she had rested to inspect the house.

Haverton Hall's rooms might not possess quite the
vastness of the *palazzo's* marble-floored rooms, nor the
fading grandeur of the Prague palace, but Sylvie had
already lost count of the number of salons and ante-
chambers they had walked through on the lower floor.
The gallery felt as though it stretched for miles, and as
she studied the dusty wooden floor of the ballroom her
heart sank at the thought of inspecting its lofty plasterwork ceiling and its elegantly inlaid panelling. And they
still had the upper floors to go over! But she couldn't
afford to show any weakness in front of Ran and have
him crowing over her. No way. And so, ignoring the
warning beginnings of a throbbing headache, she took a
deep breath and began to inspect the panelling.

'The first thing we're going to need to do is to get a
report on the extent of the dry rot,' she told Ran in a
firmly businesslike voice.

He stopped her. 'That won't be necessary.'

Sylvie paused and turned to look angrily at him.

'Ran, there's something you *have* to understand,' she

told him pointedly. '*I* am in charge here now. I wasn't asking for your approval,' she told him gently. 'The house has dry rot. We need a specialist's report on the extent of the damage.'

'I already have one.'

Sylvie started to frown.

'When...?' she began.

But before she could continue Ran told her coolly, 'It was obvious that the Trust would need to commission a full structural survey of the place to assess it, so in order to save time I commissioned one. You should have had a copy. I had one faxed to the Trust's New York office last week when I received it.'

Sylvie could feel her heart starting to beat just a little bit too fast as the angry colour burned her face.

'You commissioned a survey?' she questioned with dangerous calmness. 'May I ask who gave you that authority?'

'Lloyd,' came back the prompt and stingingly dismissive reply.

Sylvie opened her mouth and then closed it again. It was quite typical of Lloyd that he should have done such a thing and she knew it. He would only have been thinking of saving time in getting his latest pet project under way; he would not have seen, as she so clearly did, that what Ran was actually doing was not trying to be helpful but deliberately trying to upstage her and challenge her authority.

'I take it you haven't read the report,' Ran was continuing, talking to her as though she were some kind of errant pupil who had failed to turn in a piece of homework, Sylvie decided as she silently ground her firm white teeth.

'I haven't received any report to read,' she corrected him acidly.

Ran shrugged.

'Well, I've got a copy here. Do you want to continue with your inspection or would you prefer to wait until you've had a chance to read through it?'

Had the question been put by anyone else, Sylvie knew that she would have gratefully seized on the excuse to defer her self-imposed task until after she had had a rest and the opportunity to do something about the increasingly painful pressure of her headache, but because it was *Ran* who asked her, *Ran* whom she was fiercely determined not to allow to have any advantage over her, she shook her head and told him aggressively, 'When I want to change any of my plans, Ran, I'll let you know. But until I do I think you can safely take it that I don't...'

She saw his eyebrows lift a little but he made no comment.

It had been a hot week and the air in the ballroom was stifling, the dust thick and choking as it lay heavily all around them.

Sylvie sneezed and winced as the pounding in her head increased. The bright early evening sunlight streaming in through the windows was making her feel oddly dizzy and faintly nauseous... She tried to look away from it and gave a small gasp of pain as the act of moving her head made the blood pound agonisingly against her temples.

Only rarely did she suffer these enervating headaches. They were brought on by stress and tension. Turning away so that Ran wouldn't see her, she tried to massage the pain away discreetly.

'Careful…' Ran warned her tersely.

'What?' Sylvie spun round, colour flaring up under her skin as Ran motioned towards a piece of fallen plasterwork she had almost walked over.

She was feeling increasingly sick and dizzy in the sharp bright light. Despairingly she closed her eyes and then wished she hadn't as the room started to spin dangerously around her.

'Sylvie…'

Quickly she opened her eyes.

'You're not well; what is it?' she heard Ran demanding tersely.

'Nothing,' she denied angrily. 'A headache, that's all.'

'A *headache*…?' His eyebrows shot up as Ran studied her now far too pale face and saw the tell-tale beading of sweat on her forehead.

'That's it,' he told her forcefully. 'We can finish this tomorrow. You need to rest.'

'I need to do my job,' Sylvie protested shakily, but Ran quite obviously wasn't going to listen to her.

'Can you make it back to the car?' he was asking her. 'Or shall I carry you?'

Carry her… Sylvie gave him a furiously outraged look.

'Ran, there's nothing wrong with me,' she lied, and then gave a small gasp as the quick movement of her head as she shook it in denial of his suggestion caused nauseating arrows of pain to savage her aching head.

The next thing she knew, Ran was taking her very firmly by the arm and propelling her towards the door, ignoring her protests to leave her alone.

At the top of the stairs, to her infuriated chagrin, he turned round and swung her up into his arms, telling her through gritted teeth, 'If you're going to faint on me, Sylvie, then here's the best place to do it.'

She wanted to tell him that fainting was the last thing she intended to do, but her face was pressed against the warm flesh of his throat and if she tried to speak her lips would be touching his skin and then...

Swallowing hard, Sylvie tried to concentrate on banishing the agonising pain in her head but it was something that she couldn't just will away. As she knew from past experience, the only way of getting rid of it was for her to go to bed and sleep it off.

They were downstairs now and Ran was crossing the hallway, thrusting open the door and carrying her out into the fresh air.

'What are you doing?' she demanded as he walked past her Discovery towards his own car.

'I'm taking you home...to the Rectory,' he told her promptly.

'I can drive,' Sylvie protested, but to her annoyance Ran simply gave a brief derogatory laugh.

He told her dismissively, 'No way...' And then she was being bundled into the passenger seat of a Land Rover nearly as ancient as the one she remembered him driving around her stepbrother's estate, and as she struggled to sit up Ran was jumping into the driver's seat next to her and turning the key in the ignition.

'Ran...my luggage...' She was protesting, but he obviously had no intention of listening to her. With the Land Rover's engine noise making it virtually impossible for her to speak over it, Sylvie gave up her attempt to stop him and subsided weakly into her seat, hunching her shoulders as she deliberately turned her head away and refused to look at him.

As he glanced at her hunched shoulders and averted profile, Ran's frown deepened. In that pose she looked so defenceless and vulnerable, so different from the professional, high-powered businesswoman she had just shown herself to be and much more like the girl he remembered.

The Land Rover kicked up a trail of dust as he turned off the drive and onto the track that led to the Rectory.

Girl or woman, what did it matter so far as *he* was concerned? He cursed under his breath, his attention suddenly caught by the sight of several deer grazing placidly beside the track. They were supposed to be confined to the park area surrounding the house and not cropping the grazing he needed for his sheep. There must be a break in the fence somewhere—the new fence which he had just severely depleted his carefully hoarded bank balance to buy—which meant... There had been rumours about rustlers being in the area; other farmers had reported break-ins and losses.

Once he had seen Sylvie settled at the house he would have to come back out and check the fencing.

Sylvie winced as the Land Rover hit a rut in the road, sitting up and just about managing to suppress a sharp cry of pain—or at least she thought she had suppressed it until she heard Ran asking her curtly, 'What is it? What's wrong?'

'Nothing... I've got a headache, that's all,' she stressed offhandedly, but her face flushed as she saw the look he was giving her and she realised that he wasn't deceived.

'A headache?' he queried dryly. 'It looks more like a migraine to me. Have you got some medication for it or...?'

'It isn't a migraine,' Sylvie denied, adding reluctantly, 'It's… I… It's a stress headache,' she admitted in an angry rush of words. 'I…I get them occasionally. The travel…flying…'

Ran's mouth hardened as he listened to her.

'What's happened to you, Sylvie?' he asked her quietly. 'Why should it be so difficult for you to admit to being vulnerable…human…? What *is* it that pushes you, drives you, forces you to make such almost superhuman demands on yourself? Anyone else, having flown across the Atlantic and driven close on fifty miles without a break, would have chosen to rest and relax a little bit before starting to work, but not you…'

'That may be the British way, but it's different in America,' Sylvie told him sharply. 'There, people are rewarded, praised, for fulfilling their potential and for—'

'Driving themselves into such a state of exhaustion that they make themselves ill?' Ran challenged her. 'I thought that Lloyd was supposed to…' He stopped, not wanting to put into words, to make a reality, the true relationship he knew existed between Sylvie and her boss. 'I thought he cared about you…valued you…' he finished carefully instead.

Sylvie was sitting upright now, ignoring the pounding pain in her head as she glared belligerently at Ran.

'Lloyd doesn't…he isn't…'

She stopped, shaking her head. How could she explain to Ran of all people about the thing that drove her, the memories and the fears? As a teenager she had done so many foolish things, and even let down the people who had loved and supported her; her involvement with Wayne was something she knew she would always regret.

She hadn't known at the time, of course, just what he was. In her innocent naiveté she had never guessed that he was anything other than someone who had bought a handful of recreational drugs to pass on to people at rave parties.

When she had run away from university, though, to join Wayne and the band of New Age travellers who had invaded her stepbrother's lands, she had quickly learned just what a mistake she had made, and she knew that she would always be grateful to Alex and his wife Mollie, not just for the fact that they had helped her to extricate herself from a situation she had very quickly grown to fear, but also for the fact that they had supported her, believed in her, *accepted* her acknowledgement that she had made a mistake and given her the opportunity to get her life back on track.

She and Wayne had never actually been lovers, although she knew that very few people would believe that, nor had she ever used drugs; but she *had* been tainted by his lifestyle, *had* had her eyes opened painfully to certain harsh realities of life, and after Alex had interceded for her with her mother and with the university authorities, getting her a place at Vassar where she had been able to complete her education, she had promised herself that she would pay him and Mollie back for their kindness and their love and support by showing the world and her detractors just how worthy of that support she was.

At Vassar she had gained a reputation as something of a recluse and a swot; dates and parties had been strictly out of bounds so far as she was concerned and her dedication had paid off with excellent exam results.

And now, just as she had once felt the need to prove

herself to Alex and Mollie, she felt a corresponding need to prove herself worthy of Lloyd's trust in her professional abilities. It was true that sometimes she did drive herself too hard...but the scornful verbal sketch of herself that Ran had just drawn for her quite illogically hurt.

Given that she had striven so hard to be considered wholly professional, to be capable and strong, it was quite definitely illogical, she knew, to wish forlornly that Ran might have adopted a more protective and less critical attitude towards her, that he might have shown more concern, some tenderness, some...

'Why the hell didn't you *say* you weren't feeling well?'

Ran's curt demand broke into her thoughts, underlining their implausibility, their stupidity, their dangerous vulnerability.

'Why should I have done?' Sylvie countered defensively, adding tersely, 'I hardly think that either the Trust or the owners of the properties it acquires would thank me for wasting both time and consequently money by bringing up the subject of my own health during business discussions. You and I may know one another from the past, Ran, but so far as I am concerned the fact that we have dealings with one another in the present is entirely down to the business and professional relationship between us.'

It was several seconds before Ran bothered to respond to her unrehearsed but determinedly distancing little speech, and for a moment Sylvie thought that he was actually going to ignore what she had said, but then he turned towards her and said, 'So what you're saying is that it's to be purely business between us, is that it?'

It took every ounce of courage that Sylvie possessed,

and then some, for her to be able to meet the look he was giving her full-on, but somehow or other she managed to do so, even if the effort left her perilously short of breath and with her heart pounding almost as painfully as her head, She agreed coolly, 'Yes.'

Ran was the one to look away first, his face hardening as he glanced briefly at her mouth before doing so.

'Well, if that's what you want, so be it,' he told her crisply, returning his attention to his driving.

His response, instead of making her feel relieved, left her feeling... What? Disappointed that he hadn't challenged her, hadn't given her the opportunity to...to what? Argue with him? Why should she *want* to? What was it she felt she had to prove? What was it she wanted to be given the opportunity to prove?

Angry with herself, Sylvie shook her head. There was nothing, of course. She had made her point, said what she wanted to say and now Ran knew exactly how she viewed their working relationship and exactly how she viewed him. He could be in no doubt that, were it not for the fact that he was the owner of a property the Trust had decided to acquire, she would have no cause, nor any wish, to be involved with him.

Up ahead of her she could see a grove, a small wooded area; Ran drove into it and through it towards the mellow high red-brick wall and through its open gates.

The house which lay beyond them took Sylvie's breath away.

She was used to grand and beautiful properties, to elegance of design, to scenery and settings so spectacular that one had to blink and look again, but this was something else.

This was a house as familiar to her as though she had already walked every one of its floors, as though she knew each and every single one of its rooms, its corners. This was a house, *the* house she had created for herself as a girlhood fantasy. A house, *the* house, the *home* which would house and protect the family she so much longed to be a part of.

Totally bemused, she couldn't drag her gaze away from its red-brick walls, her professional eye automatically noting the symmetrical perfection of its Georgian windows and the delicacy of the pretty fanlight above the doorway. An ancient wisteria clothed the facing wall, its trunk and branches silvery grey against the rich warmth of the brick; its flowering season was now over but its soft green tendrils of leaves were coolly restful to her aching eyes.

Prior to her mother's second marriage to Alex's father, they had lived in a smart apartment in Belgravia—her mother had been a very social person, involved, as she still was, in a good many charities and a keen bridge player, but Sylvie had never really felt comfortable or at home in the elegant London flat. Before his death her father had owned a large house in one of London's squares and Sylvie still missed the freedom that living there had given her.

To comfort herself she had created her perfect house and the perfect family to go with it, mother, father, daughter—herself, plus a sister for her to play with and a brother too, along with grandparents and aunts and uncles and cousins. It had been the house that she had given most of her mental energy and imagination to lovingly creating, though. A house for a family, a house that wrapped itself lovingly and protectively around you…a house with enough land for her to have a pony. A house… The house… *This* house..!

Ran had stopped the Land Rover. Shakily she got out, unable to take her eyes off the house, barely aware of Ran's expression as he watched her.

Just for a second, seeing that luminous bemused expression on her face, he had been transported back in time…to a time when she had looked at *him* like that, a time when…

Grimly he reminded himself of what Sylvie had just said, of the terms she had just set between them. She had made it more than plain, if he had needed it underlining, which he had not, that the only reason she was here in his life was because of her job and that, given the choice, she would far rather be working alongside someone else…*anyone* else.

The gravel crunched beneath Sylvie's feet as she walked slowly, as if in a dream, towards the Rectory's front door.

Already she knew what would lie beyond it—the soft-toned walls of the hallway with its highly polished antique furniture, its glowing wooden floors, its rugs and bowls of country-garden flowers. In her mind's eye she could see it all as she herself had created it, smell the scent of the flowers…see the contented look in the eyes of the cat who basked illegally on the rug, lying there sunning himself in a warm beam of sunshine, ignoring the fact that his place and his basket were not here but in the kitchen.

Automatically her hand reached out for the door handle and then she realised what she was doing. Self-consciously she stepped back, turning her head away so that she didn't have to look at Ran as he stepped past her to unlock the door.

It was cruelly ironic that Ran, of all people, should own this house that so closely epitomised all that she herself had longed for in a home as a young girl.

The front door was open. Ran paused to allow her to precede him inside but, as she did so, Sylvie came to an abrupt halt. Faded, unattractive wallpaper and chipped dark brown paint assaulted her disbelieving gaze. In place of the polished mellow wooden floor she had expected was a carpet, so old and faded that it was no longer possible to even guess at its original colour, but Sylvie suspected with disgust that it must have been the same horrendous brown as the paintwork.

True, there was some furniture, old rather than antique, dusted rather than polished, but there were certainly no flowers, no perfumed scent, nor, not surprisingly, was there any cat.

'What is it?' Ran asked her.

Hard on the heels of the acute envy she had felt when she had first seen the exterior of the house came a pang of sadness for its inner neglect. Oh, it was clean enough, if you discounted the air possessing a sharp, almost chemical smell that made her wrinkle her nose a little, but it was a long, long way from the home she had so lovingly mentally created.

She heard Ran moving around in the hall behind her.

'I'll take you up to your room,' he told her. 'Have you got something for your headache?'

'Yes, but they're in my luggage which is in my hire car,' Sylvie told him grimly.

In the excitement of seeing the house her headache

had abated slightly, but now the strong smell in the hallway had made it return and with interest. She could no longer deny that lying down somewhere dark and quiet had become a necessity.

'It's this way,' Ran told her unnecessarily as he headed towards the stairs.

Once they might have been elegant, although now it was hard to know; the original staircase no longer existed and the monstrosity which had replaced it made Sylvie shudder in distaste.

The house had a sad, forlorn air about it, she recognised as she reached the large rectangular landing, carpeted again in the same revolting dun-brown as the hallway below.

'Did your great-uncle live here?' Sylvie asked him curiously.

'No. It was let out to tenants. When my cousin inherited he moved in here, and after his death... I thought about selling it, but it's too far off the beaten track to attract the interest of a buyer, and then once I'd made the decision to hang onto the land and farm it seemed to make sense to move into the house myself. It needs some work doing on it, of course...'

Sylvie said nothing but her expressive eyes gave her away and Ran continued coldly, 'Well, yes, I can see that to someone such as yourself, used to only the very best that money can provide, it must be rather a comedown. I'm sorry if the only accommodation I can offer you isn't up to your usual standards...' Ran's eyes darkened as he reflected on the elegance of Alex's home and the luxury she must have enjoyed with Lloyd, but to Sylvie, who was remembering how Ran had once seen her living in the most basic and primitive conditions, when she had been part of the group of New Age travellers who had set up camp on Alex's estate, the look he was giving her seemed to be one of taunting mockery.

'You're down here,' Ran was saying as he led the way down a corridor with doors off either side of it, pushing one of them open and then standing to one side as he waited for her to enter.

The bedroom was large, with two long windows that let in the glowing evening sunlight. The old-fashioned wooden furniture, like the tables in the hallway, was spotlessly clean but lacked the warm lustre that it would once have had from being lovingly polished by several generations of female hands. The empty grate in the pretty fireplace, which she would have filled with a collection of dried flowers or covered with an embroidered firescreen, was simply that—an empty grate. The curtains and the bedding were modern and, she suspected, newly purchased for her visit. The same depressing brown carpet as downstairs covered the floor.

'You've got your own bathroom,' Ran told her as he crossed the floor to push open another door. 'It's old-fashioned but it works.'

As she looked into the bathroom past him, Sylvie said wryly, 'It may be old-fashioned to you, Ran, but this type of plain white Edwardian sanitaryware is very much in vogue right now.'

'There are wardrobes and cupboards on that wall,' he told her unnecessarily, indicating the bank of built-in furniture. 'I haven't had the chance yet, but tomorrow I'll bring up a desk from downstairs.'

'I'll certainly need somewhere to put my laptop,' Sylvie agreed. 'But I will also need to have a room somewhere, I think preferably up at the Hall itself, to work officially from. But that's something we can discuss later.

'Where's your housekeeper?' she asked him. 'I'd like to meet her…'

'Mrs Elliott… She'll be here in the morning. I can introduce you then.

'Look.' He glanced at his watch and then told her, 'I'm afraid I'm going to have to leave you. I have to go out, but if you'd like something for that headache…'

'What I'd like is my own medication,' Sylvie told him acidly, 'but, since that's not available, thanks but no, thanks. I need my luggage,' she added pointedly.

'If you give me the keys to your Discovery, I'll go and get it for you,' Ran told her promptly. 'Just give me ten minutes to make a couple of phone calls.'

As she handed over the keys to her car Sylvie wondered where it was he was going to be spending the evening and with whom.

Ran was a very masculinely attractive man; even she had to admit that.

'I doubt that Ran will ever marry,' Alex had once commented.

'Why not?' Sylvie had questioned curiously, her adoring teenage heart thumping frantically at the thought of being married to Ran, of being his wife, of sharing his life, his *bed*… A delicious shiver of anticipatory pleasure had run through her as she'd willed her stepbrother to say that there was a mysterious someone in Ran's life, far too young for him as yet, a special someone… herself…

But instead, disappointingly, prosaically, Alex had told her, 'An estate manager's salary and tied accommodation in a small cottage are hardly up to the standard or style of living that the women Ran dates are used to, and he's far too proud to want to live off his wife…'

'The women…?' Sylvie had flared unhappily, whilst her mother, who had been listening to their conversation, had chipped in disparagingly.

'Ran would be far better off marrying some farmer's daughter, a girl who's been brought up for that kind of lifestyle…'

Sylvie remembered how Alex's eyebrows had risen at this display of snobbery from her mother. But now, of course, Ran's prospects had changed. She knew how much Lloyd had paid him for the house and the estate. There had been death duties and other commitments to meet, of course, but even so he would have been left with a sizeable sum, much larger than the inheritance she had received from her father, which her over-anxious mother had been convinced would make her a target for potential fortune-hunters.

Yes, with the money he had at his disposal, and the living he would no doubt make out of the land, Ran would financially have a great deal to offer a woman.

Not that a man's financial status had ever counted for anything with her. Love in a cottage might be an ideal, a daydream, a fantasy now relegated to her childhood, but secretly Sylvie still adhered to the belief 'Better a humble home where love is than a mansion without it'— and, of course, there had never been any doubt in her mind whatsoever that when it came to the material things in life what Ran had to offer the woman he loved…

The woman he loved.

She bit her lip as Ran started to walk away from her. Once he had gone she stared out of the bedroom window. It overlooked the formal gardens to one side of the house. Like the house, they had an air of neglect; of being unloved. Sylvie's vivid imagination soon filled the neglected borders with lush herbaceous plants and restored the overgrown rose garden to what must have been a haven of peace and perfume.

The air in the bedroom felt stale, but when she tried to open one of the sash windows all she managed to do was to break one of her nails. Cursing herself under her breath, she winced as the pain inside her head increased. Perhaps she had been rash in refusing Ran's offer of some headache tablets.

Quickly she opened the bedroom door and hurried back down the stairs.

She found Ran in a huge ill equipped kitchen at the back of the house. As she pushed open the door he was heading towards it carrying a tray of tea.

'Who's that for?' Sylvie demanded suspiciously.

'You,' Ran told her promptly. On the tray Sylvie could see a small packet of a familiar brand of headache tablets. The temptation to tell him that she didn't want either his tea or his tablets was so strong that she had to fight hard to ignore it. Where on earth had such perversity come from—and when she had come downstairs especially to ask him for them?

'I can manage it for myself,' she told him ungraciously, and she held out her hands for the tray. The look he gave her made her flush but doggedly she stood her ground. Even so, she doubted that he would have handed the tray over to her if the telephone in the hallway had not rung.

As he went to answer it Sylvie headed for the stairs.

'Vicky…' she heard him saying warmly, and then, 'Yes…it's still on… I'm looking forward to it too,' he confirmed, his voice dropping and deepening. 'Look, I have to go...'

Sylvie was halfway up the stairs when she heard him replacing the telephone receiver.

'Sylvie—' he began.

But she cut him short, turning round and telling him crisply, 'Don't let me delay you if you've got a date, Ran. I've got plenty of work to read up on.'

'You need to sleep off your headache,' Ran told her curtly.

'On the contrary. I need to work,' Sylvie corrected him sharply as she continued on her way upstairs.

Ran stood and watched her. God, but she got under his skin. Why did he let her? Why hadn't he simply told her that the only date he had this evening was with a damaged fence?

Angrily he turned on his heel and strode towards the front door.

As he closed it behind him Sylvie's body slumped slightly; tension had invaded each and every one of her muscles and it wasn't just her head that pounded with stress now, it was her whole body. Wearily she made her way to her bedroom, took two of the tablets, drank her tea and then, having removed her outer clothes, crawled into bed in her underwear. It was only when she was on the verge of sleep that she remembered that she had neglected to ask Ran to do something about the window she had been unable to open.

CHAPTER FOUR

RAN grimaced as he studied the very obviously cut-through pieces of fencing wire. No accident, that. Someone had quite definitely used wire cutters on them, which meant...

The lambs which had been born early in the spring had all gone now, his breeding stock the only flock that remained. It was an unpalatable thought though, that the deer roaming the home park made a tempting target for rustlers, all the more so because those animals were tame and not used to being hunted.

The last time he had seen Alex, the two of them had discussed the pros and cons of tagging their deer. Like him, Alex had a small herd on his estate, but since their marriage Mollie, his wife, had added a new strain to them in the shape of the same miniature deer that the Duchess of Devonshire had bred so successfully.

As Ran glanced towards the ha-ha which separated the parkland from the main gardens to the Hall he could hear the peacocks screeching their warning that someone was approaching the house.

Frowning, he got up, dusting the twigs and grass from his jeans as he headed back to the Land Rover.

It was almost ten o'clock, hardly the time for anyone to be visiting the Hall for any legitimate reason. Still frowning, he started the Land Rover's engine.

Sylvie had woken up abruptly, wondering where on earth she was and why she couldn't breathe properly.

The dying sun had heated the already stuffy air in her bedroom to the point where she could actually taste its staleness in her mouth. The sharp intensity of her earlier headache had, thankfully, eased, but she knew there was no guarantee of its not returning if she continued to breathe such unhealthy air.

What she needed was some fresh air. After sluicing her face with cold water she pulled on her jeans and T-shirt, grimacing slightly as she did so. New York had effected some changes in her, she reflected wryly. Once she would have been quite happy in grubby clothes, but now...

Lloyd often teased her for the preppy look of loafers, jeans and white T-shirts which had become her trade-mark, but, as she had loftily told him, they made good sense for her job in that they always looked workmanlike and enabled her to climb scaffolding and straddle plat-forms whilst at the same time looking smart and busi-nesslike enough to command the respect of the some-times very chauvinistic men she had to deal with. Women too, especially in Italy, the home of style with a capital S, had been discreetly impressed with her work-ing 'uniform', she had noticed. Now it was second na-ture to her always to wear immaculate white T-shirts and equally immaculate jeans, and the act of putting on clothes she had already been wearing all day was not one she enjoyed.

She had a spare set of car keys in her purse—another trick she had learned from her work. Spare keys to any-thing and everything were a necessity, as she had quickly discovered the first time she had allowed one of the workmen to accidentally lock her out of a building

and then go home with the keys—it would be a simple
enough matter for her to walk back to Haverton Hall and
pick up her Discovery. The last thing she wanted was to
be dependent on Ran for a lift to the place in the morning, and besides—a small triumphant smile curved her
full mouth—it would be good to be able to point out
haughtily to him that whilst he had been out enjoying
himself with his girlfriend *she* had been working.

She had a well-developed sense of direction and the
walk to the Hall, which someone else might have found
a daunting prospect, was nothing to her.

Humming happily to herself, Sylvie set out.

It was a warm summer's evening, with just enough
remaining light for her to avoid the occasional cloud of
midges hovering on the still air.

Being on foot gave her the opportunity to assess the
land far better than she had been able to do from inside
Ran's Land Rover. She had spent enough time on Alex's
estate to appreciate that it was going to take a considerable amount of good husbandry on Ran's part to bring
this land into the same productive state as her stepbrother's. Oddly, she envied him the challenge, but not
so much as she envied his wife the pleasure she would
have in lovingly restoring the Rectory; in making it the
home that Sylvie knew it could be. Oh, yes, she envied
her that.

Only that? Sylvie paused, shaking her thick hair back
from her head. Of course only that. She couldn't possibly envy her Ran, could she—Ran and the children he
would give her? No, of course she couldn't.

It was almost dark when Sylvie eventually reached the
Hall, its bulk throwing long shadows across the gravel,

cloaking both her and the Discovery as she walked towards it.

The sound of other feet on the gravel momentarily made her freeze until she recognised the familiar shapes of half a dozen inquisitive peacocks and peahens. The cocks were sending their shrill cries of warning up into the still night air.

Sylvie laughed as she heard them, relieved, and shook her head at them as she told them cheerfully, 'Yes, I may be an intruder now, but you're going to have to get used to me. You and I shall be seeing an awful lot of one another, you know.'

She stayed with them for several minutes, watching them and talking to them. Soon, no doubt, when it became fully dark, they would be roosting somewhere out of the way of any predatory hunting foxes.

Turning her back on them, Sylvie stared thoughtfully at the house, trying to visualise how it would look once the stone had been cleaned. That alone would cost a small fortune and would, no doubt, take almost as long as it would take for the interior to be renovated. She must ask Ran to give her any formal records from when the hall had originally been built and the work done on it since then. She wasn't sure, but she suspected that the stairway she had seen had been, if not the work of Grinling Gibbons, then certainly the work of one of his more innovative apprentices.

The tiny sprays of coral, the seashells and unbelievably realistic fish carved into the wood related, no doubt, to the fact that the money for the original house had come from the very profitable overseas trading its owner had been involved in. As a prominent member of King

Charles II's court, and one of his favourites, he undoubtedly had had access to many money-making activities.

Idly Sylvie wondered what it would have been like to live in such a time and in such a house. It was one of her indulgences that whenever she became involved with a new property she couldn't help daydreaming about its past, its history, picturing herself as part of it... imagining how and what she would have chosen had she been its chatelaine and then translating that into...

Ran parked his Land Rover out of sight and sound of the house. The peafowl, on their way to their roosting place, saw him and started to flap their wings until he threw down the grain he had brought with him to silence them. No point in giving the intruders the same warning he himself had so helpfully received.

Abandoning her study of the Hall, Sylvie stepped back into the shadows and made her way back towards her parked car. As he rounded the corner of the building, for a moment Ran thought that its frontage was deserted, and then he saw someone moving in the semi-darkness.

Immediately he acted, crouching down low and using the shadows to conceal his presence as he ran light-footed and quietly towards Sylvie's car and whoever it was who was trying to break into it. There wasn't any time to waste—the Discovery's driver's door was already open. Launching himself towards the figure about to climb into it, Ran brought the thief down in a rugby tackle, pinning him down on the ground beneath him as he grunted, 'Got you.'

Sylvie didn't see her assailant spring out at her but she certainly felt him as the speed of his attack carried her to the ground, his weight keeping her there as his hands moved quickly and lightly over her body.

Frantically she tried to struggle, kicking out at him, clawing his back as he pinned her legs, imprisoning her beneath his own, and then reached out to imprison her hands. As she twisted and turned beneath him, trying to throw off his weight, Sylvie felt too furiously angry to be afraid, but then, suddenly, as he secured both her hands in one of his and ran his free one experimentally over her body, she froze, all her feminine instincts and fears awakened.

'Keep still,' Ran warned his quarry abruptly. It had come as a shock to discover that she was female. He had assumed that the attempted theft of the car was being carried out by a young boy.

As she heard and recognised Ran's voice, Sylvie's fear immediately changed to a mixture of relief and fury.

'Let go of me,' she demanded immediately.

'Sylvie…?' Ran stared at her in disbelief. 'What the hell…?'

He had relaxed his grip on her hands but his weight was still holding her pinned to the ground and Sylvie wriggled protestingly beneath him, complaining.

'Sylvie,' Ran repeated, still obviously shocked by her presence. 'I thought… I heard the peafowl and thought someone was… I thought you were trying to steal the car… I couldn't tell who you were in the dark,' Ran told her curtly as he read the disbelief in her eyes, her expression revealed to him as the moon grew in strength now that the dusk had given way to proper darkness.

'What are you doing here anyway?' he demanded sharply.

'I needed some fresh air; the windows in my room won't open and I…I decided I might as well walk over here and collect my car… And what about you? I thought *you* were supposed to be going on a date, not creeping around frightening people to death,' Sylvie accused him angrily.

She was becoming acutely and very uncomfortably conscious of the way he was lying on top of her, her legs still entangled with his from when she had tried to escape from him, but now...

Sylvie drew a sharp self-admonitory breath at the direction her thoughts were taking. It was becoming increasingly difficult for her to breathe and not just because of Ran's weight on top of her. She was all too aware of how, when she did breathe, her breasts were pressing against his chest and even more dangerously conscious of the way her pelvis was accommodating itself to the shape of him. She could smell the warm summer night air on his skin and with it the much, much more intimate musky male scent that was him. Somehow or other during their struggle her T-shirt had become separated from her jeans and she was hideously aware that it was too late to regret now the fact that in redressing herself she had not bothered to put back on the sensible white bra she had discarded when she had gone to bed. Instinctively her free hand went to her body to check just how far up her T-shirt had ridden.

'What is it?' Ran asked her, his attention caught by the movement of her hand.

'You're heavy, Ran, you're *hurting* me,' Sylvie told him, not entirely truthfully, as she tried to bury herself in the night's cloaking shadows, but it was too late and she could see from the sudden narrowing of his gaze as it followed the action of her hand that he realised, as she had just done herself, that her wretched T-shirt had ridden up far enough to expose the lower curve of her breasts.

The last thing, the very last thing she wanted was for Ran to study her body in any way at all, so why…why, the moment his gaze fell to her breasts, did they suddenly decide to react to his presence by swelling and firming, her nipples sensually flaunting peaks of explicit womanhood?

'You're not wearing a bra…'

'Thank you, Ran, but I *am* already aware of that fact,' Sylvie snapped at him through gritted teeth, her face hot with colour as she tried to reach the edge of her T-shirt to tug it down. But before she could do so Ran forestalled her, his own fingers curling round the thin white fabric.

Sylvie was in no doubt that Ran *did* intend to pull it down to cover her breasts. She could read his intentions quite plainly in his eyes. So how on earth what happened next *did* happen she was at a complete loss to know.

She moved, and so did Ran's hand. Sylvie froze tensely as she felt his knuckles brush the underside of her breasts; immediately she made an awkward lunging movement away from his touch, forgetting that Ran had hold of the edge of her T-shirt. As she moved Ran tugged and then Sylvie tugged back and Ran let go.

Sylvie wasn't sure which of them it was that made the small hissing sound, expelling their breath as her T-shirt, Lycra added to the cotton to ensure its smooth neat fit, reacted automatically to their tugging action and shot upwards, fully exposing her naked breasts.

Sylvie heard Ran curse and then saw him go very still; motionless herself, Sylvie waited. The sensation of Ran's hand gently cupping her naked breast made her close her eyes in self-defence as she tried to stem the rapture that flooded through her. It wasn't just *what* he was doing, it was the fact that she had once longed for him to touch her, to hold her like this so very, very much, and it was as though all that long-ago feeling and all that long-ago need had suddenly risen up inside her.

'Ran...' She heard herself whisper his name, but the hands she put out to him were there to hold him, not to push him away, and as she felt him lower himself slowly against her again the shudder that ran through her was one of desire and not rejection.

Very slowly and gently his fingertips stroked her breasts, shaping them, exploring them. The night air felt velvet soft and sensual against them but nowhere near as soft nor as sensual as Ran's hands.

Carefully he caressed her and she could see the fierce gleam in his eyes as he looked briefly into hers and then he was bending his head towards her, kissing her with a fierce, passionate intensity that left her totally defenceless. Helplessly she opened her mouth to the hungry demand of his, making a tiny soft keening sound deep in her throat as she responded and matched his passion.

There was something earthy, primitive, inevitable and unstoppable about what was happening. A soft breeze whispered through the trees bordering the gravel and hypersensitively Sylvie heard it, felt its warmth against her skin. The rough cloth of Ran's shirt teased her breasts, making her ache for the feel of his hands against them again. His hands...his mouth... She heard him groan, his fingers biting into her skin as he drew her close, so close that she could feel the hard, aroused pulse of his body. Instinctively her own rose up as though seeking even closer contact with him. His mouth burned hotly against her throat as he kissed it, his head moving lower and lower still until she could feel its demanding heat against her breast.

Sylvie whispered in need, arching up towards him, almost sobbing in relief as his mouth finally closed over her nipple, caressing it gently, his tongue laving it and then flicking erotically against it before he started to suck on it with a rhythmic urgency that echoed the pulsing heat of his arousal.

Once, long ago, she had dreamt of Ran wanting her like this, *needing* her like this, all aching, fierce, demanding male passion. Tiny shock waves of desire were flooding sensuously through her, she wanted him so badly; eagerly she drew him closer and then froze as somewhere in the woods a fox screamed noisily to the moon.

Ran too tensed, lifting his mouth from her body as he turned his head in the direction of the noise.

Suddenly, abruptly, protected no longer by the heat of his passion nor the warmth of his body, Sylvie realised what she was doing. The gravel of the drive which previously she had not even noticed pressed sharply into her skin, and her face flushed with mortification as she realised how she must look, how she must *seem* to Ran, so pathetically eager for his kisses, for *him*, that she…

'Don't touch me,' she warned him shakily as she yanked down her top and struggled to her feet. 'I feel sorry for your…for Vicky…if all it takes to make you unfaithful to her is…'

'You?' Ran supplied tersely for her.

Sylvie's flush deepened, pain filling her body as she turned away from him so that he wouldn't see how much he was hurting her.

'We both know that what just happened had nothing to do with... That it wasn't *me*... I could have been *anyone*. My body could have been *anyone's*. You were...'

'So turned on by the sight of your semi-naked breasts that I couldn't resist seeing if they felt and tasted as good as they looked,' Ran told her softly. 'You forget, Sylvie... I've seen them before, and not just seen them but—'

'Stop it, stop it,' Sylvie begged him, instinctively placing her hands over her ears to blot out the sound of his taunting words. That was the last thing she wanted to be reminded about now...the very last... Tears blurred her vision. Frantically she blinked them away; she wasn't going to let Ran see her crying... No way...

Shakily she made her way towards the Discovery whilst Ran watched her broodingly. What the hell could he say to her? She had every right to be furiously angry with him. That gibe about Vicky had been uncalled for, though. Vicky wasn't his love...he didn't *have* a love... There was no relationship, no commitment in his life...unlike her.

Did she respond to Lloyd the same way she had to him, with that aching, intoxicating blend of female need and almost out-of-control hunger?

Ran closed his eyes as he heard Sylvie start the engine of her car.

He had made his fair share of mistakes in his life and had his due portion of regrets, but there was nothing he regretted more than... He swallowed and looked out into the darkness. He hadn't needed what had happened tonight to tell him that there was unfinished business between him and Sylvie.

As he started to walk towards where he had left his car the fierce male ache in his body made him clench his teeth. Right now there was nothing, *nothing*, he wanted more than to finish what they had started. Nothing he wanted more and no one he could have less.

Sylvie's body might still be responsive to him, but Sylvie herself hated him. He knew that. She had told him so often enough.

'Wayne's the man I love,' she had said, throwing the words at him like weapons, and he, too furious, too jealous to respond, had simply walked away without explaining to her that she was a wealthy man's daughter and he might have nothing, but at least, unlike her precious Wayne, he genuinely cared about her, hadn't just been using her!

He had spent the next two days searching Oxford from top to bottom for her, but by then it was too late—she had disappeared. The next time he had seen her she had been with the band of New Age travellers who had invaded Alex's land, quite plainly enjoying flaunting her relationship with its leader in front of him.

'What's wrong?' she had taunted him. '*You* didn't want me...you told me so and you were right, Ran, you're not the one for me...not very much of a man at all compared with Wayne,' she had purred with a sensuously knowing look that had made him feel as if someone was ripping out his guts.

'She and Wayne seem to be lovers,' Alex had confided to him unhappily, and now another man had taken over that role in her life, that *place* in her bed, and he had no right...

Helplessly he stared at the stars. Why the hell had he done it, given in to the temptation to resurrect for himself all the old ghosts, all the old pain? Hadn't he already spent enough nights lying alone in his bed, aching for her, wanting her?

Perhaps Alex was right; perhaps it was time that he looked around for a woman to settle down with, and perhaps once this business was finished and Sylvie was finally out of his life that was exactly what he would do… Perhaps…

CHAPTER FIVE

SYLVIE frowned as she started to double-check what she had just been reading. In a detailed account for the work involved in treating both the wet and dry rot to Haverton Hall, she had only just noticed that slipped in at the back was an additional sheet reporting on some dry rot infestation in the Rectory, Ran's private property, and with it was a brief note confirming that the work on the Rectory would be put in hand before the contractors started working on Haverton Hall itself.

Sylvie could feel her heart starting to thump heavily with a mixture of anger and pain as she re-read the sheet. It wasn't unknown for the owners of the properties the Trust took over to try to drive as hard a bargain as they possibly could. It had fallen to Sylvie on more than one occasion to tactfully inform very grand personages that odd pieces of furniture they had listed as antiques had turned out, on further inspection, to be in fact extremely good copies and therefore not worth the value which had originally been attributed to them. On such occasions a very large supply of tact plus an even larger helping of erring on the side of generosity was called for, but for some reason the possibility of having caught Ran out in such a way evoked within her such strong and confusing emotions that she had to get up from her makeshift desk in front of her bedroom window to pace her bedroom floor whilst she mentally rehearsed exactly how she was going to confront him with her discovery of what he had done. The sum involved wasn't particularly large—and, had Ran gone about things in a different way, she knew perfectly well that the Trust would probably have large-mindedly and generously offered to bear the cost of the work on the Rectory. It was the fact that he had tried to *cheat* them…to deceive and trick her…that Sylvie found so unacceptable, the fact that he probably thought he *had* deceived her, the fact that he was probably secretly laughing at her behind her back. Well, he wasn't going to be laughing when she confronted him, she decided angrily.

A knock on her bedroom door stopped her in her tracks, her body tensing as she called out tersely, 'Come in,' whilst mentally deciding how to mount her attack. But when the door opened it wasn't Ran who walked into her room but the housekeeper, Mrs Elliott.

'Oh, Mrs Elliott,' Sylvie faltered.

'Ran asked me to check with you what you would like for dinner this evening,' the woman told her. 'He landed a fine wild salmon this morning and he said it was a particular favourite of yours…'

Sylvie closed her eyes.

Damn Ran. What was he trying to do to her reminding her, of things, of a past, she would much rather forget?

'That's very kind of you, Mrs Elliott,' she told the other woman crisply, 'but I shall be eating out this evening.'

Previously she had not given the least thought to where she might eat her evening meal, and she knew that her behaviour in refusing Ran's salmon was both illogical and slightly childish, but she hadn't been able to help herself.

Where was Ran anyway…strategically keeping out of

her way? Well, he couldn't do that for ever, and she
certainly intended to tell him what she had discovered
and to demand an explanation of his misuse of the
Trust's funds. No doubt he had imagined that he could
slip the bill for the work on his own property through
with the bill for the cost of the work on Haverton Hall
without anyone being any the wiser. Well, he was going
to learn very quickly his error. Which reminded her—
she really ought to go up to the house and have a word
with whoever was in charge of the company he had hired
to deal with the dry rot. Sylvie pursed her lips. By rights
the contract ought to have been put out to tender, but
she had to admit that by acting so promptly and getting
both the report compiled and the work started Ran had
saved her a good deal of groundwork—and enabled
work to be done on the Rectory at the Trust's expense?

Ten minutes later Sylvie was on her way downstairs
when she heard voices in the hallway, and as she
rounded the curve of the staircase she could see Mrs
Elliott talking with a tall, elegant woman in her late
thirties.

'So you'll tell Ran that I called,' she was saying to
Mrs Elliott.

'Yes, I will, Mrs Edwards,' the other woman was responding respectfully.

Thoughtfully and discreetly Sylvie studied her. Tall,
slender, expensively dressed, immaculately made up, she
was the type of woman whom Sylvie could remember
Ran favouring and she immediately guessed that she
must be Ran's current woman-friend. There was certainly that very confident, almost proprietorial air about
her that suggested she was far more than simply a mere
visitor to the house. She turned away from Mrs Elliott

and then saw Sylvie, her expression changing slightly and becoming, if not challenging then certainly assessing, Sylvie recognised as she continued on her way downstairs.

'I'm just on my way to Haverton Hall, Mrs Elliott,' she told Ran's daily calmly, adding with an impetuosity she later refused to examine or analyse, 'Please thank Ran for his offer of dinner.'

Out of the corner of her eye she could see the way Ran's woman-friend's eyes darkened as she watched her, and she had just reached the front door when Mrs Elliott stopped her, announcing, 'Oh, I'm so sorry, I almost forgot; Ran asked me to tell you that if you wanted to finish going over the big house he'd be back around three.'

'Did he? That's very thoughtful of him. How very obliging of him,' Sylvie responded acidly. 'When he does return, Mrs Elliott, please tell him that there's no need for him to put himself to so much trouble. I have my own set of keys to Haverton Hall.'

Without waiting for the older woman to make any further response, Sylvie pulled open the front door. How dared he? she fumed as she hurried towards her hire car. She had no need of either his company or his permission to view the Hall. Furiously she started the Discovery, sending up an angry spray of gravel as she reversed and then headed for the drive.

She was over halfway to Haverton Hall before she felt calm enough to slow down a little, her face burning as hotly as her temper. It was not up to Ran to tell her what she could and could not do—not any longer.

As she brought the Discovery to a halt outside the house she hastily averted her eyes from the spot where last night... What had happened last night was something she had no intention of dwelling on nor trying to analyse; it had been a mistake, an error of judgement, a total and complete aberration and something which had, no doubt, been brought on by some kind of jet lag, some kind of inexplicable imbalance, and it really wasn't worthy of having her waste any time agonising over it.

Unlocking the huge door, she turned the handle and took a deep breath as she pushed it open and stepped inside. Resolutely ignoring the echoing sound of her own footsteps, she hurried to where she and Ran had left off their inspection the previous day. In her bag she had an inventory and a plan of the house, but an hour later she was forced to admit that it was proving far less interesting inspecting the rooms on her own than it had been yesterday, with Ran's informative descriptions of the rooms and their original uses.

From previous experience she knew that in a very short space of time she herself would be completely familiar with the house's layout and its history, but right now... She gave a small scream as a mouse scuttled across the floor right in front of her. She had always had an irrational fear of them—they moved so fast and so far, and she had never totally got over an unpleasant childhood experience of having one jump towards her as it ran from one of the stable cats.

She was working her way along the upper floor when she suddenly heard Ran calling her name. Stiffening, she stood where she was. Mrs Elliott must have told him that he would find her here. In her bag she had the report and the costings he had commissioned for treatment of the wet and dry rot. Firmly she walked towards the door, opened it and called out, 'I'm up here, Ran...'

'You shouldn't have come here on your own,' he cautioned her as he came down the corridor towards her.

'Why not? The house isn't haunted, is it?' she mocked him sarcastically.

'Not as far as I know,' he agreed, 'but the floors, especially on these upper two floors, aren't totally to be trusted, and if you should have had an accident—'

'How very thoughtful of you to be concerned, Ran,' Sylvie interrupted him. 'Almost as thoughtful as it was of you to commission these reports.'

As she spoke she removed the reports from her bag and waved them under his nose. 'Or am I being naive and would "self-interested" be a much truer description?'

Ran started to frown.

'I don't know what you're trying to imply, Sylvie,' he began, but she wouldn't let him go any further, challenging him immediately,

'Don't you, Ran? I read the reports from the surveyors this morning. Tucked in at the back of the estimates you'd obtained was this…'

Coolly she handed him the costing for the work on the Rectory.

'So?' Ran shrugged after he had scanned the piece of paper she proffered.

'This particular costing relates to work that needs to be carried out on the *Rectory*, your *own private* house,' Sylvie pointed out patiently.

'And…?' Ran demanded, frowning at her before telling her, 'I'm sorry, Sylvie, but I'm afraid I'm at a loss to understand exactly what it is you're driving at. The Rectory needed some work doing on it to put right the dry rot the surveyors found, and—'

'You decided to slip the bill for that work in amongst the bills for the work that was needed on Haverton Hall, to *lose* it amongst the admittedly far greater cost of the work needed here!'

'What?' Ran demanded ominously quietly, his expression as well as his voice betraying his outrage.

'I don't like what you're trying to suggest, Sylvie,' he told her sharply.

She shook her head and told him thinly, 'Neither do I, Ran. But the facts speak for themselves.'

'Do they?' His mouth twisted bitterly. 'I rather think it's your overheated imagination that's doing the "speaking" through your totally erroneous interpretation of them,' he told her through gritted teeth.

'You can't deny the evidence of this report,' Sylvie reminded him sternly.

'What evidence?' Ran demanded. 'This is a report and an estimate for work on the Rectory—work which I have had carried out at *my own* expense; the only reason the report and costing is there at all is because I omitted to remove it when I had the documents copied for you…'

'*You've* paid for the work on the Rectory yourself?' Sylvie queried in disbelief.

Ran's mouth thinned.

'Perhaps you'd like to see the receipts,' he challenged her.

'Yes, I would,' Sylvie responded doggedly, refusing to let him cow her even though she could feel her face starting to burn self-consciously and her stomach beginning to churn as she contemplated just how foolish she was going to look if Ran did produce such receipts.

'Mrs Elliott tells me that you're going out for dinner this evening.'

Sylvie stared at him, thrown by his abrupt change of subject.

'Yes. Yes, I am,' she agreed.

'There isn't a decent restaurant for miles,' he told her, 'and certainly not one that offers fresh wild salmon; it's always been one of your favourites...'

'Perhaps my tastes have changed,' Sylvie said a little loftily, adding robustly, 'Unlike yours...'

As he started to frown she explained sweetly, 'I saw your...*friend*. She called at the Rectory just as I was leaving. I'm sure she'd be more than delighted to share your salmon with you, Ran,' she told him coolly. 'Now, about those receipts...'

Inwardly Sylvie shivered a bit as she saw the anger flare in his eyes but outwardly she stood her ground. It was, after all, her job to make sure that the Trust wasn't cheated by *anyone*.

'Of course,' Ran told her formally, inclining his head as though in defeat, but then, just as Sylvie started to draw a relieved breath, he gave her a dangerously vulpine smile and told her softly, 'But I'm afraid it will have to be this evening as I have a business meeting tomorrow morning and then I shall probably be away for several days...'

'With your...friend...?'

Later Sylvie could only despair over whatever it was that had led her to make such a dangerously betraying and provocative remark, but inexplicably the words were out before she could stop them, causing Ran, who had been on the point of turning away from her, to turn back and slowly scrutinise her from head to foot before asking her softly, 'If you mean Vicky, is that really any of your business...*or* the Trust's...?'

He had caught her out and Sylvie knew it. It most certainly was not part of her duty as the Trust's representative to ask any questions about his personal life, and she was mortified that she had done so.

'If you want to see the receipts for the work on the Rectory then it will have to be this evening, Sylvie,' Ran was repeating briskly. 'Shall we say about eight-thirty?'

Before she could say anything else he had gone, striding across the dusty floor and leaving her to watch his departing back.

It was a good ten minutes after she had heard the noise of his Land Rover engine die away before Sylvie felt able to continue with her work. Her intelligence told her that their antagonism was coming between her and the normally wisely efficient way in which she dealt with even the most awkward of the Trust's clients, but her emotions refused to allow her to back down, to climb down. If she was wary of him, suspicious of him, then she had every right to be.

And every right to as good as accuse him of trying to defraud the Trust?

She started to nibble anxiously at her bottom lip. If she was wrong about him trying to get the Trust to cover the cost of work he had had done on his own home, and if he chose to complain to Lloyd—

Irritably Sylvie reminded herself why she was here.

Although the house wasn't any larger than others she had dealt with, it certainly seemed to possess far more small interconnecting rooms here on its upper storeys. She rubbed the dust from the window of one of them and peered out at the countryside spread all around her. From here she could see the river where Ran must have caught his fish. It wound lazily in a long half-loop through the parkland which surrounded the house. Although the terrain here in Derbyshire was very different from that which surrounded Alex's home, it was disturbingly easy, looking down towards the river, to remember the many happy hours she had spent with Alex and Ran as a young girl, watching them as they worked together, helping them fish and later learning from them their countryside skills.

One of the ways in which, hopefully, ultimately, Haverton Hall could generate its own income would be, as Ran had suggested in the initial approach he had made to the Trust, for the house to be let out to large corporations and groups along with its fishing and shooting rights. The Trust adopted a policy that no game existing on its lands could be killed simply for sport—a very strict culling programme was put in place where necessary and the art of tracking animals was taught as a skill for its own sake rather than with a view to killing. That had been a condition which she herself had insisted on persuading the trustees to adopt, and it made her stop and frown slightly to herself now as she was forced to remember how it had been Ran who had first shown her that it was not necessary to kill to enjoy such traditional country sports.

Ran…

Sylvie was still thinking about him some time later when an exhausting drive through the virtually uninhabited countryside which surrounded the house had only produced three small villages, not one of which boasted a restaurant.

In the small pub in the third village the landlord shook his head when she asked about food and apologised.

'We don't have the trade for it round here, although I could perhaps see if there's any sandwiches left over from lunchtime.'

Smiling wanly, Sylvie shook her head. She was hungry, very hungry in fact, and had been looking forward to sitting down to a proper hot meal.

'There's a good place over Lintwell way,' the pub manager was continuing helpfully, 'but that's a good twenty-five miles from here.'

Twenty-five miles. Sylvie's stomach was already starting to rumble. Against her will she had a mental vision of Ran's salmon, pink and poached, served with delicious home-grown baby new potatoes and fresh vegetables and, of course, a proper hollandaise sauce. Her mouth watered.

It was gone seven o'clock now, though, and if she were to drive to Lintwell and back and eat as well that would mean she would be late for her meeting with Ran and there was no way she was going to allow him the opportunity to accuse her of being unprofessional.

Refusing the landlord's offer of the afternoon's leftover sandwiches, she made her way back to her car. She would just have to go without a meal tonight, she told herself firmly; after all, it wouldn't be the end of the world. She was hardly going to starve... But oh, that salmon and... Ran was quite right. It was her favourite.

It was almost eight when Sylvie pulled up outside the Rectory's front door.

Her earlier hunger had turned into a gnawing irritation that was making her head ache and her temper on edge.

Low blood sugar, she told herself sternly. All you need is a sweet drink.

All she *needed* maybe, but not all she wanted. What she wanted...

What on earth was the matter with her? she derided herself as she opened the front door. Other women her age daydreamed and fantasised about having men, not meals.

Eight o'clock. She just had time to get showered and changed before her meeting with Ran. She wanted to run through her figures again, but if, as he said, he had paid for the work himself and he had the receipts to prove it... Perhaps she *had* been too quick to accuse him...

'Sylvie...'

She froze at the bottom of the stairs as she heard Ran's voice. When she turned her head he was standing in an open doorway several feet away from her.

'Mrs Elliott is going to serve dinner at eight-thirty so you've got half an hour to get ready...'

A dozen questions and just as many denials and arguments sprang immediately to Sylvie's lips, but somehow she managed not to utter them and she was at the top of the stairs before she managed to ask herself why she had not simply told Ran that she had eaten already.

Why? The audible rumble of her stomach as she opened her bedroom door gave its own answer. Even so, it galled her to know that Ran had guessed she would have to return to the house without having found somewhere to eat. But just let him try to make something of it, Sylvie decided fiercely as, having had her shower, she changed into a long silky black jersey dress, brushing her hair and quickly re-doing her make-up before checking the time.

Almost eight-thirty. Taking a deep breath, Sylvie checked her appearance in the mirror and then, holding her head high, headed for the bedroom door.

Her jersey dress, plain black and unadorned, might not, to anyone but the *cognoscente*, reveal the fact that it had cost her the best part of a month's wages and carried the label of one of New York's top designers—the uninitiated might be deceived by the simple design and the way the heavy fabric discreetly hinted at rather than clung more obviously to Sylvie's slender figure. But even the most self-confessed sartorial ignoramus would have reacted to the way Ran looked when Sylvie saw him waiting for her at the bottom of the stairs.

Used as she was to seeing him wearing casual work clothes, and perhaps because that was the image she held engraved in her mind's eye—jeans fitting snugly against the hard muscle of his thighs, checked work shirt rolled up at the sleeves and just open enough at the neck to reveal the silky dark expanse of body hair which so temptingly and tormentingly made one's fingers long to unfasten a few more buttons and explore just how thick, just how silky that soft dark hair actually was—Sylvie had forgotten how very male Ran could look in formal clothes.

And although he hadn't gone so far as to change into a dinner suit he *was* wearing a pair of well-cut dark trousers and a crisp white shirt.

The fact that he was just shrugging on his jacket as she came down the stairs afforded Sylvie an unwanted glimpse of the lethal maleness of the muscles in his torso and made her hesitate betrayingly just for a second before continuing her journey downwards.

He had changed his clothes simply to have dinner with her.

Why? Because he knew very well the effect his appearance would have on any susceptible woman and because he intended to use that fact to distract her, confuse her when she needed all her attention, all her concentration to ascertain the truth about that invoice? Or was she letting her imagination run away with her? Was the woman he had dressed so elegantly for not her but—?

Was he perhaps seeing the other woman after their meeting had finished?

'We've just got time for a drink before dinner if you'd like one,' Ran told her calmly, but his glance, Sylvie was sure, had rested for just a betraying fraction of a second on the soft thrust of her breasts before it had lifted to her face. Her heart started to thump giddily.

'No... No drink, thanks,' she refused, giving him a thin smile as she added deliberately, 'I generally find that alcohol and business don't mix.'

Giving a small shrug, Ran opened the dining-room door for her and waited for her to precede him inside. As she did so, Sylvie caught the clean, sharp scent of his freshly showered body and the giddying thump of her vulnerable heart became a frighteningly heavy ache.

'I...I've brought the estimates down with me,' she told him quickly, lifting the papers she was holding in front of him, but Ran shook his head.

'After dinner,' he told her dismissively, adding, '*I* generally find that good food and poor communication don't mix.'

Poor communication. Sylvie gave him a fulminating look before taking the chair he had pulled out for her.

The salmon was every bit as delicious as Sylvie had imagined and so, too, was the home-made summer pudding served with fresh cream that followed it. The cheese they ate to finish the meal was made locally, Ran informed her, adding that he had been wondering if he might not produce something similar himself, but that he had decided the costs involved were prohibitive.

To have dinner alone with Ran like this would once have made her feel so excited, so...so thrilled because she had been so besottedly in love with him. Of course, she would hardly have been able to do justice to the meal because then her fevered imagination would have been thrilling her with images of the two of them together alone, after dinner, Ran taking her in his arms and...

'I've asked Mrs Elliott to serve coffee in the library...'

The crisp, businesslike tone of Ran's voice cut across her treacherous thoughts. Guiltily, Sylvie pushed them away, reminding herself severely of just why she was here.

'Here is the separate estimate I asked for, for the work which needed doing here, and here is the receipt I obtained for that work.'

Her facial muscles rigid, Sylvie willed her hand not to tremble betrayingly as she took the papers from Ran and then looked at them. She was furious with herself for giving him the opportunity to put her in the wrong.

Her eyes strayed to the date at the top of the receipted

invoice. She wasn't going to give in yet. Standing up, she handed the papers back to Ran and told him dismissively, 'What I can see is a signed and dated receipt, Ran.'

'Showing that the invoice was settled several weeks ago...'

'*Purporting* to show that it was settled several weeks ago,' Sylvie pointed out stubbornly. 'For all I know this date could have been written on the invoice last week...or...' She paused meaningfully before adding with a triumphant smile, 'Or even today...'

She had started to walk away when Ran stopped her, grabbing hold of her arm and swinging her round to face him as he exploded, 'Are you *really* trying to accuse me of falsifying this receipt? For God's sake, Sylvie, what the hell kind of man do you think I am?'

Pointedly Sylvie ignored his question and stared down at where he was still holding onto her arm instead as she demanded icily, 'Let go of me, Ran.'

'Let *go* of you...? Do you realise what you're saying, what you're *accusing* me of doing? You're not a teenager any more, Sylvie, and if this is some kind of petty attempt to—'

'No, I'm not.' Sylvie interrupted him furiously. 'I'm the Trust's representative here at Haverton and as such it's my job to protect the Trust's interests and its investments... If I think that someone, *anyone*, is trying to cheat the Trust or misuse its funds, then it's my job to—'

'Your *job*...?' Ran laughed savagely. 'You sound very high-minded for someone who's slept her way into her "job" via her boss's bed.'

There was a second's pause and then a white heat, a zigzag of pure fury and frustrated womanly pride, hit

Sylvie like a bolt of lightning. Immediately she reacted in the only way her outraged female instincts knew, lifting her hand and slapping Ran's face in furious rejection of his insult.

Sylvie didn't know which of them was the more shocked—she who had delivered the blow or Ran who had received it. For a single beat of time they both stood completely still, staring at one another. Sylvie could feel her heart racing, she could see the white, slowly reddening imprint of her hand against Ran's dark skin and she could see too the vengeful male fury darkening his eyes. Too late to regret her behaviour, or to turn and run; Ran was still holding onto her arm, and as she tried to pull away he dragged her towards him, his eyes glittering with fevered rage.

Sylvie knew, even before it happened, just what he was going to do. She was already closing her eyes and whispering helplessly, 'No,' as she felt the hard, bruising pressure of his mouth against her own.

To be kissed like this, in fury, in punishment, and with a blind, searing male desire to dominate, was something totally outside all her experience. Her body had no defences against it, no knowledge of how to deal with it. Panic and anger surged through her body. She was no helpless Victorian virgin, she was a modern woman, able to give as good as she got. Fiercely she returned the anger of Ran's furious kiss. He was already prising apart her closed lips with his tongue, demanding entry to the intimacy of her mouth, not with the tender touch of a lover but with the forceful pressure of a warrior, a victor. Wildly Sylvie tried to evade him, but he was holding onto her too strongly and all her attempts to break free did was to bring her body into even closer contact with

his. She still fought to break free, pummelling his chest
with her fists and then, when that did no good and there
was no longer any space between their bodies for her to
do so, angrily raking her nails down his back.

Somewhere, deep down, in the murkiest of murky waters of her subconscious, lay the knowledge that this
wasn't just about the insult he had given her, nor her
angry reaction to it; that this explosion of furious emotion this need to reach out and hurt him, to damage and
destroy what was left of the love she had once felt for
him, had its roots, its being, in something very, very
different from mere insulted female pride.

'Little vixen,' she heard Ran muttering thickly against
her mouth as he caught hold of her hand. 'Your elderly
lover might need the stimulus of having his back
scratched raw when you make love but I certainly don't.'

Shocked into awareness of what she was doing by his
words, Sylvie went still.

Lloyd might not be her lover, but that didn't really
matter; it was the impact of what Ran had just said to
her that hurt and wounded so badly, the fact that he was
comparing the anger and mutual hatred they were both
expressing with an act that, to Sylvie, was one which
should be highlighted and hallmarked with tenderness
and true emotional love. Suddenly all the anger drained
out of her. She felt sickened, not just by Ran's words
but more importantly by what she herself had done. A
vixen, Ran had called her, but when animals mated they
did so for a specific purpose; their coming together was
never an act of cruelty or cynical disregard for everything that sharing the intimacy of one's body with another should be.

Sylvie could feel her eyes starting to fill with tears.

Ran had pulled back from her to look at her, and, taking advantage of his slackened grip, she pulled herself free of him and started to walk quickly, if a little unsteadily, towards the library door.

Startled, Ran called out to her, following her out into the hallway, watching as she disappeared up the stairs. Should he go after her, apologise, explain...? That look he had just seen in her eyes had shocked him. It was more the look of a hurt child than a mature, experienced, worldly woman, and besides... There had been no call for him to make that remark to her about Lloyd. Her relationship with the other man was, after all, her own affair, even if he... God... For a moment there the feeling, the sharp dig of her nails into his skin through the fabric of his shirt, had made him ache so badly for the feel of her naked body beneath his own, the feel, the scent, the taste of her. And if he could have his time again... But what was the point in thinking about, *reliving* old memories, old mistakes?

He had done what he had thought was best at the time, the honourable thing to do...

CHAPTER SIX

WEARILY Sylvie looked at the luminous face of her watch. Half past one in the morning. She had been awake for the last hour, stubbornly courting sleep, angrily refusing to allow her thoughts to take control, to force her to remember.

She was too hyped up for sleep, too *afraid* to sleep just in case she... She what? Dreamed of Ran?

She looked across at the desk in front of the window. One of the small pleasures of living in the depths of the country was that one did not need to close the curtains at night. There was nothing Sylvie liked more than being able to see the night sky.

When her mother had first married Alex's father and they had gone to live in his ancestral home, she had been overwhelmed at first by the darkness of the huge house. It had been Ran who had guessed her fears and apprehensions after he had found her sleepwalking that night. Ran who had been staying at the house instead of his cottage one weekend, 'babysitting' her in the absence of her mother, and who had taken her, not back to bed, but to his own room where he had made her a hot drink and talked to her, showing her the telescope he used to watch the night sky.

The binoculars beside it he had used for another, more mundane purpose. As the estate manager one of his jobs had been to keep a sharp look-out for poachers. The night had no fears for Ran, and through him she too had learned to appreciate its special beauties. It had been Ran who had taken her to watch the badger cubs at play, earning her mother's anger. Sylvie quickly stopped that line of thought. Since she couldn't sleep she might as well try to do some work; that at least would be a far more profitable way of spending her time than thinking about Ran.

Her mouth still felt slightly swollen and sensitive from the way he had kissed her earlier. Her face started to burn as she recalled again the comment he had made to her about her being a vixen—and about Lloyd being her lover.

What would he say if he knew that she had only had one lover and that lover had been a man who hadn't really wanted her, a man she had had to coax and beg to take her to bed, a man who had told her that he felt no love for her, that what had happened between them had been a mistake, an error of judgement best forgotten?

No. No. No. Angrily, Sylvie buried her face in her hands, but it was too late; there was no pushing back the memories now, they were here, surrounding her, flooding out any kind of denial or rational thought.

She had been at university by then; had, in fact, gone there unwillingly. So intense and all-consuming had been the ferocity of her teenage love for Ran, so burningly immediate and sharp-fanged her desire for him, that she had not been able to bear the thought of putting any kind of distance between them. Every spare minute she had, every excuse she could use, she *had* used to be with Ran. As Alex's stepsister it had been easy enough for her to spend her free time at the estate, joining the group of local teenagers who were helping Ran with some of his environmental projects had given her even more opportunity to be with him. Not that Ran himself had seemed to be aware of her feelings, even though she had done everything she could to show him how she felt.

There had been that afternoon she had fallen into the muddy lake they had been cleaning. Ran had pulled her out, grinning at her mud-covered clothes and hair.

'I need a bath,' she had complained, grimacing.

'A *bath*?' Ran had laughed. 'There's no way Alex's housekeeper is going to let you into the house like that. I'd better take you back to the cottage with me and hose you down outside before I let you go back, otherwise we'll both be in real trouble.'

His cottage... How she had trembled at the thought, imagining not the prosaic cleaning-up operation Ran had so teasingly referred to but something far more intimate, her body soaking in a tub of blissfully hot water whilst Ran lovingly soaped her clean...

'What's wrong?' he had asked her, frowning at her. 'You've gone very red. Are you feeling ill?'

Ill... Sick with love, with *longing* for him, would have been the appropriate answer, but she had been too naive, too shy to make it. Instead she had shaken her head and dutifully climbed into his battered Land Rover for the drive back to his small estate cottage.

The sensual intimacy she had so dangerously imagined had proved to be just that—a fantasy.

Ran had made her remove her clothes in his small back porch, sternly admonishing her not to move off the old towel he had put down on the floor and to give him a shout once she was undressed and wrapped in the towel he had left her.

'I'll put your stuff in the washer—Alex's housekeeper will kill me if she sees it—and then you can have a quick shower upstairs. You'll have to go home in my stuff but at least it will be clean.'

'These towels are awfully thin,' she had remarked critically once she was standing wrapped in the protection of the largest of them, and Ran had returned to scoop up her filthy clothes.

'Mmm… I use them to dry the dogs,' Ran had told her unromantically, grinning at her when he saw her expression. 'They're the ones who should be pulling a face,' he said. 'When *they* come back covered in mud they get hosed down outside before they're even allowed in.'

'I'm not a dog, I'm a…' A woman, she had been about to say, but then she had stopped as Ran had stooped to pick up her white briefs from the stone floor, her face turning an unsophisticated shade of pink when she saw how small they looked held in his strongly masculine hand.

The wet had seeped right through her jeans to her briefs, but Ran's eyebrows had risen as he'd studied them and then her.

'It's all right… I can go home without them; it won't matter under…my…your jeans,' Sylvie had told him helpfully, far too innocent and young then to understand just how sensuously provocative it could be for a woman to go naked beneath her clothes—and even more so when the clothes, the *jeans* she was wearing, were his and not her own.

'It's okay; I think I've got something you can wear,' Ran had told her laconically.

She had been young and naive but not so young nor

so naive as not to be able to guess where the tiny pretty lacy briefs Ran had given her might have come from, and the knowledge that they must have belonged to another woman had cast a shadow not just over the whole day, but over everything.

She had once heard Alex joking with Ran about his taste for older women.

'I'm not in the market for commitment or marriage,' Ran had returned. 'But I'm not about to turn myself into a monk either,' he had admitted frankly. Neither of them had known that she was listening as she hesitated outside Alex's library door on her way past.

'So a woman who knows what life's all about, who's been married and decided that it isn't for her, suits me fine.'

She hadn't been able to hide her massive crush on Ran before she'd left for university, in fact had openly offered her love to him, but he had determinedly pushed it away—just as he had also determinedly pushed her away.

She had noticed it again at Alex's annual Christmas party. Her mother had been there, turning her nose up at such little country pursuits, but Sylvie hadn't cared. She'd been determined that Ran was going to dance with her and that she was going to claim a Christmas kiss from him.

She had been wearing a new dress and high heels. She had put her hair up and worn make-up. Alex had looked at her with tender amusement when she had come downstairs, but there had been no tenderness in Ran's eyes later that evening when he had removed her arms from around his neck, refusing to give her the kiss she had begged him for. It had taken three glasses of wine before she had had the courage to approach him and, horrendously, she could feel her eyes starting to fill with tears as he'd unlocked her arms from around his neck and started to turn away from her.

'Ran, please...' she had pleaded, but he had ignored her, stony-faced and blank-eyed, as he'd walked away from her.

And, as though that hadn't been bad enough, to compound the evening's heartache and humiliation, she had seen him less than an hour later dancing with the newly divorced wife of one of Alex's tenants, holding her tightly against his body as he caressed her under the dim lights, bending his head to kiss her with heart-shaking passion before leading her outside.

She had been so jealous, so burned up with pain that even her skin had felt raw and tender.

Later, naively, she'd told herself that Ran hadn't meant to hurt her, that he probably still thought of her as a child and not a woman, and so she had gone on clinging to her self-created delusions.

All through her first year at university, as much as she had wanted to hate Ran, she had also yearned for him, dreaming of him, longing for him, promising herself that one day it would be different, one day he would look at her and love her.

She had refused dates from the boys she met on her courses and only attended the regulation student parties because the other girls had teased her into it. Naturally gregarious, although no one could ever come to mean to her what Ran meant, she had nevertheless made several platonic friendships with various boys she had met at university. One of them she had particularly taken to; shy and self-effacing, David had only come to university because of family pressure. As the youngest of his family he'd been expected to follow in the footsteps of his elder sisters and brothers, all of whom had graduated with honours.

'What did you really want to do?' Sylvie had asked him.

'Paint,' he had told her simply.

Sylvie's discovery that he was taking drugs had saddened but not particularly shocked her. They were, after all, a feature of university life, although she herself had stayed clear of them.

It had been David who had persuaded her to attend the rave party where he had introduced her to Wayne. She had guessed that Wayne was his supplier but had naively assumed then that Wayne was no more than a generous-minded individual who had the contacts to supply his friends with drugs, and that it was they who pressured him into obtaining them for them rather than the other way around. Without directly saying so, Wayne had implied that they were two of a kind, individuals who stood out from the crowd. His street-wise sophistication had reminded her in some odd way of Ran. Perhaps because, like Ran, Wayne was older than her and the friends she'd mixed with. She had listened half enviously when he had told her of his plans to spend the summer with a group of eco-warriors, travelling the country.

Sylvie had always been idealistic, and Wayne's description of the way the group were dedicated to preventing the destruction of the countryside by greedy power barons had increased her sense of comradeship with him and with the group he was joining.

Just as importantly, Wayne had seemed to understand

the problems she was having in convincing her mother that she was now an adult.

'She's such a snob,' she had told Wayne ruefully, wrinkling her nose.

'She wouldn't much approve of me, then,' he had countered, and although she had shaken her head Sylvie had been forced to admit that he was right. She had confided to Wayne how uncomfortable it often made her feel that she should be so privileged. Alex gave her an allowance and her mother was constantly visiting her and fussing over whether or not she was eating properly and wearing the right kind of clothes. Her mother had never wanted her to go to university. She had bemoaned the fact that girls like Sylvie no longer had the opportunity to ''come out'' properly, as she had done as a girl. Alex had been the driving force behind her moving off to university. Time, he said, for her to grow and find out about herself.

It had not been long after her disclosure that she received an allowance that Wayne had asked to borrow money from her. Of course she had given it to him. He was a friend…

And then, after she had given Wayne the money he had asked for, she had discovered that she needed to buy some new course books, and that stupidly she had not realised that she had an advance rent bill due for the small flat she lived in.

She had had to telephone Alex to ask him for an advance on her forthcoming allowance. She had felt uncomfortable about doing so, but after a small pause, when she had stammeringly explained that she had loaned some money to a friend, he had said quietly that she could leave the matter with him.

Naively she had assumed that that meant that he would send her a cheque, and suddenly she'd had more important things to worry about than money. David, her friend, was dead. He had collapsed at a rave party and been rushed into hospital, but it had been too late to save him.

His family had taken him home to bury him and they had also made it plain that they did not want any of his university friends to attend his funeral.

'They blame us for what happened to him,' one of his other friends told Sylvie angrily. 'They're the ones who are at fault. He never wanted to come here...'

Sylvie was too upset to make any comment when Wayne asked for another loan, and he was moody and sharp-tempered with her, mocking her upbringing and taunting her with her naiveté and innocence.

That hurt Sylvie but she said nothing. She knew that he would soon be leaving the city to join the eco-warriors, who were beginning to drift away from the site of their recent defeat over a large motorway extension and to make their way south to meet up with another group, who were trying to persuade the Government to give permission for some land previously owned by the Army to be opened to the general public.

To Sylvie it sounded a good cause.

'Come with us,' Wayne suggested, and then he laughed sneeringly as he added, 'But no, of course you won't... Mummy wouldn't like it, would she?'

Sylvie said nothing. She was still too numbed by David's death. University life, which at first had seemed to promise so much freedom...which she had hoped would be the passage which would carry her effortlessly into womanhood and Ran's love...was proving to be far more painful and difficult than she had envisaged.

She had lost weight and hope, and now her work was beginning to suffer too.

The weather was hot and sticky, with the threat of thunder forever present in the air. They needed a good storm, Sylvie reflected early one evening as she returned to her small flat. She wasn't hungry, and the prospect of an evening spent over her books didn't appeal in the least. She missed David and their discussions and she missed Ran even more.

The day had been so hot and the flat was so airless that she showered in a vain attempt to get cool, pulling over her naked body an old cotton shirt which had once belonged to Alex, too drained and lethargic even to think of getting properly dressed. Half an hour later Wayne arrived, carrying a bottle of wine which he insisted on opening even though she told him that she didn't want anything to drink. In the end it was easier to give in than to argue, but she stood her ground over the drug he offered her, firmly shaking her head.

'Please yourself,' he told her easily, but Sylvie noticed that he didn't have one himself either.

'Any chance of letting me have that money?' he asked her a few minutes later as he lounged on her small sofa, watching her as she tried to work. There was a look in his eyes that made her feel uncomfortable, and not just because she couldn't give him the loan he wanted; no, it was more than that, and suddenly she was acutely conscious of her nudity beneath Alex's shirt.

'I'm sorry, I can't...not at the moment,' she apologised. 'I...I'm waiting for Alex to send me a cheque.

Wayne, I don't want to be a bad host, but really I have to work...'

'You want me to leave...'

'If you don't mind,' Sylvie agreed, waving her hand in the direction of the books she had spread out on the small table in front of her.

For a moment she thought he was going to argue with her, but to her relief he didn't, walking instead towards the door. Eager to see him leave, Sylvie went with him. As she opened the door for him she saw the Land Rover pulling to a halt a little further down the road and her heart started to race with frantic excitement. As though aware of her loss of attention, and angered by it, to her shock Wayne suddenly reached for her, grabbing hold of her and forcing her back against the open door, his mouth hot and wet on hers as he kissed her roughly.

Immediately Sylvie pulled away, but not in time to stop Ran, who was stepping out of the Land Rover and walking towards her, from seeing what had happened, nor from witnessing how she was dressed, she saw uncomfortably as she felt his glance scorch her shirt-clad body.

To her relief Wayne's mobile phone had started to ring and he was already heading for his car, his back towards her as he talked in a low voice into the telephone.

As Ran's long-legged, determined stride brought him closer to her door, Sylvie could only stand and watch.

'Ran!' she exclaimed weakly when he reached her. 'What a surprise. I didn't know... I didn't expect...'

'Obviously not,' was Ran's terse response as he stepped past her and into her small hallway, firmly closing the door behind him as he told her sardonically, 'I'm sorry if my arrival is inopportune, although something tells me that it would have been a lot less opportune had I arrived, say, half an hour ago.'

Sylvie's face flamed as she saw the way he was looking at her and realised what he meant. Ran thought that she and Wayne were lovers.

'It's not…we weren't… Wayne is just a friend…' she finally managed to tell him defensively.

Ran's eyebrows immediately shot up.

'A friend! Tell me, Sylvie, do you normally receive your *friends* wearing just one of their shirts…?'

'This isn't Wayne's shirt; it's one of Alex's old ones,' she protested, hot-faced.

What was Ran doing here? Why had he come to see her? Her heart started to thump frantically.

'Alex's shirt?' Ran was frowning at her as he studied her.

'Yes… I…I like to wear it… It makes me think of home…of Alex and you. I miss you both,' she told him daringly, holding her breath as she waited for his response.

There had to be *some* reason for his being here and his reaction to Wayne's presence… Was she daring to hope too much in thinking that beneath his anger he might *just* be a little jealous? She was a woman now, she reminded herself, not a child, and—

'Home…?' Ran cut across her increasingly buoyant thoughts. 'I doubt your mother would enjoy hearing you describe Otel Place as your home.'

Sylvie bit her lip. It was true that her mother did not approve of her attachment to Otel Place and would have preferred it if, like her, Sylvie had been a city person.

'I'm an adult now,' she told Ran bravely. 'I make my own decisions, my own choices…'

'I see… And entertaining your friends wearing nothing but one of Alex's shirts is one of those choices, is it, Sylvie?'

Her face burned. There was no hint of jealousy in his voice now, only a familiar older-brother note of censure.

'I…I wasn't expecting Wayne to come round. It was so hot. I had a shower and…'

'Wayne… This wouldn't be the friend who's borrowed half your last quarter's allowance from you, would it?' Ran challenged her.

Sylvie blanched. Alex had obviously told him about that; she wished that he hadn't.

'I… He'll pay me back.' She defended both Wayne's request and her own acceptance of it.

'Things have certainly changed since *my* time at university,' Ran told her cynically. 'Then it was the man who did the chasing, the pursuing, not the woman who had to secure the man's attentions by offering him money.'

Sylvie stared at him, unable to keep either her shock or the pain his words had caused her from showing in her eyes.

'It isn't like that… I *haven't* been pursuing Wayne. I don't…'

She stopped abruptly and looked away from him. How could she tell Ran of all men…people…that she didn't run after his sex, when he had good reason to believe otherwise after the ways she had so blatantly revealed her feelings for him? Now he was looking at her in that horribly cynical way, his mouth twisting in mocking contempt.

'Alex asked me to come,' he told her as she remained silent. 'He's had to go away on business but he asked me to come and give you this...'

As he spoke Ran was removing a cheque from his wallet which he handed to her.

Swallowing hard, Sylvie took it from him.

'You could have posted it to me,' she told him in a small voice.

'Alex wanted it delivered in person.'

'It's a long drive... I could... Would you like something to drink...to eat...?'

'Coffee will be fine,' Ran told her shortly, following her as she automatically started to walk into her small living room.

The bottle of wine Wayne had brought with him was still on the table, her own glass nearly empty, and Sylvie saw the hard look Ran gave it as he walked past her work table.

A wooden divider separated the living room end of the room from the small kitchenette, and Ran leaned against it as Sylvie bustled about making them both a cup of coffee.

'You've lost weight,' Ran told her abruptly when she finally handed him his mug. 'It is just sex this friend of yours is dealing in, isn't it, Sylvie...?'

As the meaning of his words sank in Sylvie put down her own mug of coffee, her face burning with indignation.

'I'm not taking drugs, if that's what you're suggesting,' she told him angrily. 'I'm not *that* stupid, Ran.'

She closed her eyes momentarily, thinking painfully of David and the waste of his young life. No, drugs would never be something she would be tempted to use, and it hurt her that Ran thought she might.

The buoyancy and joy she had felt earlier had all gone, evaporated, burned away in the raw heat of Ran's anger and contempt. Suddenly she felt slightly tired and sick—the combination of no food, alcohol and too much painful emotion, she guessed miserably.

As tears filled her eyes she reached out impulsively, her fingers curling round the soft fabric of his shirt as she pleaded despairingly, 'Ran, *why* does it have to be like this between us? Why…can't we be friends…?'

'Friends…?'

She shrank back as she heard the bitterness in his voice.

'And what kind of friendship do you propose that we should have, Sylvie? The same kind you share with your *friend* who's just left? What's wrong? Isn't he satisfying you in bed? Do you need someone to compare him with? Because if so…'

Sylvie had had enough.

'That's not what I meant at all,' she cried out. 'I hate you, Ran… I hate you,' she told him tearfully, the child surfacing over the adult she had wanted to be…had wanted him to see…as she pummelled furiously at his chest, desperate to break down the barrier he had thrown up between them.

'Sylvie, stop it.'

As Ran caught hold of her small fists and held her away from him Sylvie realised what she was doing. Shamefaced, she started to look away from him, tensing in his hold when she heard him curse softly under his breath, and then suddenly he was sliding one hand into her hair, holding her head still as he bent his own towards hers, his breath fanning hotly against her face, her lips, his mouth...

His mouth!

In the shock of feeling Ran's mouth actually caressing her own, Sylvie immediately forgot everything which had preceded it— their quarrel, his anger and contempt—and remembered only her love for him!

Instinctively she moved closer to him, opening her mouth beneath his, responding joyously and passionately to his kiss, naively believing that despite everything that had happened he *must* care for her after all; he couldn't be kissing her like this and not do so, could he?

Innocently she pressed her body even closer to his, shivering in ecstatic pleasure as she felt her own response to his nearness. Beneath Alex's shirt, her breasts swelled and hardened; blissfully she anticipated Ran touching them, caressing them.

'*Ran.*'

His name was a soft plea whispered against his lips, her tongue-tip delicately touching them, exploring, tasting. She could feel him shuddering against her and, greatly daring, she darted her tongue into his mouth, seeking and then finding his, motivated, driven by instinct rather than knowledge; but the effect of her innocent exploration on Ran was so explosive that initially it took her off guard, half shocking and wholly exciting her. His hands started to move possessively over her body, down her back, shaping her waist and then moving lower to urge her lower body even closer to his as his tongue lunged repeatedly into the soft moistness of her mouth, carrying her inexorably to the point where she no longer had any control over either her emotions or her physical responsiveness to him, teaching her just what a world of difference existed between her own shyly tentative exploration of his mouth and his passionate male possession of hers.

Against her body she could feel the hard outline of his, and her whole body burned with virginal excitement as it registered and recognised the sensual heat of his physical arousal; the reality of what was happening between them rolled over her, engulfing and totally possessing her as she gave herself up willingly to its domination. She wanted to see him, touch him, taste him, *absorb* the reality of him with every single one of her senses. She wanted, needed, *craved*, to be fully a part of him; to have her whole body melt in the heat of their mutual passion so that she could be totally absorbed into him. She wanted...

With a small moan she wrenched herself away from him, her whole body trembling as she looked into his eyes and told him, *begged* him, 'Ran... Not here... I want... Take me to bed...' she whispered, her face flaming with the directness of her own request. But there was pride in her eyes, not shame, as she looked at him. Why *should* she feel ashamed of loving him so much? After all, he was the one who had kissed her...held her...

'Sylvie...'

The unexpected harshness in Ran's voice unnerved her a little, but she refused to pay any heed to it. Instead she walked up to him and, holding his eyes, very deliberately reached out and touched his body, intimately, there, just where she could see the way his arousal, his erection, was straining against his jeans.

She felt his reaction jolt right through him, as though her touch had burned him, but the drift of her fingertips had been as light as the wings of a butterfly.

'You want me, Ran,' she whispered shakily, 'and I want you…'

And then, without waiting for his response, she turned her back on him and walked very slowly and very deliberately to her bedroom door.

Once there she turned round and looked at him gravely.

He was still standing where she had left him, his face unfamiliarly pale, his eyes blazing with…

Quickly she looked away and then, before her courage could desert her, she tugged open the buttons of her borrowed shirt and shrugged it off.

Standing still and naked in full view of Ran whilst he watched her in silence was probably the hardest thing she had ever had to do, she acknowledged, but, somehow, doing it made her feel strong and brave and very, very womanly.

There was an odd glittering brilliance in Ran's eyes, and her stomach muscles tensed as she saw the way his jaw tightened as he looked away from her.

'Ran…' she commanded softly.

'Sylvie, for God's sake…'

Ignoring the tough grimness in his voice, she turned her back and walked fully into her small bedroom. Seconds later he had followed her there, slamming the bedroom door shut as he bent to retrieve her discarded shirt.

'Here. Put it back on,' he ordered curtly.

Sylvie looked at him.

He was standing just over an arm's length away from her and she could see that despite the hardness of his jaw his body was still aroused.

Uncertainly she licked her lips, tiny flames of excited

nervousness flicking along her spine as she saw the way his glance followed her involuntary movement.

'*You* put it on *for* me, Ran,' she whispered provocatively, taking a step towards him, and then another, and then, before she could stop herself, she discovered that *she* was the one looking at his mouth, and then at just where…

She heard him groan, saw out of the corner of her eye Alex's shirt as he hurled it away and then, blissfully, she was in his arms, her naked body pressed close against his fully dressed one as he covered her face, her throat, her mouth with hot, fevered kisses.

In his arms Sylvie shivered in mute delight. Every nerve-ending in her body was singing in joy and triumph.

'Oh Ran… Ran…' She whispered his name ecstatically as she wrapped her arms around him. 'I want you so much… I *love* you so much…' she told him, but she doubted he heard the words because they were silenced before she could properly form them as he continued to kiss her.

'I want you to take your clothes off,' she told him huskily when she finally could speak. 'I want to see all of you, Ran… I want…'

There was a hooded and unbelievably exciting look about his eyes as he stepped back from her and started to comply with her shy demand, never removing his glance from hers as he thrust off his clothes, his shirt first, revealing the hard-muscled expanse of his chest with its male pattern of silky dark hair. Sylvie caught her breath as she watched him. She had seen his bare torso before, had seen him in fact wearing little more than a pair of swimming shorts, but somehow this…this was different. Then his attitude towards his own semi-nudity had been laid-back and totally sexless; now...

Sylvie licked her lips a second time as she caught the burning look he was giving her.

His jeans followed his shirt and her stomach quivered, her heart leapt like a spawning salmon. Against the stark whiteness of his boxer shorts his skin gleamed, warmly tanned, and his body...his maleness...

Quickly she averted her eyes, suddenly conscious of her inexperience, her naiveté, her virginity, but her self-consciousness was quickly forgotten, swept away in a dizzying tide of longing and excitement. In another handful of seconds, less, she would be free to do what she had longed to do for what felt like for ever, free to look, to touch...to...

'Ran...'

Helplessly she closed the distance between them, rubbing her face blissfully against the soft warmth of his chest, breathing in the male scent of him in bemused adoration before shyly pressing her closed lips to his skin.

He felt so good, smelled so good; tentatively she opened her eyes and then her mouth, licking exploratively at his skin. In her ear she could feel the rapid increase in Ran's heartbeat. His arms tightened around her and then, suddenly, he was picking her up, carrying her over to the bed, laying her on it, touching her skin, stroking her body, kissing her in all the ways she had imagined and showing her at the same time just how far short of the wondrous reality her imagination had fallen.

In his hands her breasts swelled and ached, her nipples taut, begging to be touched, kissed, sucked.

Unable to stop herself, Sylvie started to moan softly

as his mouth tugged gently on her breast, her body arching, twisting, filled, *driven* by such an intensity of need that she herself was lost in it.

'Ran… Ran…'

Frantically she moaned his name against his hot skin, touching, licking, kissing as much of him as she could reach.

'Ran…*now*…please…*now*,' she heard herself demanding, even though part of her mind wondered just why she felt so overwhelmed by her own sense of urgency, by her own need to have the hot male strength of him buried deep inside her. She just knew that she did.

She could feel him touching her intimately with his fingers as he kissed her but she pushed them away. Everything that was female and intuitive within her urged her to reject something that was only a substitute for what her body, her nature, her essence, demanded, instinctively refusing a satisfaction which could not give her what nature had designed her for.

No completion, no conception could take place through what he was offering her and her body; her senses, her nature demanded what they believed was their due.

Without any previous experience to guide her Sylvie responded to her own instincts, lifting her hips, rubbing herself against him, moaning her urgent need until she felt Ran's hands move to her hips, holding her, lifting her as he finally moved against her.

A small tremor of shock made her gasp out loud, her body tensing and her eyes widening as she felt the reality of his body within hers. She had never really thought about the practicalities of sex…and he felt so…so male…so…so big…

She felt him check slightly and saw him frown, saw the recognition of her inexperience, her virginity, dawn in his eyes, but as he tried to draw back from her Sylvie wrapped herself around him, holding him, and then it was too late; then his body took over, demanding the satisfaction hers had been promising it.

It was everything and more that Sylvie had imagined—bliss, heaven…perfection, even if afterwards, as she curled up happily next to Ran, she did feel slightly sore… Slightly sore but oh, so deliciously pleased with herself. She was a *woman* now. Ran's woman… They would be married at Otel Place, of course, and Alex would give her away… Happily she drifted off to sleep.

In the morning when she woke up she was in bed alone, and at first she thought she must have dreamt the entire incident, but when she went padding into her living room she found Ran standing there fully dressed, staring out of the window. Overjoyed, she rushed over to him, flinging her arms around him, but instead of responding as she had expected, instead of turning round and holding her, kissing her, picking her up and carrying her back to bed, he firmly disengaged her arms and pushed her sternly away.

'What is it? What's wrong?' she demanded, not understanding. 'Last night—'

'Last night was a mistake,' Ran interrupted her curtly. 'It should never have happened and I wish to God… Why didn't you *tell* me you were still a virgin?'

'I… I…' Sylvie could feel her eyes starting to fill with tears.

This wasn't how it should be—Ran aloof, cold and distant, almost accusing.

'Ran, I love you,' she told him shakily. 'I want us to be together…married…'

'*Married?* You're a child still, Sylvie… Your mother…'

'I'm not a child, I'm nearly twenty,' she protested frantically.

'You're a *child*,' Ran insisted, 'and if I'd known… Why didn't you *tell* me? *Why* did you let me think that you and Wayne were lovers?'

'I *did* tell you but you wouldn't listen. I thought you'd be pleased…that you'd *want* to be the first…the only one…' she told him pathetically.

'*Pleased?* Oh, my God.' Ran started to laugh, a harshly bitter laugh. 'The only thing that could make this appalling situation any worse would be to discover that you're pregnant…'

Sylvie's face went white. Last night, lost in the throes of her love and their shared intimacy, she had craved the conception of his child, and to have to listen to him now, telling her that that was the last thing he wanted, that she was the last *person* he wanted, was the cruellest blow she had ever experienced.

'I'm on the pill,' she told him quietly, ducking her head as she explained, 'There were… I had… My doctor recommended it for other reasons.'

It was the truth, and it made her blood run cold now to remember how unwilling she had been to take it. Thank God she had. To have exposed a child, her child, to the dislike, the bitterness she could see in Ran's eyes and hear in his voice would have been more than she could bear.

All her dreams and her hopes lay in ruins around her, destroyed by Ran's rejection of her.

'Go and get dressed, please,' she heard him demanding. 'I have to leave soon, but first we need to talk.'

Get dressed!

Suddenly she felt as acutely self-conscious, as guilty as the first Eve must have done. As she tugged on her clothes in the privacy of her bedroom she knew that she had paid a heavy price for the intimacy of Ran's lovemaking—the loss not just of her innocence, but the destruction of her love, her faith, her belief in herself as a woman. She felt as though she never wanted to see Ran again, as though she could never bear to face him again, as though someone had wrenched away a protective curtain. She saw that last night could have been nothing more to him than the mere satisfying of a sexual itch, that *she* had been nothing more to him than someone, a *body*, to relieve his sexual frustration with.

As she walked back into the living room he handed her a mug of coffee. Taking it from him, she was careful to make sure that not only did her fingers not touch his but that they did not even touch the mug where his had done. She felt scorched, besmirched, *soiled* from the experience of knowing just how little he had actually wanted her. What she wanted more than anything else now was to get him out of here, out of her flat, out of her life, out of her heart for ever.

'Sylvie...'

'I don't want to talk about it, Ran,' she told him proudly, turning her back to him. 'It happened. It was a mistake, we both know that, but a girl has to lose her virginity some time...' She gave a small painful shrug.

'Wayne will be pleased. Like you, he didn't want to be the first...'

What on earth was she saying...implying...? Sylvie wondered sickly as her pride demanded, commanded, forced her to retaliate, lie and to convince Ran that he hadn't hurt her, that he couldn't possibly have the power to hurt her.

'You begged *me* to make love to you so that you could have sex with Wayne?'

She could hear disbelief and something else in the harsh fury of Ran's voice, but shakily she ignored it, holding up her head as she turned round to confront him.

'Yes, that's right,' she agreed.

'I don't believe you,' Ran told her flatly, adding grimly, 'You said you loved me. You were even talking about marriage...'

Sylvie gave a small dismissive shrug.

'Isn't that what a *virgin* is supposed to do?' She pulled an uncaring face. 'How could I possibly love *you*, Ran? Why *should* I love you? All you ever do is criticise me. I want you to leave...'

'Sylvie, you can't just—'

'Wayne will be coming round soon,' she fibbed, adding carelessly, 'He's been telling me for ages to find someone to...to lose my virginity with. He's very experienced and he likes his lovers to know...to know what sex is all about...Wayne's the man I love.'

What was she *saying*? Sylvie could hardly believe the lies she was hearing herself speak, but Ran seemed to have no difficulty in accepting them.

Slamming down his barely touched mug of coffee, he came towards her.

Immediately Sylvie backed away.

'I don't know why you're making such a fuss,' she told him, adding flippantly, 'It's no big deal after all—'

'No...maybe not to you,' Ran interrupted her grimly.

'Not to you either,' Sylvie told him. Her phone started to ring and she hurried towards it, telling him over her shoulder, 'That will be Wayne...'

It wasn't, and she knew that the poor double-glazing salesperson must have been astonished and probably shocked by the tone of her conversation as she overrode his sales pitch, telling him that she had done what he wanted and that she couldn't wait to see him, to be with him properly, if he knew what she meant. Blowing noisy kisses into the receiver, she ended the call and then turned to Ran, telling him coolly, 'Wayne's on his way, so unless you want to stand and watch to see just how quick a learner I am...'

She was still smiling—the hurting, false, ridiculous smile she had pinned to her face as she'd challenged him—when she heard the door slam behind him, and then continued to wear it for several minutes after he had gone, despite the fact that tears were flooding from her eyes.

It was later that morning that she actually bumped into Wayne, completely by chance. In the two hours since Ran had left she had had more than enough time to dwell on what had happened and what she had said, and by the time she saw Wayne she had convinced herself that it was totally impossible for her ever to see Ran again...ever to see *anyone* again who was even remotely connected with him.

'Hi there, doll,' Wayne greeted her with a grin. 'Looks like it's time to say goodbye. I'm meeting up with the eco-warriors this afternoon.'

Swiftly Sylvie made up her mind, seizing on the opportunity to make her escape, not just from Ran but from everything that was associated with him—her love, her shame, and her fear that he would somehow guess that she had lied to him.

'I'm coming with you,' she told Wayne determinedly, adding before he could argue, 'My stepbrother has sent me some money so I can afford to support myself.'

'How much has he sent you?' Wayne questioned her interestedly.

An hour later, having packed everything that she would need, Sylvie locked the door of her flat behind her and went to join Wayne, who was waiting in his car.

She was a new Sylvie now, a different Sylvie. Ran, her love for him, the life she had once led—*all* were in the past and best forgotten.

CHAPTER SEVEN

A NOISE in the garden outside her window brought Sylvie out of her reverie. Startled, she let her unfocused gaze sweep the moonlit darkness and then sweep it again, her body stiffening as she saw Ran turn away and disappear into the shadows.

How long had he been standing there watching her? She knew from his clothes that he must have been working, probably checking for poachers who, she guessed, were as much a potential threat here as they had often been on her stepbrother's estate.

Shivering, she headed back to her bed. It was gone three o'clock in the morning and as she touched her face she realised that it was wet with her tears.

Why in heaven's name did she have to be so pathetic...standing there with tears pouring down her face whilst she relived the pain of the past? Oh, but she envied Ran. Her mouth twisted into a bitter smile as she tried to imagine *him* ever crying a single tear over her.

What had happened to her will-power, her strength; to the promise she had made herself before coming here—that things were going to be different, that never again would Ran be allowed to treat her with the same contempt he had shown her when they had faced one another as foes, enemies, on opposite sides, when she had allowed the eco-warriors to invade Alex's land, to destroy the pretty woodland glade that she had once

119

worked so hard to help create…just as Ran had destroyed her love and also destroyed her?

He had hated her for that almost as much as she had hated him. She had seen it in his eyes when he'd insisted on joining the others to see her off to America.

'Why are you here?' she had taunted.

'Why do you think?' he had responded, and of course she had known. He wanted to be sure that she really was leaving.

And now she was back—back to make the unwanted and agonisingly painful discovery that some things *didn't* change, that some loves didn't die.

She wasn't twenty any longer; it was impossible for her to run away now, to take refuge in disappearing, as she'd tried to escape herself and her love. She had a job to do, responsibilities, and besides, what had running away the first time actually achieved? It hadn't stopped her loving him, had it?

In the protective darkness of the moonlit garden Ran leaned back against the trunk of a concealing tree and closed his eyes. The discovery that Sylvie was going to be representing the Trust had reinforced all the irony he had felt when he had first learnt of his unexpected inheritance. He might not be a millionaire, but his lifestyle now and his prospects were certainly a far cry from what they had been when Sylvie's mother had insisted on Alex speaking to him about Sylvie's youthful crush on him.

He had been aware, of course, of her feelings, aware of them and aware too that at seventeen she was far too young, far too emotionally immature for the sort of relationship that he, as a man in his twenties, might have wanted.

'What the hell does Sylvie's mother think I'm going to *do*?' he had demanded angrily as he'd paced the floor of Alex's library.

Sympathetically Alex had shaken his head as he'd told him quietly, 'This isn't exactly easy for me, Ran. You're my friend as well as—'

'Your *employee*...' Angrily Ran had grimaced. 'No doubt as far as Sylvie's mother is concerned I'm only one step removed from being a servant,' he had expostulated scornfully.

Wisely, Alex had said nothing, allowing him to express his ire and distaste instead.

'You must share her concern,' he had concluded, 'otherwise you wouldn't have raised the subject.'

'Yes, in some ways I do,' Alex had agreed steadily. 'Not, I hardly need say, because I think you are in any way socially inferior to Sylvie. I know your family background, Ran, and your lineage, and if there's any shortfall of social acceptability here it's far more on Sylvie's side than yours. But I hope you know me well enough to know that that kind of attitude is totally abhorrent to me. No, my concern lies in a rather different direction and, in all honesty, it's Sylvie I should more properly be speaking to and not you, but...well, she isn't my sister, there's no blood tie between us, and teenage girls and their emotions are, I'm afraid, somewhat outside my own limited experience. So...the truth is that Sylvie believes herself in love with you with all the ferocity that teenagers do believe in such things. For your sake as much as for hers I feel that such feelings are best not...encouraged. She's young and very vulnerable and I should hate to see her hurt...to see either of you hurt,' he had amended gently when he had seen Ran's expression.

'What the hell do you think I'm going to do to her?' Ran had exploded. 'Take her to bed and…?'

'Is it really so impossible that you might be tempted to?' Alex had asked him quietly. 'I'm not criticising or condemning, Ran; physically she's mature and she loves you—or believes she does—'

'She's got a crush on me that she'll soon grow out of,' Ran had interrupted him grimly. 'That's what you want me to say, isn't it? And I should keep my hands off her until she does grow out of it…out of me… But what if *I* feel differently, Alex? What if *I* want…?' He had shaken his head, angry with himself as well as with Alex. *More* angry with himself than he was with Alex who he knew was only doing what he saw as his duty by his stepsister.

'You're right, she's a child still, and the sooner she grows up and forgets all about me the better,' Ran had told him hardily. 'And as for taking her to bed,' he had thrown at Alex as he turned to leave, 'well, there's always a cure for that.'

And so there had been, for a while at least, until he had grown sickened and shamed by the emptiness of the sexual encounters he was sharing with women who meant as little to him emotionally as he did to them. And, even with that form of release, keeping the promise he had made to Alex and himself hadn't been easy. There had been times, far too many of them, when he had nearly weakened, like when he had fished her out of the muddy lake and taken her back to his cottage. Oh, God, the temptation then to take what she was so innocently offering him, to take on the role not so much of seducer as sorcerer, transmuting the frail strength of her youthful crush on him into the enduring bond of real adult love.

But, despite the temptation which kissing her had presented, somehow he had always managed to tell himself of the differences that lay between them in age, experience and in prospects. He loved his job and wouldn't have wanted to change it for anything or *anyone*, but there was no denying that to expect a girl, brought up as Sylvie had been with every conceivable luxury, to move into the kind of accommodation estate managers normally occupied, to live the often lonely lifestyle that would be hers when he was working... He just couldn't do it. Had she been older, wiser...poorer...it might have been different. And so he had resisted the temptation to give in to her desire and his own love, and he had praised himself for his selflessness, until the fateful day he had taken her Alex's cheque.

To see her there, outside her flat, dressed only in a man's shirt—a shirt through which, with the hot summer sunshine slanting down on her, he could see quite plainly the shape and fullness of her breasts and even the dark aureoles of her nipples—to watch her with another man, a man who he had immediately assumed was her lover, had created within him an anger, a bitterness, a jealousy that had rent wide apart his self-control.

To discover later, *too* late, that there had been no other lover, to realise what he had done and why, had filled him with such self-loathing that he could hardly endure the weight of his own guilt.

'I love you,' Sylvie had told him innocently. 'I want us to be together...'

He had spent the previous week with Alex, discussing

ways and means in which they could reduce the cost of running the estate. Amongst them had been his own suggestion that they rent out his cottage and that he move into rooms in the main house. He knew that if Alex accepted his suggestion he wouldn't even have a proper home to offer her. He could just imagine how her mother would react to that, to the idea of her daughter living in rooms above the stables of the house where she had been brought up. And Sylvie was still so young, still so naive…still at university with the whole of her life in front of her. What right had *he* to use what had happened between them to tie her to him? No, better to let her think that he didn't want her than to have her turn to him five or even ten years down the line to tell him that she had made a mistake; to accuse him of putting his own emotions before her needs, of taking advantage of her youth and inexperience.

And he'd been glad he had done so when she had dropped the bombshell about her relationship with Wayne.

Somehow that was something he had just not expected, but he had seen from the expression in her eyes and the vehemence in her voice that she meant every word she was saying. And so he had walked away, telling himself that it was for the best for her, best that somehow, some time, some *way* he should learn how to forget her.

But, of course, he had never done so.

And now here she was, back in his life, a woman now and not a girl, and what a woman, how much of a woman, *the* woman whom he loved—and who hated him.

It had hurt him more than he could bear that she

should think he would actually try to cheat anyone… Did her precious Lloyd know how lucky he was or how much he, Ran, would give simply to hold her in his arms and hear her telling him that she loved him? He would give everything he had, everything he was…

What a fool he was. She didn't love him, she *loathed* him.

Watching her just now on his way back from checking on the fences, on the look-out for potential poachers, he had ached so badly for her, so very, *very* badly. There was no point in him going to bed; soon the false dawn would be lightening the night sky, and besides, there was only one reason he wanted to be in bed right now and it had nothing to do with sleeping or being alone.

Kissing her tonight had opened the floodgates on his love for her and his body still ached with the longing it had evoked. How the hell he was going to get through the next few months he had no idea. Grimly he turned away from the house and the temptation of Sylvie's bed-room, Sylvie's bed, Sylvie herself.

CHAPTER EIGHT

'Hi, HON, it's me, Lloyd.'

Sylvie smiled warmly as she recognised her boss's voice.

'Lloyd,' she responded, 'how are you?'

'Fine, I guess. Listen, I've got to come over to England on some other business and I thought whilst I was there I'd drive up to Derbyshire and see how you're getting on with Haverton Hall.'

Sylvie laughed. She wasn't in the least deceived. Lloyd was like a child with a new toy whenever he acquired a new property, saying every time that he wasn't going to visit it again until all the renovation work had been complete and then being totally unable to resist checking on how things were going. Or not so much checking on how things were going, but sneaking another look, like a child sneaking a look at a hidden-away Christmas present just to check that it was still there and that he was actually going to receive it. As Sylvie well knew, no matter how many properties Lloyd acquired, he still continued to fall in love with new ones, and Haverton Hall was well worth falling in love with.

This morning she had an appointment with the firm who were going to work on the restoration of the carving and the plasterwork. Based in London, the artisans the firm employed had all completed their training at the same Italian firm that Sylvie had used when renovating the *palazzo*. She had seen samples and photographs of their work and knew that no matter how expensive they might be—and they would be—they were the right people to work on Haverton Hall.

'When are you arriving?' she asked Lloyd, still smiling.

'I'm booked on today's Concorde,' he told her.

Sylvie heard the door to the small office she had organised for herself at Haverton Hall open behind her, but she didn't turn round. She didn't need to; she knew from the reaction of her own body that it was Ran who had walked in. Ever since the night he had kissed her and they had argued, they had treated one another with cold distance. She had gone downstairs that morning to discover a neat file of papers and bank statements awaiting her which proved conclusively that Ran had paid for the work done on the Rectory himself.

She had apologised, very formally and very curtly, and then pointed out that he wouldn't have been the first client to take advantage of Lloyd's generosity.

'*I* haven't taken advantage of it,' he'd reminded her acidly, before walking away from her.

Since then, the contact between them had been as minimal as both of them could make it.

'Oh, Lloyd, that's wonderful,' she told her employer truthfully. 'I've missed you.' It was true. She had missed him and suddenly something occurred to her. 'Look, I've got to come down to London to see some people. Why don't we drive back together? I'm going to have to stay overnight anyway... The Annabelle?' she responded, when he told her where he was planning to stay, and then teased him, 'Isn't that a bit romantic...?'

'I've heard some good things about its designer,'

Lloyd responded mock-sternly. 'My interest in the place is purely professional.'

By the time Sylvie had completed her telephone call Ran had gone. Good; the less contact she had with him the better. She much preferred her solitary evening meals to the trauma of spending any time with him, even if she did sometimes wonder *where* he was eating and with whom and if he stayed with her all night. It had to be Vicky, of course. The woman was forever telephoning him, purring smugly down the line whenever Sylvie answered, demanding, 'Tell Ran to ring me; he's got my number.'

She was sure he had, Sylvie had decided acidly, him and every other man who was subjected to the divorcee's high octane blend of sexuality.

The shop occupied by Messrs Phillips and Company, master gilders and restorers, was down a narrow alley, a small courtyard of buildings that time seemed to have forgotten.

Walking into the courtyard was like walking back in time, Sylvie decided as she gasped in delight at the Elizabethan framework of the narrow buildings with their outward-jutting upper storeys.

'They belong to one of the royal estates,' the chief partner in the business, Stuart Phillips, informed Sylvie. 'And they're very strict, not just about the maintenance of the building but about who they take as tenants as well. We got our tenancy after we had been commissioned to work on one of the royal palaces.'

An hour later, after Sylvie had discussed Haverton Hall and the work required on it, he turned to her and told her, 'We *can* do it, but it's going to be very costly.'

'Very costly is fine,' Sylvie assured him and then smiled at him as she added softly, '*Exorbitantly* costly isn't; there's enough work here to keep you in business for nearly twelve months...guaranteed work.'

'Our order books are already full,' he told her urbanely.

'Not according to my contacts,' Sylvie retaliated. 'The way I heard it, one of your biggest contracts has been withdrawn due to lack of funds.'

'I don't know who your informants are...' Stuart Phillips began huffily, but Sylvie stopped him.

'Let's be honest with one another, shall we?' she suggested firmly. 'We're both busy people with no time to waste on silly point-scoring. You're the best in the business in this country and I *want* the best for Haverton Hall, but...there are other firms...'

'We shall need a guarantee that the contract will be seen through to its end,' he told her, frowning. 'I don't like carrying all my eggs in one basket...'

'You shall have it,' Sylvie assured him.

'Mmm... From the records you've shown us the original workmanship was done to a very high standard, especially the wood-carving.'

'If not Grinling Gibbons himself, then certainly one of his most skilful pupils,' Sylvie agreed.

'The records you've got of the original designed decor are excellent; they even list the furniture and each room's colour scheme,' he assessed.

She had Ran to thank for that, Sylvie acknowledged. Normally it fell to her lot to search painstakingly through the records to put together a composite picture of what a property had originally looked like. On this occasion Ran had done all that spadework for her. Not that she had allowed him to see how impressed she was. She wasn't prepared to do *anything* that would allow him to think he had some sort of advantage over her.

When the time came for her and Stuart Phillips to part company Sylvie had his agreement to concentrate exclusively on the work on Haverton Hall, even though she had had to agree to a substantial bonus payment to get him to do so. She made sure she held tightly to budget where she could, but she would never take the less expensive option when it came to employing the best craftsmen. It would be worth it, she exulted as she left the courtyard. Haverton Hall was worth it.

She had arranged to meet Lloyd at his hotel for afternoon tea. He loved that type of tradition and, as he happily informed her an hour later when she was shown up to his private suite, 'No other country serves an afternoon tea quite like England...'

'I should hope not,' was Sylvie's tongue-in-cheek response, then she started to tell him about her visit to the gilders.

'You're sure they'll be as good as the Italians?' he asked her at one point, suddenly very professional and alert.

'Better,' Sylvie told him simply. 'You see, the original work on the house was carried out by *English* workmen who had trained in Italy, rather like Messrs Phillips, artisans, and my guess is that their workmanship, although Italian in conception, would have had a decidedly English interpretation to it—where an Italian craftsman might have carved cherubs and allegorical scenes from the great masters, an English craftsman would have carved animals and birds, things from *nature*.'

'Why don't you stay here tonight?' Lloyd suggested

once they had finished talking about her visit to Messrs Phillips and Company. 'I can ring down and book you a room.'

Sylvie shook her head.

'No, thanks; I've already arranged to stay overnight with my mother.'

Knowing that Lloyd had a business dinner organized, Sylvie left just after five o'clock, having arranged to pick him up at ten in the morning.

She drove to her mother's, suffering the latter's perfumed embrace after her mother's maid had let her into the apartment.

'Darling, it's my bridge evening this evening. I could cancel it but...'

'No, please don't.' Sylvie checked her mother with a smile.

'Well, at least we can have dinner together and you can tell me all your news. How is dear Ran? So exciting, his inheritance...the title...'

Sylvie's smile faded.

'Ran's fine,' she told her mother, adding dismissively, 'We don't see an awful lot of one another; we're both busy.'

'Oh, darling, such a shame,' her mother protested.

'I...' Sylvie gave her a direct look. 'At one time you thoroughly disapproved of him.' And my feelings for him, Sylvie could have added, but she didn't.

Her mother made a small *moue*. 'But, darling, that was before...'

'Before what?' Sylvie challenged her wryly. 'Before he inherited the title...'

'Well, these things *do* make a difference.' Her mother

defended herself as Sylvie gave her a quizzical look. 'Ran is now an extremely eligible man.'

'Mother! These days a woman doesn't need an eligible man,' Sylvie told her. 'We can support ourselves.'

'Every woman needs a man to love her, Sylvie,' her mother told her sadly. 'I still miss your stepfather.'

Immediately Sylvie was contrite. Her mother was old-fashioned and out of touch in her ideas, her thinking, but she had genuinely loved both Sylvie's own father and her second husband, Alex's father, and Sylvie knew that despite the business with which she filled her days she was sometimes lonely.

'Have you seen Alex and Mollie recently?' she questioned, wanting to turn the conversation into happier channels.

'Oh, yes,' her mother responded immediately and warmly, 'and they've invited me to Otel Place for Christmas.'

Several hours later, as she prepared for an early night, Sylvie wondered what Ran was doing. Not going to bed on his own if his recent behaviour pattern was to be followed. Angrily, she closed her eyes. What did it matter to her who Ran spent his nights with or how?

What did it matter?

All the world, *that* was how much it mattered, but no one but her must ever know that.

Even before he had kissed her she had known the truth. Just the way her body, her senses, her being, had reacted the moment she had set eyes on him again had told her that what she had tried to dismiss as a mere childish crush had somewhere, somehow, against all the odds and certainly against her own will, turned into real adult love. She ached for Ran—to be at one with him, at peace with him, to be *loved* by him, to share his life, to bear his children—with such an intensity that sometimes she didn't know quite how she was going to be able to go on bearing it.

Live one day at a time, that was her present motto; just get through each minute, each hour, just go on telling herself that ultimately it was going to get better, that once the work on Haverton Hall was finished and she was out of Ran's orbit she would be able to rebuild her defences and, with them, her own life. That was what she told herself, but deep down inside she wasn't sure she truly believed it.

'We'll have to call at the Rectory first,' Sylvie warned Lloyd as she drove north. 'I don't have the keys to Haverton Hall with me.'

'That's fine by me,' Lloyd assured her. 'How are you and Ran getting along, by the way?'

'He's a client of the Trust,' Sylvie pointed out severely.

'So you haven't fallen in love with him, then,' Lloyd teased her. Somehow Sylvie managed to force a responsive smile. Lloyd meant no harm. He took a paternal interest in her and often told her, only semi-jokingly, that it was time she fell in love. He had no idea about the real state of affairs between her and Ran, the real state of her heart, her emotions.

'Say, this is really beautiful countryside,' he commented as they drove through Derbyshire.

'But still not as beautiful as Haverton,' Sylvie teased him.

Immediately he was off, enthusing about the house and its architecture.

Sylvie's heart sank when she pulled up outside the Rectory and saw that Ran's Land Rover was there. There was another car outside as well and Sylvie's heart dropped even further when she recognised it. Perhaps with her away and the opportunity to have the house to themselves, Ran and Vicky had decided on a change of venue and had spent the night together here.

Ran had given her a set of keys to the Rectory, and rather than disturb him she used them to unlock the door, but to her discomfort, as they walked through the hall, Ran and Vicky were just coming downstairs.

'Hi there,' Lloyd began genially, but before Ran could say anything his telephone began to ring.

'Excuse me a moment, will you?' he said apologetically, leaving the three of them together as he hurried into the library to answer the telephone.

'I don't think we've met,' Vicky began coyly, ignoring Sylvie to smile provocatively at Lloyd.

'Lloyd, Vicky Edwards.' Sylvie introduced them mechanically. 'Lloyd is my boss and—'

'So you work for the Trust as well, do you?' Vicky commented.

'Lloyd *is* the Trust,' Sylvie told her, thoroughly exasperated by the other woman's manner.

'Oh…how very interesting,' she responded softly, immediately crossing the hall to Lloyd's side, turning her back on Sylvie. 'You must tell me more…'

Quite how Vicky managed to invite herself to join them when they went to Haverton Sylvie wasn't quite sure, but invite herself she most certainly had.

Lloyd obviously didn't share her own dislike of her, she recognised as she saw the bemused male appreciation with which he was regarding the older woman.

By the time Ran rejoined them Vicky was purring seductively to Lloyd.

'So you're staying at the Annabelle. I've heard it's the last word in luxury...'

'It sure is,' Lloyd agreed enthusiastically. 'My suite is really something else, isn't it, Sylvie?'

'Yes, it is,' Sylvie agreed colourlessly. Out of the corner of her eye she could see Ran switching his concentration from Lloyd and Vicky to her, frowning as he did so.

It wasn't *her* fault that his lady-friend, his *lover*, was showing an interest in Lloyd... Sylvie had seen women expressing such an interest before, of course; Lloyd was an extremely wealthy man and a very, very charming one. In the past he had often made a joke of their pursuit of him, warning Sylvie that it was part of her job to keep them at bay. For his age he was extremely fit and physically he looked attractive. He still had a full head of silver hair and his eyes held a warm twinkle, but to prefer him to Ran... Or was it perhaps his bank balance that was attracting the other woman? Sylvie wondered unkindly.

In the end, all four of them drove over to Haverton Hall in Ran's Land Rover, with Vicky pulling a small face as she coaxed Lloyd to sit in the back with her.

'This really is the most uncomfortable old thing, Ran,' she complained, adding to Lloyd in a sugary sweet voice, 'I keep telling him he should buy himself a decent four-wheel drive. In all the years I've known Ran, he's never owned a decent car. You Americans make such wonderful ones…so luxurious and comfortable…'

'Well, I guess we have the country for them,' Lloyd agreed with a smile. 'You and Ran are old friends then?'

Vicky pouted.

'Well, we certainly go back a long way—although I only moved to Derbyshire a short time ago and, by coincidence, I discovered that Ran was one of my new neighbours and we were able to renew old acquaintances.'

Some coincidence, Sylvie reflected ironically, irritated by Vicky's behaviour. What on earth did Ran see in her? Surely he could see what type of woman she was—how unworthy of him she was?

When they arrived at Haverton Hall, Vicky made a big performance of climbing out of the Land Rover, thanking Lloyd effusively for helping her, leaning heavily on his arm as she complained about the uneven gravel on the forecourt.

'You should have worn flat shoes like Sylvie,' Ran told her.

'Flat shoes…? Ugh, no, never.' She shuddered. 'I *always* wear high heels,' she confided to Lloyd. 'I think they're so much more feminine.' Lifting her foot, she held out one slim, elegant ankle for his inspection.

'Very pretty,' Lloyd approved, 'but you'd better hang onto me. We don't want you to hurt yourself.'

As they toured the house, Sylvie's irritation with Vicky grew. Every time she made a comment, Vicky had to chip in, diverting Lloyd's attention from the house to herself, accompanying each successful attempt to do so with a look of acid triumph in Sylvie's direction. Really, the woman was totally impossible. They weren't in competition for his approval...his *affections*, for goodness' sake. She was simply trying to do her job. If Ran's lover wanted to flirt with Lloyd, that was totally her business and Ran's. All that Sylvie wished was that she had chosen another time to do so.

'The Annabelle sounds the most fabulous hotel. I'd love to see it... I've been planning to go to London for some time... I need some new clothes and there's no-where in Derbyshire.' Vicky gave a small, fastidious shudder as they finally headed back to the Land Rover.

'You were? Say, why don't you come back with me, then? Sylvie's going to drive me to Manchester airport and—' Lloyd began politely.

'Come to London and stay at the Annabelle as your guest...?' Vicky pounced immediately. 'Oh, how wonderful and how kind of you. I'd love to...' she breathed huskily.

Sylvie, who guessed that Lloyd had simply been suggesting that they travel together, could only marvel at the other woman's sang-froid and her cheek. *She* would never have dared to behave as Vicky had just done. But Lloyd, far from looking displeased, was almost beaming from ear to ear.

Sylvie waited until they were back at the Rectory and Vicky had disappeared to 'tidy herself up' before taking Lloyd to one side, out of Ran's earshot, to warn him discreetly, 'Lloyd, Vicky is Ran's girlfriend and I don't think—'

'So far as I am concerned, Vicky is a free agent. If she wants to go to London with Lloyd then that's up to her.' Sylvie bit her lip as Ran interrupted her. He had been on the other side of the hallway, but then his hearing had always been extremely sharp. It went with his job.

'I'm afraid I'm going to have to go home and collect a few things,' Vicky apologised gushingly to Lloyd as she came back downstairs. 'I don't want to keep you waiting.'

Grimly Sylvie watched as she batted heavily mascaraed eyelashes in Lloyd's direction.

'No problem,' he assured her. 'There are a few things Sylvie and I need to discuss and I guess Ran too. You take all the time you need, my dear.'

'I expect the Annabelle is very dressy,' Vicky murmured appreciatively.

'Charming woman,' Lloyd commented warmly after she had gone.

'Yes, she is,' Ran agreed.

'About as charming as a piranha,' Sylvie muttered between clenched teeth behind their backs before reminding Lloyd curtly, 'I've got preliminary estimates for some of the work here if you want to see them. I have faxed copies off to New York, but...'

'Sylvie, you're so efficient,' Lloyd told her, smiling benignly at her. 'I keep telling her, Ran, that she needs to relax a bit more...have fun... When was the last time *you* spent a day shopping for yourself?' he challenged her before she could say anything.

'I shopped in Italy,' she told him dismissively.

'Yes, I know. I was there, remember...? I took her to Armani,' he told Ran. 'And what did she do? She told me that the clothes were far too expensive. What do you do with a woman like that?'

'They *were* too expensive,' Sylvie told him defensively. Too expensive for her at any rate, and although she knew that Lloyd would happily have offered to buy an outfit for her he was still her employer and she had no intention of taking advantage of his generosity. Even so, it hurt to know that he was comparing her to Vicky Edwards and perhaps finding her less feminine, less womanly, and in front of *Ran*. It was plain what both of them were thinking: that somehow she was less *fun* than the other woman—less of a *woman*. Well, let them think what they liked, she decided angrily. *She* was there to do a job, not to…to flirt and bat her eyelashes.

'She's a wonderful girl,' she heard Lloyd telling Ran as she went to get the papers she wanted him to see. 'But she works too hard, takes life too seriously.'

After she had dropped Lloyd and Vicky off at the airport, her head aching from listening to the other woman's flirtatious comments, instead of heading back to Derbyshire, Sylvie drove on impulse to Manchester itself and parked the Discovery outside the Emporio Armani boutique that a kindly taxi driver had directed her to.

A pretty, dark-haired girl who could have been Italian but wasn't brought her the trouser suit she had seen in the window.

The diffusion range might be cheaper than the designer originals but it was still expensive. Even so… As she turned and twisted in front of the mirror, studying her reflection in the flatteringly cut suit, Sylvie admitted that she couldn't resist it. Neither could she resist the matching shirt that went with it.

So, she was dull and boring and unfeminine, was she? Well, she might not wear three-inch heels, and she certainly didn't flutter her eyelashes, but she was still a woman...very much a woman...more than woman enough to ache with longing for Ran. Oh, yes, she was more than woman enough for that!

CHAPTER NINE

'YOU'VE been a long time. What happened?'

Guiltily Sylvie spun round, dropping her Armani carrier bag as she did so. She had arrived back at the Rectory five minutes ago and had decided to go straight to her room, but she had just reached the top of the stairs when Ran emerged from his room, his curt comment coupled with her own guilt startling her.

'You've been shopping,' he said sharply in disbelief, answering his own question as he saw the bag she had just dropped and the contents spilled out from it onto the carpet.

'What if I have?' Sylvie retorted defensively, bending down to gather up her purchases but not fast enough to match Ran, who had bent and got there before her, scooping up the soft, expensive cloth and then, pausing, shocking her by removing it completely from the carrier. He studied what she had bought and then lifted his gaze to her flushed face.

'New clothes. Now, then, I wonder what motivated you to do that?' he asked her softly.

'What I choose to do with my time and my money is no business of yours,' Sylvie snapped sharply at him.

But he ignored her, taunting her softly, 'What exactly are you trying to do, Sylvie? Compete with Vicky? You can't. You don't have the right type of...assets.'

Furious with him, and with herself because his taunting remarks weren't just making her angry, they were hurting her badly as well, Sylvie exploded into angry self-defence.

'If by "the right type of assets" you mean I don't use my womanhood, my sexuality, as some kind of...of cheap means of attracting men, then I'm glad to say that I don't,' she agreed.

'Really? Then why go and buy this?' Ran challenged her softly, indicating the trouser suit.

'I bought it on impulse,' she told him quickly. Too quickly, she realised as she saw the cynical look he was giving her. 'Anyway,' she added protectively, 'it's hardly the kind of outfit a woman would buy to...to attract a man...'

'No?' Ran gave her a sardonic smile. 'Oh, come on, Sylvie, we both know better than that. There's something powerfully alluring about the sight of a woman wearing a trouser suit, something very, very sensual and appealing—much more so than an over-tight dress on an over-exposed body. You bought this outfit because you're jealous of Vicky. Because you—'

'Me...jealous...of her?' Sylvie virtually spat at him as she grabbed her new purchase from him and stuffed it back into the bag. 'No way,' she told him, shaking her head almost violently in denial. 'Why should I be jealous?' she added dangerously, too upset to question the wisdom of inviting him to humiliate her still further by revealing his awareness of just how she felt about him. 'Just because years ago I was stupid enough, adoring enough, *vulnerable* enough to...to care too much about you, that doesn't mean that I'm jealous of your lover. In fact...'

'My *lover*?' Ran stopped her as they both stood up, frowning down at her as he informed her curtly, 'I was referring to the fact that you're jealous because you're afraid of losing *Lloyd* to Vicky. He's your lover and—'

'My lover...? Lloyd?' Sylvie stared at him in disbelief.

Suddenly Sylvie had had enough. There was no way that Ran could possibly, genuinely, believe that she and Lloyd were lovers; he was just playing some kind of peculiar and cruel game with her. Well, he was going to have to play it on his own. Grabbing hold of her shopping, she darted past him, almost running into her bedroom and slamming the door behind her, her heart thudding with angry pain.

As she closed her eyes and leaned against the door she had just closed, she could feel them starting to burn with the useless demeaning tears of her unwanted love.

What was Ran doing now—laughing inwardly at her because he knew that her jealousy, her pain, her *love* were all for him, or was he too wrapped up in what he thought to spare any time to consider her feelings? Had he accused her of being jealous out of his own feelings of jealousy against Lloyd?

This job, which she had taken on with such high hopes, such a surge of determination and conviction that through it she would finally and for ever slay the dragons of her tormented youthful love for him, had now turned into a hydra-headed monster which she could never hope to overcome. How on earth was she going to be able to concentrate on what she had to do when she was forced to work in such close proximity to Ran?

No. It was impossible, she acknowledged half an hour later as she sat at her desk trying to concentrate on the work schedule she had in front of her. No matter how hard she tried to visualise a situation where she and Ran could work together in harmony, her emotions untouched by his presence, all she could actually see was a situation that was going to get worse and worse as she became more and more helplessly trapped in her love and his lack of it. The best remedy, the only remedy she could honestly see that would work would be for her to go to Lloyd and ask him to find someone else to complete this project, she admitted unhappily.

It wasn't a course she wanted to take. She prided herself on her professionalism and it would mean taking Lloyd into her confidence about her feelings for Ran—she knew, of course, that he would respect them, but even so...

If she stayed on the possibility was—no, the *probability* was, she corrected herself fiercely, that sooner or later she would make a mistake that could prejudice the progress of the work on the house. This was a project that was going to demand her total concentration and attention and how could she give it when all the time she was thinking about Ran, when her feelings for him were already dominating her mind and her emotions?

It wasn't going to be easy. She hated letting Lloyd down; in fact, it felt as though in asking him to find someone else to take over this particular project for her she was letting *herself* down; but she feared that if she stayed the way in which she could potentially let herself down, damage herself and her self-esteem, her very *self*, could be far more traumatic.

The anger and contempt which Ran had displayed towards her this evening had shown how very little compassion he was likely to have for her. No, there was no other way.

It was with a very heavy heart that Sylvie prepared

for bed. There would be other houses, other projects, and no one but her would ever know how much it would hurt knowing that it was someone else who would have the pleasure of restoring Ran's ancestral home to what it must once have been, just as it would be another woman who would ultimately stand beside Ran and their children in love and pride as they went through their lives together.

Ran wasn't sure just what had woken him up first—his training, his work, meant that he was always alert to any sound that heralded some unfamiliarity, his perceptions and senses so keenly attuned that he was aware of such changes even in his sleep.

Alert and wide awake, he lay in the darkness listening. The illuminated face of his alarm clock showed that it was just gone half past one in the morning. The house had no alarm system. Lucy, his gun dog who slept downstairs, might be getting on in years now but she would have been barking if someone had been trying to break into the house, and besides, the outside lights had not come on.

Through his open bedroom window he could hear an owl hooting as it flew past. No alien sounds disturbed the natural busyness of the country night.

He started to relax and then he heard it—a door opening upstairs. Immediately he was out of bed and, reaching for his robe, pulled it on—he slept nude—before striding across to open his bedroom door quietly.

He saw her immediately, a slim white wraith who seemed to float rather than walk down the corridor, but, ethereal though she looked, Sylvie was no ghost. Even before he reached her he knew that she was sleepwalking; all the tell-tale signs were there, and of course he knew from her girlhood exactly what to do. So why was it so hard, then, to take her gently in his hold so that he could turn her round and walk her back to her bedroom?

The best thing to do, they had all been told after the first frightening occasion when she had been found wandering the long gallery at Otel Place, totally oblivious to what she was doing, was to guide her gently back to bed, if possible without waking her; but now, as he touched her, Ran could feel her start to tremble violently, her face turning towards him, her body stiffening as he tried to turn her round. Cursing under his breath, he glanced towards his own still open bedroom door. Perhaps if he could get her in there... The old family doctor at Otel Place had recommended that she be allowed to wake up naturally rather than be abruptly woken from her sleepwalk and he had also informed them that often these bouts of 'walking' could be attributed to some kind of disturbance or trauma that the walker might have suffered. Ran did not need to look very far to find the cause of tonight's disturbance, and inwardly he cursed not just Vicky but Lloyd as well.

Didn't the man know just how lucky he was—what he, Ran, would give to change places with him?

Sylvie was still trembling against his body, her eyes wide open and unseeing as she stood stiffly beside him, almost transfixed. Not wanting to risk waking her, Ran urged her gently towards his own bedroom, talking very quietly and softly to her, just as though she were still the girl he remembered.

'It's all right, Sylvie,' he assured her gently. 'Everything's all right... Come on, now...'

Obediently she moved, leaning on him slightly. If he

could get her into bed without her waking up he could sit with her to check that she was going to sleep on and then he could spend the rest of the night in one of the other rooms. In the morning… He started to frown. Too late to regret now the jealousy which had prompted him to speak so harshly to her earlier, but the sight of that suit, the knowledge of just how it would look on her body, had filled him with such furious jealousy that he had overreacted.

Tenderly Ran guided her into his bedroom and towards the bed. The light gown she was wearing was plain and white, in soft cotton. In it she looked almost like a girl…youthful…virginal…

He closed his eyes. The last thing he needed right now was to start thinking about—to start *remembering*. Forcing himself to suppress the thoughts, the memories and the emotions which were running riot inside him, he stopped to pick her up, intending to lay her down on the bed, but as he did so a dog fox out in the woodland beyond the garden howled to his mate; the sound carried into the bedroom on the still night air, shocking him into immobility and Sylvie into immediate wakefulness.

'Ran…what…?'

He could hear the shocked anxiety in her voice as she stared round his moonlit bedroom.

'You were sleepwalking.' He tried to reassure her. 'I heard a noise…found you on the landing…'

Sleepwalking. Sylvie focused distractedly on Ran's face.

It had been years since she had last walked in her sleep, but she didn't for one moment doubt that Ran was telling the truth. After all, there was no reason why he should have spirited her from her own bed and carried her here to his—was there? If he had wanted to take her there, all he had to do... But even so... She started to shiver.

She only walked in her sleep in times of intense personal stress...intense personal *dis*tress...

'It's all right, Sylvie,' she heard Ran saying gently. He was still holding onto her. Sylvie could feel the warmth of his arms, his body through the robe he was wearing and through her own fine cotton nightgown. Bemusedly she looked at him, her eyes huge and shadowed in the small oval of her pale face.

Outside a peafowl, one of the small colony which had migrated from Haverton Hall to the Rectory, its slumber no doubt disturbed by the mating call of the fox, screamed loudly, causing Sylvie to go rigid with tension.

'It's all right, Sylvie,' Ran repeated soothingly. 'It's only a peafowl.'

She knew that, of course—their noise was, after all, familiar to her—but for once she felt too weak to bother arguing the point with Ran.

His bedroom was on the opposite side of the house from hers and furnished very differently, with heavy early Georgian furniture that looked imposingly traditional and masculine. The room suited Ran, she thought abstractedly; it suited his maleness, his completeness. A wave of longing swept over her. Unable to stop herself, she turned in towards his body, lifting her hand towards him.

Later she wasn't even sure if she had actually *meant* to touch him or if the gesture had simply been one of longing, but as he turned his head towards her her fingertips grazed his mouth. She felt his breath against them, warm, tormenting her with all that could never be.

She started to look away and then, to her shock, she felt Ran taking hold of her wrist, circling it with his thumb and fingers, holding her hand where it was whilst he very deliberately pressed a kiss to each of her fingertips in turn.

Wild-eyed, Sylvie watched him, almost forgetting to breathe in her shock.

'Ran,' she protested half-heartedly, but as she said the word she was already moving closer to him, instinctively seeking the warmth and the comfort of his body heat, his body.

If it felt like heaven to have his arms close around her, that was nothing compared to what it felt like to have him lift his hands to her face and cup it whilst he oh, so gently kissed her mouth, a slow, tender, lingering kiss…a *lover's* kiss. Silently Sylvie pressed even closer to him, lifting her own arms to hold him, her mouth and then her whole body, trembling with the effort it took her not to give in to what she was feeling.

She could feel her eyes fill with tears, feel them, too, starting to flood over and roll down her face.

'Sylvie.' She could hear the emotion in Ran's voice as he lifted one fingertip to touch them. 'Don't cry…please don't cry. *No* man is worth your tears…'

'It just hurts so much,' Sylvie told him, unable to hold back what she was feeling any longer. Somehow the night and their seclusion had stripped away the barriers she had fought so hard to erect against her love for him.

'I hate feeling like this,' she whispered. 'I hate loving so much and so…so…unwontedly… It's so demeaning and it hurts so badly.'

She heard Ran groan as though something about her agonised and honest admission touched him very deeply and then he was holding her, rocking her in his arms as he told her huskily, 'You mustn't be hurt, Sylvie. Please, don't be hurt…'

And then, totally unexpectedly, he was kissing her, not with the gentle tenderness he had shown her before, but with a fierce sensual passion that took her breath away and with it all her resistance. Her body went weak, pliable, compliant, yearning towards his as his mouth moved demandingly on hers. She could feel the fierce, heavy thud of his heart, the sudden swift betraying arousal of his body.

He was and always had been a very male man, she reminded herself. He might not love her, she might not be the woman he wanted, but she was here in his arms, loving him, wanting him, and she could sense how little it would take to overturn his self-control.

Swiftly, dangerously, stabbing right at the most intimate female heart of her, came the thought that she might never have his love but she could have tonight…her memories and perhaps even more. A woman alone need not feel ashamed to give birth to a child these days…she need not even name its father… A child…*Ran's* child… Already she was responding to him, inviting him, inciting him, her hands reaching out to move under his robe, shaping the hard muscles of his shoulders, his arms.

This time when the peafowl cried neither of them paid any attention to it. Beneath the insistent thrust of Ran's tongue, Sylvie's lips parted.

She just wanted comfort, that was all, Ran warned himself as he felt her mouth tremble beneath his. She didn't want him…love him…

But it was already too late. He wanted her, he loved

her, and, God forgive him, he couldn't stop himself from giving in to his need to show her all that a man's love for a woman could and should be.

He kissed her face, her throat, her shoulders as he slid the soft whiteness of her nightdress from her body, only partially managing to stifle his groan of longing as he looked at her clad only in moonlight.

Beneath Ran's heavy-lidded gaze, Sylvie felt her willpower melting. He wanted her; she could see it in his eyes, feel it in the fierce tremble of his fingertips as they traced the outline of her body. Even with her eyes closed, she could feel how much he wanted her.

Shakily Sylvie mirrored his touch on his body, tracing the deep V left by the open neckline of his robe. When she touched the knot which secured the robe she lifted a love-dazed glance to his and commanded huskily, 'Take it off.'

Silently Ran did so, never removing his gaze from hers as the robe slid to the floor.

Before, the last time, the *only* time, she had been too caught up in the intensity of what was happening and her own needs and emotions to do anything more than register the fact that he was there, that his body was…*his*… But now, this time…

Like a gourmet examining a banquet, a sumptuous repast which had been set out before her, she studied every bit of him, feasting her eyes and her senses on him. He was magnificent…he was perfect…he was Ran. Her love, her life, the father of her child, their child… A fierce thrill ran through her.

'Ran.'

She said his name urgently, almost harshly. As she stepped towards him he stopped her, circling her wrists with his hands, holding her slightly away from him whilst he looked at her in turn. She could see the fierce hunger in his eyes as he focused on her breasts and an excited kick of pleasure gripped her.

There was something so dangerously erotic about standing there naked in front of him, her hands virtually pinioned, that it fed her own senses, her own need…to the point where she could feel her arousal beating a heavy pulse of longing so strongly within her body that she was forced to surrender to it.

Her eyes, soft with emotion, echoed the need, the feeling that was pulsing through her body, touching her, she felt, to her very soul as she looked deep into Ran's eyes. The huge wave of emotion that caught her up and rendered her powerless to do anything to withstand it contained far, far more than just physical desire or the immediacy of the moment. She felt a sense of fate, of destiny almost, as though all the previous emotions, all the love she had known for him had brought her here, to this moment. He might not share her love but he was here with her; she could see in his eyes that somehow something within him was aware of her and responsive to her, even if it was only man's most basic need for a woman that drove him, and against all logic and rational thinking Sylvie knew that what happened between them tonight would be something precious and almost sacred, that the child she now longed so deeply to conceive would be special and loved, so very, very loved.

Odd to think how fate worked, and she could see as clearly as though she were there the small pack of pills in the bathroom, still containing the ones she had accidentally omitted to take since her arrival in Derbyshire, not by design or plan and certainly not because she had

had any intention, any pre-warning that this was going to happen.

'You're beautiful, do you know that?' she heard Ran declaring rawly as, still holding her wrists, he leaned forward and slowly kissed her face, her eyelids, her lips, each one in turn, with something that was almost reverence. Then he moved on to her throat…her breasts…before releasing her wrists and scooping her up in his arms as though he couldn't bear not to have the full length of her held tightly against his body any longer. He slid his hand into her hair and opened her mouth with a kiss so intense and passionate that Sylvie felt as though she was dissolving into him, becoming a part of him.

Just how long they stood like that, how long they kissed, she had no idea; all she did know was that when his mouth finally lifted from hers the room was full of the charged sound of their breathing, the oxygen content of the air somehow diminished so that she felt positively light-headed and dizzy, aching from head to foot with need and longing.

But Ran was ignoring her body language, her silent plea for the intimacy of his body weight lying heavily and sensuously against hers on the bed behind her. Instead he was picking her up and gently placing her on the bed.

'It's all right,' she heard him saying softly to her. 'Everything's all right.' And he was cupping her feet in his hands, slowly massaging them so that tingles of sensation and heat shot through her veins like liquid fire. The feeling of his lips brushing her toes, so unexpected and shockingly intimate, made her gasp in shock, but when she instinctively tried to pull away he stopped her, his tongue weaving a rainbow patter of sensation against her skin as he caressed her toes, the narrow indentation of her fine-boned ankles, the exquisitely sensitive place just behind her knees and then the soft, quivering flesh of her thighs. All of them felt the slow, lingering touch of his mouth whilst the heat of an arousal so intense that she could hardly endure it covered her body in a soft sheen of reaction to what he was doing.

Only when she heard him groan as her thighs trembled in involuntary and uncontrollable response to his touch did she feel him remove his mouth from her, and only then did she realise too that the sound she could hear, had heard, whilst he caressed her was the raw, sobbed sound of her own breathing.

'Ran...'

Unable to stop herself, she moaned his name with all her pent-up need and longing openly displayed, but although he raised his head and looked sombrely at her, although she could see quite plainly as he moved the evidence of his own need, his response to her wasn't to cover her, to move over her and within her as she so longed for him to do, but instead to slide his hands along her thighs, holding, parting, lifting them and then moving round her. His thumbs traced the V between her thighs, following the line of soft hair that grew there before he buried his head against her, breathing in her scent, moaning her name over and over again as he caressed her sex with his tongue and his lips.

The hot molten weight of her own need completely swamped her. The pulse she had felt before had become a thunderous roar, an avalanche of frantic need that gathered and tightened until it overwhelmed her completely, exploding inside her in a series of sharp bursts of pleasure that left her trembling and panting, dizzy and elated, and yet somehow not quite fully satisfied...not complete. She was driven instead to reach for Ran, to cover him with kisses as she drew him closer to her, his torso, where his body hair felt slick and damp with his passion, his throat, where he groaned as she ran her tongue-tip hungrily over his Adam's apple, his jaw, his ears, his mouth.

Fiercely she wrapped herself around him. Her arms, her legs, holding him in an embrace that went back to Eve, knowing instinctively that he would be unable to resist it...or her...

The feeling of him moving against her was just as she remembered it only more intense, like comparing a faded photograph to the sharp colours of reality. Sylvie caught her breath on a cry of primal female pleasure as he moved within her, her body urging him deeper, her eyes liquid with emotion as she whispered to him how much she wanted him, how much she needed him.

'Yes, Ran, yes,' she said, twisting and turning, volubly as well as physically inviting him to possess her as deeply and intimately as only a woman in love did invite a man.

Instinctively she knew that what they were experiencing and sharing went far, far beyond mere sex, that each thrust of his body within hers brought them both ever closer to eternity, to creation itself.

As she felt her body open up completely to receive him, Sylvie gripped him tightly, her eyes open wide, fixed intently on his as she begged him, 'Now, Ran; let it be now...'

And as he responded to her, as she felt the hot liquid pulse of his release within her, her own cycle of rhythmic orgasmic contractions began again, only this time they were so much deeper and stronger; this time they weren't for mere pleasure, she decided, half dazed with the intensity of what she was experiencing. This time they were harvesting the gift he had given her, the precious gift of life.

As his body subsided within hers, Ran still held her, stroking her hair, brushing his lips against her forehead, whilst she breathed in the hot, satisfied male scent of his skin.

'It's been a long time,' she heard him saying unevenly as his heartbeat still thundered against her body.

'Yes,' she agreed quietly. There was no need for her to lie, to pretend; even if it was only temporarily, the barriers between them had been swept to one side by what she had experienced. Oddly she almost felt proud of the truth, of loving him so intensely that she had never been able to share herself with anyone else.

'I'm not… Sex for sex's sake just isn't for me…'

There was a brief silence. She lifted her head and looked uncertainly at Ran. What was he thinking? Was he wishing she had been less open and honest, that she had pretended that what they had just shared meant nothing, that *he* meant nothing? But when she looked into his eyes they were too dark for her to be able to read his expression properly. All she could see was his faintly twisted smile before he touched her face gently and told her, 'I meant that it had been as long a time for *me*, Sylvie…that I hadn't…couldn't… I was trying to explain…to excuse the fact that…that I wasn't as controlled as I should have been.'

'You were…you felt good to me,' Sylvie told him

simply and truthfully, compelled to add, 'But then, I don't have…you have…'

'Been less thankfully in control on either of the occasions we've been like this…?' Ran suggested ruefully. 'You're very kind, Sylvie, and…' His body suddenly tensed and when he moved she could see in his eyes something that made her own stomach muscles lock in sensual expectation.

'And I'm afraid I am likely to give you another demonstration of just how lacking in self-control you make me,' he told her with a soft groan as he took hold of her hand and placed it on his body, commanding her huskily, 'Feel.'

Instinctively Sylvie let her touch become a soft caress, her heart thudding as she felt him grow and harden still further beneath her fingertips.

'Oh, God, Sylvie, Sylvie,' she heard him protest, and he took hold of her, kissing her passionately as their bodies immediately and instinctively moved closer together.

It was fully daylight when Sylvie eventually woke up, her face flushing with hot colour as she opened her eyes to find Ran propped up on one elbow watching her.

'How long have you been awake?' she asked him, nervously clutching hold of the bedclothes, her colour deepening as she started to remember in full the events of the previous night.

'Long enough to know that you snore,' Ran told her ungallantly.

'Snore? I do *no* such thing,' Sylvie protested indignantly, letting go of the duvet in her ire.

'No? Well, then, you growl…' Ran teased her.

'I do not growl! I don't make *any* kind of noise at all,' Sylvie protested.

'Oh, yes, you do,' Ran told her immediately, his manner completely changing, the amusement in his eyes replaced by a look of shockingly burning intensity as he leaned closer to her and half whispered against her mouth as his fingertips brushed the tip of her breast.

'When I touch you here you make a little sound deep in your throat, and…'

'No. No, I don't want to listen to any of this,' Sylvie cried out frantically as the full reality of her situation hit her.

Last night she and Ran had made love…last night she had ignored all the rules, all the laws of dignity and common sense and self-preservation which she had sworn she would adhere to, and…

And last night, lost in the fathomless deep waters of love and longing, she had prayed that she might conceive Ran's child, had prayed for it and ached for it. A deep shudder racked through her. Logic told her that it was far too soon for her, for *anyone*, to know that she had done so, but somehow she did; somehow she sensed that already the seed that would be Ran's child was growing there, implanted deep within her.

Immediately tears filled her eyes, tears of love for the child she knew would be her whole life, and tears also for the fact that he would never know the love of his father, for already she had decided that this child must be *her* child, *her* responsibility, that Ran must never know of its existence, that her child must not be a child whose father only acknowledged him out of duty, a child who knew that its mother was not and never had been loved by its father.

'You're crying.' She could hear the accusation in Ran's voice and immediately tried to blink away her tears. 'I'm sorry about last night,' she heard Ran telling her gruffly. 'I *do* understand... It must be hard for you loving a man who doesn't...'

'Love me back,' Sylvie supplied chokily for him. If, in the past, she had thought that his anger and contempt were hard to bear, they were nothing now that she was faced with his pity and compassion. 'Yes. It is,' she agreed. 'But I'm a woman now, Ran, not a child, and if I choose to love the wrong person, then that is my choice and my *right*. The last thing I want or need is your pity,' she told him sharply, pride making her hold up her head.

'Last night shouldn't have happened,' Ran told her quietly, 'but I...'

'Couldn't help yourself,' Sylvie finished lightly. 'Yes, so you said at the time. It's obviously something we should both...forget...'

Sylvie looked away as she spoke, knowing quite well that she was lying, that she would have the most important reason there could be for *not* forgetting it, for not being *able* to forget it, but that wasn't a piece of information she had any intention of sharing with Ran.

'I...I should like to go back to my own room to get dressed before Mrs Elliott arrives,' she told him with formal dignity, adding, when he continued to look at her, 'I want you to turn your back, Ran, so that I can get out of this bed...'

The look he gave her made her face burn.

'Yes, I know that you've already seen...that... But that was last night,' she snapped self-consciously. 'That was then...this...this is now; this is different...'

'Yes, it is, isn't it?' Ran agreed heavily, and then, to

her relief, he turned away so that she could slip out of the bed and snatch up her nightdress which she pulled on before heading for the door, opening it without pausing to look back because she knew that if she did look back—

Last night had been the most perfect, the most wonderful night of her life, but now it was over and soon, too, with Lloyd's agreement, her time here would be over, and only *she* would know that when she left Haverton Hall, when she left *Ran*, she would be carrying a small and very precious piece of him with her.

CHAPTER 10

'I'M SORRY to disturb you but Ran said that he thought you might like coffee.'

Forcing a welcoming smile to her lips, Sylvie took the tray from Ran's housekeeper.

She had been working in the library all morning, painstakingly going through the accounts and costings for the work she had already commissioned for Haverton Hall.

But now, even though she hadn't eaten any breakfast and she knew that she ought to be hungry, the *only* hunger she had was the never-ending hunger for Ran's love. And, as he had made more than plain to her, that was something she could never have.

Half an hour later she was just on her way downstairs, intending to drive over to Haverton, when her mobile rang. Answering it, she was surprised to hear Lloyd's voice on the other end of the line.

'Lloyd. I wasn't expecting to hear from you today. I thought you'd be…otherwise engaged,' Sylvie told him tactfully.

'Well, I guess I thought I would be too,' she heard Lloyd responding with a rueful note in his voice. 'Like they say, though, there's no fool like an old fool. Still, it was fun while it lasted, and I guess I had my money's worth.'

From the tone of his voice Sylvie immediately recognised that Lloyd had quickly become disillusioned with Vicky.

'I'm going to miss you, hon, when I'm back in New York,' Lloyd told her with the warm affection that was so much a part of his personality.

'I'll miss you as well,' Sylvie told him gravely, and meant it. 'Lloyd, I need to talk to you,' she added quietly. 'There's…there's… I can't stay here… I…I want to come back to New York…'

Biting down hard on her bottom lip, Sylvie willed herself not to lose control. Lloyd would wonder what on earth was the matter with her. She hadn't intended to blurt it all out like that. She had told herself that she would wait, assemble all her arguments and then talk to him calmly and quietly, and yet here she was, letting her emotions run away with her, giving in to the urgent need she felt to protect herself from the pain that being so physically close to Ran was causing her.

'Say, honey, you sound upset. What's wrong?' she heard Lloyd asking her anxiously.

'I can't discuss it over the phone,' Sylvie told him. 'I need to see you… Oh, Lloyd, I'm so sorry…' She gulped as she heard her voice thickening with tears.

'Don't be,' she heard Lloyd telling her gently, and then, to her relief, he said, 'I'll be there with you just as soon as I can fix up everything down here and then we can talk.'

'Oh, Lloyd,' Sylvie wept.

How typical it was of Lloyd that he should put everything else on hold to come and see her, Sylvie acknowledged after their call had ended. He would understand, she knew he would, but she still felt guilty about letting him down.

The door to Ran's study was open and Ran himself entered the hallway just as she was about to cross it. As he glanced at the mobile she was still holding in her hand, Sylvie realised that he must have overheard her talking to Lloyd.

'Lloyd's coming back,' she told him huskily.

'Yes, so I gathered,' she heard him responding flatly, with something that almost sounded like anger hardening his voice. Sylvie couldn't bring herself to look at him. Already the tenderness they had shared last night felt as though it was all something she herself had imagined, created out of her own need; it had gone.

'I...I have to go to Haverton,' she told him shakily as she made to walk past him.

Ran watched her go. It tore him apart to see the pain she was in. Last night she had turned to him in need, in simple human need, driven by her longing, her *love* for another man, a man who had left her to be with another woman.

Did Lloyd have any conception of what he had done, of what he *was* doing, or did he simply think that his wealth gave him the right to ignore other people's feelings? Did he think that the damage he had done to Sylvie, the hurt he had caused her, simply didn't matter?

Yesterday he had left her to be with someone else and now, today, he was coming back.

'I need to see you,' he had heard Sylvie whisper emotionally to him, and as he had heard the betraying tremble in her voice he had closed his eyes. He knew all about that need, had known about it from long before the night he had taken Sylvie in his arms in a mixture of fury and longing, breaking every promise he had ever made himself as he made love to her, *with* her, and discovered, with a mixture of joy, pain and shame, that he was her first lover.

'Wayne's been telling me for ages to find someone to lose my virginity with,' she had thrown tauntingly at him, and she had gone from him to Wayne, abandoning everything and everyone to be with him—her family, her education, even, it had seemed to Ran at times, her principles.

But then she had changed her mind, begged Alex for his help and support, to help her get her life back on track.

He had seen her off at the airport with Alex and his new wife, an impulse decision, giving in to a need for which he had berated and despised himself.

He had ended up going home afterwards and slowly getting drunk—not something he was in any way proud to remember, but it had been the only way he could find to anaesthetise himself against his pain.

Not even to Alex, his closest friend, had he been able to talk about how he felt, about how much he loved her. Alex was, after all, her stepbrother.

He had thought that he was prepared for the reality of knowing that she would spend her life with someone else, but that had been when that reality was at a safe distance. Knowing she loved Lloyd was one thing; having to witness that love, having to hold her whilst she cried for him, having to listen to her pleading with him for his return—no amount of preparation could protect him from that kind of pain.

And now Lloyd was on his way back to see her. Would she tell him about last night, about the intimacy *they* had shared? Morally there was no reason why she should do so but...

Last night, when he had held her, touched her, loved her, when he had felt her body's response to him, answered not just its sensuality but its deeper and far more intensely urgent demand for something that went far beyond even the physical, sexual satisfaction he had felt...known... He opened his eyes and walked across to the window of his study to look out into the garden. Long-ago ancestors of his had designed and planned this garden, lived in this building; his title, his land, the great house which was now too big and too expensive for any one family to run—all that tradition now rested on him and with him.

Once, long ago, it would have been considered his duty as the last male of his line to produce a child, a son, a legitimate heir. But that was something he could never do. He could not marry another woman when it was Sylvie he loved, not for his own sake and not for any wife's either, so there would be no legitimate heir. The only child he would ever have was the one he knew already that he and Sylvie had created between them last night. *Their* child. But he could not compel Sylvie to allow him to be a part of that child's life. Not when he knew that she didn't love him. Twice now she had turned to him for comfort when, in reality, she had loved another man. There could not, must not ever be a third occasion.

Lloyd was more than likely to arrive before evening and Ran knew that he simply could not endure being there to see him reunited with Sylvie.

He walked back to his desk and reached for the telephone.

In the pretty sitting room which his wife had made so much her own, Alex grinned in appreciation as their son headed eagerly towards him, swinging him up into his arms as Mollie looked on placidly. Alex looked lovingly at her. She was in the early stages of pregnancy with their second child and suffering from morning sickness.

'I've just had a phone call from Ran,' he told her.

'Mmm… How is he—and Sylvie…?'

'He wants to come down for a few days. Apparently he wants to pick my brains for ideas on making the estate more self-sufficient.'

'Do you think he and Sylvie will ever work things out?' Mollie asked him anxiously.

Alex raised his eyebrows.

'Why ask me? *You're* the one who thinks that they are madly in love with one another.'

'I don't *think*, I *know*,' Mollie corrected him sternly. 'But the pair of them are just so…so stubbornly determined not to admit to one another how they feel.'

'Has it ever occurred to you that you might *just* be wrong?' Alex asked her tenderly.

'No, because I'm not. You're Sylvie's brother, Alex, and Ran's best friend; you have a duty to do something to help them.'

'Oh, no! No! No way…' Alex denied, shaking his head and looking alarmed. 'They are both adults.'

'Maybe. But they're both behaving like children. We have to do *something*, Alex; you *saw* the way Sylvie was breaking her heart over Ran when we went to see her in New York just after she went there… It was pitiful to see the look in her eyes when she finally managed to ask after him… And Ran's just as bad.'

'Look, they're at Haverton Hall together…alone,' Alex stressed. 'If that doesn't give them both the opportunity to sort themselves out…'

'Maybe being alone isn't what they need, maybe they need someone to talk to, to show them…' Mollie suggested meaningfully, giving him a coaxing smile.

'No way,' Alex told her firmly, but Mollie had made up her mind. One way or another, something would have to be done, and if Alex couldn't be persuaded to do that something, well, then—

Determinedly she started to think.

It was later in the afternoon when Sylvie returned from Haverton Hall to learn from Mrs Elliott that Ran had announced that he had to go away for several days.

'Did he say where he was going or when he would be back?' Sylvie asked her stiffly.

The older woman shook her head.

'He just said that he would telephone,' she informed her.

Had Ran genuinely gone away on business or had he gone because of *her*? Sylvie wondered painfully. He had been kind towards her when he had talked about the pain of unrequited love, kinder than she had ever known him be before, but that didn't alter the fact that he didn't love her and that her presence here in his home must be creating problems for him. Well, she wouldn't be creating those problems for very much longer, she decided, her determination to convince Lloyd to hand over their Haverton Hall project to someone else even stronger than it had already been.

Lloyd himself rang whilst she was upstairs updating her files, explaining that he had been delayed a little longer than he had expected and that it would be late evening before he arrived in Derbyshire.

Ran had instructed his housekeeper to prepare a room for Lloyd before he had left—the room next to her own, Sylvie discovered, when Mrs Elliott, the housekeeper, informed her of Ran's instructions.

Her mobile rang and she answered it, expecting to hear Lloyd's voice but hearing instead that of her step-sister-in-law.

'Mollie, how are you?' she asked, genuinely pleased to recognise her caller.

'Queasy,' Mollie responded, but Sylvie could tell from the happiness in the other woman's voice just how pleased she was about her recently announced pregnancy.

'Just you wait until it's your turn,' Mollie warned her. 'It's no joke. We had salmon for supper and it's my favourite and I couldn't touch a bite…'

Her turn! Sylvie gripped her mobile tightly. How would Mollie and Alex react when she told them that she was pregnant? They would want to know who the father of her child was, of course, although both of them were modern enough, *loving* enough, to accept her decision to keep the father's identity to herself and to bring up her child alone.

'How are things going up there?' Mollie asked her. 'How are you and Ran getting on…?'

To Mollie's intuitive ears the silence that hummed down the wire between them before Sylvie answered her spoke volumes.

'We aren't,' Sylvie told her shortly. 'And in fact…' She paused and then decided there was little point in keeping her decision from Mollie who was, in many ways, despite the distance which separated them, probably her closet friend; not just a stepsister-in-law.

'I…I've decided to ask Lloyd to take me off this project, Mollie. I can't…it isn't… My being here just isn't going to work… Ran and I…' She stopped.

'You still love him, don't you?' Mollie asked her gently.

For a moment Sylvie didn't think she was going to be able to reply but almost against her will she felt compelled to respond honestly to Mollie's gentle question.

'Yes. Yes, I do,' she admitted. 'More than ever. He's...he's everything I've ever wanted, Mollie. The *only* man I've ever loved, the only man I ever *will* love...in every sense of the word,' she admitted in a very low voice. 'There hasn't... I haven't... Isn't it incredible in this day and age,' she continued, her voice full of angry despair, 'that at my age the only man I've ever been intimate with, the only man who's ever touched me...made *love* to me...is Ran? And both times... He doesn't love me, Mollie. I *know* that. He never has, and that first time he was angry, and his reactions were... Both of us were angry and what we did...what we had... But this time it was so...so loving...so tender...so meaningful. But in reality he was just comforting me... He—'

'Did he *tell* you that?' Mollie interrupted her softly.

'Not in so many words. He talked about how painful it is to love someone who can't love you back, and...and about how there's no need to...to feel ashamed of having that love; of needing that person.

'I can't stay here, Mollie,' she burst out passionately. 'I'm afraid of what might happen, of what I might say...do... Ran was so kind, so...gentle and tender... I want to keep that memory... I don't want...'

'He must feel something for you if...'

'If he took me to bed?' Sylvie supplied dryly for her. 'He *wanted* me, yes, but... Lloyd was up here and he took Ran's latest lady-friend back to London with him. Oh, I don't think their relationship was particularly serious, but obviously Ran's a man, and as such...'

'He took you to bed because he wanted sex; is that what you're saying?' Mollie asked her shrewdly.

'Well, I think that was a large part of it,' Sylvie agreed.

'But he must have felt something for you, Sylvie, to talk to you the way you say he did. If he really didn't care, didn't *want* to get involved, then surely the last thing he would do would be to allow that kind of intimacy to take place between you.'

'Yes... No... Oh, I don't know. I just know... I just know that I'm afraid if I stay here I'll... I can't cope with it, Mollie; it's safer for me to put as much distance as I can between us...'

'Have you told him you're leaving?' Mollie asked her.

'Not in so many words,' Sylvie admitted. 'He knows that I've asked... Lloyd's coming up to Derbyshire to see me, but Ran isn't here at the moment. His housekeeper says he told her that he's had to go away for a few days, but he hasn't told her where or when he'll be back... I suspect that he's trying to avoid me...'

'Just like he was when he took you to bed,' Mollie suggested wryly. 'Have you ever asked him how he feels about you, Sylvie?'

For a moment Sylvie was too shocked to answer.

'No! No, of course not—I *couldn't*. How could I? Would you have asked Alex that?'

'Perhaps not,' Mollie acknowledged. 'But Alex's and my relationship is very different to yours and Ran's. We hadn't known one another very long. Whilst you and Ran...'

'The difference is that you and Alex love one another, whilst Ran and I... I have to go, Mollie. I just can't talk about it any longer,' Sylvie told her emotionally.

As she ended the call she prayed that Lloyd would get here soon. God and Lloyd willing, she could leave Derbyshire before Ran came back.

As though on cue she saw the lights of a car drawing

up outside the house, sweeping across her bedroom window. Lloyd at last...

Taking a deep breath, she went downstairs to meet him.

Half an hour later, after she had told Lloyd everything, he gravely handed her a handkerchief and asked her, 'You really love him that much?'

'Too much. Stupid, aren't I?' Sylvie said shakily, reiterating urgently, 'Lloyd, I hate letting you down, but I *can't* stay here—not now.'

'You aren't letting me down, honey. Your happiness means an awful lot to me. I guess I kinda think of you as the daughter I've never had. If I didn't have this meeting I'd wait to take you back with me.'

'No. No, you can't do that. I'll tie up all the loose ends I can whilst Ran's away. The least I can do is to leave everything in order for whoever takes over from me here.'

'See you in New York, then, hon,' Lloyd told her before taking her in his arms and hugging her.

A little later he had gone. Soon she would be gone too...

Her throat tight, Sylvie blinked away her tears.

CHAPTER ELEVEN

'IT'S a beautiful spot here, isn't it?' Mollie commented as she walked across the grass to join Ran where he stood studying the pool in the centre of the small tree-filled glade.

Once, before her marriage to Alex, this glade had been the scene of disturbing desecration when it had been taken over by a band of travellers, eco-warriors, led by the drug dealer Wayne, who had convinced a then idealistic and innocent Sylvie that his sole object in travelling was to assert the rights of the homeless.

It had been Sylvie who had brought them to this pretty glade on her stepbrother's land, and ultimately Sylvie who had played a major part in the drama which had unfolded when she had realised just how dangerous and unsavoury a character Wayne actually was.

It had taken months to restore the glade to what it had once been. Now it was a favourite spot for local visitors. In the spring it was filled with the colour of hundreds and hundreds of bluebells, but now they were over and the trees were just beginning to show the beginnings of the turn of colour which heralded the end of summer.

'It's hard to believe now just how much this place has been transformed,' Mollie remarked as she stood at Ran's side.

'I wish I'd seen Sylvie the day she fell into the mud when you were cleaning out the lake and you had to pull her out... How old was she then, Ran?'

'Seventeen,' he responded immediately, causing Mollie to give him a swift, thoughtful look.

'Mmm… When we were talking the last time Sylvie was home she mentioned how upset she was when her mother insisted that she had to leave Otel Place. She wanted to stay on here with Alex after his father's death, but her mother wouldn't permit it.'

'She was a young girl on the verge of womanhood. A bachelor household just wasn't the place for her.'

'Even though one of those bachelors was someone she loved very deeply, someone she has never stopped loving…someone she *still* loves very deeply?' Mollie suggested.

'Alex felt that it was best that she stayed with her mother,' Ran told her doggedly.

'I wasn't referring to *Alex*,' Mollie returned gently. 'It was because of her love for *you*, Ran, that Sylvie wanted to stay here.'

'She was a child,' Ran told her angrily, turning away from her so that she couldn't see his face. 'What did she know of…love? She was so young, Mollie, and I was just her brother's manager; I couldn't afford…'

'To let her see that you loved her back?' Mollie suggested softly.

Ran turned round and looked angrily at her.

'What I intended to say was that I couldn't afford to give her the kind of lifestyle she was used to, and even if I had been able to do so she was too young, for God's sake, a child still…'

'She wasn't a child at nineteen,' Mollie reminded him, adding more meaningfully, 'And you didn't treat her as one either, Ran. You and she were lovers,' she told him directly. 'You were her first lover, but you left her, let her—'

'*No! She* was the one who left me,' Ran told her fiercely. 'She told me herself that the only reason she'd given herself to me was because Wayne didn't want a virgin…and…'

'And you *believed* her?' Mollie derided him quietly.

Ran looked at her.

'She was saying goodbye to him when I arrived and if you'd seen her with him…'

'Looks can be deceptive,' Mollie pointed out. 'People can go to extraordinary lengths to conceal what they really feel if they believe that exposing those feelings could lead to them being rejected and hurt.

'After all,' she added quietly, '*you've* concealed the fact that you love Sylvie from her, haven't you?'

Immediately Ran tensed, his jaw tightening.

'Alex told you?' he demanded. 'That was supposed to be—'

'Alex hasn't told me anything,' Mollie assured him. 'He didn't need to tell me, Ran; I guessed.'

'How?'

'By knowing the kind of man you are and subtracting that from the way you behave towards Sylvie, and coming up with a figure that just doesn't add up, not unless you add another ingredient to it,' she told him with a small smile. 'Why don't you tell her how you feel…?'

'She knows,' Ran told her shortly. 'Look, Mollie, I appreciate your concern,' he said. 'Maybe once, as a child, a young woman, Sylvie did love me, but that's all changed now. She's not a young girl any more, she's an adult. There've been other men in her life, men who—'

'*What* other men?' Mollie challenged him, and then added boldly before he could answer, '*You* are the only lover Sylvie has ever had, Ran, the only one she's ever wanted...'

'No...that's not true,' Ran denied, but Mollie could see the way he changed colour, his face paling beneath his outdoor tan. 'She and Wayne were lovers and now she has Lloyd.'

'No,' Mollie denied firmly, and then added more gently, 'No, Ran. Wayne and Sylvie were *never* lovers. She told me that at the time and I know it was the truth. She's said very much the same thing since, very recently.'

'How recently?' Ran pounced, and then shook his head. 'This isn't about other men, other loves. I would still feel the same way about her no matter how many other men there'd been in her life, but I can't, *won't* impose either myself or my love on her. She loves Lloyd.'

'Yes, she does,' Mollie agreed, 'but she loves him as a friend, Ran, not as a man.'

'You wouldn't say that if you'd heard her talking to him on the phone as I did, pleading with him to see her...'

Mollie took a deep breath. Before following Ran out here to talk with him there had been certain limits she had imposed on her revelations, certain boundaries she had told herself she must not and would not cross, certain confidences she would not share, but now she knew that she was going to have to break that self-imposed sanction.

'Pleading with him to see her because she wants to be taken off the Haverton Hall project,' Mollie told him quietly. 'She's desperately afraid, Ran, afraid of the way she feels about you and afraid of... She told me herself that she just doesn't think she can take any more. She said it was impossible for her to do her work properly when all she could think about was you. She wants Lloyd to allow her to work on something else, something that doesn't involve her in any kind of contact with you… It's up to you, Ran,' she told him simply, 'If you love her…'

'I saw the way she reacted when Lloyd left her to go to London with Vicky,' Ran told her tersely.

'Lloyd has never been her lover, Ran,' Mollie reasserted. 'She doesn't love him in that way, but if you doubt my word, if you really want to know the truth, there's only one person you need to talk with, isn't there? If you don't believe me, Ran, then think about this: why should a woman, any woman, not just allow but encourage a man to make love to her when she has been deliberately celibate for years and when she believes that he cares nothing for her? Why, unless it's because her own emotions are so strong, so powerful, that they are outside her own control? Very few human emotions come into *that* kind of category, Ran.

'Oh, and by the way…' Mollie paused and turned round as she started to walk away from him. 'I nearly forgot. Sylvie telephoned last night. She's spoken to Lloyd and he's agreed that she can leave Haverton whenever she wishes. She's booked on a flight from London tomorrow.

'Sometimes, for a woman, just being loved isn't enough.

Sometimes we need more than an act of faith and sometimes we need to be told, shown, to see it, to hear it, touch it, taste it.'

'What's the matter with Ran?' Alex asked Mollie curiously half an hour later as he walked into her sitting

room. 'I've just passed him on the lane; he said he was
going back to Haverton. He said something urgent had
come up.'

'Mmm…did he…?'

'Mollie…' Alex said perceptively. 'What's been going on? What have you—?'

'Oh…' Putting her hand to her mouth, Mollie got up
and raced for the door.

Morning sickness—what a euphemism, Alex decided.
Poor Mollie suffered from it all day. Sympathetically he
went to follow her.

Her bags were packed, a note left for Ran explaining
that someone else was going to take over her work, her
files were all in order; there was nothing left for her to
do other than get into her hire car and drive it to the
airport. Still Sylvie couldn't quite bring herself to go.

Irresolutely she made her way upstairs, pausing outside Ran's bedroom. She had the house to herself. Mrs
Elliott had left for the day. Impulsively she opened the
door and went inside. The room was just as she remembered it from that single night she had spent here. She
went over to the bed, smoothing a trembling hand over
the pillow which had been Ran's.

Tears burned behind her eyes but she refused to shed
them. Instead she walked determinedly towards the door
and through it.

Outside the air was warm with the heat of the late
summer sun. She could see the lavender which grew in
huge drifts alongside the drive.

Silently she turned to give one last look at the house.
Where Haverton was a mansion, this was a true home.
Very gently she touched the warm mellow brick before

wheeling round and hurrying unsteadily towards her hire car. She had booked herself into a London hotel overnight ready for her morning flight to New York. It was time for her to leave. There was, after all, no reason for her to stay.

All the way north as he drove, Ran told himself that he was a complete fool, that Mollie was wrong.

'If Sylvie does love me, there's nothing to stop her saying so,' he had told Mollie sharply.

'Nothing, apart from the fact that she believes you don't love *her*,' Mollie had agreed.

Did she believe that? How *could* she? Only the other night, holding her in his arms, he had indirectly referred to his feelings for her.

His body ached with tension and the sense of urgency which had driven him north, not allowing him to pause or stop. The hills basked in the heat of the late afternoon sunshine as he drove the last few miles home.

He saw the Discovery before he saw her, his heart giving a huge leap of relief when he saw that it was still there, that *she* was still there. And then he saw her.

She was wearing the smart cut trouser suit and carrying her document case. Instinctively he pressed his foot down harder on the accelerator.

Ran was travelling at such a speed that at first Sylvie couldn't make out the shape of the car, never mind the driver, for the clouds of dust that surrounded it, but instinctively she knew it was Ran and immediately, for some idiotic reason, her first impulse was to get away before he saw her. But as she tugged frantically at the huge Discovery's door Ran was already bringing his car to a swerving halt in front of her, blocking her exit. He got out of the car and strode towards her, his face grim and unreadable.

'Ran... I...I was just leaving... I—'

'Why?' he demanded, cutting across her husky, nervous words.

'Why?'

'Why are you leaving, Sylvie? Is it because of Lloyd? Because he's your lover and you can't bear to be away from him...?'

Sylvie was too shocked to prevaricate.

'No!' she exclaimed immediately. 'Lloyd isn't my lover.'

'Then why the hell were you so upset when he took Vicky off to London with him?' Ran exploded.

'I... She... It was obvious what she was doing, how mercenary she is, but you defended her, you encouraged her to flirt...you praised her...you...'

'I couldn't wait for her to take Lloyd out of the way so that you could see just how undeserving of you he is,' Ran finished quietly for her.

Sylvie stared at him. The sun was shining down hotly on her head, which must be the reason she was feeling so peculiar, she decided dizzily. There could be no other explanation for the look she had just imagined she had seen in Ran's eyes.

'You can't really have thought that Lloyd and I were lovers,' she told him shakily. 'He's my friend. I like him... love him, yes, as a person, but...' She stopped and wet her suddenly dry lips with the tip of her tongue.

'Don't do that, Sylvie,' she heard Ran demanding rawly. 'Come with me,' he commanded, suddenly reaching out and taking hold of her hand before she could stop him, hurrying her across the gravel and into a part of the garden she had not explored as yet, down a yew-enclosed alleyway.

Through a doorway in the yew hedge Ran guided her into a small secluded garden which was entirely planted with white roses, so many of them that their scent made Sylvie feel light-headed.

'My great-uncle planted these roses in memory of the only woman he loved. She died of pneumonia shortly before they were due to be married and this garden and his memories were all that he had left of her.

'I don't want memories to be all I ever have of you, Sylvie. I love you,' he told her rawly. 'I have *always* loved you and will *always* love you. I haven't told you before because I didn't feel I had the right… First you were too young, then there was Wayne, and then…'

'You love me…?' Sylvie stared at him in disbelief. 'But only the other night you told me that you didn't, couldn't…' she reminded him. 'You said that you knew how painful it was for me to love you but that—'

She stopped as she heard the sharp explosive sound he made.

'No,' he corrected her. 'What I was trying to say was how painful it was for *me* to love you knowing that you didn't love me back.'

For a moment they stared at one another in silence and then, uncertainly, as though she was afraid to believe what she was hearing, Sylvie lifted her hand to his face, her fingers shaking as they touched his skin.

'You love me, Ran? I didn't… I can't… I'm afraid to believe it just in case…' She stopped and pressed her lips together, trying to stop them from trembling.

'Oh, God, Sylvie, what have I done—what have *we* done?' Ran demanded hoarsely as he reached for her. 'I

loved you when you were sixteen, when I had no *right*
to have the kind of feelings I had for you; I loved you
when you were seventeen and you almost drove me
crazy with what you were so innocently offering me. I
loved you when you were nineteen and you flung your
virginity at me like a gauntlet, giving me your body but
denying me your love.'

'I thought you hated me,' Sylvie whispered. 'You
were so angry with me when I came to Otel Place with
Wayne and the travellers.'

'That wasn't anger, it was jealousy,' Ran told her
dryly. 'You'll never know how many, many times the
only thing that kept you out of my bed was that ''anger''. It was either alienate you or...'

'Why didn't you...? Why didn't you take me to bed
then? You must have known how much I wanted it, how
much I wanted *you*,' Sylvie said.

'No. No, I didn't. Oh, yes, I knew you'd had a crush
on me at one stage, but when I saw you with Wayne,
when you told me that you wanted him...'

'I thought you were rejecting me. I had my pride, you
know,' Sylvie told him ruefully. 'You'd pushed me away
so many times before—'

'For your own sake,' Ran interrupted her. 'As your
mother had already pointed out to me, I had nothing to
offer you.'

'*Nothing*...?' Sylvie protested emotionally, her eyes
shining with suppressed tears. 'You had *everything*, Ran,
were *everything* to me...still are everything.'

As he took her in his arms and kissed her, white petals
from the roses drifted down onto them both.

'Like confetti,' Ran said softly when he finally, reluctantly lifted his mouth from hers. 'Traditionally we should be married from the private chapel at Haverton Hall, but it's badly in need of restoration and I can't wait that long.' As he kissed her again he whispered against her mouth, 'Perhaps our first child can be christened there.'

Immediately Sylvie opened her eyes.

'You know…about that,' she guessed. 'You…you felt it too…'

'Yes,' Ran acknowledged. 'How could we have been such fools, Sylvie, so blind? Surely that alone should have told us both, shown us both. What we shared that night, what we *created*, could only have come from mutual love.'

'Yes,' Sylvie admitted huskily. 'I still can't quite believe it…' she added, brushing white rose petals off his arms. 'It's…it's still so… It's less than an hour since I thought that I'd be driving away from Haverton and you, for ever. What made you come back? What—?'

'You did,' he told her promptly, and then relented when he saw her face.

'Mollie talked to me…made me think…see…'

'Mollie? But she never said a word when she rang me—' Sylvie began indignantly, and then stopped. 'Oh, Ran,' she whispered, 'I can't bear to think how close we came to…to not having this…not having one another.'

'It wouldn't have ended here,' Ran comforted her.

'I don't know what Lloyd's going to say when I tell him that I've changed my mind and I want to stay at Haverton…'

'For ever,' Ran told her.

'For ever,' Sylvie agreed.

'Let's go inside,' Ran said abruptly, 'I want to hold

you…make love with you…*show* you how much I love you…how much I need you.'

Ten minutes later, as she lay in his arms on his bed, tracing the strong shape of his nose, she told him huskily, 'There's only ever been you, Ran. I couldn't bear…didn't want…'

'Do you think it's been any different for me?' he demanded rawly.

Uncertainly Sylvie looked at him.

'But you're a man,' she protested. 'There was always someone…one of your sophisticated women-friends…'

'*Friends*, yes,' Ran agreed, 'but lovers, no. Oh, I had some meaningless encounters in the early days, but I've not slept with anyone for a long time. It isn't so very much different for a man, Sylvie, not when he loves a woman the way I love you. Perhaps that was part of the reason why… Will it be a boy or a girl, do you think?'

'I don't know,' Sylvie answered. 'What I do know, though, is that he or she will be a creation of our love.'

'We shall have to marry quickly and quietly,' Ran told her. 'Your mother won't like that…'

'I'd like to be married at Otel Place,' Sylvie said softly. 'Where we first met. I do like this room, Ran,' she added dreamily. 'It's very you.'

'Do you? I'm very glad to hear that since from now on you're going to be seeing an awful lot of it,' Ran told her mock-solemnly before drawing her down against him and cupping her face so that he could kiss her.

They were married five weeks later at Otel Place with just their immediate family in attendance and, of course, Lloyd, whom Sylvie had especially wanted to be there.

Alex gave her away whilst her mother, who had been

overjoyed to discover that she was to marry Ran, sobbed into her handkerchief. Alex and Mollie's child was their only attendant, carrying the ring with solemn determination on a velvet cushion embroidered with Ran's family's arms. Sylvie's dress was cream and gold.

'White has never suited me,' she had told Mollie, adding, tongue-in-cheek, 'Besides, it wouldn't be appropriate.'

'I should hope not,' Mollie had agreed. 'After the years you and Ran have been apart, I'm surprised he let you out of bed long enough to *get* married,' she'd added forthrightly.

Sylvie had laughed and then asked demurely, 'What makes you think that he's the one keeping me in bed? I love him so much, Mollie,' she'd added seriously, 'and it's all thanks to you that we're together.'

'Well, don't try to repay me by naming this after me,' Mollie had warned her as she'd gently patted Sylvie's still flat stomach.

Sylvie had stared at her.

'You know? But how…? I…'

'I saw the colour you turned at breakfast the other morning,' Mollie had told her wryly. 'And besides… Well, let's just say that Ran has that certain look about him. He loves you so much, Sylvie.'

Involuntarily Sylvie's glance now went to her new husband, her heart starting to thud heavily. Much as she loved her family, right now the *only* person she wanted was Ran. Quietly she made her way towards where he was talking with Alex, linking her arm through his as she suggested softly, 'Let's go home, Ran…'

'I really think that Haverton is my favourite of all our buildings,' Lloyd confessed to Sylvie as they both stood together in the ante-chamber to the small family chapel where Sylvie and Ran's baby son and Lloyd's godson had just been christened.

'You say that about every one of them,' Sylvie teased, but Lloyd shook his head.

'No, Haverton *is* special,' he insisted. 'You've done a fine job here, Sylvie. Are you sure I can't tempt you to come back to work for me? There's a palace I've seen in Spain…'

'No.' Laughing, Sylvie shook her head. 'I have another project to occupy me now,' she reminded him, looking lovingly towards her son, who was being cradled by his father.

The work on Haverton had been finished just in time for Rory's christening. The official opening of the house to the public was scheduled for the end of the month.

Ran hadn't put any pressure on her to make her project on Haverton the last one. She *wanted* to be with Rory and, of course, with Ran. Maybe in years to come she might pick up her career again, although she doubted it. She was the Trust's official caretaker for Haverton, and looking after the house and its grounds was going to prove more than stimulating enough.

Already, even before the house officially opened, she had bookings for a string of weddings, carrying right through the coming year, never mind the conferences and private parties who had expressed interest in hiring the house. It was extremely satisfying to know that simply on the interest that had already been shown in the house her costings indicated that it would earn enough to pay for its own upkeep.

'Even if you had managed to run away from me,' Ran had told her only the previous night, 'sooner or later I would have seen Rory, and once I had I would have known that he was mine and then…'

'And then…?' Sylvie had demanded challengingly.

'And then I would have remembered how he came into being and then somehow I'd have found a way to become a part of his life— and yours,' Ran had told her quietly.

'Because he's your son?' she had asked him.

'Because you're my woman…my love…' Ran had corrected her.

Sometimes, even now, she couldn't believe how lucky she had been, how wonderful her life was. Living at the Rectory was fulfilling part of her childhood dream—the house so closely mirrored the secret home she'd used to create for herself. But it wasn't, of course, her home, wonderful though it was, that made her feel that she had been so especially blessed… She looked tenderly at Ran.

If the Rectory was her dream home then Ran was certainly her dream man, although to describe him as such in no way did either him or the depth and intensity of the love they shared true justice.

Ran was her man, her mate, her soul and the real heart of her life… Without him… Without him she wouldn't have her beautiful kitchen floor covered in mud as it had been the other morning when he had come in shouting triumphantly that the poachers he had suspected of taking their stock had finally been caught poaching from a neighbour's property.

She smiled secretly to herself. Rory was six months old and she suspected that well before he reached his second birthday he would have a sibling, a brother or a sister.

'What are you smiling for?' Ran asked her as he came

over to her with Rory and kissed her lovingly on the mouth.

'You know that avenue of limes we planted at Haverton to mark Rory's birth?'

'Mmm…'

'Well, do you remember you said that we'd plant a cross walkway to mark the birth of our second child?'

'Mmm…'

'Well,' Sylvie told him with a twinkle in her eyes, 'I think you'd better think about ordering saplings now…'

'Sylvie…?' Ran queried, but she was already turning away from him to speak to someone else. 'Just you wait until later,' he mock-growled in her ear, but as she answered the interested questions of one of his elderly aunts about the restoration work on Haverton Ran looked down into the alert eyes of his son and told him softly, 'Something tells me you're going to have to get used to the idea of being a big brother, Rory.'

TAKEN FOR REVENGE, BEDDED FOR PLEASURE

INDIA GREY

A self-confessed romance junkie, **India Grey** was just thirteen years old when she first sent off for the Mills & Boon® Writers' Guidelines. She can still recall the thrill of getting the large brown envelope with its distinctive logo through the letterbox, and subsequently whiled away many a dull school-day staring out of the window and dreaming of the perfect hero. She kept those guidelines with her for the next ten years, tucking them carefully inside the cover of each new diary in January, and beginning every list of New Year's resolutions with the words "Start novel." In the meantime she also gained a degree in English Literature from Manchester University, and, in a stroke of genius on the part of the gods of romance, met her gorgeous future husband on the very last night of their three years there. The last fifteen years have been spent blissfully buried in domesticity and heaps of pink washing generated by three small daughters, but she has never really stopped daydreaming about romance. She's just profoundly grateful to have finally got an excuse to do it legitimately!

This one's for Daisy, who makes the hard times easier and the good times better.

With love and thanks.

CHAPTER ONE

WAVES lapping on a silver-sanded beach... A warm breeze sighing through palm trees... Or how about, *a wide blue sky filled with marshmallow puffs of pure white cloud...?*

Nope. No good.

Bella Lawrence's eyes snapped open and she bit her lip, focusing hard on the dainty French wirework chandelier currently under the auctioneer's hammer. There was absolutely no point in trying to think calm thoughts at the moment; not while her heart was beating at roughly twice its normal speed and her hands were slick with sweat.

Not while she could still feel his eyes on her.

She wasn't sure when he'd come in, only that he hadn't been there when she'd taken her place at the start of the auction. She'd felt a growing awareness of heat on her skin and a tingling sensation in the pit of her stomach, and when she'd turned her head he'd been there. Looking.

At her.

Maybe she had lipstick on her teeth...

Sweeping her tongue nervously across them, she allowed herself another very swift glance from under her eyelashes, and felt her stampeding pulse rocket again. He was standing by the wall, making no attempt whatsoever to look interested in the rapid-fire voice of the auctioneer or the bids criss-crossing the crowded room. There was a compelling stillness about him that made her long to lift her head and gaze at him openly, letting her eyes linger on the breadth of his shoulders and the hard planes of his lean, tanned face. She needed to look at his mouth too, she thought desperately, staring hard at the chandelier. At first glance it had looked almost indecently perfect—the deeply indented upper lip sloping steeply upward from a full, sensual lower one—but she knew that if she looked again she might not be able to drag her eyes off him.

Maybe she knew him from somewhere?

Ha. Like she wouldn't remember a face like that.

Taking a deep, steadying breath Bella twisted her rolled-up auction programme between her hands and tried to redirect her thoughts, as the expensive therapist her brother Miles had insisted on finding for her had urged her to do. When she felt her emotions running high, threatening to overwhelm her, she was supposed to think of something calming. Obediently she tried the beach thing again.

He was still looking at her.

Surreptitiously she untucked her short bobbed hair from behind her ear and let it swing forward over her face in a dark curtain, shielding her from the impassive scrutiny of his stare. The problem was silver-sanded beaches were such a cliché, and if she ever found herself on one she'd no doubt be bored to tears. There had to be some difference between feeling calm and feeling half dead with boredom, didn't there?

It was a question she had asked herself repeatedly in the last five months.

Bella shifted restlessly on the hard auction room chair and unfurled her programme. Two lots to go. The wire work chandelier was dismissed in a crack of the gavel and an earthenware confit jar took its place. If she leaned forward she could just catch a glimpse of the porter waiting at the edge of the room, carrying a large, heavily framed painting. The painting that in a few minutes would hopefully be hers, and then she could leave the stuffy, overcrowded room and the unsettling…arousing stare of the stranger.

Which, she had to remind herself sternly, would be a *good* thing.

She fixed her eyes on the painting, trying to focus on the greyish rectangle of the house against its backdrop of green— anything to stop herself turning to look again at the man. This picture was completely and without a doubt the perfect present for Grandmère, and by bringing Bella to the auction rooms the very week that it had come up for sale it seemed that fate, for once, was on her side.

Although, actually, believing in fate was another habit she was supposed to be giving up. The expensive therapist said that it was important that she started to take responsibility for her own actions and reactions instead of blaming vague outside forces like fate or destiny. Or horoscopes. She sighed. It wasn't easy. In fact in her darker moments she worried that all those things she was trying to give up weren't so much habits as personality traits. Parts of herself.

What would be left afterwards?

The gavel dropped on the jar and Bella sat up. This was it. With a renewed sense of purpose and determination she kept her gaze averted from the dark stare of the stranger and focused all her attention on the auctioneer.

'Lot four-six-five,' he announced in a bored voice, as if he wasn't about to sell a momentous piece of Bella's family history. 'Charming amateur oil on canvas of a beautiful French manor house. Who'll start the bidding at twenty pounds?'

There was a shuffling of feet on the front row. A woman with dyed red hair raised her hand wearily.

'Twenty pounds at the front here. Thirty with you, sir…'

A rapid flurry of bids followed, raising the price to ninety pounds. Since leaving art college and going to work for Celia in her Notting Hill antique shop Bella had become something of an expert at auction tactics, and knew to wait for the right moment before joining the bidding. It came a second later when the auctioneer asked for a hundred pounds and the woman in the front row shook her head.

'A hundred pounds anywhere?'

Decisively, Bella raised her hand.

She was immediately outbid by a dealer she recognised two rows in front of her.

'One hundred and twenty?' asked the auctioneer. Bella nodded, and could have shouted with elation when she saw the dealer give a cursory shake of his head as the auctioneer upped the bid.

'One hundred and twenty pounds then, with the dark-haired young lady. Going once at one hundred and twenty…'

Bella thrust her hands into the pockets of her black linen jacket and crossed her fingers so tightly that it hurt. She couldn't afford to go much higher.

'Going twice…'

Just get on with it… she begged silently.

'For the third and final—' The auctioneer broke off in surprise. 'Sir? Just in time, thank you. That's one hundred and thirty pounds from you, sir?'

Bella didn't have to look to know who had made the bid.

Somehow she just managed to bite back the extremely uncalm shriek of frustration that sprang to her lips. Glaring down at the floor, she uncrossed her fingers and balled them into tight fists. There was no point in resorting to superstitious good luck charms in a situation like this.

No.

This called for a skilful combination of bluff and bravery.

Tipping her head back she resisted the temptation to turn and fix the man with a death stare, instead focusing all her attention on assuming an attitude of supreme confidence, tinged with a hint of bored irritation. She'd seen this happen before. Utter insouciance was key. She had to look as if she was buying at any price; as if she was the kind of woman who was used to getting what she wanted.

Fortunately, there was no time to dwell on the bitter irony of that.

'One forty.'

Was that really her voice? Excellent. She actually sounded as if she knew what she was doing, and the realization brought a small smile to her face.

The moment of euphoria was very short-lived; his response was instant.

'Two hundred.'

Feeling her mouth fall open in helpless and no doubt deeply unattractive outrage, Bella couldn't stop her head from being pulled round in the direction of his voice. It was low and husky and completely indifferent—in fact, everything she had intended to convey herself, only genuine. He was looking straight at her.

She felt herself stiffen as her eyes locked with his.

'Miss? Do I have two ten?'

For a second Bella had forgotten about the auctioneer. And the picture. In fact, in that moment she would have been hard pushed to remember her own name. The man's eyes were dark—incredibly dark—and even at this distance she could detect a dangerous glitter in their depths. As she stared at him she saw one of his eyebrows move upwards a fraction. Questioningly. Challengingly.

'Yes.'

'Two ten with the—'

'Three hundred.'

Bella closed her eyes for a second as the man's voice cut through the auctioneer's patter. He said the words quietly, almost apologetically, as if her defeat was a foregone conclusion. But there was boredom and an edge of impatience there too, and she sensed that he wanted this whole business over and done with as quickly as possible.

'Three ten.'

The words were out of her mouth before she could stop them. It was futile—that much was obvious from the impeccable cut of his dark suit and the indefinable aura of wealth that enveloped him like expensive cologne. But his palpable indifference caused a sensation like a thousand red-hot needles piercing her skin.

He'd barely even glanced at the painting. He couldn't want it as she wanted it. Which left the possibility that he was doing this just to annoy her, and two could definitely play at that game.

'Five.'

'Sir?' The auctioneer was flustered by this unexpected turn of events and his sudden loss of control. 'Is that three hundred and fifty-five?'

'Five hundred.'

His mouth was quite incredible, she thought distractedly. It was a good thing his chin was exceptionally firm and square as his lips were so full and finely shaped they were almost feminine. As she watched they twitched into a smile which he quickly suppressed. It was as if he was enjoying some kind of private joke.

With her.

She felt as if she'd been hypnotized. Part of her mind remained aware, rational, firmly sceptical, while the rest of her threw off all inhibition and common sense and plunged into the thrill of the unknown without hesitation.

A ripple of interest ran through the room, like a sudden sharp breeze in a still summer field. Bella could feel eyes on her as people in the rows in front of her turned round to look. Only the man leaning against the wall remained supremely unruffled, his gaze fixed on hers, his face an impassive mask that was almost insolent.

Adrenalin burned and fizzed in Bella's veins. Tearing her gaze away from the stranger, she found the painting again. She had learned enough in the two years before she dropped out of her course at art school to be well aware that this was not an exceptional piece—there was a heavy-handed, painstaking quality about it that strictly limited its value. But it was the subject that mattered. This anonymous, half-forgotten painting depicted her grandmother's ancestral home. It was part of her heritage, and the thought filled her with renewed purpose.

'Five hundred and fifty.'

As if in slow motion she turned back to look at him, and saw his shoulders rise and fall slightly as he sighed. 'Six hundred.'

'Six fifty.'

'Seven hundred.'

There was something mesmerising about his voice and the dark, dark eyes that never wavered from her face. Bella shivered. This wasn't about oil on canvas. Or cash. This was personal.

'Seven hundred and fifty.'

The numbers had no meaning. The rest of the room could have dissolved in a heap of ashes for all she cared. Darkness gathered and swirled in her head, and through it all she could see, all she was aware of, was the man standing a few feet away from her, his eyes searing into hers. She felt the colour rising into her cheeks and ran her tongue over lips that felt dry and oddly swollen. Suddenly she was unbearably hot, as if the blood in her veins had been heated slowly over a low flame.

Hastily she shrugged off her jacket, letting it fall onto the chair behind her and revealing the sober little black dress she wore beneath. She had lost all sense of time. Only the thud of her heart marked each passing second as she stared at him. His hair was dark too, an untamed halo of curls, like a knight crusader. Or a gypsy…or… Or a pirate. His mouth, she saw now, had a brutal sensuality about it that made her think of plunder, and was entirely at odds with the crisp perfection of his bespoke suit. The expression *a wolf in sheep's clothing* drifted though her dazed, distracted mind.

He lifted his head, tilting it back against the wall, but still his eyes pinned her to the spot like a butterfly in a case. Slowly, deliberately, hardly moving those beautiful lips, he spoke with a light foreign inflection that was straight from every clichéd feminine fantasy, and he seemed to address her and her alone.

'One thousand pounds.'

Bella couldn't breathe.

'Miss?' The auctioneer's voice was stiff with surprise, and it seemed to be coming from a long way away. 'Any advance on one thousand? One thousand and ten?'

A terrible, languid recklessness stole through her. This must be what it felt like to jump from a plane, in the moment before the parachute unfurled: dizzying, terrifying, yet strangely peaceful. There was nothing to do but give in to the feeling, the irresistible pull of invisible forces beyond all control.

The painting was lost; that much was certain. There was no way she could compete. But there was more at stake now, and she wanted to push him just that little bit further, break through that infuriating, intriguing, madly provocative calm. She wanted to make him *feel* something. Even if it was only anger...

Defiantly she met his gaze in a look of silent, brazen challenge.

'Yes. One thousand and *five* pounds.'

With an inner smile of triumph she waited for him to come back, upping the price. The room was very still.

'Sir? One thousand and ten?'

The stranger's eyes held her own, then with agonizing slowness travelled downwards. Her throat felt as if it was full of cement, and through the panicky darkness that gathered at the edges of her vision she thought she registered the slowly spreading smile on his lips. Then, as if from a great distance, through veils of horror and disbelief Bella saw him shake his head.

Her stomach tightened reflexively, as if she'd just been punched, and all the air was driven from her lungs in an instant. Her mouth opened in shock. Through the swirling haze of horror she was aware only of his eyes. Amusement and triumph shone in their dark depths.

'One thousand and five pounds, then.' The auctioneer's gavel hovered. 'All finished at one thousand and five…? Going once…'

With contemptuous grace the man levered himself up from the wall and stepped forward. His gaze was still locked on her, but suddenly all the amusement had gone from it.

'Second time at one thousand and five…'

Bella's heart raced and her lips felt numb and bloodless. She was suddenly horribly afraid that she might faint, and was just stumbling blindly to her feet when she saw the man give the auctioneer a curt nod.

'Back with you, sir, at one thousand and ten?' asked the auctioneer.

He nodded again, and turned away from her. Bella sucked in a wild gulp of air. The sharp rap of the auctioneer's gavel shattered the bubble of unreality in her head, and broke the spell. Ducking her head, she pushed past the rows of curious onlookers and fled, too shattered by the emotions still rampaging through her to even feel relieved.

Eyes narrowed speculatively, Olivier Moreau watched her leave.

Interesting, he thought grimly. *Very, very interesting.* On several levels.

Notoriously cynical and quickly bored, he wasn't a man whose interest was easily captured. But by offering approximately ten times too much for an anonymous painting that could be described, at best, as average, she'd got it.

And the hectic sparks in her wide, dark eyes interested him too. She'd wanted that painting very much—enough to almost lose all sense of rationality in the process. She'd been out of control there for a moment and it had scared her. He'd seen it, sensed it.

The thing that interested him most was *why?*

She'd been in such a hurry to leave that she'd left her jacket lying on the chair, and on his way out he leaned over and scooped it up. It was of soft black linen, and as he held it he caught a soft breath of jasmine in its folds which caught him unawares and re-kindled the spark of desire that had been smouldering in the darkness inside him since the moment he'd first seen her.

At the porter's desk he handed over his bidding number and a thick wedge of banknotes. Waiting for his receipt, he looked down at the linen jacket in his hand, noticing, with a faint, sardonic smile, the very exclusive designer label in the back. Very grown-up, he thought idly, picturing it lying against the creamy skin of her neck. Very expensive, but disappointingly conservative and predictable. He would have liked to see her in something more individual.

And what an enticing carnival of vivid images *that* thought introduced…

He crushed the fabric back into one hand, decisively squashing a wicked picture of dark, shining hair against crimson silk as he walked out into the humid London afternoon.

It had been a summer of seemingly endless rain, and once again the sky was low and sullen, but Olivier barely noticed as he stood at the top of the steps. He felt restless and unsettled, as if something momentous was about to happen; something he hadn't quite planned for.

Maybe it was the painting, he mused grimly. Maybe this was it—the one he'd been looking for all these years.

Or maybe it was the girl.

* * *

Stopping dead in the middle of the pavement, Bella swore suc-
cinctly as she realised that she'd left her jacket behind in the
auction room.

Knickers.

She was about to turn round when she hesitated. So what if
the jacket was Valentino, and it belonged to her grandmother?
So what if the heavens were about to open and she was only
wearing a flimsy black dress? She should have been home ages
ago—Miles always rang to check that she'd got back all right,
and he'd worry if she wasn't there when he called, so really she
should hurry…

She didn't move, paralysed by indecision and by the humiliating realization that her reluctance to go back to the auction
house had nothing to do with lack of time and far more to do with
lack of courage. Defiantly she turned round and began to retrace
her steps as frustration swelled inside her, making the back of
her throat prickle and her eyes sting. Now would be an excellent
time to burst into tears, but unfortunately crying was another
thing she'd given up, along with believing in fate and letting her
emotions completely get the better of her.

Well, she'd certainly slipped up there. Big style. Her emotions
had just had a field day, and all because of a dark-eyed glance
from a good-looking man.

Except it hadn't been just a glance, had it? It had been an open
challenge, a direct invitation, an intimate caress. Remembering
it now made the skin on the back of her neck tingle as every tiny
hair rose and shivered. She thought of those eyes, the measuring
way they had lingered on her face, assessing her, then their
speculative swoop over her body. She had felt more alive in that
moment than in all the dead days of the past five empty months
put together.

Life had felt full of excitement and possibility again.

She squeezed her eyes tight shut, trying to summon up that

damned white sandy beach as a vortex of unwelcome emotion opened up in front of her. Instead she saw dark eyes, a full, beautiful mouth. With a harsh sound of frustration she opened up her eyes again.

The image remained. Only now it was even more disturbing for being real.

'Don't tell me—you're trying to remember where you left this?'

The man from the auction room was standing a few feet away from her, a smile of sardonic amusement on his face, her jacket held in his outstretched hand. Bella's cheeks flamed. How long had he been watching her standing in the middle of the street with her eyes closed? He must think she was a complete headcase.

Which was something she usually preferred to conceal...

Hiding her embarrassment behind a screen of chilly hauteur, she snatched the jacket. 'I see. Not content with taking my painting, you also want my clothes now?'

It was a ridiculous thing to say. *Ridiculous.* What Miles would call 'a Bella classic'. The man laughed.

'That depends. Were you thinking of taking anything else off?'

Hot, treacherous, forbidden desire instantly shot through the shame, dissolving the carefully assembled shreds of Bella's self-control like Cinderella's dress on the stroke of midnight. She opened her mouth to make a stinging retort, but for a split second found herself speechless with resentment that he had managed so effortlessly to disturb her careful equilibrium. And then, of course, sense reasserted itself and she knew that any kind of emotional response would be a mistake.

Waves... White sandy beach...

With a huge effort she swallowed back the tide of wonderful, terrible words that threatened to flood from her and hid them behind a small, cold smile.

'Of course not. Thank you for picking it up. Now, if you don't mind I'm late and I have to hurry…'

Without looking up at him again she made to turn and walk away, wanting only to distance herself physically from the disturbing, charismatic pull of his presence and reassemble her defences, regain her comfortable numbness. But as she did so he reached out and took her arm, and the sensation of his fingers against her bare skin was like an electric shock. It ricocheted through her, making her flinch.

'Wait,' he said quietly. 'You said "my painting". In what way is that painting yours?'

Rigid with discomfort, his fingers still clasped around her arm, Bella looked down. 'It isn't,' she said stiffly. 'I'm sorry, that was a stupid thing to say. The painting's yours now. I know that.'

'But you're not happy about it, are you?'

She didn't reply. His voice was very low and, even standing in the middle of the street with traffic roaring past them along Piccadilly, disturbingly intimate. He shifted his position slightly, so that he was standing right in front of her, and she could see nothing but the solid wall of his chest. It was hard. Broad. Real. Very real. His fingers were still clasped around her arm; not too tightly, but she felt powerless to break away.

'You wanted it very much,' he said quietly. It was a statement, not a question.

'Yes,' she whispered.

'Why?'

'It's…nice,' Bella said tonelessly, thinking of calm, neutral things. Not thinking of his mouth, or how it would feel to kiss it.

'*Nice?*' Letting go of her arm, he took a step backwards and made a sharp expression of disgust. 'The hell it is.'

'I beg your pardon?'

Olivier looked at her narrowly. Close up she had the kind of flawless, upmarket beauty that left him cold: short, glossy hair the colour of cherished old mahogany, skin like vanilla ice cream. Earlier on, in the auction room, he had thought he sensed a rawness and a passion in her which intrigued and excited him, but now he saw he'd been wrong. There was nothing but good breeding and good bones.

'You don't have to be an art expert to see that it's rubbish,' he said brutally. 'It's not worth a quarter of the hugely inflated price I just paid for it.'

That seemed to ignite some spark within her again. 'Then why did you bother?' she flared. 'Why couldn't you just let me have it? I'm not remotely interested in what it's worth or how collectable it is. I wanted it for reasons that have nothing to do with *money*.'

'Meaning?'

Her chin rose an inch. 'My grandmother grew up in the house in the picture. That's why I wanted it.'

The sky had darkened, and a warm breeze shivered through the leaves of the trees in the park opposite as the first drops of rain splashed onto the hot pavement. Everything was suddenly very still, as if the regular spin of the world had faltered for a second or two. Olivier almost wanted to reach out to hold on to something to steady himself as for the briefest moment the iron self-control, the bedrock of his being, shivered and shifted.

He took a slow breath in and summoned a bland smile to his stiff face. It felt like ice cracking on a frozen lake.

'Really? And your name is…?

'Bella. Bella Lawrence.'

Lawrence. Hearing the name was like a shot of adrenalin: painful, sickening, but exhilarating. He gritted his teeth, scrutinizing her. 'Well, Bella, what a…*coincidence* that you found a picture of it. You must have been thrilled.'

If she noticed the acid in his tone she didn't react. Nothing disturbed the blankness of that porcelain-pretty face. 'Yes,' she said sweetly, 'particularly since it's her birthday tomorrow and it would have been a perfect present.' She flashed him a saccharine smile. 'Obviously I didn't bargain on some millionaire city boy coming in at the last minute and paying silly money for it, so I'll just have to think again.'

Millionaire city boy? She'd underestimated him considerably. And because she was a Lawrence that stung.

She turned to go, but he had no intention of letting her disappear yet.

'What makes you think I'm a millionaire city boy?'

He didn't move. He didn't even raise his voice, but she turned back to him and Olivier felt a lick of triumph. As her eyes skimmed over him he took his phone from his inside pocket, barely glancing at it as he speed-dialled. Bella Lawrence shrugged.

'The suit. The shoes. The arrogance. Am I right?'

'Sort of.' Without taking his eyes from hers, he gestured with a terse movement of his head to a gleaming dark green Bentley that was just pulling up at the kerbside. 'Can I offer you a lift anywhere?'

Her eyebrows rose. 'Very impressive,' she said sarcastically. 'So you're half millionaire city boy, half magician. What else can you do?'

He gave her a lethal smile. 'Unfortunately, Mademoiselle Lawrence, my talents are too numerous to list now, while we're in grave danger of getting soaked to the skin and I'm late for a meeting. But if you'd like to get into the car I'd be only too happy to enlighten you.'

He opened the car door and stood back. The rain was falling harder now, releasing the scent of hot asphalt and damp earth and making the skin on her bare arms glisten, but she didn't move.

'No, thank you,' she said politely. 'I don't think it would be a good idea.'

'Ri-ight.' His fingers drummed an impatient beat on the roof of the car. 'And I suppose you'd argue that choosing to get completely and unnecessarily soaked is a stroke of genius, would you?' He sighed and stood back. 'Look, you said yourself that you're in a hurry—if it makes you feel better you can have the car to yourself. My office is just around the corner in Curzon Street. I'll walk. Just tell Louis where you want to go.'

He took a couple of steps backwards, still watching her, silently willing her to accept the offer. He would find out where she lived eventually, but it would be so much easier to do it this way. The pavement was virtually empty now, as everyone with any sense had rushed to shelter in doorways or disappeared into the dark mouth of the tube. Bella Lawrence stood beside the open door of the Bentley in her expensive black dress, her hair slick with water.

She frowned suspiciously. 'Why?'

'The painting—let's just say it's the least I can do. Please.'

She glanced up at the angry sky and hesitated. And then, bristling with resentment and indignation, slipped into the car and leaned forward to pull the door briskly shut. She didn't look at him.

'My pleasure,' he murmured sarcastically to himself as the car drew smoothly away from the kerb and was swallowed up by the Friday afternoon traffic.

Though 'pleasure' wasn't quite the right word for it, he reflected as he thrust his hands into his pockets and strode through the rain.

Satisfaction.

That was it.

CHAPTER TWO

GENEVIEVE DELACROIX'S face was pale, delicately tinted with a faint rose-pink blush, as if in the aftermath of passion, and her rosy lips were curved in a lazy smile of repletion. Reclining on the velvet-draped couch, she was completely naked, apart from a large and heavily jewel-encrusted gold cross hanging on a length of red velvet ribbon around her neck.

Her eyes, dark blue and watchful, seemed to bore into Olivier's back as he stood at the glass wall of his apartment, looking down over the most expensive view in London. Eight storeys below him cars sailed noiselessly along Park Lane, and above him planes bound for Heathrow studded the indigo sky with flashing points of light, outshining the stars. But Olivier noticed none of this. The image of the painting swam in front of him, superimposed on the glittering cityscape in the polished sheet of glass.

His instinct about the 'charming amateur painting' in the saleroom had been correct. Although it was unsigned, its subject matter—Le Manoir St Laurien—and the distinctively painstaking style of the brushwork had left him in no doubt that it had been painted by his father.

But Julien Moreau was no amateur. Had things been different he would have been one of the most important painters of his generation.

Olivier took a gulp of cognac from the glass in his hand, draining half the contents in a single mouthful, and then, steeling himself as if against a blow, he turned to face the picture behind him. The one that had lain hidden beneath the other work.

La Dame de la Croix.

For years he had searched for this painting. His contacts in the art world spread across the globe and encompassed all the major auction houses, galleries and collections, but since he knew that the portrait of Genevieve Delacroix was likely to have been concealed behind one of Julien's flawed, later attempts, his contacts had been of little help. He had tried to keep an eye on the catalogues of smaller salerooms, but it had been like searching for a needle in a haystack. The odds had been impossibly stacked against him.

And yet he had done it. The painting was here, propped up on a tall steel bar chair in front of him, as fresh and vivid as if the paint was still wet.

Olivier Moreau prided himself on his ability to achieve. He was a man who got what he wanted through a combination of intelligence, focus and ruthlessness, but he knew that none of that was enough to have pulled off today's coup.

That had been down to luck. Or maybe fate, or some long-overdue divine justice. Karma, some people might call it; after all, it was about time the mighty Lawrences were made to face up to what they'd done, and now the painting was back in his possession he could begin the process of exacting retribution.

He took another mouthful of cognac and let his gaze run speculatively over Genevieve Delacroix's luscious flesh. Hypothetically, in the long years when he had dreamed of recovering this picture, he had always imagined he would simply reveal it, and the shocking scandal behind it, to the world in the most high-profile and damaging way possible.

But now that didn't seem enough.

In his work Olivier operated on a principle of 'absolute return'. His success lay in his ability to exact profit—maximum profit—from every available opportunity, and in this instance fate had very kindly presented him with not one opportunity, but two. *La Dame de la Croix* and Bella Lawrence had both fallen into his lap on the same day. He wouldn't be the man he was if he let a chance like that pass without exploiting it to the full.

Fate…justice…karma—it hardly mattered what you called it. In truth they were all just euphemisms for revenge. The Lawrences didn't know it yet, but it was payback time.

An eye for an eye.

A tooth for a tooth.

A heart for a heart.

Genevieve Lawrence was standing in the hallway rearranging the flowers that had just been delivered by one of London's most exclusive florists when Bella came downstairs.

'Morning,' Bella said with an apologetic smile, kissing her grandmother's perfumed cheek.

Genevieve cast an amused glance at her little gold watch. 'Only just, *cherie*,' she said in her voice of silk and silver. It might have been a lifetime since the young Genevieve Delacroix had left France to marry the dashing and distinguished Lord Edward Lawrence, but her accent was still as strong as ever. 'I take it you slept well?'

'Yes, thanks,' Bella lied. There was no point in telling Genevieve that sleep had proved so elusive that she'd ended up sitting by the window and sketching in the moonlight. The man from the auction house, whose face was still so vivid in her mind, had proved frustratingly difficult to capture on paper. The sky had been streaked with pink when she'd finally given up trying and crawled back into bed. 'Is there still lots to do for tonight?'

Pulling a dripping long-stemmed lily from the vase, Genevieve sighed. 'There does seem to be a lot of last-minute things to attend to. For one thing, these flowers are all wrong. Now I remember why I haven't entertained like this since your grandfather died.'

Bella made a soft, sympathetic sound. After almost fifty years of marriage, Genevieve had been widowed two years ago. 'Will it be awful for you, to do it without him?'

'Awful? Not at all,' said Genevieve matter-of-factly, looking critically at the arrangement of lilies and white hydrangeas. She didn't elaborate, and Bella realised with a flicker of surprise how little she knew her grandmother. Up until five months ago she had been nothing but a remote, elegant figure who had always stood silently by Edward Lawrence's side: coolness and shade to the full-on dazzle of his forceful presence. It was only since Bella had come, at Miles's insistence, to live in the house in Wilton Square, following the business with Dan Nightingale, that she had begun to see the person behind the impeccable façade. And to like her.

'It is a shame that your mama and papa cannot be here, though,' Genevieve continued, adjusting a glossy, tropical-looking leaf. 'I had a call from your mother this morning to say there has been more trouble overnight and the diplomatic situation is too tense for your papa to leave just now.'

Bella was slightly ashamed at the relief that leapt within her. Used to being the invisible member of the dynamic and high-achieving Lawrence family, she had felt completely smothered by the attention which had been focused on her since the Dan Nightingale thing, and she had been dreading seeing her parents for the first time since it happened. Miles's stifling concern was quite enough to deal with.

'They must be very disappointed,' she said guiltily.

Genevieve gave a little lift of her narrow shoulders. 'You

know the Lawrence men, *cherie*. Work comes first. But we will manage without them, I dare say. Now—have you decided what you will wear tonight?'

Bella's eyes lit up. 'Well...I got this gorgeous little silk smock dress in Portobello Market the other day. It's bright red with fuchsia-pink flowers around the hem, with kind of pink sequins and gold embroidery on them...' The words came out in a rush of enthusiasm and her hands fluttered in the air, sketching fluid lines. 'And it's short—but not, you know, indecently short, and it's got this deep scooped neckline and sweet little sleeves...' The words petered out.

'It sounds fabulous, *cherie*.'

'Yes...' Subdued again, Bella paused. 'You know, I think maybe it would be better if I borrowed your black Balenciaga, though.'

Genevieve's fine eyebrows rose questioningly. 'Would it be foolish to ask why?'

'I think that Miles would rather I—I don't know...I think I should just keep it low key. After all that's happened...'

Picking at the spiky leaves of a discarded palm leaf, Bella didn't notice the concerned glance Genevieve cast her; however, she did detect the faint note of reproach in her grandmother's voice. 'Bella, *ma chère,* you cannot spend your life trying to be what your brother wants you to be.'

Bella gave a crooked smile. 'No, but perhaps I have less chance of messing up that way. After all, I made a huge fuss about being given the chance to be myself and live my own life, and look what happened.'

'You made a mistake,' said Genevieve mildly. 'Is that so bad?'

Bella's smile faded. The huge, marble-tiled hallway felt suddenly cold. 'Given that it could have caused a scandal which may have cost Papa *and* Miles their jobs, I think that's as bad as I'd like it to get,' she said quietly. Without realizing it she had completely stripped the palm frond, and its shredded leaves were scattered over the polished surface of the table. 'I don't want to make things any more difficult for Miles than I have already. It's a pretty important time for him just now, with the election coming up and everything, and the last thing he needs is his drop-out, headcase sister mucking things up for him again.'

'But, *cherie,* this is a private party for my birthday, not a political rally for Miles. You can wear what you like.'

'I know, but you have to admit, *Grandmère,* that you have some pretty influential friends. I think I should stay in the background as much as possible.' She gave a short laugh. 'In fact it would probably be better all round if I didn't come...'

She had been sweeping the torn leaves into a little pile, but now Genevieve stopped her, laying her hand over Bella's quite firmly. 'Stop this, Bella.'

'Sorry... It's not that I don't want to be there for your party, it's just that you have to admit I'm a bit of a liability,' Bella said lightly. She gave an awkward smile. 'Even Ashley, PR Genius and Totally Nice Person, would have her work cut out making an art school dropout, shop girl and psychiatrist's dream ticket seem like a political asset.'

'Oh, Bella,' Genevieve sighed. Suddenly she seemed very sad. 'You have such *talent*. If only you could see that.'

'For art,' said Bella soberly. 'That's all, and that avenue is fairly conclusively closed since—'

Genevieve cut her off. '*Non.* Not just for art. For empathy. For understanding people, and seeing through the façade to what lies beneath. For *loving.*'

Bella laughed, but there was a faint tinge of bitterness to it. 'I think Miles would say that's my problem, not my talent.'

'*Non!* Don't let him make you believe that!'

The sudden rawness in Genevieve's voice made Bella's heart miss a beat. Her words echoed for a moment round the grand room, seeming out of place amongst the gleaming marble and polished wood, the perfectly arranged Sèvres china and Georgian silver. The orchid she had been holding fell to the floor as Genevieve took Bella's hands in hers.

'I do not want to watch you throw away your happiness to appease your family. Please, *cherie,* tell me you won't. Don't make the same mistake that I made.'

As the car glided through the security cordon at the entrance to Wilton Square, the noise and activity of the city was left behind and Olivier felt as if he was entering a charmed world. Beyond the dark shapes of the trees in the central garden Genevieve Delacroix's ivory mansion blazed with light, and music spilled from windows which had been thrown open against the sticky air. The party had been going for an hour or so, and Olivier had timed his arrival carefully to allow him to slip in relatively unnoticed.

The enormous black front door was opened by a stiff-backed butler in white tie and tails, and Olivier handed over the gold-edged invitation he had managed to procure from a contact in the Treasury who owed him a favour. The butler took it with an impassive nod, gesturing for him to leave the gift he carried on a mahogany sideboard groaning under the weight of exquisitely wrapped parcels. Placing the painting of Le Manoir St Laurien, carefully reinserted into its frame, amongst them, Olivier followed the direction of the noise.

The spacious first-floor sitting room was packed with cabinet ministers, high-powered media figures and ancient aristocrats, and their loud, almost unintelligibly well-bred voices drifted assuredly above the music of the band downstairs. So this was the world of Bella Lawrence, he thought as his eyes moved around the elegant panelled room. Luxurious, expensive, exclusive… things that she no doubt took for granted and barely noticed. It was what she'd been born to.

Without being particularly conscious of it, he found his gaze skimming over the distinguished, easily recognizable faces of politicians and TV celebrities, searching for one face in particular. But the vicious kick of desire in the pit of his stomach when he saw her caught him off guard.

She was wearing another slim-fitting, severe black dress, which disguised rather than emphasised her figure, and high heels that made her endless legs seem as gracefully unsteady as a colt's. She carried a large plate of canapés, which she was offering to a noisy group of media types. Her face was hidden by the silken curtain of her hair, but there was a stiffness in the set of her shoulders and a downward tilt to her head that told him she wasn't smiling.

This was her world. So why did she look so out of place?

'Caviar blini?' he heard her murmur to a prominent TV news journalist, who took one without glancing at her or breaking off his conversation.

Eyes narrowed, Olivier watched.

Warm waves…sandy beach…top TV newsreader lying on it while I smash a plate of caviar blinis over his head…

Bella's smile was a painful rictus grin as she moved on, wondering how soon she could beat a hasty retreat to her room and curl up with a book. *Any time now,* she thought resignedly, *for all the notice anyone's taking of me.*

As she moved further into the room she could hear Miles's voice—confident, urbane, totally in command—and once again the randomness of the gene lottery was brought home to her. How could it be that he was so…*assured,* and she had never felt a moment's assurance in her whole life? She kept her head bowed, her back towards him, hoping to pass by unnoticed and be spared the inevitable embarrassment of being introduced to whichever political worthy he was talking to.

'Ah, Bella! There you are…I was just talking about you.'

If Bella had been wearing boots at that moment her heart would have sunk into the bottom of them. Fortunately, her shiny black high-heeled shoes were too tight to leave any room for anything else, so she summoned a smile and turned round.

'This is my little sister, Bella,' Miles said heartily to the vaguely familiar-looking man standing beside him. 'Named after the suffragette Christabel Pankhurst.'

Taking a caviar blini, the man smiled politely. 'Of course. And as one of the distinguished Lawrence family I imagine you're just as much of a trailblazer as your namesake?'

Bella felt her smile falter. *Oh, yes, absolutely*, she wanted to say. *I'm the first member of my family to fail at anything and become a dropout.* Just as she was wondering how to frame this sentence slightly more positively, the slim brunette at Miles's side stepped in.

'Bella's the artistic one in the family, Prime Minister. She's incredibly talented, so although Miles needs help to match a pair of socks, I actually have hope that we might just end up having children with a glimmer of creativity...'

Prime Minister. Oh, knickers. That was why she recognised him...

Bella cast a grateful glance at the girl who had spoken. Ashley McGarry was Miles's fiancée. She was also extremely gorgeous, owned her own incredibly successful PR firm and was just about the nicest person Bella knew. Which was good, because it would have been hard to forgive her for the gorgeousness and success otherwise.

'So, what kind of art do you do?' the Prime Minister asked her politely.

Bella squirmed. 'I paint furniture.'

The PM looked surprised. He'd clearly expected something a little more cutting edge. Ashley came to the rescue again. 'Bella has one of the most enviable jobs in London, working in a gorgeous shop in Notting Hill that sells French antiques and vintage stuff.' She turned to Bella with an encouraging smile. 'I went back the other day to see if that fabulous mirror was still there, but Celia had sold it. I was so disappointed.'

Don't worry,' said Bella. 'Her daughter's twins are due any minute, so she's asked me to do the autumn buying trip to France. I'm going to take her car and tour the markets around Paris, so I can look out for another one for you then.'

Miles looked up. 'You're going to France, Bella? On your own?'

Suddenly the atmosphere was very tense. Ashley laid a hand on Bella's arm but this time said nothing. Bella felt as if someone was slowly pouring cold porridge down her back. How could she be having this conversation now? *In front of the Prime Minister?*

'Yes, Miles,' she said miserably, looking at the floor. 'I'll be fine.'

'We'll talk about it later.'

'There's no need—I've said I'm going, and that's that.'

Miles turned back to the Prime Minister and said with forced cheerfulness, 'My sister hasn't been…well. She's still recovering and she needs keeping an eye on.'

It was too humiliating. Bella seemed to spend her whole life these days trying to forget what had happened, but it was impossible when to everyone else it was the single most significant thing about her. Speechless with suppressed rage, she whirled round, the plate clasped in front of her like a weapon, and walked straight into someone stepping towards her.

As if in slow motion she watched caviar blinis sail gracefully through the air and rain down all around her. The plate jolted against her hipbones, coming between her and the body of the man with whom she had collided. In a daze of embarrassment and misery she sank instantly to the floor and started to pick up scattered canapés, desperate to clear up the damage and get out.

The man she had bumped into dropped to his knees beside her.

'It's fine,' she muttered miserably, without looking up. 'Please don't bother. I can manage.'

'Leave it.'

His voice was very low, and very French. And very filled with barely suppressed anger.

She froze. Then, full of foreboding, she dragged her gaze upwards. Her indrawn breath made a little gasping sound. She was looking straight into the dark, gleaming eyes of the man from the auction house.

'Wh—what? I don't understand...' she whispered hoarsely. 'What are you doing here?'

'Taking you away.' Removing the plate from her hands, he put it on a side table and gently pulled her up. She was suddenly aware of Miles behind her, looking at her with obvious dismay that she'd managed to make a fool of herself again. She could hardly blame him. She was standing liberally smeared in first-class beluga caviar just a few feet away from the Prime Minister and some of the most important, most famous and influential people in the country.

And in front of possibly the best-looking man on the planet.

Without warning, hot tears stung her eyes, but before they spilled over she felt the man from the auction take her chin in his fingers and gently tilt her head up.

'Oh, no you don't, beauty. You're not going to cry,' he murmured as he bent towards her, and in a heartbeat his mouth closed over hers, warm and firm. For a second she felt herself stiffen, but her gasp of shock was lost in his kiss.

The bright, tasteful room full of people dissolved, the loud music of the band faded away, and along with it her shame and humiliation. She was in a dark, secret world of lips and hands, and the only sound was the frantic drumbeat of her heart. Or his heart. Or both together...

After a second, a minute, a lifetime, he lifted his head and with one hand in the small of her back moved his mouth to her ear.

'OK, *cherie,* smile nicely and head for the door.'

Bella opened her mouth to protest, but he swept his thumb swiftly across it.

'Don't speak,' he murmured huskily. 'Don't say a word. You can thank me later.'

CHAPTER THREE

OLIVIER followed her through the crowded room.

Already, he noticed, she was walking taller, holding her head higher. There was a provocative sway to her hips. In short, a glimmer of the brilliant spark he had noticed yesterday in the auction room had returned.

With just one kiss.

Dieu, what he would do to her with a whole night.

The thought brought the ghost of a smile to his set face. He had decided already that seducing Genevieve Lawrence's grand-daughter, sleeping with her, would be a matter of cold-blooded score-settling, but if the change he'd just witnessed was anything to go by it would almost be too pleasurable to count as vengeance.

How would it feel to touch the flesh that had been so forbidden to his father? How would it feel to possess such a price-less pearl…the daughter of the Delacroix dynasty…and then cast it away as if it were worthless? Would it make up for what they had done?

On the landing outside the sitting room she stopped and turned to him. There was a pink stain in her cheeks and an intense, almost feverish glitter in her eyes.

'*Thank you?* I'm supposed to thank you for this?' She looked down at herself. Beads of caviar gleamed darkly on the pale skin of her arms and the ivory swell of her breast. 'Of *course*. Caviar body paint is *such* a good look…'

Olivier smiled lazily. She might be being sarcastic, but she was actually completely right. She looked good enough to eat. 'Believe me,' he drawled, 'it's a lot better than being completely humiliated in public by some overbearing bastard treating you like a child.'

'Do you mind?' she gasped. 'That was my brother!'

'And that makes it all right for him to treat you like that?' Olivier asked coolly.

'He's protective. He just—' Bella broke off, shaking her head in confusion. 'Look, I don't know what this has to do with you…'

'I don't like bullying. Now, which is your room?'

'Why?' she demanded.

He paused, looking at her thoughtfully. Standing there with her eyes sparking with fury she looked oddly sweet, and he couldn't help but admire her defiance. The prospect of seducing her was like a sudden and unexpected blow to the stomach. 'Let's just say I don't like people who use their natural advantages to repress people who don't have the same power,' he said quietly.

She laughed suddenly: a short, joyful peal that broke the tension. 'I didn't mean that.' She looked up at him and their gazes locked. 'I meant, why do you want to know which is my room?'

'Because I think you need to get out of that dress.'

The sparkling laughter faded from her eyes, and was replaced by something much more intense.

Gently, not wanting to frighten her, he reached out and cupped her breast in the flat of his hand, feeling the ripeness and heat of her skin through the severe black crêpe. A small shiver ran through her. Slowly, lazily, he ran his thumb over the bare skin above the low-cut neckline of the dress where her cleavage spilled out, scooping up black beads of caviar that glistened against the creamy flesh. Her eyes stayed fixed to his the entire time, and he saw the momentary flicker of her eyelids at his touch.

Removing his hand, he put his thumb to his lips and sucked off the caviar.

She drew in a soft, shuddering breath. 'Up there,' she said in a low voice. 'My room is up there.'

'Then allow me…' Olivier almost expected her to protest as he took her hand and led her to the stairs, but passively she allowed him to lead her. Even so, he had the impression that a fierce battle was going on beneath that graceful exterior. This little rich girl had been brought up to be polite and well behaved, but all the etiquette and good breeding couldn't quite conceal the wildness that heated her blue-tinged blood.

Just like her Grandmother. Just like the original *Dame de la Croix*.

He followed her across the thickly carpeted upper landing. She opened a door, revealing a pretty room with a window set into its sloping roof. Outside a blue August twilight was gathering over the treetops in the residents' garden opposite, casting deep, inky shadows in the room. Just inside the door she stopped and turned to him.

'Wait!' She looked agitated. 'I don't know anything about you. I don't even know your name…'

'Olivier Moreau.' Solemnly he held out his hand and said with a tiny hint of sarcasm, 'Millionaire city boy.'

He was rewarded with a smile so brief it had disappeared before it was properly there. 'You said I was only half right about that. Who are you really?'

'I'm a hedge fund manager.'

'What does that mean?'

He paused, weighing up how to answer. 'I buy and sell… things.'

'What things?'

He shrugged. 'Anything. But I like dealing in the complex, indefinable things best. Rain, air quality, confidence…'

'Or other people's heritage?' she added bitingly.

He acknowledged the dig with a small smile. 'Exactly. As long as it gives me a good return on the investment. What else can I tell you? I'm French, but I've been based in London for the last four years. I collect art. I'm not married and I have no children. Is there anything else you'd like to know?'

'Why you came here tonight.'

She walked away from him into the room, but he stayed where he was, lounging easily against the doorframe. He didn't want to rush her, or pressure her. There was no need.

'I wanted to see you again,' he said simply. 'After yesterday.'

She was standing by the wardrobe with her back to him, her head bent as she fumbled with the buttons on the back of the dress. In the melting blue light her neck was as pale and delicate as the petals of a lily.

'What for?'

Her directness was unexpected, but Olivier admired her for it. Slowly he moved across the twilit room, desire licking through him in instant, automatic response as he reached out to help her. His libido obviously had little respect for history or family loyalty, he thought dryly, noticing that she stiffened slightly as he slid the button from its tiny satin loop.

His fingers moved down to the second button. 'I wanted to give you what's rightfully yours.'

'The painting?' There was a pause as the dress slid from her shoulders, revealing the flawless expanse of her bare back. It glimmered milk-white in the moonlight for a moment, and then she turned round so she was facing him.

'Of course.'

In her 'take-me' heels, with the caviar-smeared black dress clutched against her breasts, she looked dishevelled and wanton, but when she spoke the icy hauteur in her voice shattered the enchantment.

'No, thanks.'

He felt an uncomfortable jolt of surprise but instantly concealed it, looking at her steadily. 'Why not? You said it was your grandmother's house. If that's the case then she should have it.'

'It's too expensive.'

He moved slowly towards her, genuine interest gleaming in his eyes. Having a woman turn down a gift on the grounds that it was 'too expensive' was a bit like having a goldfish decide against a bowl of water on the basis that it was too wet. He was intrigued.

'I thought you said yesterday that you didn't care how much it was worth?'

'I did,' she said with cold disdain. 'But that's irrelevant now. You're a businessman, Mr Moreau, and I assume that part of your success rests on knowing your market. You no doubt think that all this—' she made a sweeping gesture with one arm, causing a corner of the dress to fall down, revealing a tantalizing glimpse of voluptuous flesh '—means I'm some wealthy, profligate trustafarian, and you can sell the painting to me at a profit because you know how much I wanted it.' She shook her head emphatically. 'Well, I just hope that your projections in the boardroom are a lot more accurate than the ones you've made about me, because that's a huge miscalculation. It makes no difference how much I want the painting because I can't *afford* it.'

She stopped, her chin raised in awkward defiance, her dark hair framing a face that burned with fury and bitterness and passion. For a moment neither of them spoke, and above the distant thud of the band Olivier could hear Bella's laboured breathing. In the half-light her shoulders looked fragile and translucent as they rose and fell rapidly.

'Great speech,' he said dryly after a long pause. 'However, completely unnecessary. I said I came to *give* it to you.'

'Why? Why would you do that?'

The space between them seemed to pulse with possibility.

Watching her closely, Olivier could see that the hostility that crackled around her like static was due in part to a deep-seated uncertainty. Insecurity, perhaps. Having seen her arrogant, over-bearing brother at work, it wasn't hard to work out where that had come from.

He gently lifted the fallen edge of her dress, tucking it back in place and hiding the ivory swell of her breast, careful not to let his fingers brush her skin.

She shivered.

'You want it,' he said simply, looking at her thoughtfully. He saw the heat flare in her eyes and knew she had all but forgotten, as he had intended her to, that he was referring to the painting.

He turned, hiding his slight smile of triumph, and walked casually across the room. 'I left it downstairs. I hope your grand-mother likes it,' he said, and closed the door quietly behind him.

Going down the wide stairs, he counted each step. Would she come after him before he reached the first floor, or would she manage to hold out for longer and leave it until he'd reached the hallway?

There was, of course, no question that she would come after him.

He reached the front door and, ignoring the imperious man-servant who had welcomed him on the way in, stepped out into the warm evening. He had to hand it to her. She was pushing it to the limit. Unhurriedly he crossed the empty street to where his car was waiting, and was just reaching out a hand to the open the door when he heard the clatter of her heels on the marble floor behind him. At the sound of her voice he found he was smiling.

'Wait—please wait!'

He arranged his face into an expression of bland enquiry before he turned round.

She had put on a short dress of vivid scarlet silk, loose and flowing like a smock, and as she ran down the steps towards him the silk rippled against the curves of her body like water cascading over a statue in a fountain. The transformation from the bland, dutiful girl he had watched up there in the drawing room to this vibrant beauty was breathtaking. It was as if she had been brought back to life.

She came to an abrupt halt by the pillared entrance portico.

'I'm sorry for being so suspicious and cynical,' she said, and her voice vibrated with suppressed emotion. She was trembling. 'I've learned the hard way, I'm afraid. It made me forget that there are good people out there too. I'm sorry, please—forgive me.'

Olivier found himself taking a couple of steps towards her, so he was standing in the middle of the carless road.

'Apology accepted.' He raised an eyebrow. 'Was there anything else?'

'Yes.' Keeping her chin held high, she came down the steps to where he stood. Her eyes flashed with feeling. 'I never said thank you.'

The height of her heels meant that she didn't have to stretch upwards very far to press a kiss on his cheek, but they also made her unsteady. As she leaned over she wobbled slightly, and Olivier found himself grasping her arms as the warmth and softness of her lips met his skin.

He didn't let go of her straight away. 'There's no need to thank me,' he said with a trace of mockery. 'According to you the painting was morally yours all along.'

She gave a breathy laugh and looked down as he let her go. 'All right, then…not just for the painting. For extracting me from an extremely embarrassing situation, and making my brother see I'm not a child any more.'

Olivier glanced up at the row of tall windows behind their elegant wrought-iron balconies on the first floor. Miles was still there, and as Olivier watched he glanced down. Olivier felt a small dart of triumph as he saw the expression of anger and disapproval on Miles Lawrence's handsome face.

'It was my pleasure,' he said dryly.

'He only does it because he cares, but unfortunately it's a very thin line between being caring and being controlling—especially where my love-life is concerned. No one is ever going to be *good enough* for his little sister, of course…'

Loathing rose up in Olivier's throat as she said that. *Not good enough*. Times had changed, the world had moved on, but it seemed that Miles Lawrence still held fast the same outdated, elitist principles of his forebears. The principles that had ruined Julien Moreau's life.

'Charming,' he murmured sardonically. Bella jumped slightly as he trailed a caressing finger down her cheek, adding lightly, 'Don't look now, but he's watching.'

Her eyes widened a little as understanding dawned. It was like dipping a brush of black ink into clear water, Olivier thought idly as the darkness of her pupils spread and deepened. Her head tilted back a little and her lips parted as slowly, deliberately, he bent his head and their lips met in the lightest butterfly touch.

He had her.

Lifting his hand to cup her face, he dipped his head again and closed his mouth over hers. His fingers slipped into the silk of her hair, and he felt her tongue dart between his open lips. He had her, and tasting Delacroix flesh was every bit as easy and as sweet as he'd anticipated.

Bella slid her hands inside his dinner jacket, placing her palms flat against his ribs where she could feel the steady rhythm of his heart. His body was warm, reassuringly solid, and the expensive, dry, masculine scent of him filled her head and blotted out the city smells of dust and diesel and night-scented stock from the square's garden. She felt as if she was melting, and the violent trembling that had gripped her since she had run down the stairs after him eased, replaced by a delicious languor like honey in her veins.

The summer evening enfolded them as they stood alone in a

halo of light from the windows, and the music of the band eddied around them. They were playing a mellow, dreamy song, and Bella felt her hips undulating lazily beneath Olivier's warm hand.

Desire beat an indolent tattoo in her blood. She felt heavy with it, drenched and pulsing, as if there was an unhurried inevitability about it. The panic that she had felt before had completely disappeared. Suddenly she didn't care what her family thought of her. What must Miles be saying now? That she was irresponsible…?

Olivier's mouth moved to her cheek, the hollow beneath her ear, the curve of her neck.

Mmm…yes. Irresponsible, definitely…

She slid her hands over his shoulders, arching her back as his lips raised goosebumps up her arms.

Impulsive?

Oh, yes. There were impulses that she had barely dared to imagine raging through her like forked lightning, and she wanted nothing more than to give into each and every one of them.

Easily led…

'Oh…'

She felt a sharp stab of dismay as Olivier lifted his head and pulled back from her a little. Her skin tingled and sang with the need to feel his lips against it again.

The expression on his face was impossible to read as he looked down at her, but his voice was wry and slightly mocking. 'Do you think that showed him?'

For a moment Bella didn't understand what he meant, and then disappointment and shame hit her as she remembered that this was just an act to annoy Miles. She gave a shaky laugh, desperate to make light of the terrifying and utterly genuine lust that rampaged through her.

'Not sure…' she said lightly. 'Maybe sex on the back seat of your car…just to be completely certain he got the message that I'm a big girl now…?'

There was a part of her—a distant, dutiful part—that was completely horrified by what she'd just said but was helpless to intervene. The expensive therapist would have a fit, but Bella felt as if she had torn off a mask and was finally revealing herself. It felt good. She was tired of being invisible; she wanted to be noticed.

His mouth curved into a lazy, wicked smile that simultaneously dazzled her and made her squirm with painful, pulsing longing.

'I'm sure my driver would enjoy that,' he murmured.

She met his gaze and smiled challengingly. 'I didn't mean with him.'

For a moment neither of them moved. The laughter that had been bubbling inside her was obliterated by a tide of drenching urgency. From behind them, in the house, there was a ripple of applause as the band finished the song, and then silence.

His eyes were so dark it was impossible to see where the pupil ended and the iris began. The band started up again, in a persuasive flourish of strings. As if in a dream she stroked the flat of her hand down the silk lapel of his jacket, swaying slightly against him.

Unsmiling, Olivier held out his hand.

With slow deliberation Bella touched her palm to his. For a moment they stood there like that, while the music curled around them, and then Bella let her fingers close around his. His hand felt big in hers, strong and unbending, and as she moved towards him his other hand came up to her waist, bunching up the thin silk as it slid across her back. She held his shoulder, but despite the formality of their position she couldn't help tilting her pelvis towards him, arching her back so her hipbones bumped against his.

And then they were dancing. His hooded eyes glittered down at her, but his face remained completely still.

He was guiding her steps gently, expertly, and the click of her heels echoed dully off the high buildings around them as they swayed against each other in the empty street. Above them the sky had darkened to a rich sapphire-blue, and the sounds of the city seemed very far away. There was just the music and the presence of this man, this stranger with his dark, hypnotic eyes and his aura of quiet, persuasive strength.

He had the stillest face she had ever seen, she thought hazily. His exceptional beauty concealed everything, like armour. She had a sudden fierce, searing need to get past it to the man beneath.

'I have to go.'

His words cut crudely through her thoughts. He was pulling away from her, distancing himself, and she felt instantly desolate.

'Why? Where are you going?'

'I'm due at a reception at the Tate. I've donated a picture to their forthcoming exhibition, and it's the private view tonight. I have to be there.' He hesitated, looking at her measuringly. 'But you could come with me, if you'd like to?'

'I can't. My grandmother—it's her party and—'

She broke off. Miles had appeared in the doorway, his face a scowling mixture of irritation and concern. 'Bella, come back inside at once,' he said with barely concealed impatience, then gave a nervous half laugh. 'That dress is completely inadequate for hanging about outside. You'll catch your death of cold.'

Olivier's eyes were on her. She could feel their dark, silent challenge. She looked from him to Miles, and was suddenly aware that her big brother, who had always seemed so omnipotent, so completely in control, was *afraid*. And then she looked back to where Olivier stood, strong and certain, and Genevieve's words from that morning came back to her.

Don't throw away your happiness to appease your family.

She would understand.

Hesitantly she walked forward towards Olivier, and took his hand, feeling his power give her strength. 'I'd like to come with you—if I may?' At his brief nod of assent she turned back to Miles, and so missed the dark gleam of triumph in Olivier Moreau's eyes.

CHAPTER FOUR

'I'M GLAD you changed your mind.'

Olivier kept his gaze fixed casually ahead. Bella seemed to have pressed herself into the furthest corner of the car seat and was sitting stiffly, her hands tucked between her thighs and the soft leather upholstery.

'I don't think Miles would say the same thing. I'm going to have a lot of explaining to do later.'

The easy sensuality of a few minutes ago had melted away, and replacing it was that dull listlessness which he'd noticed yesterday in the street and earlier at the party. It exasperated him beyond belief.

'Why?'

'He'll be worried about me.'

Olivier's jaw tensed. 'Of course,' he said sourly. 'I'm not *good enough* to take his little sister out.'

She shook her head and gave a sort of rueful laugh. 'Not really. Not just that. It's because I…' She stopped, and in the orange glow of the street light he saw her bite her lip.

'Go on.'

'Nothing.' She turned to look out of the window, so all he could see was the sharp line of her cheekbone and the hollow beneath it. 'I've given him cause to worry in the past, that's all.

Poor old Miles is the one who has to bail me out and pick up the pieces.'

'What about your parents? Where are they?'

'My father's a diplomat. He's posted in Cairo at the moment, but my parents have always lived abroad. Because Miles is nine years older than me he's always taken on the role of looking after me.'

Olivier tapped a finger impatiently on the butter-soft leather upholstery. *Looking after her?* Was that what he called it? From what he'd seen, Miles was just one in a long line of arrogant bastards who treated his sister like a possession. Like an object, with no right to thoughts and feelings and opinions of her own.

Hatred rose in his throat, hot and acidic, and then the irony of his reaction reasserted itself.

Touché.

The car slowed and came to a halt in a line of traffic waiting to pull up in front of the gallery's Millbank entrance. As it moved forwards again, to swing across the road, the sudden motion threw Bella against Olivier for a moment, and he automatically put a hand out to steady her. He could feel her heat through the slippery silk of her dress. Lust tore through him, jagged and painful, like shrapnel.

He got out of the car as soon as it stopped, without waiting for Louis to open the door, but the moment he did so a volley of flashbulbs erupted around him. As always, he ignored them, but as he turned to help Bella from the car the look of startled uncertainty on her face sent an unexpected wave of protectiveness surging through him. Pulling her into his body, shielding her face with his hand as the cluster of paparazzi struggled to get a shot, he pushed through them. Her heart beat wildly against his own ribs as he guided her up the steps to the entrance.

Dieu, he thought with bitter self-mockery, he was really beginning to embrace the idea of himself in the role of hero rather too enthusiastically. He'd be trading the Bentley in for a suit of armour and a white charger next.

Once inside the echoing marble hallway, he let her go immediately, relinquishing her trembling, slender body with savage relief. There was no doubt at all that seducing her would be a pleasure, as well as an appropriate way of closing the circle, but he hadn't bargained on listening to her family problems first. He didn't want to get to *know* her, he thought derisively. That just added unnecessary shades of grey to an issue that was essentially black and white.

There were old debts to settle between their families. She would be part of the payment. It was as simple as that. Taking her, and then discarding her as if she was nothing...nobody...that would go a long way to evening out the score. It would be a transaction, like so many others he handled day in, day out. She wasn't a fellow victim of the Lawrences' self-seeking ruthlessness and prejudice, for pity's sake. She was one of them.

He had to remember that, and remember what they had done to his father, and take the opportunity so generously presented to him by the hand of fate. The only thing he expected to feel—would allow himself to feel—was satisfaction when it was all complete.

Hopefully on two levels.

Bella blinked dazedly in the bright light of the vast space. The evening had taken on a dream-like quality, and she felt disorientated and bewildered. Everything had moved very fast; one minute it seemed she had been handing round canapés to self-important public figures, and the next she had been hurtling away from the party—away from her home and her family—with a man who was almost a stranger.

A stranger who made her feel more herself than she ever had with the people who were supposed to know her best. She was filled with a sudden longing to be back in Olivier's arms, crushed against the hardness of his chest, but he was already striding away from her across the polished floor. She felt her gaze rest hungrily for a moment on his broad shoulders and narrow hips as she followed him into the high, echoing hall where the reception was taking place, then, with some effort, tore her eyes away and looked around.

The octagonal room was packed with people, ranging from elderly *grandes dames,* dripping with grimy heirloom diamonds, to *nouveau* celebrity patrons and aggressively fashionable artistic types. The scene looked like the society page of a glossy magazine brought magically to life, and her hands fluttered nervously at the sequinned hem of her dress. Black was the predominant colour, and she found herself thinking wistfully of the vintage Balenciaga dress, now covered in caviar and lying on her bedroom floor. Her Portobello market smock suddenly felt very bright, very short, and very flimsy.

Olivier was coming back from collecting a couple of glasses of champagne from the table by the door, seemingly oblivious to all the heads that turned in his direction. No wonder people stared, she thought helplessly, making an effort not to look at him as he handed her a glass. He was, quite simply, the most compelling man she had ever seen. The most good-looking too, though that was almost incidental. There was a brooding, focused, self-contained quality about him, which she had noticed yesterday in the auction room, and which seemed to set him apart from everyone else.

He wasn't a team player, she thought with a shudder.

Champagne bubbles burst on her tongue. In the crush of people, Olivier's closeness was ten times more exhilarating than the alcohol, and her skin still tingled and burned where he'd held her against him. She felt that beneath her dress her flesh would bear marks where she'd touched him.

She took another hasty sip of champagne, only this time her

hand was so unsteady that the glass clattered slightly against her teeth. And then his hand closed around it, around the glass, and it should have steadied her but it didn't. It drove her wild.

'OK?'

She nodded, smiling ruefully and feeling the colour seep along her cheeks. 'Spectacularly wrongly dressed, but never mind.'

His face didn't show a flicker of reaction. 'I disagree. You're perfectly dressed. You're far too fiery and beautiful to be hidden away in black, so hold your head up and smile.'

Bella couldn't look at him as shimmering rivulets of pleasure ran through her. *Fiery and beautiful.* It made her sound like the person she wanted to be.

She laughed. 'No way. I don't even have lipstick on.'

Just then someone behind her pushed past, knocking her forwards slightly so that the back of the hand in which he held his champagne glass brushed her breast. Instantly the pleasure sharpened to piercing desire.

'Look at me.'

His voice was husky, the French accent more pronounced than ever. Slowly she lifted her head. His face was so completely expressionless that he looked almost bored, but there was an intense glitter in the depths of his eyes. And then, with a languid intimacy that made her forget that they were in a room full of people, he lifted his hand to her face, pressing his thumb to her mouth, rubbing, massaging her lips as they parted beneath his touch.

By the time he let his hand fall to his side again she was breathless and flushed.

'There.' He almost smiled. 'You look like you're wearing lipstick now.'

'Thank you.' Bella felt as if she was opening, unfurling, blossoming in the heat of his exotic presence. Her mouth felt bee-stung and effortlessly sexy, and taking a sip of champagne from the narrow flute felt like an act of outrageous wantonness. She felt shimmering and incandescent.

Fiery and beautiful.

She smiled, letting the chilled champagne slide down her throat. 'Maybe we should look at the paintings now?'

Before she combusted with desire.

He gave a curt nod of assent. 'I take it you've been here before?' he said, putting a protective arm around her to guide her through the crowd.

'Of course. This is one of my favourite places, but I've never been here at night before.' She tipped her head back, looking up at the majestic dome above them and thinking of the silent rooms spreading out on all sides, the familiar paintings hanging in the darkness. 'It's different...'

'Different? How?'

Because I'm with you.

'More exciting.' Her eyes held his. 'More intimate.'

One dark brow quirked upwards a fraction. 'Intimate? With all these people here?'

'Because it's dark. Everything is more intimate in the dark.'

He moved through the crowd and she followed, unsteady on her glorious, insane skyscraper heels and her legs that felt as if they were made of marshmallow. At one point they nearly got separated as the groups of people shifted and moved together after he passed, but he didn't let go of her hand—gripping it more tightly and turning back, making a passage through the crowd for her. Eventually they reached the door to the long gallery. It was quieter in here, with only a few small groups of people viewing the paintings.

'I never asked,' Bella said slightly breathlessly, desperately trying to regain her sense of reality and rationalise away the persistent, distracting throb of her desire. 'What is the exhibition?'

'It's called "Five Hundred Years of Flesh",' he said, looking down at her with that cool, focused stare that seemed to strip her bare and make her shiver. 'It's an exhibition of the nude in art.'

Her eyes widened. Still with her hand in his, he drew her into the cavernous space and placed her so she was standing in front of him. For a moment she gazed silently around as the drowsy beat of longing quickened into something even sharper, more urgent. On all sides naked bodies reclined and stood—beckoning and inviting, aloof and superior, or simply bored. And behind her, close enough for her to sense his heat and feel the primitive pull of his maleness, stood Olivier.

He dipped his head and spoke in a husky whisper, his breath caressing her neck. 'Where would you like to start?'

The question, deliberately ambiguous, unleashed a tidal wave of hot, wanton need within her, and she let out a low sigh of surrender. He put his hand on the back of her neck, sliding his fingers into her hair, his thumb massaging the base of her skull as she squirmed helplessly, pinioned with longing.

'Here,' she said throatily, threading her fingers through his and leading him further down the gallery to one of the most famous nudes of all. Manet's *Olympia* reclined on a bed, gazing straight out at the onlooker. A beautifully embroidered shawl was crumpled beneath her, and she wore one delicate high-heeled slipper. Behind her a maid was showing her a blowsy bouquet of wrapped flowers, and a cat arched itself at her feet, but she was oblivious to both.

Bella smiled into Olivier's eyes. 'Why waste time on the apprentices when you can go straight to the master?'

'*Olympia*.' Olivier barely glanced at it. Instead his gaze followed his own fingers as they trailed down the inside of her arm. 'Why this one?'

'I like her.'

Lifting her hand, he nodded slowly. His face was as still as ever, the habitual creases between his dark brows giving him an air of extreme concentration that almost pushed her over the edge. Her rapid, ragged breathing was loud in the quiet gallery, but she was powerless to do anything about it.

He brought her palm up to his mouth. 'Tell me why,' he said thoughtfully, his lips brushing her skin. 'Tell me what you like about her.'

Bella had to force herself to bring her head up, to open her eyes and concentrate on the painting, and not the ripples of ecstasy that were running along the nerves of her arm and spreading downwards. Olympia's eyes met hers across the two metres and the hundred years that separated them, and she seemed to absolutely understand how Bella was feeling.

'She has great taste in accessories...' Bella murmured drowsily, uncurling her fingers and spreading out her hand as Olivier's lips brushed the hollow at the crook of her elbow. 'The bracelet, and those perfect shoes. I like it that she's wearing them in bed.'

Olivier lifted his head, and then looked down at Bella's feet in their shiny black shoes with the high, high heels. Her insteps seemed to arch themselves involuntarily as she imagined him touching them. 'One of them. She's only wearing one of them,' he said huskily. 'She seems to have lost the other one. But go on.'

Bella was finding it hard to breathe. 'I...love...the shawl...I can imagine how the silk must feel against her skin...'

She cupped her hand against his face, feeling the hardness of his jaw and the slight roughness of stubble beneath her tingling palm. 'Do you like her, Olivier?'

He smiled properly then: a slow curving of his beautiful, sulky mouth that conveyed neither joy nor amusement, but something more subtle. An acceptance of challenge, perhaps.

'Yes.'

'Why? What do you like about her?'

'She was a prostitute, a member of the lower class,' he said, taking a step backwards and positioning himself behind her.

Without being distracted by the movement of his mouth as he spoke, she picked up the faint trace of sardonic bitterness in his tone. 'The painting was so shocking not because of her body, but because of her status. She was too real. Too *common*. The critics were horrified by her because she made sex seem so simple.'

Bella started as his fingers brushed her neck.

'But I like that she's not afraid…' he said more softly, moving his fingertips lightly along her jaw. 'I like it that she knows how powerful she is. And…' Holding her chin, he gently pulled her face round so she was looking up at him. 'And I like that the expression in her eyes is exactly the same as yours is now.'

Her indrawn breath made a sharp hissing sound, like rain on hot stone, and then she twisted round, finding his mouth with hers. She was holding the lapels of his jacket, clutching and twisting at the thick silk as savage instinct took over. The kiss was hard and urgent, a crashing finale to the slow crescendo of the last hours. The images around the walls merged and spun in a blur of colour as Bella abandoned herself to the kind of all-consuming pleasure that a thousand years of visualizing white sandy beaches couldn't possibly suppress. He tasted of cold champagne, but infinitely more intoxicating, and he filled her head and her mouth and her whole body.

There was a noise at the entrance to the gallery: a burst of laughter and raised voices as more people came into the room. Olivier straightened up, his hands still holding her face as he looked over her shoulder. The next moment a woman with a press badge round her neck had appeared beside him.

'Monsieur Moreau? Please excuse me, but I wonder if you'd give me a few words for a piece I'm doing on the exhibition for the weekend papers?'

Dazed and breathless, Bella slid away, raking a hand through her hair, pushing it back from her hot forehead as she wandered along the wall of paintings.

She was hopeless. A completely lost cause. What had just happened there was categorical evidence that when will-power had been dished out she'd been daydreaming at the back of the class. The friction between her hot thighs as she walked was exquisite and agonizing, and at that moment she felt as if she could conquer the world. Ever since she had been too young to know anything about sex, Miles had made her feel it was something scary, something dangerous, and she'd come to associate desire with loss of control. But tonight she'd learned he was wrong.

She no longer felt afraid. She just felt *alive*. And for the first time since she'd woken up in the hospital she was ridiculously glad about that.

Turning her head, she looked back at the woman in the painting. Olivier was right. Her pose was demure, her face serene, but her eyes spoke of sex. Something shifted and settled inside Bella's head. It was like the feeling of remembering something that had been floating just out of reach. With Olivier's touch on her body she felt like Olympia—sexy and powerful and passionate. It felt good, not frightening or destructive.

She was aware of a sensation of release, a lightening of tension as she looked up to find Olivier. He was still talking to the woman reporter, his face very still, very controlled.

She wanted him.

She *wanted* him, and Miles and the therapist were wrong. There was nothing unstable or unhealthy about it—she glanced back at Olympia. It was a strength, not a weakness. It was about *taking control*, not losing it.

Out of the corner of her eye she was aware of another group of people coming along the row of paintings, talking loudly. Something about one of the voices drew her attention and she looked up.

Instantly she felt the blood drain from her face and the air rush from her lungs. Standing a few feet away from her, an expression of suppressed amusement on his face, as if he was trying not to laugh at some hilarious private joke, was Dan Nightingale.

Olivier's patience was running out now. 'A few questions' was rapidly turning into an in-depth interview, and he wasn't in the mood. He was damned good at compartmentalizing his life and focusing absolutely on the task in hand, so was extremely disconcerted to find himself answering questions on his collection of twentieth-century art while simultaneously imagining peeling off the red silk dress of the girl standing at the other end of the room.

Yesterday in the street he had written her off as a vapid posh girl, and that was exactly how she'd appeared earlier this evening as she handed round the canapés in that anonymous black dress.

Not now. In scarlet silk, her chilly aristocratic perfection was transformed into something warmer and infinitely more appealing. It brought out the passion he had glimpsed in her in the auction room and gave her an air of wild Bohemianism that was irresistible.

Or maybe that wasn't the dress. Maybe that was her—the real Bella Lawrence. The girl her stiff, conventional family was so desperate to suppress. She reminded him of a butterfly who had been squeezed tightly in someone's fist so that her beautiful, vibrant wings were crushed and torn. But who still wanted to fly.

'So, Monsieur Moreau—can you tell me about your latest acquisition?' the journalist asked with a girlish flutter of her eyelashes.

Olivier thoughts flickered to the painting he'd bought yesterday. The house at St Laurien, and the other, secret painting hidden beneath it. *La Dame de la Croix* could easily have taken its place here, amongst the works of masters.

Had things been different.

Tersely he said, 'I don't want to give details at the moment.'

The journalist nodded, her eyes sliding slyly in Bella's direction. 'How about the one over there? She's very pretty…'

His face hardening ominously, Olivier followed her gaze to where Bella was now talking to a man with tousled blond hair. He was dressed in the unofficial uniform of the perennial art student—appallingly cut black suit and open-necked black shirt.

Something needled Olivier about how he was standing in front of her, leaning over her, dominating the space around her in a way that was almost territorial.

'I have nothing more to say,' he growled at the journalist, and, giving her an almost imperceptible nod of dismissal, he strode past her and made his way towards Bella and the blond man.

On second glance, Olivier thought scathingly, he was hardly a man. He was a boy, a pretty blond boy, as flaky and insubstantial as a pop pin-up, though clearly Bella thought otherwise. The eyes that had looked at him so adoringly only minutes before were now gazing with similar rapt fascination into the face of this...*boy*.

Anger pierced him, sharp and sudden. He'd almost been taken in by her little-girl-lost routine. He and the rest of the male population, apparently, he thought acidly as he watched the blond boy reach out and tuck the dark silk of her hair neatly behind her ear in a gesture which was unmistakably intimate.

Olivier felt as if he'd been punched in the stomach. It wasn't just anger. No, at least there was something pure and energizing about anger. The emotion which knocked the air from his lungs and made him want to double up was darker and more sinister.

Jealousy.

He'd started the evening with one aim in mind, he reminded himself bitterly. To seduce her. That was what he'd set out to do, and he'd almost allowed some ridiculous, uncharacteristic and completely misplaced sense of chivalry and sentimentality to stand in his way.

He should be grateful to this upstart for showing him how foolish he was being before it was too late. Bella Lawrence wasn't the innocent she pretended to be, and the big bad brother thing was clearly something she played up, to bring out the macho, chest-beating instincts in the men she flirted with.

She was as clever as she was beautiful, and she had played him like a fool.

As he approached she looked up at him, and he saw nameless emotion blazing in her midnight eyes.

'Are you ready to go?' he asked with savage courtesy.

'Yes, please.' She came towards him without hesitation. At least she had the decency to look uncomfortable at being caught out flirting with another man, when her lips were still swollen from his own kisses. Affections that were so easily transferred were essentially worthless. He summoned a glacial smile. At least he could now enjoy what was on offer without guilt.

Bella just concentrated on putting one foot in front of the other and keeping herself upright as they walked through the gallery. But if it hadn't been for the steel band of Olivier's arm around her, she wasn't sure she could have made it. It was a relief to step out into the purple and gold London night, but in the time it took for her to take a deep lungful of air Olivier's car had appeared from nowhere and she was being firmly guided towards it.

She'd been right when she'd said he was a magician, she thought distractedly. He made things happen. Unlike her, who had things happen *to* her.

Against the throb of the expensive engine, she sank back into the seat and said quietly, 'I'm sorry.'

Her throat felt tight, as if there was something lodged at its base. Seeing Dan had been a shock—but mainly because it had hammered home to her in one swift, devastatingly accurate blow how flimsy her feelings for him had been. She'd been in love with the idea of him, that was all. He was nothing, she could see that with painful clarity now, but it only made what had happened as a consequence seem all the more pointless.

Looking out of the window, Olivier pulled his silk bow tie undone. He was utterly offhand. 'What for?'

For being such a fool five months ago.

She bit her lip. 'Sorry that *he* turned up. He was just someone I—I knew, at art college—'

Olivier cut her off abruptly. 'There's no need to explain.'

Bella felt herself shrink a little inside. Die a little. She had *wanted* to explain, but immediately she bundled the thought up and shoved it to the back of her mind again. It was all rather ironic: there was Miles, forking out a fortune for the best therapist in London, and Bella would rather stick needles under her fingernails than confide anything remotely significant to her. Yet here, in the hushed comfort of the moving car, she was overwhelmed by the need to talk about it to this strong, remote stranger.

Clamping her teeth together, she looked out onto the lit-up city.

No. Better to bury it. To forget, even though there were times when the effort of denial was almost too much. It wore her down, all this pretending, all this repression of thoughts and feelings. It was a constant battle, but tonight she'd been free of it just for a little while. When Olivier had held her, and kissed her, nothing else had mattered. The grey fog inside had been burned away; she had forgotten to be afraid.

The headlights of a passing car illuminated his inscrutable face for a moment. Bella felt suddenly wrung out with longing for him, and for the blissful oblivion he had given her. She wanted to forget again.

Shyly she looked up at him from under her lashes, half ashamed of the strength of her desire. 'Where are we going?' she asked huskily.

Olivier turned his dark gaze on her. 'That all depends on what you want to do.'

It wasn't an entirely deceptive statement. He had already chosen the outcome of the evening—that was a given—but the lead-up to it was still open for her to influence in any way she liked.

In the sodium glow of the streetlights he watched her eyes widen and her ripe lips part. Was she still thinking of that other man, the one who had stood too close to her and touched her hair? he wondered cynically. Of course he had no way of knowing, but there was one sure-fire way of obliterating him from her mind if she was…

He picked up her hand from the seat beside him and laced his fingers through hers.

'Are you hungry?'

Mutely she shook her head, so her sleek, silky hair gleamed in the lights beyond the hushed interior of the car.

'Are you tired? Do you want to go home?'

The question was a formality; they both knew that. She was sitting up very straight, her thighs pressed together, the seat belt separating her firm, high breasts. Everything about her seemed to quiver with suppressed energy. She was like a taut string, waiting to be played.

'No,' she whispered, so quietly it was little more than a sigh.

But Olivier heard, and smiled. Leaning forward, he slid back the glass that separated them from the driver.

'Louis, the apartment, *s'il vous plaît*.'

CHAPTER FIVE

BELLA HAD never seen anything like Olivier's apartment.

Three of the walls were dark crimson, covered with startlingly modern canvases, and the fourth was made entirely of glass. Apart from a hugely oversized white sofa and tall, steel-legged bar-type chair by the window, the long room was virtually empty, giving no distraction from either the stunning art or the glittering view of London spread out below.

It also gave nothing away about the man who owned it. Bella had wanted to see past the sophisticated designer armour plating that Olivier wore to the man beneath, and this place told her nothing.

Going over to the window, she pressed her palms against it. She felt slightly dizzy and let out her breath in a slow, uneven exhalation that fogged the glass and momentarily reduced the sparkling lights to a dull shimmer. Olivier had come to stand behind her, and when the cloud of her breath dissolved again she could see the contours of his face reflected in the glass. She felt hollowed out with wanting him.

'It's quite a view,' she said hesitantly. 'You must never get bored with looking at it.'

'Wrong,' he said, very softly. 'I'm bored with looking at it now. I'd much rather look at you.'

His hands came to rest lightly on her hips, massaging her body gently through the slippery silk of her dress. She felt boneless, helpless, as her head fell forward, her burning cheek coming to rest against the cool glass. Moving upwards, his fingers found the buttons at the back of her dress, and a moment later it slid from her shoulders and pooled at her feet in a whisper of scarlet.

For a second she was aware of nothing but the ecstasy of air on her heated skin, and then the fact that she was pressed against a window and wearing nothing but the briefest black silk bra and lace pants filtered into her lust-drenched brain. But Olivier's fingers were tracing a delicate pattern of bliss down her spine, and though she opened her mouth to protest the words wouldn't seem to form.

'The window…people can see…'

'Shh…' He dipped his head to her shoulder so she felt the warmth of his breath on her quivering skin. 'Not without the lights on. We're too high up. No one can see you.' Taking hold of her shoulders, he turned her gently around so she was looking up into his perfect, impassive face. 'Except me.'

There was a low vibration of arousal in his voice which was completely at odds with the composure of his expression. It thrilled her. Unconsciously she raised both her hands to her head, clutching at her hair, sliding her fingers through it as she submitted to his smoky, appraising stare.

There was nowhere to hide from him, or from the savage force of the feelings he aroused in her, and in that moment she knew this was what she had been born for and that there was no point in fighting it any longer. She had unleashed the tornado within, and now she had to learn to ride the storm.

She felt her mouth blossom into a sensuous smile. 'You're sure?'

'Of course. I'm never anything but.' He slipped a finger beneath her bra strap. 'Take this off.'

His arrogance should have infuriated her, but it didn't. It was the most powerful aphrodisiac imaginable.

Without taking her eyes from his, she reached round and unhooked her bra, letting the straps fall down her shoulders. But before he had a chance to glimpse what it concealed she threw him a glance of pure wickedness from beneath her hair and turned round again, so she was facing the glass. Only then, with the artful grace of a practised stripper, did she stretch out her arms and toss the bra aside. Pressing her hands flat against the window, she flexed her shoulders and moved her feet, still in their shiny high heels, a little wider apart.

It felt indescribably delicious. Wicked, dangerous, exhilarating. London lay spread at her feet, silent and sparkling. She felt omnipotent.

Fiery and beautiful.

The sound Olivier made was somewhere between a moan and a sigh. Reflected in the glass, his face was a mask of inscrutability, but Bella caught the ferocious gleam of desire in his eyes and it nearly undid her. His fingers traced a path around the top of her tiny lace panties, dipping lightly beneath the elastic, then retreating and circling, unhurried.

A shiver of desperate need ran through her, so powerful it was like a foretaste of anticipated bliss. The movements which a moment ago had been artful and calculated were now completely instinctual. Arching her back, she felt her pelvis tilt helplessly back towards him as her breasts pressed against the chill glass windowpane. He grasped her bottom in his big, powerful hands, sliding his fingers beneath the flimsy lace of her pants and pulling them downwards in one swift movement.

Fluidly, confidently, as if she were performing a movement in some passionate dance, she stepped out of them on her high heels and spun round. She was spreadeagled against the glass, her arms out, her head thrown back, her hair partially covering her face. Her breath was coming in staccato gasps.

Her swollen lips formed one word.

'*Please…*'

Olivier could barely hold back a primitive hiss of triumph as elation exploded like fireworks in the darkness of his heart. She was ready to beg him. This was what he had waited for. What he had wanted.

But in that instant he knew it wasn't enough.

He wanted to possess her wholly. And, more than that, he wanted to take her to such delirious heights of ecstasy that she would never forget him.

In a single stride he had crossed the space between them and, placing his hands on the glass on either side of her head, brought his mouth down on hers. Her lips parted beneath his as her trembling fingers grasped at the buttons of his dress shirt, but the starched fabric was unyielding. He both heard and felt her snarl of frustration against his mouth as she pulled with increasing desperation, until the buttons were torn apart and her hands found his bare skin, moving outwards, pushing the crisp cotton back over his shoulders to expose as much of his chest as she could to her sensual, questing touch before moving down to his belt.

The strength of her passion and her lack of inhibition were completely unexpected, and shook him more than he wanted to admit. He found himself holding back, unable to risk touching her body because he knew that if he did his careful veneer of control would be shattered.

He couldn't let that happen. He wouldn't let her do that to him. He had to stay in command.

Reaching behind him, he grabbed the steel bar chair that he had used to prop the painting on earlier and pulled it roughly towards them. Clasping her narrow ribs, he hitched her up, so that her bottom was resting on the edge of the chair, her long legs in their shiny high heels still reaching the floor. She was breathing in a series of soft gasps that curled like caressing fingers around his taut nerves. Her hands travelled across his back, beneath his shirt, making trails of scorching want.

He had to keep himself distant.

Kneeling on the floor in front of her, he parted her legs gently and brushed the backs of his fingers up the long length of her quivering thighs.

She was so perfect it almost hurt him to touch her.

He gritted his teeth against the tide of sheer, annihilating lust that threatened to engulf him as his thumbs reached the moist darkness at the top of her thighs. Dipping his head he breathed in her delicate musky scent and let his tongue slowly, languorously explore her secret folds. Braced against the chair, she cried out in a high, pure sound of complete abandon, which was like a sledgehammer on his fragile shell of control.

'Now, Olivier,' she gasped. *'Please...'*

That was it. Holding back now was impossible. Olivier straightened up in front of her. Oblivious to the lights of the city sparkling before him, he focused only on her dazzling, desire-darkened eyes as he reached into his back pocket for the small foil packet he had placed there so calculatingly earlier. Swiftly, she took it from him, tearing it open with her teeth and sliding the condom onto him with fingers that shook with impatience. There was no time for him to undress properly, and he thrust into her with savage hunger as she arched towards him, wrapping her legs around him and letting her head fall back against the glass in wordless ecstasy.

She was amazing.

Astonishing.

His kept his hands flat on the window on either side of her head while she held his shoulders with her hands and gripped him tightly between her strong thighs. Her mouth was near his ear, and he could feel her breath against his neck, hear her moans of bliss.

And then suddenly she gave a wild gasp and her legs tightened around him. Without thinking he gathered her into his arms, cradling her naked, pliant and beautiful body against him, and unleashed his own climax.

He'd expected to feel triumph or exhilaration; some sense of victory.

The vicious self-loathing and despair that wrapped itself around his heart as he held her against him rocked him to the core.

'Thank you, oh, *thank you*.'

Exhausted, and high on unimagined bliss, Bella breathed the words into the warmth of his chest. Her voice sounded cracked and dry. And stupid, she thought distantly, keeping her head pressed against him. What a stupid, gauche thing to say. She hoped he hadn't heard.

'You have the most amazingly good manners,' he remarked tonelessly, disentangling her arms from around his neck. 'I don't think I've ever slept with anyone before who said please and thank you during sex. You were obviously brought up extremely well.'

He'd heard. Knickers.

Bella put her feet on the floor and wondered if her shaking legs would take her weight if she tried to stand. 'I was,' she said, hoping her voice didn't betray the desolation she felt at the sudden loss of contact with his body. 'I'm cursed with eternal respectability and politeness.'

He had his back towards her as she took a couple of tentative steps, rotating her hips and flexing her stiffened spine.

'Looking at you now, I find that hard to believe.'

The harsh note of mockery in his voice made her freeze inside. Her head shot up. He had turned and was leaning against the glass, looking at her, and apart from his unbuttoned shirt he showed no outward sign of what had just taken place. With the glittering city behind him he looked completely unruffled, completely in command. He was master of all he surveyed, whereas she…

She was naked, apart from a pair of skyscraper heels…

And somehow they only made her feel *more* naked.

She crossed her arms across her chest, appalled by the cold sarcasm of his tone. She'd hardly expected hearts and flowers and sincere declarations of undying love, but this…this *total* withdrawal was like being shown a glimpse of heaven and then having the door slammed in her face. Her dress was lying on the floor at his feet, and she was just trying to decide whether it would be less humiliating to ask him to pass it to her or to go and pick it up herself when he said blandly, 'What were you thanking me for, anyway?'

She shook her head in embarrassment. 'Nothing. Doesn't matter.' Moving towards him, she stooped quickly to get the dress and, clutching it against her, straightened up again. Before she could back away he had caught her around the waist with one hand. 'Tell me.'

His eyes bored into hers. There was no warmth in them, just a peculiar intensity that felt like despair. She looked down, struggling to think of some way of answering him that would sound light and amusing and casual, but the feel of his hand on her hip and the nearness of him scattered her thoughts like petals in the wind, so there was nothing left in her head but the truth.

The embarrassing, undeniable truth.

'I wanted to thank you for making me feel like that,' she said hoarsely. 'I didn't ever quite *get* it before, with…other boyfriends… I didn't know it could be like that. That…powerful.'

Her voice had dropped to a whisper, and she could feel the colour flaming in her cheeks. Abruptly he pulled his hand away, and she saw it clench into a fist as he brought it back to his side. His face was an emotionless mask.

Obviously the pleasure had been purely on her side.

He nodded curtly, then gave a brief, ironic smile. 'Any time. I'll get Louis to take you home.'

As she watched him pick up his jacket from where he'd

thrown it onto the huge white sofa and take his phone from the inside pocket, keeping the hurt from showing on her face was one of the hardest things Bella had ever done. She felt numb with shock, still anaesthetised by the after-effects of the violent pleasure that had just ripped through her, and it was only this that enabled her to summon a smile and hold her head high. Part of her was achingly bewildered by his sudden glacial detachment, but part of her understood completely.

She had sensed it at the gallery. Olivier Moreau was not a man who gave anything of himself to anyone. He was a lone wolf. The sex was spectacular, but intimacy was not part of the package.

How hideously humiliating that she'd behaved as if it was.

Louis was taking his time to answer. He clearly hadn't expected Olivier to require his services so soon. He wasn't the only one, thought Bella wretchedly, making her way to the door.

'Could you tell me where the bathroom is?'

Holding the phone against his ear, Olivier nodded vaguely in the direction of the corridor. 'Second on the left.'

With her dress still held around her, Bella tiptoed out and pulled the door closed behind her. Out in the corridor, she swiftly slipped the scarlet silk back over her head, smoothed a shaking hand over her hair, then took a deep breath.

A flickering pulse of anger had begun to beat unsteadily in her battered heart, and the insides of her wrists stung and burned. She rubbed them together.

Not again. She wasn't going there again. She was stronger now—more powerful. A sudden image of Olympia flashed into her mind's eye, and Bella recalled the serenity and the sense of quiet self-possession that exuded from her, making it perfectly clear that she was at the beck and call of no man.

Bella's high heels made no sound on the muffling thickness of the cream carpet as she walked quickly down the corridor and let herself out of the front door.

CHAPTER SIX

Normandy, France. One month later.

CELIA'S ancient MG sports car was—like its owner—eccentric, charming and totally unreliable. It had a fold-down hood in cracked black canvas that was remarkably difficult to work, a radio that only picked up two channels, and a throaty, spluttering cough that sounded like the death rattle of a lifelong smoker.

Bella adored it.

She had forgotten how much she also adored France. Leaving behind the industrial grimness of Le Havre, and rejecting the blandness of the autoroute, she chose instead the smaller roads that followed the meandering path of the Seine through the luscious heart of Normandy, and found herself in the middle of a Pre-Raphaelite landscape. Autumn was at its spectacular, flaming height, and the low sun lit everything in such a way as to make it look improbably lovely.

Fiery and beautiful.

The words materialised in her mind involuntarily, and she gritted her teeth and shifted up a gear.

That night in London just over a month ago had marked a turning point for her in many ways. Since then she had stopped trying to hide or deny out of existence negative thoughts or uncomfortable feelings. Not all of them anyway—just the ones centring on Olivier Moreau, which, admittedly, accounted for a fairly high percentage.

For as long as she could remember she had dealt with problems by retreating into a place inside her head where she was safe, and it felt as if Olivier had opened up that secret place and left her nowhere to hide. In the most blissful, brutal way possible he had forced her to feel again. Pleasure and pain, ecstasy and agony, heaven and hell. The aftermath had been difficult and humiliating and shocking, but those brief moments when she had stood naked and defiant before the entire city had done more for her fragile sense of self than a lifetime of stilted sessions with the expensive therapist could ever have achieved. Much to Miles's dismay she had cancelled her weekly appointments.

Maybe she just needed more sex, she mused sadly, gazing out over the lush Normandy countryside. But not with Olivier Moreau. With someone much more tender and romantic and human.

A wicked voice inside her broke crudely into her thoughts.

But just as skillful...

She came to a junction and slowed down to read the signpost, giving a groan of dismay as she discovered that Paris was still sixty kilometres away. The mellow afternoon sun was beginning to sink behind the glorious auburn fringe of beech trees on the horizon. She arched her aching back and was just wishing she hadn't decided to take the scenic route after all when she noticed the name on the signpost pointing in the opposite direction.

St Laurien.

It must be fate. Bella found herself turning not in the direction of Paris but off the main road and into a dense thicket of woodland, which cut out the mellow sunlight and plunged her into fragrant gloom. It was getting ridiculously late to be going on a nostalgic sightseeing tour, but she couldn't resist the temptation to have a quick look at the house where her grandmother had grown up. The house in the painting.

All of a sudden a dark shape hurtled out of the undergrowth at the side of the road. There was noise—a crashing of branches, a clattering of hooves—and Bella caught a fleeting, terrible glimpse of white rolling eyes and blood-red steaming nostrils as she pulled the steering wheel of the car around so hard it felt as if her arms were being yanked from their sockets. She came to a halt, skewed across the road.

Suddenly it was very quiet and very dark. Making a conscious effort to relax, trying to ease the iron bands of panic that had instantly closed around her chest, Bella took a couple of deep, deliberate breaths and unfastened her seatbelt.

It had been a horse. A riderless horse.

She got slowly out of the car and slammed the door. Her heart was thudding painfully against her ribs and she found she was very reluctant to leave the relative safety of the little red MG.

'Hello?'

Her voice echoed through the trees and dissolved into the thick gloom. She tried again. 'Hello? Is there anybody there?'

No one answered. But by that time she had already seen the body crumpled on the leaf-strewn ground.

For a moment she had a horrible certainty that the man was dead.

His face, lined with age, was an unearthly white, and blood from a cut on his forehead ran down into his silver-grey hair. But as she crouched down beside him his eyelids flickered and he made an attempt to sit up.

'Please don't move.' Gently she settled him back onto his bed of coppery leaves. 'You've had a fall. From your horse. I'm going to go back to my car and phone for help.'

Bella's heart was hammering against her ribs as she dialled for an ambulance, concentrating hard as she dredged up long-forgotten phrases from French lessons. When she got back to the man he was very still, and looked as if he was falling into deep sleep. She half remembered that was bad, and sat down beside him on the damp leaf-scented earth. He was wearing thick leather gloves, which seemed at odds with the warmth of the day, but she took his hand in his and held it tightly, willing him to stay with her.

Instinctively she started to speak, not bothered that he might not understand English, but more concerned with striking the right note of comforting optimism. 'So,' she began, her cheerful tone belying the anxious thud of her heart, 'you live nearby?'

He gave an almost imperceptible nod. *'Le Vieux Moulin...'*

The Old Mill. 'It sounds pretty,' she said enthusiastically, wincing at the banality of the comment but at the same time aware that it hardly mattered. This was life and death, not speed dating, and the important thing was to keep him conscious until help arrived, not dazzle him with her sparkling conversation. 'Do you have family?'

'Fils.'

'A son?' Excellent. She felt the weight of responsibility starting to slip from her and she squeezed his hand harder. 'If you give me his number I'll call him...'

The old man shook his head. The movement seemed to hurt him because his face was suddenly flooded with pain.

'Non. Non...'

'OK... Don't worry, please. It doesn't matter if you can't remember it. If you tell me his name I can find it.'

With great difficulty the old man opened his eyes. They were dark and troubled. *'Non*...please, you must not. He is very important...very successful...he must not be bothered because of me...'

Bella gave a small laugh. 'I'm sure he wouldn't like to hear you say that. You've had a bad fall. I'm sure he'd want to be with you.'

'No. He is busy...very busy. His job...very well paid. *Très important.* Please, you must not telephone. He will not come.'

'Shhh...' Bella soothed, holding both of his gloved hands in hers reassuringly. 'OK, it's all right. Don't worry about that now. The ambulance will be here soon, and they'll get you to hospital where they can have a good look at you.'

It was as if she'd given him an electric shock. At the mention of the word hospital the man struggled to sit upright, his face contorting with agony. *'No! C'est impossible...* My horse, my home...I cannot leave. There is no one else to look after things...!'

Bella put her hands on his shoulders. They were broad, but even beneath the thick tweed of his jacket she could feel the sharp bones, and the dark eyes that fixed on her were filled with anguish that wrenched at her heart.

'Don't worry. Please, don't worry. I'll take care of everything.'

The words were out of her mouth before she'd had time to think. Instantly she felt the tension leave his frail body and he slumped backwards onto the ground, a look of relief on his paper-white face.

It was too late to backtrack now. Bella bit her lip and wondered what she'd let herself in for.

'So, she finally showed up.' Fabrice de Roche leaned back in his executive leather chair and let out a low breath of appreciation. 'I must say, Olivier, *mon ami,* there aren't too many women I'd wait fifty years to get a look at but this one's worth it. Genevieve Delacroix...what a beauty.' He tilted his head to one side, narrowing his eyes. 'Especially from this angle.'

One of Paris's top fine art dealers, Fabrice was a connoisseur of both women and paintings, but behind his insouciant charm beat the chilly heart of a businessman. His interest in *La Dame de la Croix* was professional as well as personal.

'Where did you find her?'

'A sale in London,' Olivier said tersely, and then, noticing Fabrice's look of surprise, added, 'Minor auction house, in a sale of French rustic junk. It was hidden under another canvas, an unsigned one. Something Julien painted after the fire.'

'Ah. So that's how it managed to disappear for so long. I wonder how it came to be on the market?'

Olivier gave a wintry smile. 'I assume he covered it up with the intention of protecting it. My mother was never very rational when it came to Genevieve Delacroix, and I imagine if she'd found it she would certainly have destroyed it. Unfortunately she also had a spiteful habit of giving anything he painted latterly to *brocantes* and *vide-greniers* just to emphasise to him how worthless it was, so probably that's what happened to this one. Who knows where it's been all this time?'

Fabrice nodded slowly, his dissipated blue eyes running over Genevieve Delacroix's elegant body. 'So, you need to know how much it's worth? I take it, as the other painting wasn't…ah…of the same standard, you picked it up for a song?'

'A thousand. Sterling.'

Once more Fabrice's face showed surprise. 'That's a lot for a minor work of…well, shall we just say "limited artistic merit".' Fabrice leaned forward, frowning slightly. 'Which suggests someone else was on to it.'

'How could they be? No one else knows for certain that it survived the fire.'

'Not for sure….' Fabrice let the words hang in the air for a moment before continuing. 'But you're well aware of the rumours about this painting. It's almost mythical. And let's just say that the Lawrence tribe have got fingers in a lot of pies.' Fabrice sat back again and inhaled deeply. A reformed forty-Gauloises-a-day man, his conversation was punctuated with pauses like this, as though the cigarettes had gone but the habit remained. 'With an election looming in Britain—in which Miles Lawrence with his very public views on morality and old-fashioned values is set to play a key role—they also have a lot to lose if this resurfaces now. Did you see who else was bidding for it?'

Olivier stood up abruptly and went to the window, which

wasn't perhaps a good idea. As he looked out across Paris as the autumn dusk fell, a vivid image of Bella Lawrence superimposed itself onto the glittering cityscape below…

'Yes.'

'Do you think it was someone connected with the Lawrences?'

…Bella Lawrence, beautiful and brazen, wearing nothing but a look of defiant invitation and a pair of high-heeled shoes.

'It was.'

Until now, uncertainty hadn't featured much in Olivier Moreau's emotional repertoire, but then neither had wanting something and knowing it was out of his reach. The night when he'd made love with Bella Lawrence had changed a lot of things.

Though, of course, 'made love' was completely the wrong term. He had had sex with her, thoroughly and ruthlessly. Passionately. In his head he heard her voice again as she stood in front of him, naked and glorious, and said that she'd never known sex could be so powerful. At the time he'd made some cutting response, but the truth was he'd felt it too.

He had wanted to touch her on some deep level, to brand her so she wouldn't forget him, and then he had wanted to drop her. But it turned out that *he* was the one who couldn't forget, and *he* was the one who had been left high and dry when she'd walked out so bloody unexpectedly.

Damn her.

Fabrice cleared his throat. 'In that case, my friend, I'd say they're onto it. May I suggest you double up on security and make sure you have watertight insurance? I take it that's why you want a valuation… You're not thinking of selling?'

Olivier turned back to Fabrice. 'Not mine to sell,' he said shortly. 'It belongs to my father.'

'Shame. So, what do you intend to do with it?'

Olivier frowned. A muscle was flickering in his tense jaw. 'Veronique Lemercier's an ex-girlfriend of mine.'

'The journalist?' Fabrice gave a low whistle as he pulled a bottle of Armagnac and two glasses from a drawer. 'Bit of a viper, isn't she? If she takes up the story, within a few days Genevieve Delacroix will have more exposure than a Hollywood celebrity. In every way.' Smiling, he splashed generous measures into each glass and pushed one across the desk. Oblivious to Olivier's black gloom, he raised his glass.

'Nice work, Olivier. Revenge, as they say, is sweet.'

Sweet?

Fortunately at that moment Olivier's private mobile rang, and he took the call, leaving Fabrice with his simplistic preconceptions intact. Revenge might be sweet, but it sure as hell left a very bitter aftertaste.

It was completely dark by the time Bella found herself bumping the MG up the potholed drive to Le Vieux Moulin. The ambulance hadn't been able to find them, and she felt as if she'd waited hours, during which time the old man had drifted in and out of consciousness. Sometimes there had been minutes at a time where he'd been perfectly lucid, and at others he'd been so silent that Bella had had to check and check again that he was still breathing.

By the time the paramedics had arrived it had been dark, and he had been very weak. Bella had taken off her coat and wrapped it around him, but he'd still seemed frighteningly cold and very frail. Once she'd seen him safely into the ambulance, and reassured him that she would take care of everything, she had spent a terrifying and utterly fruitless time trudging through the forest in search of the missing horse, until it had become too dark to see properly and even the sound of her own breathing had been enough to scare the life out of her. When she had got back into the car to continue the search by road she had felt failure and guilt gnawing at her as keenly as the cold.

Driving now into an uneven cobbled courtyard, she saw a huge, oddly shaped building rising up in front of her. The dim headlamps of the MG showed a muddle of lime plaster and timber, mullioned windows and steeply sloping roofs. A light burned in one window, spilling pale gold beams onto the mossy cobblestones.

Bella left her bag in the car and tentatively crossed the yard to the house. Her whole body was stiff with exhaustion, and her heart was hammering painfully against her aching ribs.

Why on earth had she agreed to do this?

Because, she thought grimly, sliding the key into the lock and pushing open a heavy wooden door, *this man's son is too busy and successful to bother with him and he has no one else. Because he's alone and frightened, and I want to help him.*

The dim light from the open door to her right illuminated a room that looked like something from a period drama, or the inside of an old galleon. Gnarled timbers criss-crossed walls of lime-washed plaster that bulged alarmingly, and the air was damp and chill, scented with age-old woodsmoke and apples. Bella shut the door quietly and moved hesitantly forward, feeling a prickle of unease.

The house was very quiet, very still. As if it was waiting for her.

Hardly daring to breathe, she tiptoed to the doorway of the room from which the light was coming. It was the kitchen—long and low-ceilinged, warmed by an archaic iron cooking range which stood in an inglenook fireplace big enough to stand up in. Possibly there was a time when this kitchen would have been considered state-of-the-art, but that time certainly hadn't been within the last two centuries.

How could someone still live like this?

She exhaled a long, shaky sigh as she moved forward, trailing her fingers over the worn surface of the scarred pine table in the centre of the room. There was a painting hanging on the wall beyond the fireplace and, wrapping her arms around herself to ward off the chill of apprehension, she walked towards it. It reminded her of—

Suddenly she was grabbed from behind.

Sheer, suffocating terror annihilated every thought or sensation as an arm closed like a band of steel around her waist and she was pulled against a hard, lean body. A thousand half-formed images and ideas blurred in her stupefied brain, but none broke through the smothering blackness of fear. She opened her mouth to scream just as a hand clamped over it.

For a second she thrashed and kicked wildly, then felt herself being yanked roughly round so she was facing her assailant.

The scream of panic that had risen in her throat dried up and her racing heart performed an elaborate back-flip as she found herself looking not into the crazed glare of a serial killer, but into the dark eyes of Olivier Moreau.

CHAPTER SEVEN

FOR A moment she felt a terrible, compelling urge to collapse against his strong chest and cling to him, but then her adrenalin levels subsided and reality reasserted itself. Pushing herself violently away from him she shrank back, breathing raggedly and staring at him in horror.

'My God. It's *you...*'

His dark brows quirked upwards a fraction and his mouth twitched into the faintest of glacial smiles. 'God?' he drawled. 'I'm flattered.'

'Don't be,' she snapped, wrapping her arms around herself. 'I didn't mean it like that. What are you doing here?'

Through a haze of confusion and hostility she watched him cross the room and take a couple of glasses from the crowded old dresser. He was dressed in a dark city suit and an ice-white shirt which looked totally out of place in the rustic simplicity of the kitchen, but the assured precision of his movements told her he was on familiar ground. Though it was a million miles from the sterile sophistication of his London apartment, Bella sensed straight away that he belonged here.

When he spoke his voice was like sharpened icicles. 'I came to see my father. He's in hospital—as you've no doubt already heard. I assume you thought that while the house was empty—'

'Your father?'

It came out as an exhalation of disbelief and disgust. Contempt blazed from her dark blue eyes, and in that moment she looked every inch an aristocratic Delacroix.

The anger that had burned slowly inside Olivier since the night she'd run out on him was fanned into white-hot flame.

'Yes.' He spoke almost without moving his lips. *'My father.* Don't try to pretend you hadn't worked that out already.'

Slowly Bella raised her head and met his gaze.

'Yes,' she said slowly, struggling to make sense of the events of the last baffling hours. 'I suppose I should have done. When he said that his son was too busy…too *important* to bother with him… perhaps I should have worked out that he was referring to you. After all, there can't be many people who are that bloody *cold.'*

Olivier's eyes narrowed dangerously. 'It was you who found him?'

'Yes, of course,' she said distractedly, thrusting a hand through the raven's wing of hair that fell across her face. 'What else would I be doing here?'

'I think that's obvious,' he said bitterly, taking down a bottle of red wine from the rack on the dresser and studying the label. 'It's rather a convenient coincidence, wouldn't you agree?'

Bella gave a breathy exhalation of incredulous laughter. *'Convenient?* Are you *kidding?* I could be reclining in a hot bath in a Parisian hotel right now, but instead I have spent the entire afternoon in the middle of nowhere on some kind of impromptu Extreme Survival Exercise.' She shook her head in utter disbelief. 'I suppose a *thank you* would be too much to expect?'

Olivier looked at her steadily. His eyes gleamed. 'I wasn't as well brought up as you were.'

Heat exploded in Bella's cheeks. And her knickers. He was watching her carefully, and she knew that he was thinking of the same thing. Remembering the same words. Dropping his gaze, he uncorked the wine in one smooth, expert movement. 'Though,' he continued, with a languid smile, pouring it into two glasses, 'while we're on the subject, I would have expected you to know better than to leave without saying goodbye.'

Bella lifted her chin defiantly. 'I thought I'd spare you the bother of having to make polite conversation while we waited for Louis to bring the car.'

'I told you—I don't do polite.'

'Obviously not,' she snapped. 'You don't do human very well either. Tell me, if I cut you would I find blood in your veins, or ice?'

He held a glass to her and for a moment they both stared at the dark ruby glint of the liquid in the low light. 'I'm sure you'd like to test the theory,' he drawled.

'Don't tempt me.'

He gave her a chilly smile. 'And don't judge me. Maybe you would find ice. But maybe it's better that way.'

She took the glass and held it against her chest, so that the light shone through it and cast a blood-red shadow across her heart. 'I'm not sure your father would agree with that.'

He looked at her steadily, coldly. 'You know nothing about my father.'

Anger and indignation flashed in her eyes. 'I know that when he was frightened and in pain he didn't want to *bother* you! He could have been dying, but according to him you're too important, too successful to be inconvenienced with a little detail like that!'

Olivier shrugged. 'Well, the hospital decided otherwise,' he said offhandedly. 'They notified me when he was admitted and I left a meeting to get there.'

It was so easy to provoke her, he thought, watching with savage satisfaction as fury and indignation stained her cheeks a deep rose. All her emotions were so near the surface that as soon as you scratched her they came spilling out. She couldn't lie to save her life, he'd bank on it, but Fabrice's warning still rang in his ears. How much did she know about *La Dame de la Croix?*

'How *noble,*' she snapped, then stopped abruptly and pressed her fingers to her temples. When she dropped her hands a moment later Olivier saw that she had drawn that thick, muffling veil back around herself, and she was looking at him with the same dull eyes that had so exasperated him in the street that day, and at Genevieve Delacroix's party. It was some kind of defence mechanism, he could see now. The thought was oddly unsettling.

She gave a tiny, brittle smile. 'Look, you're here now, so there's no need for me to stay,' she said flatly. 'I promised your father I'd look after the house and try to find his horse, but since you've taken the trouble to show up, *you* can do it.'

She made to move past him to the door, but he caught her arm. 'Don't be ridiculous.'

'I'm sorry?' she said coolly. 'Is it ridiculous to expect you to do something for your own father?'

'I was referring to you leaving tonight. You're not going anywhere. But, just for the record, my relationship with my father is absolutely nothing to do with you.'

'Maybe not.' She hesitated, as if deciding whether to continue, and then said, 'I don't care that you treated me like some executive toy to be picked up and used for an evening's entertainment and then thrown away without a second thought. At a stretch, that *could* be seen as the behaviour of a typical arrogant, high-handed, chauvinistic, self-satisfied male. What does make me angry is that you seem to apply the same emotionless principle to your father. In my eyes that's utterly unforgivable.'

The room was suddenly very quiet and very still. The space between them seemed charged with some kind of invisible energy. It gleamed in the depths of Olivier's eyes and sounded a low, sinister note of warning in his voice when he spoke. *'Unforgivable?'*

'Yes.'

He smiled. A cruel, beautiful smile. 'You're quite an expert. Am I to assume that your family is perfect?'

'You know it's not.' The note of anguish in her voice was barely detectable. 'But at least I'm loyal to them.'

Tipping his head back, he crossed his arms and regarded her with lazy speculation. 'Oh, yes,' he said with quiet brutality. 'Very loyal and very obedient. And I'd say that was your biggest problem.'

She wanted to speak. Wanted to defend herself or disagree. But she couldn't. Her lips parted, she looked up into his narrowed, penetrating stare and the words melted on her tongue.

He had seen inside her.

For a long moment they simply gazed at each other, and then with a note of quiet triumph he said, 'Perhaps you'd like to go upstairs to your room. I'll bring your things in from the car.'

'I can manage,' she said dully.

'I don't think so. I don't want you to do another one of your famous disappearing acts.'

It was only when she'd left, when he'd heard her going up the creaking stairs, that Olivier realised his whole body was rigid with tension. For a moment he stood motionless as the irony of her words echoed round his head.

He had to grip the edge of the table to stop himself reaching out and hurling his glass across the room, watching the wine run down the wall like blood.

Bella slept fitfully, disturbed and tormented by the thought of Olivier's presence somewhere nearby in the creaking old house. Arriving in the dark last night, she'd got an impression of a sprawling building made up of odd angles and surprising corners, and in her muddled, fretful half dreams the timbered passageways and low doorways stretched out before her in a never-ending labyrinth as she tried to escape from him.

Or to find him.

Perhaps it was just as well she'd given up believing in fate. If she still did she might start to get paranoid. The horrible coincidence of being thrown back into the company of the man she had come here hoping to forget was altogether too cruel to contemplate.

She must have fallen into a deeper sleep around dawn, because the next thing she knew the light falling through the thin linen curtains was the thick honey-gold of morning. A sense of alarm that she had allowed herself to let her guard down propelled her out of bed immediately, and, still clumsy with sleep, she pushed her feet swiftly into her long boots, zipping them up over her pyjamas before hurrying downstairs.

The deserted kitchen was warm, and buttery sunlight sloped though the mullioned windows, casting intricate criss-cross patterns on the flagstoned floor. There was no sign of Olivier, though from the heat coming from the range Bella knew that he must have been up for a while.

The thought made her heart give an uneven thud.

She went to the back door and pushed it open. A rush of sharp, apple-scented autumn air curled around her, and she closed her eyes for a second and breathed it in, savouring its perfumed sweetness. In front of her lay a small garden surrounded by a low wall of crumbling yellowish stone. A brick path cut between neat beds filled with blowsy lettuces, canes of beans and raspberries, sprawling, spidery strawberry plants. Beyond this tamed square, lush fields unfurled like green velvet, glittering with dew.

She'd been completely wrong about this place when she'd dismissed it as primitive, she thought, picking a fat, crimson raspberry and feeling its juice explode in her mouth as she leant over the wall to look at the fields.

It was. But it was also utterly idyllic.

The light, the luxuriance of colours and textures, made it an artist's paradise, and there was an air of timeless tranquillity about it that soothed some clamour within her that she hadn't even been aware of until now. It was as if the place inside her head had been conjured into real life. The safe place to which she'd always retreated.

The field beyond the wall sloped down slightly to an untidy hedge, in the centre of which stood a tree. Even from some distance away she could see that its branches were laden with fruit, and, drawing closer through the wet grass, she found that they were fat purple plums. Many of them lay in the grass at her feet and she picked one up, stroking the bloom from the cool flesh with the palm of her hand, lifting it to her face to smell its honeyed perfume before taking a bite.

It was perfect—sweet and juicy, and far too good to be left rotting on the ground. She began to collect up more, discarding the ones that were old or soft, but there were still too many to carry. Clamping the first one between her teeth, she pulled up the front of her stretchy vest top and made an apron of it, and then, crouching on the ground, began loading the others into it.

Suddenly the indolent peace of the morning was shattered by a thundering noise that shook the ground and sent a dart of panic through her. Cradling the plums in the front of her T-shirt, she leapt to her feet.

A horse came over the hedge, so close that it was almost on top of her. For an appalling, heart-stopping moment the sky was blotted out by its massive dark forequarters above her, the dull gleam of polished leather and sweating flesh. She froze, not daring to move as the rider swerved at the last minute and the flailing hooves and flying stirrups missed her by inches. She was trembling violently with shock as the horse came to a sliding, shuddering standstill a small distance away. Before it had even stopped moving the rider leapt off.

Her heart, crashing against her ribs at three times its normal speed, plummeted as she recognised Olivier. As he strode towards her she could see that his habitually inscrutable face was now set in a pale mask of fury.

'Next time you feel suicidal may I suggest something less dramatic?' he said with lethal sweetness. 'Pills and alcohol, perhaps? A nice sharp razorblade? Anything that doesn't involve me, in fact.'

Bella felt the blood leach from her head. She looked at him in mute horror.

'I'm…I'm sorry,' she whispered through white lips.

Olivier scowled. 'Are you hurt?'

She gave a tiny shake of her head. Her eyes were dark pools of anguish, and she didn't seem to notice when several of the plums she was holding in the front of her T-shirt rolled out and fell to the floor. She looked as if she was about to pass out.

Instantly he was beside her, wrapping an arm around her waist to hold her up. His fingers dug into the exposed skin of her midriff beneath her outstretched top. He gritted his teeth against an unwelcome and wholly inappropriate rush of lust.

'Bella?'

She seemed to gather herself, and looked up at him.

'I'm fine. Sorry. Sorry. I was just…'

'It's OK,' he said roughly. For a moment they looked at each other as a gulf of unspoken history opened up between them. Olivier felt as if his chest was being crushed. Slowly, as if the movement hurt him, he raised his hand to her ashen cheek.

He'd barely touched her before he snatched his hand back again and spun round away from her, thrusting his fingers through his hair as he strode over to where the horse was grazing quietly. Swinging effortlessly back into the saddle, he looked down at her. Some of the colour had returned to her cheeks, but the eyes that looked up at him were huge and filled with hurt.

Remorse pierced him. Remorse and bitterness and anger and

longing. Viciously pulling the horse round, he kicked it forward and galloped across the field towards the stables.

For a man who had spent his whole life carefully erasing emotion, all of that was a lot to deal with.

CHAPTER EIGHT

BELLA was in the kitchen when he came in from the stables. Standing at the primitive old sink, rinsing the plums she'd collected, she had her back to him and her head bent. Her dark hair fell forward, hiding her face, but the syrupy morning sunlight fell on her slender arms, glinting off the beads of water on her skin.

Olivier swallowed and busied himself looking for coffee and the battered stove-top coffeepot his father had always used.

'Was that your father's horse? You found it?' Bella asked in a slightly shaky voice.

'Oui,' he said curtly. 'I phoned the neighbouring farms this morning. Duval next door found the horse in the field with his cows at milking time. He seems none the worse for yesterday's drama.'

'That's good.' She shot him a rueful glance from behind the shiny fall of her hair. 'What about today's drama?'

'No harm done.'

The words came out more harshly than he'd intended, and he silently cursed himself as he leaned over her to fill the pot with water. *No harm done.* To the horse, maybe, but it was more than could be said for him. The encounter had shaken him more than he cared to admit.

It wasn't just that she could have been hurt. No, what had

jolted him so badly was her reaction afterwards, when he'd confronted her. She had looked so…*broken* for a second. Completely crushed. And it had made him see her vulnerability and hate himself for what he'd tried to do to her.

What he'd done.

He didn't want to be reminded. He didn't want to care. He just wanted to settle the score once and for all and get on with the future, having slain the demons of the past.

On the marble shelf of the larder he found eggs, and went outside to look for tarragon and thyme. The sharp, astringent scent they released as he picked them made him feel suddenly inexpressibly lonely, taking him back to countless other haphazard, thrown-together meals when it had been just him and Julien. He breathed in, remembering the silence, the atmosphere of sadness and loss. Of suffering.

That was the look that he'd seen on Bella's face before.

He pictured her standing there, her eyes huge and dark in her bloodless face. Haunted, that was how she'd looked.

He pushed the thought away, sneering inwardly at his own sentimentality. *Haunted?* What he really meant was that she'd looked damned hot, standing there in her pyjamas and boots with her top lifted up and a deliciously enticing sweep of her midriff exposed. She'd looked sleepy and tousled and infinitely kissable, which was exactly what he'd almost done. *That* was what bothered him, if he was going to be brutally honest. Not anything to do with *her* being haunted, but the fact that *he* felt completely bloody possessed by the need to bed her.

Again. Oh, God, *again*, and it was nothing to do with revenge or the past and everything to do with her.

He remembered the first time he had set eyes on her in the auction house, how he had automatically singled her out because of her looks. Same old routine, he'd thought. A meaningless piece of flirtation like countless others with innumerable anonymous pretty girls who had slid from his memory the moment they were out of his sight and his bed.

But it was as if some wrathful feminist goddess had specifically thrown Bella Lawrence into his path as punishment for his hubris, his arrogance. The one woman in the world who, it turned out, could undermine his rock-solid self-assurance, tear down the elaborately constructed walls he'd built around himself and pluck cords of feeling that were beyond the reach of all the others.

He hated her for making it feel so good.

Bella took down two thick pottery mugs from the dresser and laid the table with greenish-glazed plates and old bone-handled knives and forks. They felt solid and heavy in her hands, and she ran her fingers appreciatively over the worn surface of a knife. Celia would go mad for these.

Olivier came in from the garden, his big hands full of herbs, his face grim. Going over to the range, he didn't even glance at her. He was wearing a pale blue shirt, unbuttoned over a white T-shirt, and, leaning against the sink, she couldn't help staring at the way the low sun brought out strands of deep gold that she'd never noticed before in his hair, turning it from dark brown to rich, burnished tortoiseshell. It curled just above the collar of the shirt, leaving a strip of tanned skin that, in spite of herself, her fingers itched to touch.

What was the matter with her this morning? Maybe it was the restless night, or her earlier brush with death, but she felt painfully conscious of her own body; the beat of her heart and the feeling of her clothes against her skin. She was horribly aware of Olivier's body too, and the way his presence seemed to fill every corner of the low, sunlit kitchen.

There was an effortless grace to his movements, she thought despairingly as she watched him stir the eggs in the pan, noticing how the muscles rippled and flexed beneath the butterscotch skin of his forearms. Whether he was dressed in an immaculate dinner jacket and drinking champagne at the Tate, or making breakfast here in this ancient kitchen, he carried the same aura of intense, focused power and sexuality.

He turned round and glanced at her as he slid a perfect herb omelette onto her plate, and she blushed, aware that he'd caught her staring at him.

'Thanks.' She sat down awkwardly and, picking up her fork, took a mouthful of omelette. It was so light it seemed to melt on her tongue. Olivier sat down opposite and she felt suddenly shy. The peaceful domesticity of the situation was deeply unsettling, especially in the face of his cold, brooding silence.

'So,' she said in a low, halting voice, needing to fill the silence, 'when was the last time you came back here?'

She thought she saw him tense for a second, but when he spoke his voice was completely emotionless.

'I left twelve years ago and I've never been back. Amazingly enough it's still exactly the same as the day I left,' he said, glancing derisively around the kitchen.

'Did you expect it to be different?'

'No.' His gaze came to rest on her, and she had the uncomfortable sensation that he was stripping her bare. 'Around here nothing has changed for centuries. That's exactly why I got out.'

Bella lifted her chin an inch. There was something challenging in the way he was looking at her that made her feel both uncomfortable and confused. She picked up the coffee pot and poured more of the dark, fragrant liquid into her mug. 'Some people might say that's a good thing. There's something reassuring about things staying the same.'

'That depends on your perspective. It must be very reassuring if you have the upper hand. If you're the one who calls the shots.'

He spoke with a quiet ferocity that sent a shiver down her spine.

'What do you mean?'

'Places like St Laurien are still essentially feudal. All the wealth and power is held by a tiny minority, which can cause…problems.' He skewered a piece of omelette with sharp precision.

'Envy? Resentment? The need to be the dominant alpha male?' she said flippantly. 'Those kind of problems?'

Instantly his face darkened ominously and she wished she could take the words back. 'I suppose you think that peasants should just know their place?'

'No!' The brutality in his voice shocked her into indignation and she got up, busying herself by clearing the table. 'You're twisting everything I say! I just think that families should stick together, that's all. You know, look after each other. Be there.'

'I see. Like your parents are there for you?'

Her hands, stacking the plates, stilled. She stood with her head bent as his soft, deceptively innocuous words sank in, finding their target right in the insecure, lonely heart of her. Biting her lip, she forced herself to pick up the plates and turn around to put them by the sink, grateful for the excuse to escape the intensity of his all-seeing gaze.

'That's different,' she said stiffly. 'My family has a wider responsibility—I've always accepted that. It's part of who they are and what they do.'

From behind her she heard his scornful gust of laughter. 'A *wider responsibility*?' he echoed derisively. 'You mean they're too busy looking after the rest of the world to bother with you?'

'Yes, I suppose you could put it like that.' She ran hot water into the sink. 'But that's OK. I don't mind. Their role—in politics and government—means they always put the greater good before their own personal interests.'

For a moment he didn't reply. She didn't turn round but was aware of him moving across the kitchen towards her. She could feel the hairs stand up on the back of her neck as he came close, and with exaggerated calm he leaned over her and dropped his mug into the water.

She glanced up then, and felt her mouth go dry as she met his eyes. The hostility and contempt in them chilled her.

'You really believe that?' he said scathingly.

'Yes, of course. It's who they are, what they were born to.'

She made a brave attempt to keep her voice cool and strong, which wasn't easy given that he was standing close enough for her to be able to see the flecks of gold glittering in his dark eyes and the tiny crease at the corner of his lush mouth. She looked sharply away, concentrating on the dishes in the sink, and then realised she was holding his cup in her hand, running her fingers along the place his lips had just touched.

Her hands stopped moving. Heat exploded inside her.

Mercifully he moved away then, shaking his head slowly as if in disbelief. Gradually she found she could breathe again and anger temporarily overcame desire.

'You might criticise,' she said through gritted teeth, 'but at least we stick together. You just *left* your father. You cut yourself off without a backward glance.'

'You're making a lot of assumptions,' he said acidly. 'I said I've never been back. I didn't say I cut myself off from him.'

'Right—so you clearly take really good care of him,' she said sarcastically, turning round to face him as her anger gained strength. 'You're what—a millionaire? And just look at this place.' She held up dripping hands. 'Not so much as a dishwasher.'

A dangerous stillness seemed to come over him. Leaning back with deceptive nonchalance against the fireplace, he crossed his arms and looked at her steadily, almost challengingly. 'Firstly, you considerably undervalue my worth. And secondly, this might not be my ideal home, but it is my father's. He *chooses* to live here. He won't leave.'

'OK,' she said with deliberate and exaggerated patience. 'I can see why he doesn't want to leave, because it's beautiful. Or could be. But would it kill you to make it more comfortable for him? To—I don't know—forgo the odd Picasso in favour of central heating and windows that fit?'

'Who says I'd have to forgo the Picasso? As you said, money isn't the issue.'

'I see.' His unwavering, laser-beam gaze was making Bella feel deeply flustered. Turning back to the sink, she spoke through lips that were stiff with hostility. 'So you could very easily help him out, but you won't.'

Suddenly the electric tension in the kitchen seemed as thick and palpable as the shafts of low sunlight slanting through the small windows. Bella waited, her heart hammering hard, and wondered if she'd gone too far.

'Oh, dear.' Slowly he levered himself away from the fireplace and came towards her. He sounded bored, but his eyes glittered with malice. 'If only life really was that simple.'

Pressed up against the sink, there was no means of escape. 'What do you mean?' she stammered.

'You still don't get it, do you? OK, I'll spell it out to you. The mill doesn't belong to my father. He's a *tenant*.' He enunciated the word very clearly, as if he was talking to a child. An extremely stupid child. Bella felt the pressure in her head rise a couple of notches.

'Well, couldn't you buy the house for him?'

He laughed bitterly. 'I've lost track of the number of times I've tried to buy this damp, rotting pile of timber—the last offer I made was twice as much as I'd just paid for the apartment on Park Lane. It's not for sale.'

He was right in front of her now. Bella looked down at the flagstoned floor, letting her hair fall like a firewall between them and waiting for the sick fluttering in her stomach, brought on by his nearness, to subside. But a moment later she felt a lightning bolt of electricity shoot through her as his fingers burned the side of her neck, smoothing her hair behind her ear, so he could look into her face. There was nowhere to hide from the hypnotic murmur of his voice. 'Trying to get improvements done is similarly unrewarding. The tenancy contract won't allow any alterations without permission. Funnily enough, it's always refused.'

White sandy beach. Blue skies. Tenancy agreements.

Taking a deep breath, Bella looked up at him and thought of Ashley. Poised, intelligent Ashley—what would she say in this situation?

'But that's not right,' she said shakily. 'Whoever owns the mill has a duty to keep it up to current standards. There must be… legal requirements. Surely the owners have no choice but to comply?'

There was a dangerous glitter in his eyes. Slowly, he reached out for the drawstring ribbon in her pyjama bottoms and pulled her gently towards him. 'You would think so, wouldn't you?'

Bella's breath quickened. He was looking at her with a mixture of amusement and something darker…more disturbing. More arousing.

'Then you have to do something…complain to the owners.'

'I am,' he said quietly. 'Right now. This property is part of the St Laurien estate, and as such is in the joint ownership of the Delacroix and Lawrence families. So, Mademoiselle Lawrence, perhaps you'd like to tell me what you're going to do about it?'

'There must be some mistake!' Bella whispered. Backed up against the sink, her whole body stiffened with shock. Olivier, by contrast, looked completely relaxed. There was something both insolent and sinister about the quiet drawl of his voice.

'Sadly not. Do you need to see evidence? Documents?'

'No, I don't mean that. I mean there must be some misunderstanding…about the maintenance of the property. My family would never…'

'What? Exploit their position? Abuse their power?'

She attempted a laugh. 'Don't be so overdramatic. They'd never deliberately force someone to live in substandard accommodation.' She was pleased with that. It sounded good—definitely the kind of thing Ashley would say. She managed a smile. 'Look, leave it to me. I'll go over to Le Manoir and see my uncle and I'm sure I'll be able to sort it out quite simply. Now, if you'll excuse me, I'll go and get dressed…'

On that note she stepped briskly past him, intending to sweep gracefully from the room. Unfortunately she'd forgotten that he was still holding onto the ribbon that held up her pyjama trousers, and as she moved she felt a pull as the bow came undone, and a sudden loosening at her waist.

With a gasp of indignation she turned round, snatching the ribbon from his fingers and tying it back up with shaking, savage fingers. But not before she knew he'd had a glimpse of her bare behind. His gaze flickered over her. The complete lack of interest on his dark, impassive face was more humiliating than anything.

'Good idea,' he said blandly, moving away from her to get more coffee. 'Be ready to leave in half an hour.'

She blinked in horror. 'You're not coming with me?'

'Not to see your uncle, no. Under the circumstances I hardly think that would be wise, but I need to go to the hospital to see my father, and since I got Louis to bring me from Paris last night I don't have a car.' He glanced up at her dismissively. 'You can give me a lift.'

As she'd spent the last half hour berating him for neglect, Bella could hardly argue, no matter how much she wanted to. With a stiff nod she left the room, cursing all the way upstairs.

She might not have been able to refuse to take him to the hospital, but she didn't have to make it easy either, Bella thought half an hour later as she went out to the car, carrying a basket of the plums she had gathered that morning. The day was living up to its early promise, but although the low golden sun was deliciously warm, blue-black clouds had gathered behind it and the air was sharp. *So what?* she thought sulkily, wrestling with the hood on the MG. They might freeze, they might get soaked, but at least with the top down it would be noisy enough to make conversation impossible.

Olivier emerged from the house, unhurriedly checking his BlackBerry. Letting his gaze flicker casually to where Bella was waiting with ostentatious patience in the open-topped car, he stopped and said sardonically, 'You do realise how cold it's going to be driving with the top down?'

'It's fine,' Bella said stiffly. She had given her coat to Julien Moreau yesterday, but this morning, reluctantly aware of what Olivier had said to her that night at the Tate about wearing black, she had put aside her thickest sweater and jeans in favour of a short emerald-green velvet skirt with her boots, and a thin raspberry-pink wraparound cardigan. But he was right, of course. She was going to freeze. Putting down the hood of the car had been stupid, but she'd die of hypothermia before she let him see that. She cast him a supercilious smile.

'If you've quite finished fussing, can we go?'

The hospital to which Julien had been admitted was a modern building just outside Rouen, about twenty minutes' drive away. After a journey during which neither of them spoke, Bella dropped Olivier at the doorway.

She pulled up beneath a majestic sycamore tree and switched off the engine. He hadn't bothered taking the basket of plums in, she noticed resentfully, biting into one as she resigned herself to wait. He was right, it was damned cold, and holding the plum between her teeth for a moment she tucked her legs in their long boots up in front of her, wedging them against the steering wheel and wrapping her arms around them.

'Are you quite comfortable?'

She looked up with a start. Olivier was standing over her, watching her. She blushed and removed the plum from her mouth, hastily wiping away the juice that was running down her chin.

'That was quick. After twelve years you could only manage ten minutes?'

He opened the driver's door and took a step back. 'My father would like to meet you.'

The tone of his voice and the rigid set of his shoulders as he walked slightly ahead of her into the hospital left Bella in no doubt about what he thought about this. She followed him wordlessly up a long corridor, almost colliding with the solid wall of his body as he stopped outside a door and buzzed to gain admittance.

His face was like granite, the two frown lines between his brows more deeply carved than ever. For a second he hesitated, as if he wanted to speak, but then wearily he pulled open the door and gestured her through.

Julien Moreau lay against a bank of snowy pillows. His colour had returned, so that instead of yesterday's sickening pallor his skin was now a deep walnut-brown. His lined, weatherbeaten face broke into a slow, wide smile as he looked at Bella, and in that instant she caught a glimpse of what Olivier would look like if he relaxed. If he stopped being so angry.

'Mademoiselle…Lawrence. I have so much to thank you for.'

With a shy answering smile Bella stepped forward.

'Please, call me Bella.'

Julien laughed, though his eyes were filled with pain. 'Yes, I think that would be better.' And then he held out his hand.

She faltered, aware of Olivier's challenging, hostile gaze on her, focusing every ounce of her energy on keeping her smile in place as she took his hand in hers.

The skin was tight, paper-thin, puckered and stretched over

the bones. Raw, shiny, scarlet, it looked as if some time long ago the flesh had quite simply been melted away.

She held it gently, firmly, all the time smiling into his eyes. 'It's lovely to see you looking so much better,' she said softly. 'Everything at the mill is fine, and I brought you some of the windfalls from the plum tree. I hope you don't mind.'

Mistake.

Stupid, stupid mistake.

Striding back down the corridor half an hour later, Olivier thrust his clenched fists into the pockets of his jacket and quickened his pace.

He should have left her in the car. It was a mistake to make this personal. He felt like the watertight compartments of his life had been blown wide open.

Julien had been completely smitten, and the cruelty of that irony choked him. The space between himself and his father was so vast, so unbridgeable because of the devastation wrought on their family by the Lawrences...and yet *she* could come in here and touch the old man's shredded heart with just a smile.

Not that he could blame him. On Bella Lawrence's lips a smile could have roughly the same effect as a large measure of vintage cognac. He remembered again the moment when his father had held out one of his ravaged, ruined hands and Bella had taken it in her cool, pale and beautiful one.

He felt his own fingers flex as tension sizzled through every nerve. Tension and bitter, bitter resentment. Julien wouldn't have been so welcoming if he'd known that she was here to find his beloved painting and take it away from him again, he thought venomously.

The doors to the car park swept open and he took a deep lungful of cool air.

Bella slanted a shy glance up at him from behind her

curtain of dark hair. The tenderness in her eyes burned at his raw emotions like acid. 'Thank you for letting me come,' she said softly.

Her damned courtesy irritated him unreasonably. 'I didn't,' he drawled. 'You drove, remember? It was necessity, not generosity.'

'Letting me come in to meet your father, then.'

'Not my idea,' Olivier replied ungraciously. 'He asked.'

They were walking across the car park to where she'd left the battered red MG beneath the sycamore tree. As they approached a sharp gust of wind sent a flurry of gold and copper leaves spiralling from the tree, scattering them over the cracked leather seats like autumn confetti. Beside him, Bella shivered, and tugged the sleeves of her soft pink cardigan down over her hands.

'You didn't have to tell him I was here,' she said hesitantly. 'Or who I was. I thought that from what you said earlier he might not have…'

Olivier made a harsh, dismissive sound. 'Yes, well, it's amazing how far a bit of calculated feminine charm goes. Nicely done, Ms Lawrence. A flash of those big blue eyes, a flutter of those long lashes and fifty years of hostility and attrition are instantly blown away.'

There was a whooshing sound in Bella's ears. For a moment she stood perfectly still, staring incredulously at Olivier as adrenaline tingled and sizzled through her bloodstream and a crimson tide of fury washed her face.

'What did you *want* me to do, Olivier? Walk in there like the lady of the manor bestowing favour on a lowly peasant? She leaned towards him, the tense anger that had gripped her a moment ago suddenly giving way to an intoxicating languor. Dropping her voice to a low taunt, she tilted her face up to his and said softly, 'You'd actually *prefer* that, wouldn't you? You don't like being wrong about anything, and I guess you're used to people falling over themselves to please you and to be what you want them to be. Maybe I should just do you a favour and make your life easier by behaving like the *bitch* you think I am.'

And in one fluid movement she wrenched open the door of the MG and slipped into the driver's seat. For once the engine started first time, and she pressed her foot hard on the accelerator, firing it up in a roar of noise and exhaust fumes.

'Bella!'

He reached out for her but she yanked off the handbrake, shooting backwards out of his reach, and then, with a squeal of tyres, speeding forwards across the car park.

As the din of the throaty old engine died away in the distance Olivier was left standing there alone, rigid and speechless with fury. Until he'd met her, no woman had *ever* walked out on him, but now Bella Lawrence had done it twice.

There would not, he vowed, be a third time.

CHAPTER NINE

IT ONLY took a couple of minutes for Olivier to contact his PA in London and get her to arrange for a car for him. In a little under twenty minutes from the moment he had watched Bella storm out of the car park a sleek black Aston Martin appeared, with a far less exclusive car following behind it to take the delivery driver back to the hire company.

Showing not the slightest interest in the explanation of the car's high-tech computerised instrument panel and integral entertainment system, Olivier scrawled his signature across the form and got straight into the driver's seat, leaving the delivery man mouthing impotently as he drove off.

He drove fast, and with a terrible tense-jawed focus. Once out of the town he put his foot flat to the floor, sending the Aston Martin scorching through the lanes, whirlpools of leaves flying up in its wake.

The gates to Le Manoir St Laurien lay in a dip midway along a perfectly straight stretch of road, bordered on both sides by woodland. Speeding alongside the high stone wall that marked the boundary to the grand house, Olivier felt his hands tighten on the steering wheel as ahead of him the ornate iron gateway came into view.

And through it, a second later, the red MG.

It shot straight out into the road, barely pausing long enough to check that nothing was coming, and accelerated away in a billowing cloud of black exhaust fumes.

On the wrong side of the road. The English side.

Olivier let out a stream of vicious and extremely blue French.

The Aston Martin leapt forward with a roar as he slammed his foot down hard on the accelerator. The ancient MG was no match for it, but as he came up behind her he was horrified to glance down at his own speedometer and see just how fast she was going. Keeping his eyes fixed ahead, as if by watching her he could keep her safe, his fingers searched for the controls for the lights, or the horn, or anything he could use to get her attention, but the unfamiliar dashboard was designed for sleek minimalism rather than driving convenience and nothing came to hand.

Fury and frustration erupted inside him, tearing another succinct and colourful curse from his lips. Swerving to the right, he pulled alongside her, trying to catch her eye and order her to move over.

She saw him, of course. There was no way that she couldn't have. But stubbornly she kept her eyes fixed ahead. Her hair rippled out behind her, whipped by the wind, and her chin was lowered in determination. Against the steering wheel her knuckles showed pearl-white.

She was so preoccupied with their stupid fight that she was completely oblivious to the fact she was on the wrong side of the road.

His mind raced, fighting panic.

He accelerated the Aston Martin easily past her, then continued ahead of her on the correct side of the road, hoping that would make her realise her mistake, but in his rearview mirror he could see that her course hadn't altered. In front of him the road emerged from the cover of the trees and disappeared from view as it crested a hill.

Olivier thrust forwards and the needle on the Aston Martin's speedometer trembled. Reaching the top of the hill, he scanned the road ahead.

Dieu. Mon Dieu.

A farm truck was lumbering up the hill towards him, keeping steadfastly to its own side of the road… The side on which Bella was about to appear over the top of the hill behind him in that ridiculous, rusty death-trap of a car.

She wouldn't stand a chance.

He didn't have time to find the horn or flash the lights to warn the driver. Instantly, and without thinking, he swerved into the path of the oncoming truck, registering for a heart-stopping, slow-motion moment the driver's sudden expression of astonishment as he yanked the truck over to the other side of the road to avoid the idiot in the sports car. The two vehicles passed each other on the wrong side of the road, each of them missing each other by inches, at the same moment that the MG appeared over the crest of the hill, smoothly following the path of the Aston Martin.

The truck driver, recovering himself, sounded several loud furious blasts on the horn as he swerved back onto the correct side and drove on.

Heart pounding, blood thrumming in his ears, Olivier slowed down, swerving off the road and bringing the car to a standstill on a rutted and overgrown track into the woodland that sloped down to the river.

Bella pulled in behind him and watched him get out, slamming the door of the Aston Martin shut with such force that the car rocked on its suspension. Striding up to the MG, he wrenched the door open and grabbed her arm, pulling her roughly to her feet. The incandescent rage in his voice vibrated like an electrical charge in the mild, golden autumn afternoon.

'You could have been killed!'

'Like. You'd. *Care.*'

Held awkwardly against him, she spoke very quietly, enunciating each word with deadly precision. For a second his fingers tightened convulsively on her arms, and then he let her go so abruptly that she stumbled back against the side of the car. She'd never seen anyone look so angry. For the briefest second she thought he was going to hit her. Instead he thrust his splayed fingers through his hair in a gesture of barely controlled violence.

'If I didn't care,' he said in a low snarl, 'then why in hell's name would I have just risked my own neck for you?'

Bella folded her arms across her chest, as if trying to still the chaotic banging of her heart inside it. 'I don't know,' she spat, looking up at him with burning eyes. 'I really don't know why you'd do that, in view of the fact that you hate me so much.'

Clamping a hand over her mouth, she turned away from him and looked out over the fields. *Don't cry,* she told herself fiercely, and instantly felt a tide of rage rise up inside her like hot lava.

'I don't hate you.'

His words reached her as if from a great distance, barely penetrating the white noise in her head. Philippe Delacroix was as mad as a box of frogs, and the short time she had spent in the dilapidated, shadowy rooms of Le Manoir had been bizarre and frightening in equal measure, but, God, had she learned a lot.

Such as why her grandmother had been so understanding after what happened with Dan Nightingale.

Hugging herself tightly, as if that way she could keep herself together, Bella looked at the glowing trees and said as casually as possible, 'You didn't tell me that your father was an artist, Olivier.'

'I wonder why?' he said bitterly.

'Let me *think*—maybe because then I might have found out that he once painted a picture of my grandmother that was intended to ruin her reputation and bring down my entire family?'

Her voice rang with a mixture of triumph and despair. Olivier grasped her arm and spun her round, forcing her to face him. His fingers dug into her flesh and his eyes narrowed as they raked her face 'What did that bastard Delacroix tell you?'

Bella's hollow laugh was tinged with desolation. 'So you're not denying it, then?'

'The painting? Of course not—why would I deny it? You know as well as I do that it exists…' His words were ground out from between clenched teeth. 'After all, that's why you're here now, and it's what brought us together in the first place, isn't it?'

Bella stiffened and gave a ragged gasp of horror. '*What?* No! You're wrong! I…never knew. I thought…'

What had she thought? That it was fate, destiny…ridiculous romantic things like that that had made her path collide with the compelling man in the auction house? Oh, God. How could she have been so *stupid*?

Olivier's grip on her arm tightened. 'Don't tell me you didn't know about *La Dame de la Croix?* Don't tell me you weren't looking for it too?'

She seemed to try and shrink away from him, though he held her tightly. 'I'd never heard of it before now. And if I had I'd never have touched *you*,' she spat venomously. 'Because I know how it feels to be betrayed and exploited in the name of *art*. It happened to me too.'

He suddenly went very still. 'What do you mean?'

In the eyes that looked up into his Olivier saw a continent of desolation and hurt. 'Oh, yes. That's why I had to drop out of art school.' She took a shivery breath, steeling herself to continue. 'Not a painting, but photographs. *Naked* photographs of…of me, superimposed with newspaper headlines from way back when my grandfather was in the cabinet and made up into huge silkscreen prints.' Every word seemed to hurt her. 'Very modern…very clever—tapping so brilliantly into politics and the cult of celebrity, or something, but utterly *trashing* my dignity and my self-respect in the process.'

'Who did it?' he said hoarsely.

She tried to cover her face with her hands, but he was holding her wrists so tightly she ended up dropping her head almost onto his chest. 'The man I was talking to that night at the Tate. The man I thought I loved before I found out that he had only noticed me in the first place because of who I was. Because of my *name*.' She writhed and twisted in his iron grasp, trying to work herself free of his hands. 'That's why I know exactly how it feels to be stitched up and screwed over. I know how it feels to be on the receiving end of what your father did to my grandmother—'

'No!' His voice was like a gunshot in the still afternoon, and he pulled her against him, trying to stop her from thrashing around, trying to make her listen. 'It's not like that. The painting wasn't like that.'

This time she did break free, and sprang away from him, her eyes flashing with fury.

'Yeah, *right*,' she said with bitter sarcasm, and it was almost as if she was taunting him. 'Even though she was stark naked and wearing only the Delacroix cross—symbol of three hundred years of family honour—as a cheap pornographic prop. It was tasteful, I suppose. It was *art*.'

Olivier clenched his hands into fists and brought them up to his head. 'Yes,' he said in a voice that shook with rage. 'It *was*. It was…' He stopped, struggling to find the words in English or in French that would convey to her the tender sensuality…the *reverence* with which Julien had painted Genevieve. Immortalised her. Captured her and held her for ever as a beautiful, vibrant twenty-year-old with eyes full of passion…

Just like the girl in front of him.

Desire hit him like a punch, momentarily winding him. 'It was different. You have to believe me,' he almost gasped.

Her anger and bitterness seemed to have evaporated suddenly, leaving her looking just unbearably sad.

'How?' she said bleakly. 'How can I?'

He gave a low groan. 'You want me to show you?'

'*Yes.*'

He slammed her body against his as his mouth came down on hers, hard and relentlessly demanding. She felt herself go completely rigid as fury and frustration flooded every nerve and every cell, making her fingers grasp and twist at his clothes, her mouth open in a low, animal snarl as their teeth clashed and their tongues meshed.

And then suddenly she wasn't rigid any more, but arching against him; the fingers that tore and clawed did so now not from anger but from white-hot need. He was holding her face in both hands, his thumbs firm beneath her jaw, but then with a moan of what sounded like despair he dragged his lips from hers and tipped his head back, breathing hard.

Shocked, dazed with acute, agonizing desire and black confusion, Bella squeezed her eyes shut, resting her forehead against his chest and banging it gently against him.

And then, almost reluctantly, Olivier pulled away from her. His face was like stone.

'OK, then. I'll show you. I'll show you exactly what it was like. Come with me.'

CHAPTER TEN

NEITHER of them spoke as they walked along the overgrown track away from the cars. The low afternoon sun was as thick and golden as syrup, but it came from a sky that had darkened to a strange metallic purple colour, against which the turning leaves of the trees looked a surreal and beautiful acid-yellow.

Following Olivier through the wild undergrowth of bracken and brambles which pulled at her like tiny, grasping hands, Bella wanted to ask where they were going, but the words floated vaguely in her head and then dissolved again. Her heart thudded unevenly against her ribs, and she knew that it was nothing to do with trying to keep up with his pace and everything to do with what had just happened, what might happen next. She had no idea where he was taking her, only that her lips tingled and burned in the aftermath of his kiss, and her breasts felt swollen, ripe and tender.

They had only walked a little way when ahead of them, through the flaming trees, she saw a small stone building with boarded-up windows and a dilapidated roof of irregular slate tiles.

Reaching it, Olivier stopped and turned round. His face was tense, his jaw set, and the strange, other-worldly light painted a sheen of gold on his careless curls. The darkness in his eyes seemed to mirror the gathering blackness in the sky. As she caught up Bella realised they were right beside the river, and a little shingle beach led down from the doorway to the glassy green water.

'What is this place?'

Olivier stooped, turning over stones piled by the entrance until he found a key. 'It used to be a boathouse. My father used it as a studio.'

He stood back so she could go ahead of him into the gloom. Bella hesitated for a second, then stepped forward.

Inside it was velvet black, and smelled of moss and damp leaves. She shivered.

'But how could he paint here?' she said, trying to keep the tremor from her voice. 'It's so dark.'

A match flared, the sound making her start. For a second Olivier's face was illuminated by the bright leap of flame, and she felt her heart lurch as she saw the complete absence of emotion there. It was as hard and blank as stone.

He held the match to a candle, and then another and another, until soft light flickered tentatively into the corners of the room.

'It wasn't always. All around there used to be windows.'

He held the candle aloft so she could see. Bella let her gaze slide around the boarded-up spaces where light would once have spilled in, creating a perfect space to paint.

'What happened?' she said bleakly.

'There was a fire.'

'Here? Is that how he…?' Bella felt herself flinch as the image of Julien Moreau's scarred flesh came back to her. 'His hands?'

'Yes.'

Olivier moved away. His voice was a harsh rasp.

Broken glass crunched beneath the soles of Bella's boots as she took a few hesitant steps forward. At first glance the place looked completely derelict, but she noticed several indications that it was still used. There was a low bed or couch, covered by what looked like an old crimson velvet curtain, a wooden stool on which stood an empty wine bottle and a smeared glass, a damp-spotted mirror, and in the corner an easel, and a table scattered with brushes and tubes of paint.

Olivier was crouching in front of a small fireplace, coaxing a fire from a handful of dry wood, and Bella watched, transfixed as his big, capable hands hovered over the flames, shielding them from the draught, nurturing them until they took on an exuberant life of their own.

Like me, she thought. *Like he did to me the first time he kissed me.*

'Was this where he painted her?' she said in a low voice. 'My grandmother?'

'*Oui*. This was where he painted *La Dame de la Croix*.' Olivier straightened up and came to stand in front of her. 'It's one of his finest paintings. Most of the other up-and-coming portrait artists of the time were interested in pushing the boundaries, experimenting with texture and colour, and the results now seem quite…dated. Julien's approach was more in the tradition of Ingres or Courbet…more…luscious.'

Bella found herself mesmerised by his quiet, conversational tone, so that when his fingers found the tie of her cardigan and slowly pulled it undone she was unready. A small gasp escaped her.

He pulled back. 'Do you want me to show you how it was?' There was an edge of despair in his voice.

'Yes.'

'Then you have to trust me.' He hesitated for a heartbeat, and said bleakly. 'I *want* you to trust me.'

He was challenging her. She let her gaze move across his mouth, his beautiful mouth, and then looked slowly up into his eyes. They were fathomless pools in which her whole world seemed to spin. A dark chasm of need sucked at her and she knew she was lost.

'I trust you,' she whispered.

'Good.'

Time seemed to hitch and falter as he slid the cardigan off her shoulders. Longing shuddered through her, and she was aware of her fingers curling helplessly into fists. His eyes flickered downwards, over her shoulders, down across her breasts, while his exquisite face remained impassive. With one quick movement he unfastened her skirt, and it fell to the floor in a whisper of velvet. Then he turned away.

Bella didn't move.

He was standing by the easel with his back to her, his head bent. She remembered the painting in the gallery, Olympia on her silken bed with her level, knowing gaze. Heat throbbed and pulsed through her, and she waited.

He turned back towards her, and with a dart of piercing relief she saw the fierce blaze of desire in his eyes.

She made to move, aware that she was still wearing her underwear—tiny black lace knickers and a black bra, black hold-up stockings and her boots—but he said harshly, 'No.'

She stopped.

'Don't take anything more off.'

Olivier clenched his teeth. She was unreasonably beautiful. Looking at her was almost more than he could bear. If she undressed completely the self-control that was the foundation of his whole life would simply implode.

He needed to do this now. Needed to show her in a way that was more powerful than words what had happened all those years ago, and how wrongly Philippe Delacroix had presented it to her. The thought of him making it seem…meaningless, tawdry…crucified him. Bella deserved to know the truth.

Taking her fingers in his, touching her as little as possible, he led her to the velvet-covered couch and motioned for her to lie down.

Her eyes shimmered up at him, the desire in them naked and unashamed. Unquestioningly she settled herself on the couch, stretching out her long, long legs in their knee-high boots, drawing one knee up slightly, propping her head on her elbow. For a moment he gazed down at her body mutely, then crossed the small space to where the paints lay scattered on the table.

The image of Genevieve Lawrence in the painting rose up in front of him mockingly, her creamy skin brought to life beneath his father's sensuous brush, the jewelled cross lying warm and heavy on her naked breast. Quickly he squeezed smudges of thick watercolour onto a chipped china plate and picked up a jar of water, a long sable brush.

She made a small whimper as he stood over her, and he knew that it was the sound of raw longing. He knew it because he felt it too, but the darkness in the heart of him that had driven them for all these years dictated that he couldn't give in to it.

Not yet. There were too many ghosts crowding in the dark around them.

Frowning with concentration, he knelt in front of her. In the glow of the fire and the candles her pale skin shone like pearl. He registered the slight widening of her eyes as he dipped the brush in the water and tapped it against the side of the jar, but her gaze didn't waver.

As the sable brush touched the quivering skin on the slope of her neck she gave a small, shivering gasp. Olivier was aware of her tipping her head back, her fingers twisting in the red velvet as he bent over her, stroking the brush downwards over her collarbone, painting a ribbon of red onto her bare skin.

He didn't look up into her face, not trusting himself to resist the tormenting temptation of her ripe mouth, the open invitation in her lustrous eyes. Biting the insides of his cheeks to stop his focus from wandering, he kept his narrowed eyes fixed on the ivory silk of her skin and the image that blossomed there under the careful strokes of his brush.

The silence deepened, broken only by the soft gasp of her

breath. The fire was hot on his back as he worked, and at one point he threw down the brush, impatiently pulling his shirt from his belt and tearing open the buttons.

He heard her stifled moan.

It almost drove him over the edge, but he forced himself to go on, scowling now with the effort to keep the brush steady in his hand. Her chest was rising and falling hard, the creamy swell of her breast spilling over the black silk of her bra, and shivering beneath each caressing stroke of colour. The soft jasmine scent of her skin was almost unbearably enticing.

Focus. *Concentrate*.

In a small, writhing movement she shifted her legs, sliding one down over the other so the leather of her boots creaked quietly. He could feel a muscle in his jaw flickering with tension and savage, screaming want. He pushed the hair back from his face and plunged the brush into the water, wiping it impatiently on the trailing tails of his shirt before dipping it into the white paint. Nearly there. The movements his brush made now were gossamer touches, highlighting the jewel-bright hues.

At last he threw the brush down and got up, standing back to look down on her. A drowsy, languorous arousal lay over her like a veil. Her delicious, indolent beauty, now so reminiscent of the girl in the picture, was a knife in his side. He picked up the mirror that was propped against the wall behind the easel and, moving towards her, wordlessly held it up.

She lifted her head. Her eyes, opaque with desire, were almost hidden beneath the sweep of her dark lashes as she looked at what he had done.

'Ohh…'

It was a low, breathless exhalation of awe.

The candlelit reflection was of a goddess in a Renaissance painting. Lying back on the velvet couch, her head propped up on one hand, it seemed for all the world as if she wore a heavy, jewelled cross of gold and diamond and rubies on a crumpled length of crimson ribbon around her neck. It nestled between her breasts, resting slightly crookedly on the swell of her cleavage above her bra.

'So this is what it looks like?' she said haltingly.

Olivier nodded. He watched her exhale slowly and tip her head back, letting her liquid gaze linger hungrily on her own reflection. In that moment it was as if he had breathed life into the woman in the painting, and she was *La Dame de la Croix*— the mythical woman who had haunted and teased him and eluded him for so many years. He felt dizzy.

'Is it...exactly like this?' she asked softly.

'No.' His voice almost cracked. 'In the painting she wasn't wearing underwear.'

He wasn't looking at her, gazing instead into the depths of the shadows beyond her as he held out the mirror. Bella rose up from the couch in one sinuous, catlike movement and unhooked her bra, then slid her silk knickers down. The sound of her unzipping her boots stretched Olivier's last reserves of control to breaking point.

'Like this?'

She lay back on the bed again and looked up at him.

Slowly his gaze travelled over her.

'*La Dame de la Croix,*' he drawled quietly. 'Her hair was different...but otherwise you're very like her. Except for one thing...'

He put the mirror down and crossed the room to her. Bending down, he caught her chin between his fingers and captured her mouth with his, kissing her with all the pent-up fury and longing and frustration of the past hour and day and weeks. And then he tore his mouth away and stood back.

'Like that,' he said hoarsely, holding up the mirror for her again. 'Just like that.'

Heavy lidded, dazed, glittering, Bella's own reflected eyes looked back at her, and she knew that she had never felt more beautiful or more desirable. She was Olympia, but a thousand times more vibrant, a million times more sensual. She glowed with life and sex.

And suddenly, as if she were there, standing in the shadows and watching her own self, Genevieve's voice came back to her. *'Don't make the same mistake that I made.'*

Genevieve had loved the man who had painted her like that, and her family had made her give him up. The scattered pieces of the jigsaw slid into place.

'I see now how it was,' she said with quiet amazement. 'I *see*.'

Dazzled, she looked up into Olivier's face and saw the deep lines etched between his brows, the despair that gleamed in the depths of his eyes. The guttering candles cast deep shadows into the hollows of his cheeks and she reached out and stroked her fingers along one high cheekbone.

Gently, tenderly her lips brushed his cheek. His head fell back and she felt his low, hissing moan of anguish against her neck as he gathered her into his arms and pulled her roughly to his chest. Crushed against him, rocked by the urgency of his shuddering desire and unhinged by the strength of her own aching want, she fumbled with stiff fingers at his belt.

Triumph and annihilating despair mingled as Olivier gazed down on her luscious breasts, with the crumpled velvet ribbon holding the jewelled cross seeming to fall across them. He had got it right, he thought blackly. Just right.

His eyes met her blue Delacroix eyes, filled with hot, blatant need.

It was everything that he'd planned.

So why did he feel as if his heart had been torn out of him and thrown into the fire?

With sudden violence he seized her shoulders and covered

her mouth with his, and her instant leaping response was like fuel to the flames that consumed him. Swiftly she finished un-buttoning his jeans and pushed them roughly down over his hips so he felt the agonising relief of his aching arousal being freed from the confines of the unyielding fabric. He kicked them off. Her breath was hot against his ear, her hands grazed his waist, his midriff, and then finally closed around the pulsing heat of his erection.

He shouted his pleasure and his anguish into the muffling softness of her hair.

He could feel the throb and pulse of her silken body in his arms. Lying her down, he moved his hands down her ribs, across the quivering tautness of her stomach, then down... She bucked and gasped, and then went still and utterly silent as his fingers found the slippery heat beneath.

The world slowed and stretched. There was nothing but can-dlelight and bare skin and shuddering, shattering feeling. Heat exploded inside her under the delicate, insistent circling of his finger on what felt like the throbbing centre of her, and she felt as if he was touching her soul. The points of light made by the candles split into spiky, shimmering stars which seemed to ripple and sway as if they were lit beneath water.

And then they all seemed to converge into one dazzling ball of light, which gathered and pulsed and then split into a thousand glittering fragments as she felt herself shatter.

'Olivier...*now*. *Now*. I need you *now*... I can't wait any more. I *can't*...'

She was exquisite. Perfect. Helpless, engulfing need crashed through him as he folded her against his body and their hip bones clashed and ground together. Suddenly he wanted her cries of ecstasy to drown out the accusing voices in his head, the intense, focused urgency in her eyes to obliterate the ghosts of the past.

His mouth found hers and plundered it as they tumbled off

the low couch, pulling half of the velvet curtain with them. Holding her above him so he could see her face, Olivier pushed into her, hard, as he rolled onto the floor.

Pain ripped through him, sudden and shocking, as his bare back ground against the broken glass scattered on the wooden boards. Above him, wild and tousled and hopelessly beautiful, Bella writhed, her undulating hips sending screaming tremors of ecstasy through his body, so that they mingled with the searing agony of his tearing flesh.

Every thrust was torturous rapture.

His hands held her waist, and suddenly he felt her still beneath them. Then a violent shudder of bliss rocked her. Suddenly oblivious to the pain, he stopped fighting and gave himself up to glorious, thundering release. She fell forward, her hair caressing his face as she slid downwards and came to rest with her head on his chest.

The sweat cooled on their bodies as they both lay there, shuddering, gasping, shocked beyond words by the enormity of what had just happened. Gradually the frantic rhythm of their breathing slowed again, and she pressed her lips to his chest and murmured against the heated skin.

'I understand now. Thank you for making me see.'

She lifted her head and looked into his eyes for a moment before letting her head sink down again. Her voice was drowsy and infinitely soft.

'You were right. *La Dame de la Croix* isn't about hate. It never was. The picture was about love.'

CHAPTER ELEVEN

LOVE.

She was lying on top of him, her legs still straddling him, her hip bones still resting on his. Her cheek lay against his chest and beneath it he felt his heart seem to stop for a moment.

It was all about love.

Adrenalin rushed through him, and he sucked in a breath. He felt suddenly disorientated and light-headed. That was what he had wanted to make her see when he'd brought her down here, that was exactly what he'd been trying to prove, and yet he'd never actually *felt* that before. To him *La Dame de la Croix* was about power and tyranny, and since he'd had it in his possession he had not thought once about *love*.

He'd thought about revenge. That was the emotion that had brought him here, to this dark place with this girl with skin like velvet and eyes like midnight skies swimming with stars.

He had let himself become as bad as they were. As cold, as ruthless, as morally bankrupt. And the bitterest irony was that in doing so he had only proved them right. Fifty years ago the Delacroix family had thought that Julien Moreau was not good enough for their noble daughter, and that humiliation had driven Olivier to succeed.

And he had. Excessively.

But the cold, hard truth that had dawned on him just now was that he still wasn't good enough for Bella Lawrence, and he never would be.

She stirred. Raising herself up, she slid off his hips and came to rest beside him so she was looking into his face. Into him.

'You didn't tell me you were an artist too.'

'I'm not.' His voice was oddly flat, but Bella picked up a faint note of irony. 'I'm a city boy, remember?'

She pressed her lips against his warm skin and smiled. 'How could I forget? But the question is why a man with a talent like yours spends his life wearing a suit and sitting in boardrooms talking about money?'

She felt his muscles bunch and flex as he sat up stiffly. For the briefest second an expression of intense pain flickered across his face, but it was so quickly suppressed that she couldn't be sure she hadn't imagined it.

'If you knew how much I earned you wouldn't have to ask,' he said gruffly, moving so his back was against the couch, and reaching across for his shirt.

'Yes, I would,' she said quietly as the smile slowly faded from her face. 'Giving up what you care about—even if it is to earn millions—is like selling a bit of yourself.' Absently she caressed the painted cross with the tip of her finger, shivering slightly as she remembered the feel of his eyes on her, the whisper of his breath as he'd bent over her. 'You don't strike me as the kind of person to sell out, for any amount of money.'

Her words were like tiny darts that pierced his undefended heart. Wincing, Olivier got to his feet and bent to pick up the rest of their scattered clothes.

'I didn't "sell out". I decided to go into finance for a number of reasons.' He handed Bella her skirt without looking at her. 'Not just because I'm a shallow, emotionally bankrupt bastard.'

Still sitting on the floor, her legs tucked beneath her on the velvet curtain, Bella bit her lip. 'I'm sorry, Olivier. I shouldn't have said all that this morning.'

'Forget it. It doesn't matter.'

The terrible resignation in his voice sent shivers down her spine, but she couldn't leave it at that. She remembered the night of Genevieve's party, when he had danced with her in the quiet street and she had yearned to reach the man beneath the perfect mask. She recalled the sterile sophistication of his apartment and how, despite all that had happened between them there, she had felt more isolated from him than ever. Here, in this dark and broken place, she was seeing him. The *real* man behind the chilly self-assurance and the trappings of success.

She hesitated. 'Was your father disappointed that you didn't choose to pursue your art?'

'My father has no idea that I can even draw a straight line,' he said harshly.

Bella stopped in the middle of rolling one stocking up her leg. 'What do you mean?'

'I made sure he never knew. I never showed him anything I'd done. There was an art teacher at school who was very keen to encourage me, and found out all about fine art degree courses and wanted me to take exams, so in the end I just stopped going to lessons. I haven't painted anything since.' There was a matter-of-fact flatness to his voice, but as he did up his belt his hands moved sharply, viciously. 'Julien never knew I was remotely interested in art.'

Bella's throat was full of sand. 'Olivier, why?'

'Why do you think? He was a brilliant, talented artist, who in time would have undoubtedly become one of the geniuses of his generation. It was his whole life, and he lost it in the fire. How could I make him watch me achieve the things he never had a chance to?'

Bella stood up. Her heart was hammering painfully against

her chest as if it was trying to break out. Sudden, unexpected tears had gathered in her eyes and her face felt stiff with the effort of not letting them fall.

'So you channelled all your energy, all your brilliance, into making yourself a success in other ways, to make up for what you'd sacrificed for him?'

'Something like that.'

Olivier couldn't quite keep the bitterness from his voice, and he hated himself for it. Hated himself for having to lie to her, but the truth was too cruel. He'd channelled his energy into making himself a success to prove to *her* family that he was someone. To make himself every bit as powerful and wealthy as they were. To make sure that one day he could make them pay for what they'd done.

And now that time had come.

'Tell me about the fire,' she prompted softly.

Olivier felt his mouth go dry, and for a moment squeezed his eyes shut as her words seemed to hang in front of him, taunting and teasing.

Go on... Tell her, a voice inside him mocked. *Tell her about how it was started deliberately by Philippe Delacroix, that it was her own flesh and blood that knowingly, cold-bloodedly stripped Julien Moreau of everything. That's what you've wanted all this time, isn't it? To confront them with what they did?*

'There's nothing to tell,' he said harshly. 'It happened before I was born. Julien had been working for a huge exhibition in Paris's most prestigious gallery, and all his work was lost.'

'And his hands were so damaged he couldn't work again...?'

Olivier braced himself against the gentle compassion in her voice, but it seemed to curl itself around him, caressing him. He was powerless to resist.

'Yes. He went in, you see. He went in to get the only painting that mattered.' *The one painting that Philippe had wanted to destroy.*

'La Dame de la Croix.'
'Yes.'

Silently Bella came up behind him, sliding her arms around his waist and laying her cheek between his shoulders. Before he could bite it back, a low, sharp hiss of pain escaped him.

She stood back, her arms falling to her sides. When she spoke, the hurt in her voice made the pain in his back fade into insignificance.

'What's wrong?'

Slowly he shook his head. 'Nothing. Nothing's wrong.'

There was a certain poetry in it, he thought blackly. A pleasing symmetry and justice. He had set out with the intention of seducing her, of sleeping with her, purely to hurt her. That was what he had wanted the first time, back in London. Now his own pain was his punishment for that.

He was almost glad of it.

Outside it was raining.

The sky was a dark pewter colour, but the strange yellow light from the low sun persisted, and a lurid rainbow soared over the trees. The rain had stripped the branches further so they seemed to shiver in the half-light, and the broken surface of the river was choked with yellowing leaves.

Bella blinked and tipped her head back, letting the rain fall onto her flushed cheeks. After so long in secret darkness, suspended from the realities of time, it seemed bizarre that it should still be daylight, and she felt as she'd used to when she was a teenager, emerging into the noise and commotion of the street after two blissful hours of romantic fantasy in the dark of the cinema.

How she'd adored the cinema. It had been a legitimate outlet for all of the wild, passionate emotions that were so forbidden by the Lawrences. But now, stumbling out into the unearthly afternoon light and taking in a lungful of cool autumn air, she felt almost free of those bonds.

Olivier slid a hand around her neck, hooking her towards him, and her stomach tightened in a spasm of remembered pleasure. Getting dressed, putting on the armour of their clothes had created a little distance between them again, but a shiver rippled along the length of her spine as she thought of his body beneath them.

For all these years she had put herself last, swallowing the family line about duty and obedience, unquestioningly sacrificing her own freedom in order that nothing should cloud the mirror-shiny surface of the Lawrence–Delacroix family honour. She'd been a good girl for a long time, and now she was taking her reward.

And anyway, from this distance her family didn't seem so powerful or so frightening. Philippe Delacroix had been so twisted and embittered when he'd spoken of Julien Moreau, to the point where he had seemed pathetic, shut up all alone in that big empty museum of a house, still obsessed with events which were nothing but history.

She pitied him.

In fact, as Olivier gathered her into the shelter of his body, looking down at her with that inscrutable, appraising expression which drove her wild, she pitied anyone who wasn't her. And that, she realised, was a complete reversal of her normal outlook on life. All at once she was glad to be herself, rather than feeling the need to apologise for it.

'You have your top on inside out,' Olivier murmured gravely, close to her ear.

She felt a smile spread across her mouth as the heat spread downwards through her body. 'Who cares? I'm going to take it off again as soon as we get back to the house.'

'Is that a promise?'

Heat flared in his dark, faintly shadowed eyes and the smile died on her lips. Slowly, she ran her tongue over them, taking a step or two backwards and gazing up at him in unconcealed desire. His hair was dark with rain, one curl falling across his tanned forehead, and he brushed it back with his hand, momentarily compressing his lips against the rain that was running down his beautiful face.

Her senses kicked into overdrive.

This was what Miles and the expensive therapist had cautioned against. This wild, dizzying rush of joy and panic… But Bella knew it was what she had been born for. What she had been unconsciously craving all her life. Again Genevieve's words came back to her, and she knew that her grandmother had been right.

You have talent for loving…for giving…

There was so much she was just beginning to understand. She looked up into Olivier's face. The surreal acid-yellow light highlighted the two deep creases etched between his brows, and she brought her fingers up to his face, cupping her palm against his cheek.

'I've learned a lot this afternoon,' she said softly. 'You've helped me make sense of some of it.'

Painfully he shrugged off his coat, and gave her a crooked smile. 'It was my pleasure.'

He wrapped the coat around her, holding it firmly beneath her chin, and pulled her towards him. For a second he held her close against the shelter of his chest as he pressed his lips to her wet forehead. 'I've learned some things too…'

She sprang backwards suddenly, clamping her hand across her mouth and looking up at him in wide-eyed horror, and for a sickening moment he wondered if she'd guessed what he'd been thinking.

'Oh, no,' she wailed. 'Oh, God…'

Olivier's blood ran cold. 'What is it?'

Bella was already running ahead of him, clutching his coat around her, but as she ran she called back over her shoulder. 'The car! Celia's car! I left the top down!'

Olivier let his head roll back in relief. The car was easily put right. He'd replace it if necessary. Everything else was going to take a bit more unravelling.

Feeling his torn shoulders stinging as the rain soaked his shirt, he followed her thoughtfully, stopping to pick some huge, dark-gilled mushrooms from the base of a tree. He could see her up ahead, leaning into the car, her endless legs in their high boots the only part of her that was visible. His stomach flipped.

Dieu, but she was gorgeous. Vibrant and sexy and beautiful, with no trace left of the chilly dullness that she had worn like a shroud that first day in London. As he approached she was just getting gingerly into the soaking driver's seat. Starting up the wheezing, spluttering engine, she looked up at him with a smile that spread through his body like wildfire.

'Just when I thought my pants couldn't get any wetter…'

He'd vowed not to let her leave him a third time, and yet as he stood there and watched her drive off he felt no anger.

This time it was much more complicated.

Bella couldn't remember anything about the short drive back to the mill, apart from the tingling awareness of Olivier in the car behind her. Her body felt hollowed out, purged, blessed—as if she'd been through some elemental ritual or some baptismal fire and emerged cleaner, brighter, better.

Alive again.

She was herself. Maybe for the first time ever. She was simply a girl with a passion for life and a talent for love. And she was *proud* of that.

She glanced into the small rearview mirror of the MG and caught a glimpse of Olivier's face through the windscreen of the

Aston Martin behind her. It was utterly blank, completely inscrutable, but she felt fireworks of joy explode inside her. She
understood him now. Beneath the mask, beneath the expensive
suits, the beautiful shirts, she had seen the real man.

'Come on.'

With a little start of surprise she realised that they were back
at the mill, and that she had automatically stopped the car and
was sitting, lost in thought, with the engine still running. Olivier
leaned down and turned the ignition off, then opened the door
and held out his hand.

She took it and got up hesitantly. Her skirt was sodden from
the puddle of rainwater on the seat, and it stuck to her thighs.

Olivier raised an eyebrow. 'You're wet.'

Bella felt her breath catch in her throat. 'Yes,' she murmured,
as a smile blossomed on her lips. 'Very. I have to get dried off.'

Slowly, without smiling, he shook his head. 'Don't bother.'

Rain was dripping from the ends of her hair, running down
inside the turned-up collar of the coat he had wrapped around
her. It cloaked her in warmth and in his exquisite, unique scent.
The scent of his skin. Of him.

She felt her insides tremble.

'You're right,' she said huskily. 'No point.'

For a long moment they gazed at each other, and then wordlessly
he scooped her up into his arms and carried her into the house.

He shouldered open the door to the bedroom at the top of the
stairs and set her gently on her feet. Her skin flamed and fizzed,
hot and wet. She staggered very slightly as her knees refused to
take her own weight, and reached up to hold his shoulders as she
tilted her face up to kiss him. As she did so she saw him wince,
and pulled back.

'Get undressed,' he said hoarsely, stepping backwards. His
eyes were coal-black and impossible to read.

'Where are you going?'

'To run a bath.'

Left alone, Bella peeled the wet clothes off her hungry body and stood naked in the centre of the room. Her skin felt paper-thin, burning and glowing—like beaten gold.

Fiery and beautiful.

He had seen those qualities in her, even when she herself hadn't known they were there. Or maybe she had known, but had been ashamed of them. Hazily she looked up, catching sight of her own reflection in the fly-blown glass of the old dressing table mirror. Even in its murky depths the painted Delacroix cross seemed to gleam. Her eyes had a hectic, ravenous glitter and her lips were ruby dark. Engorged, like her other secret self…

Olivier appeared behind her. Their gazes locked.

She watched him place his hands on her shoulders, feeling waves of fresh heat ripple and billow through her at his touch. His thumbs massaged the base of her neck in lazy circles and a drop of rainwater fell from her sleek, wet hair and ran down her collar-bone, making the red of the painted ribbon run down, like blood.

Bella took a tiny, shivering inward breath.

'It's so perfect,' she murmured raggedly. 'I can't bear to spoil it.'

In the mirror she watched his eyes move slowly down over her quivering body with that deadpan detachment which made her heart race and liquid warmth flood into her pelvis. As they came back up to her face she caught the spark in their depths. 'Then allow me…'

He parted his lips and sucked the ball of his thumb before cupping her breast in the palm of his hand and sweeping his thumb across the jewelled cross, smudging the paint into a muddied streak.

She gasped.

'It's part of the past,' he said harshly.

In one fluid movement she was back in his arms, and he was carrying her along the corridor to the bathroom.

The high ceiling and grey-green walls of the large room were lost in swirling clouds of steam which curled around them, warm and languid, creating a secret world of blurred edges and dissolving colours. The sky beyond the frosted windows had darkened to a smoky blue, and the room was softly lit by an ancient, glass-shaded brass sconce on the wall, around which the steam made a halo of gold.

On the windowsill was a bottle of Muscadet, cool and green and moisture-beaded, and two glasses. Bella smiled. 'You think of everything.'

'Get in.'

She shook her head. 'Uh-uh. Not without you.'

Her hands went to the buttons of his paint-stained shirt, and with great concentration she began to undo them. Olivier stood, rock-like and motionless, his face stony as she gradually revealed the tanned expanse of his chest. When she reached the last one, she tugged the shirt free of his trousers and slipped it off his shoulders.

An expression of extreme suffering flickered across his face. It lasted no more than a fraction of a second, but Bella saw it before he could hide it behind his habitual inscrutable mask.

'Olivier?' she whispered.

He didn't move, didn't speak. Slowly, trailing her fingers across his hard chest she moved round so she was standing behind him.

The sound she made was somewhere between a groan and a sigh. 'My God. *My God*, Olivier.'

His shoulders were broad and phenomenally strong, tapering down to narrow hips, but the tanned skin was a mess of shallow cuts and drying blood.

Reverently she brushed her fingertips over them, remembering in a flash of anguished insight the crunch of glass beneath her boots as she crossed the boathouse floor.

'The glass—why didn't you say?'

Beneath her fingers she felt his muscles flex as he raised his shoulders in a small shrug.

'Stopping would have been much more painful,' he said hoarsely.

Bella felt raw with tenderness and ripe with longing. Her nipples, just inches from Olivier's back, stiffened and throbbed, and slick heat drenched her from within. She pressed her swollen lips to the torn skin and slid her arms around his waist. Still he did not move.

But as her fingers skimmed across his flat stomach she felt the muscles quiver and tighten, and just inching downwards a little she met the hard thrust of his erection.

A tremor ricocheted through his tense body.

It was all she needed to tip her over the edge of control. Without thinking, she found her hands were on the buckle of his belt, fumbling blindly with it as her mouth caressed and licked and explored the hard width of his shoulders. His hands were on hers, doing with ruthless efficiency what she was too dazed with desire to do properly, and the next thing she knew he had turned round and was scooping her into his arms as his lips came down on hers in a deep, devouring kiss.

He set her down gently in the steaming water, and got in behind her. In a delicious torpor of lust Bella slid down into the heat, and, tipping her head back, found his mouth again, darting out her tongue and caressing his lips in the lightest, the most promising of kisses. Lying against him, she could feel the hardness of his erection pressing into the small of her back, and for delicious moments arched herself against it, savouring the anticipation of feeling him inside her. Then lithely she flipped herself over and slipped beneath the water.

The clear greenish world she found herself in echoed with the throbbing of blood in her ears. His hard flesh felt almost cool in the heat of the water as she let her lips close over him, and ecstasy flooded her.

Long moments later she broke the surface, gasping for breath, her long eyelashes clogged with water. Like a mermaid, thought Olivier fiercely, clinging onto reason by a thread as he slid his hands beneath her arms and hauled her slippery, glistening, gorgeous body upwards in a shower of water, and then moved round so she was beneath him.

She wrapped her legs around him, pulling him onto her, and he entered her with a single hard thrust, sending a tidal wave of water crashing over the side of the bath. Gazing down into her unfocused, melting eyes was almost enough to bring him to a shuddering climax, even without the ravenous bliss of her slippery wetness around him, gripping him. He dropped his head to her breast, hearing her wild moan close to his ear as he took her deep pink nipple in his mouth.

The water slapped and sucked around them as they moved together, so deeply connected that it was impossible to tell where each of them ended and the other began. Bella's face was flushed and hazy with desire, but perfectly composed as she looked steadily, helplessly up at him. Her fingers tangled and twisted in his hair, and then suddenly let go. She lifted her arms above her head, stretching and arching, and then brought them down again to grip the iron-hard strength of his upper arms, anchoring herself as shockwaves of rapture shook her.

She clung to him in the aftermath, and Olivier buried his face in her damp neck and surrendered control. As he sank down on top of her he had the strangest sensation of having come home.

Afterwards, they lay back in the water and drank cold Muscadet from misted glasses as their pulses slowed and the darkness beyond the steamed-up window deepened. Reality had faded to a distant blur, and the future, other people, and ordinary things like work and routine were remote and incomprehensible.

Olivier's arm cradled her, holding her, his thumb gently

stroking her hand, her wrist. Feeling the thin ridge of scar tissue on the paper-fine skin, he lifted her hand in a shower of crystal droplets and looked at the pinkish scar, then pressed his lips against it.

Neither of them spoke. It was as if a fragile enchantment lay on the gentle, soft-edged world and neither of them wanted to break it.

CHAPTER TWELVE

OLIVIER stared detachedly at his BlackBerry.

For the first time ever the numbers didn't automatically make sense, and he found himself frowning, trying to process the information in front of him. In his business billions could be made or lost in the blink of an eye; he'd been out of touch with the markets for too long, and a lot had happened since he'd last checked that morning.

Not only in the financial world.

With an impatient sigh he scrolled through again, forcing his mind back into the familiar zone and laboriously checking the columns of figures. Nothing was amiss, the markets were all reasonably good. He'd taken his hand from the controls for a while, but things hadn't crashed and burned without him.

This time.

He couldn't afford to do it again. Fund management wasn't for part-timers, or people whose priorities were elsewhere. That was why he'd always been so good at it—because making money had always been his only goal.

It was what drove him. The need to escape from all this, and to prove himself. Make himself.

He set his BlackBerry down and looked around the low, lamp-lit kitchen. The scent of woodsmoke drifted in from the fire he had lit in the sitting room beyond, and steam misted the windows, hiding the darkness of the chilly night outside behind a diaphanous veil of silver. Upstairs he could hear the ancient floorboards creak softly as Bella moved about.

It was a world away from the sleek efficiency of the Park Lane apartment, or the opulent comforts of the villas he owned in St Tropez and Mustique, where he took whichever woman was currently top of his speed-dial list for a week of sex and sun whenever he felt like it.

Which wasn't that often. The women always resented the time he spent working, and he resented the time when he wasn't. They always seemed to expect something more than was on offer, and their flattery and suffocating affection, in such close quarters and without any distraction, grated on his nerves.

Because, he realised with a wrench, neither seemed to be related at all to him. Those women hadn't even glimpsed the real him, but had fallen in love with the monster he'd created; the hard-working, hard-hearted man who paid, paid, paid but gave nothing that mattered. Nothing of himself.

They were worshipping a cardboard cut-out. An effigy.

He scooped up the handful of mushrooms he'd picked earlier on the way back from the boathouse and unhooked a knife from beside the range. Its handle was wooden, worn smooth with age, but it fitted his hand in a way that the expensive, state-of-the-art titanium and steel ones in his own kitchen didn't. As far as he could remember, anyway. He couldn't recall the last time he had used one, or cooked anything more than just an omelette.

And he knew then that he hadn't made it at all. He'd lost himself. Lost touch with his roots and the person he was in some hollow quest for status and power. He'd denied and despised his background, and he'd subconsciously surrounded himself with people who would feel the same. For a moment he imagined bringing one of those other women here, where there was no plunge pool or home cinema… No steam room or in-house chef…

The idea was so unimaginably preposterous it was laughable.

'You're cooking?'

He looked up. Bella was standing in the doorway, her dark hair slicked back, her skin still dewy and flushed from the bath, and from their delicious lovemaking. She was wearing a grey T-shirt of Olivier's, which fell to mid-thigh, and the rest of her long, honey-coloured legs were gloriously bare.

Olivier felt his heart skip. Which was odd, he thought sardonically. Traditionally his response to a beautiful girl wearing hardly anything would have been a lot less poetic.

'You sound surprised,' he said dryly. Not entirely fairly, either, considering he'd just been thinking himself that it was pretty unusual these days.

She came to stand beside him. She didn't touch him, but he could feel his skin tingle in anticipation, almost as if it were willing her to.

She smiled. 'Impressed.' She picked up one of the big, dark-gilled mushrooms, and he watched as she stroked her fingers over its domed cap, then lifted it up to her nose and breathed in. Its damp softness and the musky, earthy scent that clung to it was unbearably sensual. Olivier had to turn away, clenching his jaw and picking up the knife to stop him sliding his hands beneath her T-shirt and having her again, right there on the floor.

'I can't believe that on top of all your other amazing talents you can cook as well.'

His voice was brusque as he began to slice the mushrooms with ruthless focus. 'When I was growing up it was a case of cook or starve. Julien wasn't very domesticated.'

'What about your mother?'

The knife stilled for a second. 'She left when I was about two.'

The steel in his voice made Bella wince. She longed to reach out to him, but his unsmiling self-possession didn't invite sympathy. She leaned against the table and looked down. 'Oh. I'm sorry, I shouldn't have asked. You don't have to talk about it.'

He swept the mushrooms into a frying pan, where almost immediately they began to soften and wilt. 'No big deal. She was doing an art history postgraduate course in Paris. She'd read about my father's work and decided to do her final year dissertation on him. She came here to see him. It was such a long time since he'd given up painting properly, and I imagine it was fairly bleak for him, so I suppose the attention flattered him—especially as she was so interested in his work. She tracked down quite a lot of the paintings he'd sold before the fire, and was interested in getting an exhibition for him, but all that came to nothing when she got pregnant.'

He paused and poured wine into the pan which hissed and sizzled, releasing a cloud of fragrant steam. Bella, silently aching for him, didn't dare speak.

'It was doomed from the start. I think she thought she could heal him and make him love her, but there was never any chance of that.'

'Why not?'

The steady, rhythmic motion of the spoon didn't falter as it turned over glossy pearls of rice in the pan. 'Because he was still in love with Genevieve. No one else would ever come close. He saw in my mother an opportunity to deaden the loneliness for a while, I suppose.' Olivier glanced up at her and gave a twisted half-smile. 'He used her. But he certainly ended up paying the price.'

'What do you mean?'

'She left, and he ended up with a child he never wanted from a woman he didn't love.'

The bland words, spoken so nonchalantly, gave Bella an insight into the bleak emotional landscape of Olivier's childhood. She shivered. She'd been so quick to jump to conclusions, so damning in her accusations that he'd neglected his father, when maybe the real story was quite the reverse.

'But your father must have loved you?' she said uncertainly. 'If he was lonely, a child must have been such a blessing. Were you never close?'

'I don't think he had much love left for anything after Genevieve Delacroix. His love for her was…total. That's why he stayed here.'

'In case she came back?'

'Partly that. Partly because he didn't want it to seem in any way like he had anything to be ashamed of.'

'In what way?'

'You believed what your uncle said, didn't you? That he'd tried to blackmail them and bring shame upon them. He knew that if he left it would look like he was guilty, that those rumours that they put around were true. So he stayed.'

'That must have taken courage,' Bella said in a small voice. 'Such a lot of courage, to stay when they had made it deliberately hard to do so.'

Olivier frowned. He'd never thought of it like that. To him, his father's passive acceptance of the situation, his tacit martyrdom, had always seemed like the ultimate act of submission. He had thought that by choosing to leave he was the courageous one.

But he'd just been running away—from the past and his problems and himself. He had been so focused on making himself as 'good' as the Delacroixes that he'd overlooked his father's far more genuine goodness.

He could see now how wrong he'd been.

'I'm so sorry, Olivier. It seems that my family have cast a long shadow over your life. I had no idea.'

'It doesn't matter any more. It's in the past.'

The words came out almost without him thinking about it. But the oddest thing was he thought he might believe them.

They ate sitting on the floor in front of the fire, in an atmosphere of quiet, bruised tenderness. Neither of them spoke much.

Bella set her plate down with a wistful sigh and leaned back against Julien's enormous old sofa. 'That was utterly delicious—thank you. I wouldn't even know where to start, especially with finding the mushrooms and everything. How do you know which ones are safe to eat?'

Olivier shrugged nonchalantly. 'I don't. I just guessed.'

Bella sat bolt-upright in horror. 'Oh, my God, Olivier—you didn't, did you? They could have been poisonous! I don't believe it—'

She stopped mid-sentence. In the glow of the fire she saw the lazy, heartbreakingly sexy smile that had spread across his face. 'You're teasing me, aren't you?' she said indignantly, leaning over to hit him playfully. 'You *do* know!'

'Of course. I grew up here, remember? You can take the boy out of rural Normandy and dress him in a suit,' he said sardonically. 'But can you ever really take rural Normandy out of the boy?'

She collapsed against him, and he moved his arm so she was lying with her head against his chest. It felt so good, so very, very good, that she was almost scared to move or breathe in case it broke the spell and he got up, or pushed her away.

'No. I don't think you can. The very first moment I saw you in that awful stuffy auction house I think that's what I sensed in you.'

'What? My peasant blood?' he said with heavy irony.

'No! Your…earthiness. Your barely concealed contempt for the bespoke suit and the silk tie. Later on I thought that you were a loner, but now I've seen where you come from I understand—that's not it. You're not a loner…you're self-sufficient. You can survive and adapt to anything, no matter what, and you don't need anyone else.'

There was a small pause. A log fell in the grate, and the wind rattled the ancient windows.

'Perhaps,' he said quietly, almost as if he wasn't aware he was speaking aloud.

Holding her against him, Olivier ran his other hand wearily

across his face, feeling the rasp of stubble against his palm, then he picked up her hand and closed his fingers around her wrist like a bracelet. In the firelight the scars were thin lines of silver on her golden skin, barely noticeable.

But he felt them.

'You're a survivor too.' His throat felt tight. 'Tell me what happened, Bella. What made you do this?'

She went very still for a moment, and then he felt the gentle rise and fall of her ribs as she sighed. 'Total bloody despair. And shame, and guilt, and humiliation...' She laughed softly. 'Shall I go on?'

'Yes. But first go back. To the beginning.'

Beneath his chin her hair felt like spun silk, and he could smell the delicate jasmine scent of her. She suddenly seemed so agonizingly, infinitely precious that he almost didn't want to hear what she was going to say because the thought of anyone hurting her crucified him.

'The beginning,' she said quietly. 'I'm not even sure where the beginning was. Not feeling that I belonged, I suppose. I've always known that I come from an important family—I remember seeing my grandfather's picture on the front of the newspaper when I was very little. But, unlike Miles, I wasn't really interested in why it was there. Miles was the clever one, the ambitious one. Compared to him I was a bitter disappointment.'

She lapsed into silence. Stroking her arm with his thumb, Olivier waited.

'Going to art school was the only thing I wanted to do,' she said after a while. 'I had to fight so hard for my parents to even consider it—they wanted me to do something *sensible*, but for the first time in my life I stood up to them. It was worth it. They made it clear that they had massive reservations, but eventually they agreed. God, I was so ecstatic.' He could hear the smile in her voice. 'I finally felt like I'd found myself. I had friends. I was living the life I wanted, doing something I was good at, and I was no longer in Miles's shadow. And then I met Dan Nightingale.'

The fragile joy that had shimmered in her voice was suddenly gone.

'He was doing a postgrad in printmaking and was one of those people that everyone knew. He was always surrounded by models and musicians, and doing glamorous, daring things. Out of nowhere he seemed to notice me—he just came up to me one afternoon as I was leaving the studio and asked me to go for a drink with him.'

'Inspired,' Olivier murmured scathingly, his fingers unconsciously tightening on her wrist as murderous loathing enveloped him.

'I was so flattered to be singled out like that. I guess because I'd stepped so far out of my family's sphere of influence it never crossed my mind that he would be aware of me as a *Lawrence*. I was ridiculously naïve, and a complete push-over. He was my f-first…proper boyfriend and I just fell for him completely. I thought he felt the same. I thought he was interested in me for *me*. And then…'

A convulsive tremor shook her whole body, and Olivier tightened his arm around her as if he could fend off the hurt. 'It was him, wasn't it?' His voice was almost a snarl. 'He was the one who took the photographs. Who made the prints.'

'How did you guess?' she said with bleak sarcasm. 'It turned out that he didn't care about me in the slightest, most insignificant bit. I was a means to an end—in this case a clever and controversial degree show exhibition—and he used me without a moment's hesitation. To him, like everyone else, I was a *name*. That's all. I was a *Lawrence*.' She gave a short gust of laughter. 'It was a valuable lesson. It made me confront the thing I'd been trying to deny all my life.'

'Which was?'

'That no matter how much I struggle to be myself and be seen as an individual I'm not. I'm someone's granddaughter, someone's daughter, someone's sister, first and foremost.'

Staring straight ahead into the fire, Olivier felt his jaw tense and his chest constrict. *No*, he wanted to say. *That's not true.* But the words lodged in his aching throat. How could he argue when he'd been guilty of seeing her like that himself?

'What I did was stupid. I know that now.' He couldn't see her face, but he felt her fingers twist into the front of his shirt. 'But I was so *hurt*—inside—and I think on some strange, confused level I wanted to bring that hurt out and make it visible, palpable. I don't remember much about it, except a mild surprise at the time that the sacred Lawrence blood looked much like anyone else's. And then Miles was there, and he…he took care of everything.'

The fire had burnt down, so that all that was left were white-hot embers, edged with coppery gold. They had been sitting there a long time. Olivier's torn back had stiffened, and when he flexed his shoulders he felt needles of agony pierce his flayed skin. He focused on the pain. His punishment.

His due.

'It seems I owe Miles an apology.' He spoke through clenched teeth. 'I was wrong about him.'

And just about everything else too.

Bella sighed. 'I know he's controlling and overbearing, but he worries about me. If it wasn't for him I wouldn't be here now.'

The flash of pain that sliced through Olivier as he bent to kiss the top of her head had nothing to do with his lacerated back.

'Then I owe him a thank-you, too,' he rasped.

Tipping his head back against the battered old sofa, he closed his eyes and picked his way through the ruins of everything he'd thought he knew or believed. Profound gratitude was not something he had ever expected to feel in relation to Miles Lawrence, but it was as if a cyclone had ripped through his head, laying waste to his entire mental landscape.

Instinctively he'd hated Dan Nightingale the moment he'd seen him with Bella in the Tate—that much was familiar. But the thing that killed him was that he was just as bad.

And he hated himself much, much more.

CHAPTER THIRTEEN

IN THE pale and glimmering light of early morning Bella woke, and instantly she knew that Olivier was gone. She struggled upright, frowning sleepily as she saw the space in the bed that still bore the imprint of his body, but the crumpled sheets—evidence of last night's quiet, intense passion—were cold.

She threw the covers back and got out of bed, feeling her heart start to hammer with nameless anguish. The house was filled with the hazy shadows of dawn so that everything seemed dissolving and insubstantial. It was as if someone had rubbed a finger over a charcoal drawing, blurring and smudging until there were no hard lines or angles.

'Olivier?'

It was barely more than a whisper, and the old walls absorbed it as she stood shivering at the top of the stairs, straining to hear in the silence some sound that would tell her he was there. None came. But then, looking up, she caught a glimpse of movement through a half-open door opposite.

On soft bare feet she approached. Standing at the window, Olivier was looking out at the blue-grey layers of mist that lay like veils over the fields. He was wearing jeans but his back was bare.

Suddenly she was reminded of the time in his apartment, when she had seen him silhouetted against the thousand brilliant, jewel-bright lights of London and had thought he looked so invincible, so wholly in command of it all. Now, just for a second, with the soft pearl-grey light of dawn falling on his shoulders, the lacerations on his back still painful and raw, she saw a nakedness and a vulnerability in him that took her breath away.

Without being conscious of deciding to do it, she found herself crossing the room to him, sliding her hands around his waist and folding herself around his body, echoing but reversing the position in which they'd finally fallen asleep last night.

'What are you doing?' she whispered.

'I have to go.'

Pressed against his back, she felt the deep rumble of his voice vibrate through her. But the closeness couldn't stop the chill from creeping into her when she heard those words, and the distant way in which he spoke them.

'Where?'

Gently, firmly, he disentangled himself from her embrace and turned so he was facing her. His face was blank, his dark eyes deeply shadowed.

'Paris. I have to see someone…about this.'

She watched him reach for what looked like a roll of stiff fabric from on top of a dusty chest of drawers. His expression didn't change as he unrolled it and spread it out in front of her.

La Dame de la Croix.

It was just as Olivier had shown her in the boathouse yesterday, and yet fundamentally different for being painted. Time stalled and logic faded, so that for the strangest moment she couldn't have said whether it was Genevieve's eyes or her own that gazed out from it so steadily, filled with quiet, triumphant repletion, with the Delacroix cross on its velvet ribbon resting crookedly on her breast.

'Oh, Olivier…it's magnificent,' she breathed. 'It's… *breathtaking.*'

'Yes,' he said simply.

'And it was lost for all these years. How wonderful that you found it and brought it back here.'

'And that I found you at the same time.'

'Fate. Or destiny,' she said softly, lifting a hand and skimming her fingertips lightly over his torn back as emotion knotted in her throat. She frowned. 'But I'm worried that we're also destined to hurt you.'

His eyes found hers and for a long moment they gazed at each other. His face wore that expression of pained intensity that carved deep lines between his brows and made her want to kiss them away. Slowly he shook his head.

'You've been hurt too, but it's over now. All of that is in the past.'

There was a quiet ferocity in his voice, so the words sounded more like a vow than a statement. Fear wrapped icy fingers around Bella's heart and squeezed, stalling her breath. She just wanted to be held against him, safe in his arms, but Olivier had already moved away and was putting on his shirt.

Dressed, he seemed suddenly distant from her—as if, wherever he was going, he had somehow already left.

Driving away from the mill, Bella's kiss still warm on his lips in the chilly dawn, Olivier felt impatience rise up inside him. He tensed his grip on the steering wheel and pressed his foot even harder on the accelerator.

He'd barely even left and already he couldn't wait to get back. *Home*. And that was something he'd never believed he'd catch himself thinking.

Last night, as Bella had rested her head on his chest in the firelight, he'd glimpsed a peace that had eluded him for a lifetime. He'd felt whole—as if the sharp, disjointed fragments that formed him had finally merged. For a brief time she'd made him feel good about himself, about who he was—and the mill and the past and his distant, difficult, damaged father were all part of that. She had accepted it all so easily, and it suddenly seemed pitiful that he had never been able to accept it himself.

He could now. Thanks to her, he wasn't ashamed any more—not of his past. But the horrific irony was that what he had done to her at the beginning now made a far darker stain on his conscience.

He had set out to hurt her, to do exactly the same thing as that bastard who had exploited her before. And although he was prepared to spend however long it took making up to her for it, he wouldn't get the chance if he didn't stop Veronique Lemercier's damned article.

In a couple of days the big Delacroix scandal of fifty years ago—the affair, the painting, the fire, the blackmail—would be gripping intelligent middle-class professionals all over France and England as they ate their cornflakes. For as long as he could remember, more than anything else, he'd wanted the world to know what Philippe Delacroix and Edward Lawrence had done, but all of a sudden there was something he wanted more.

To protect Bella.

At Rouen Hospital, morning visiting hadn't started, but when Olivier tersely explained that he had to talk to his father on an urgent matter the ward sister agreed to let him in. Julien was awake, and Olivier felt a sharp stab of guilt as he noticed the way the old man's eyes lit up when he saw him.

He frowned, struggling to know where to begin bridging the wide chasm that lay between them, forged by a lifetime of mis-understanding. Julien's scarred hands lay folded awkwardly on the bed, livid and shocking against the smooth white sheet.

Hesitantly Olivier placed his own over them. It was as good a place as any to start.

The sun was warm on her back when Bella turned the MG into the rutted driveway of the mill at lunchtime. It was another of those ravishing autumn days when everything seemed to be brushed with gold dust, and she found she was smiling as she turned the key in the heavy door, her arms laden with packages. She felt, bizarrely, as if she was coming home.

The now-familiar scent of woodsmoke and apples enveloped her as she crossed the warm flagstones of the hallway and went into the kitchen, depositing her armful of purchases on the table. It seemed incredible to think that she had come here so unexpectedly—and reluctantly—but that the moment when she'd first set foot in this crooked, creaking old building it had been almost as if she'd stepped into an enchantment.

This was where she'd discovered herself...and Olivier, and she knew without being able to say how or why that it couldn't have happened anywhere else.

Absentmindedly she sorted through the assortment of packages on the table. She'd had a surprisingly successful morning. Not wanting to hang around alone after Olivier had left for Paris, she had dressed and driven to a small town about ten kilometres away, where one of the markets on Celia's list was held. Her early start had been richly rewarded, and the boot of the MG was now full of brown paper parcels containing bone-white antique linen sheets, feather bolster cushions covered in vintage ticking, a couple of curled wire planters, and four exceptionally gorgeous silvered glass candlesticks for Miles and Ashley, twisted like barley sugar and glistening like moonlit frost. The perfect wedding gift. Bella knew that Ashley would love them.

But that wasn't what was causing the smile to keep returning to her face. Her hands were trembling slightly as she picked up one flat, tissue-wrapped parcel and peeled back the rustling layers with impatient fingers. The smile broadened as she smoothed back the last layer of tissue and picked up the richly-embroidered silk, shaking it out and watching its luscious colours spring to life in the sunlit kitchen.

It was Olympia's shawl.

And suddenly she was back in the Tate, with Olivier standing beside her, his lips brushing her palm, her neck. Her own words came back to her, and the sound of her own voice—husky with desire. *I...love...the shawl...I can imagine how the silk must feel against her skin...*

Tonight maybe she would find out for real.

She stood still, clutching the chilly silk to her as a wave of lust and longing crashed through her, nearly knocking her sideways. Last night's lovemaking in the creaking old brass bed had been both tender and intense, and she shivered as she recalled the new sensations he had awoken in her hungry, questing body. Lit only by the moon, his face had been as impassive and remote as ever, but his body had told a different story, and as she had taken him in her mouth and let her tongue explore and caress she had felt his control slip away. He had gripped her and cried out her name as if he were in pain.

But, Bella thought firmly, dragging herself back to the present and folding up the shawl, there had been enough of that. Enough pain, enough suffering. Now it was time for healing and for pleasure...Starting tonight, when he got back from Paris.

She had bought ingredients for dinner from a friendly *boucherie,* and intended to spend the afternoon cooking for him. The problem of mastering the range terrified her, but other than that the prospect of such quiet, intimate domesticity was profoundly, almost guiltily delicious. Firstly she would lay a fire for later, and then make a start.

The sitting room was grey and full of shadows. Bella swept out the ash and brought in more logs to replenish the basket beside the huge stone fireplace, then looked around for newspaper to lay a new one. Julien must keep them somewhere especially for the purpose, but she hadn't come across them so far...

On the lowest shelf of the huge wooden bookcase that ran

almost the length of one wall she saw a large box and, peering inside, was pleased to see a stack of newspapers. She pulled out the top one, and was about to start scrunching it up for kindling when something made her stop.

The paper was brittle and yellowed with age, and she noticed that the date at the top of the page was November 1954.

A sense of chilly foreboding stole through her as her eyes scanned the front page.

The name leapt out at her instantly, as if it had been printed in foot-high crimson letters.

DELACROIX.

Bella sat back on her heels and ran her hands through her hair. Letting them drop back into her lap, she found they were shaking. For a moment she sat perfectly still in the centre of the soft and faded rug where she and Olivier had lain last night, then she took all of the newspapers from the box.

She let out a small whimper of distress as she found another article in the next one. And the next.

Wrapping her arms around herself, she began to read.

The sun had been swallowed up by massing ranks of black clouds by the time Bella got unsteadily to her feet an hour later. She staggered a little, holding on to the bookcase for support as the blood seeped painfully back into her feet and her shocked brain struggled to assimilate all she'd just learned.

And then, bending down, she swept the scattered papers into her arms and grabbed the keys to the MG. She was white-lipped with anger.

Philippe Delacroix might have used bribery and blackmail to ensure he didn't have to answer for what he'd done to Julien in a court of law, but she was going to make him confront it now.

CHAPTER FOURTEEN

LEANING across a desk cluttered with auction catalogues and paperwork to shake the hand of the Louvre's Commissioner for Twentieth-Century Art, Olivier felt as though a great weight had been lifted from him. *La Dame de la Croix* was clipped to an easel on the other side of the room, from where Genevieve Delacroix's eyes regarded him steadily. At the door, he turned to look at it one last time.

Julien had responded to Olivier's proposition with the same calm acceptance that had enabled him to endure the other losses in his life. When Olivier had handed the painting to him he had held the roll of canvas tightly in his scarred hands, but he had not looked at it. *'There is no need,'* he had said hoarsely. *'Every detail is as vivid in my mind's eye now as it was when I painted it.'* And, recalling the image of Bella, naked and ravishing against the red velvet, Olivier had understood completely.

'Once again, *merci,* Monsieur Moreau,' the commissioner said solemnly now. 'It is a magnificent painting, and will make an extremely valuable part of our collection… in the fullness of time,' he added carefully. The terms of the donation were that *La Dame de la Croix* would not be hung until Philippe Delacroix, Genevieve Lawrence and Julien Moreau had all been dead for five years. 'Let us hope that that time does not come too soon,' he added with dutiful courtesy.

Olivier nodded briefly, his eyes still fixed on those of the woman in the painting. For a second he imagined that he saw approval there.

He walked back through the huge echoing hallways and corridors of the gallery, deliberately keeping his footsteps slow and measured, although a part of him wanted to break into a run. He had plenty of time before his lunch meeting with Veronique about pulling the article. Too much time. He felt impatient to be finished and on the way home.

Going back to Le Moulin and to Bella.

Walking along Paris's most exclusive shopping streets, he gazed unseeingly into brightly lit window displays of glittering jewellery and starkly minimalist displays of designer clothing. All of it seemed ridiculously irrelevant—a flimsy two-dimensional world of image and appearance. The world he'd used to inhabit.

But then, right in front of him, he noticed a smaller shop, squeezed between two aggressively stylish designer giants, with a narrow art nouveau frontage painted in absinthe-green. In the window were old-fashioned tailors' mannequins displaying an array of delicate lingerie in shades of turquoise and tangerine and rose.

Olivier stopped on the pavement, feeling a slow half-smile spread across his face as heat rose through his body and a kaleidoscope of luscious images rampaged through his mind.

OK, so not all the shops here were irrelevant, he thought ruefully, opening the door. This kind of shopping he could easily see the point of.

Waves…white sandy beach…palm trees…

Pacing back from the far wall to the window, Bella could feel her self-control slipping. She knew she mustn't give in to the hysteria that was lapping at her brain far more insistently than the waves on any damned white sandy beach.

She had to stay calm. Had to stay positive. Had to stay rational.

Not that there was anything remotely positive or rational about being locked in a room in a deserted château with a dangerously insane distant relative.

When she'd met him yesterday she had sensed something slightly obsessive, slightly deranged, in Philippe Delacroix's manner when he had spoken of the painting and of Julien Moreau. Not for a second, however, had she imagined the depths of that obsession or the corrosive violence of his derangement.

Obviously. If she had she would never have arrived on his doorstep with her armful of newspapers and her foolish, naïve moralising.

Her throat constricted painfully around the dry sob that rose up inside her, and for the millionth time she glanced out of the window, hoping desperately to see a black Aston Martin roaring towards the house. Where was Olivier now? Philippe had wanted her to ring him, to summon him to Le Manoir with the painting, and he hadn't believed her when she'd said she didn't know Olivier's mobile number. As she'd tried to explain to him that she and Olivier Moreau had only known each other for the shortest time, the gossamer ties that connected them had begun to feel increasingly fragile.

The fact that she didn't even know what he was doing in Paris or when he was coming back just emphasised how tenuous their relationship was. Pulling the sleeves of her jumper down over her cold, cold hands, Bella slid down the wall. As shadows gathered in the cobwebbed corners of the room she put her head on her knees and comforted herself by recalling every delicious, bone-melting moment of last night with Olivier.

It beat waves on a stupid beach any day.

Olivier had just been waiting for the girl in the shop to finish wrapping the last of his purchases in layers of pink tissue paper when his PA had called. The message she gave him had filled him with unspeakable dread.

It had seemed to take for ever to get out of Paris. Slumped helplessly behind the wheel of the Aston Martin in the midst of the Friday traffic, there was nothing to distract him from going over and over the possible implications of Philippe Delacroix's call. Alicia had said he had sounded angry and agitated, and that he wanted Olivier to go straight away to Le Manoir, where Bella was 'waiting for him'.

And he wanted him to bring the painting.

An early autumn dusk had fallen as the Aston Martin devoured the last few miles, its headlamps illuminating the gloomy, overgrown hedgerows. By the time he finally swung the car, with a screech of tyres, between the tall stone gateposts of Le Manoir, Olivier felt spacy with adrenalin. His self-control, stretched almost to breaking point on the long drive, was now hanging by a thread.

He leapt out of the car and slammed the door with barely controlled violence. He just hoped that Delacroix wasn't stupid enough to annoy him. *Or to have hurt Bella.*

That was the thought that he'd so ruthlessly squashed all the way from Paris, but now he was here it seemed to balloon hugely, blocking out everything else in his head. There was no way of rationalizing any scenario involving Bella, the painting and Philippe Delacroix. It was a combination that could only mean disaster.

Olivier's few dealings with Delacroix over Le Moulin had shown him that Genevieve's older brother had never forgotten what had happened, but instead had held onto it until it became almost an obsession. He was deluded. Deranged. And, Olivier thought with a sickening thud of anguish, very possibly dangerous.

Running up the stone steps, he applied his shoulder violently to the heavy double front doors, feeling them yield a little under the pressure. He pushed again, and the lock gave way.

The huge hallway was murky in the half-light. Striding across its chilly marble floor, Olivier shouted Bella's name. For a second he paused, listening to his voice echoing through the gloomy rooms that spread out on either side of him. And then, from somewhere up above, he thought he heard an answering call.

Relief shot through him, searing and pure. He was halfway up the wide staircase when a voice came from behind him.

'Really, Monsieur Moreau. Your manners are every bit as deplorable as your vulgar father's. Don't you know that in polite society we knock before entering?'

Olivier stopped and turned slowly round. Philippe Delacroix stood in the shadows at the foot of the stairs, looking up at him. He was dressed for the outdoors—as if he was on some shooting party from the days before the Great War, with plus fours and gaiters and a tweed jacket.

For a split second Olivier felt a flash of pity for the relic he had become. And then loathing obliterated everything.

'Where's Bella?' he said icily.

'She's waiting for you. You can see her once you've handed over what I asked for.' Delacroix spoke completely matter-of-factly, as if they were discussing a dog. 'I trust you brought the painting, as instructed. If not, I am afraid Bella will have to wait longer, and she won't like that at all. She is like my sister—very impatient.' His lips drew back and he gave a sudden burst of wheezing laughter. 'And with a similar penchant for the lower orders.'

Hitting him, going down the stairs and knocking Philippe Delacroix across his own stately hallway, would be the most tempting thing in the world, but at that moment Olivier heard a noise from along the corridor at the top of the stairs: the rattling of a door handle, accompanied by a muffled voice.

Bella's voice.

In an instant he was at the top of the stairs, striding quickly along the dim corridor. Following the sound of her voice, he pushed open doors, calling to her. At last he came to a locked door.

'Olivier! I'm here!'

'Stand back from the door,' he snarled, his voice harsh with anxiety.

It didn't give way as easily as the front door had done—locked with an old-fashioned key, it proved much more durable than the more modern latch downstairs—but the urgent need to get to Bella doubled Olivier's already considerable strength. On the fourth attempt there was a splintering of wood and the door burst open.

And she was there. Bella was there. She was standing in the centre of the empty room, her hands pressed to her mouth, her blue eyes wide with fear and joy and relief. For a moment neither of them moved. Their eyes met, and Olivier had to brace himself as a tidal wave of totally unfamiliar emotion battered him. He held back, suddenly afraid that if he went to her then he wouldn't be able to stop himself from crushing her to him and kissing the living daylights out of her.

'You came,' she croaked. 'I'm so sorry, I—'

She broke off as a hidden door in the panelling behind her opened and, like a pantomime villain, Philippe Delacroix appeared.

'*Alors*—I said to *wait*.'

It would have been farcical but for the fact there was something very sinister about the soft, reasonable tone of Philippe's voice as, addressing Olivier, he took hold of Bella's arm. It took Olivier a moment to realise that in one hand he carried a rifle.

'Why is it that no one seems capable of following the simplest commands these days?' Delacroix went on in a tone of weary regret. 'No wonder society is in such a terrible mess. It was all so much easier when people listened to their betters and did as they were told.'

'What are you doing, Delacroix?'

'I told you, Moreau. I said *quite clearly* that before you could see Bella I wanted the painting.' Philippe shook his head sadly, and in the grey twilight Olivier could see the slightly manic glitter in his small eyes. 'You may think you can get away with disregarding my orders, but you are wrong.'

'I haven't got the painting,' Olivier said tersely.

Bella's eyes blazed into his in the dingy room. 'He knows you have, Olivier. I told him. I'm so sorry—I didn't know...I didn't think...'

'See?' Delacroix said triumphantly, flinging his arms out, so that the gun made a wide arc, glinting dully in the gloom. 'There's no point in *lying*, Moreau. You have what I want and...' with one hand he waved the gun at Bella '...I have what you want. It's a very simple transaction. You give me that painting and I give you your girl.'

Olivier's mind raced. Narrowing his eyes, he measured the distance between them. He was too far away to snatch the gun, and any sudden movement would be unwise; Philippe Delacroix was a renowned shot. But he had to find some way of distracting him long enough to get Bella to safety.

Nonchalantly he shrugged. 'OK. I admit I have it. But I'm not letting it go.'

He heard Bella's soft gasp of dismay. Not looking at her, not reaching out to her then, took strength of Herculean proportions.

Bella felt dread prickle through every nerve and cell, like poison, until she thought she might black out. She kept her eyes fixed on Olivier's, trying to anchor herself in him as the shadows darkened at the edges of her vision, but the expression of cold hauteur on his face chilled her like death.

She hardly noticed the barrel of the gun pressing into her ribs.

'Think very carefully about that, Moreau,' rasped Philippe in a voice that made Bella's flesh crawl. Olivier half turned away.

'No need, I'm afraid,' he said coldly. 'The deal is off, Delacroix.

I spent years looking for that painting, and I'm not about to give it up. For anyone.'

Bella clasped her hands together to stop them shaking, tucking them beneath her chin as her eyes were stretched wide by shock and horror. Dimly she was aware of Philippe's discomfiture, the sharp jab of the rifle beneath her diaphragm, but it paled into insignificance in the face of Olivier's betrayal.

'So you used her, just like your father used my sister,' Philippe hissed venomously.

Time stood still. A thick, muffling silence fell over the lightless room. Bella felt as if she was under water. Everything seemed to slow and stall as she waited for Olivier to speak. To deny it.

'Yes. I used her.'

He was frowning slightly, and in the gathering dusk he looked entirely remote. In that instant it was impossible to imagine kissing that brutal, beautiful mouth or gripping those massive, powerful shoulders as she shivered and melted in ecstasy. His cruel words, spoken so casually, fell on her like careless hammer blows and it was as if she had dreamed it all.

'I used her to get back at you,' he went on offhandedly, taking a step towards them. 'I simply wanted to take what had been forbidden to my father. It was revenge—pure and simple.'

Bella heard her own low moan of pain, but was suddenly aware that the gun was no longer pressing into her. And then it all happened very quickly—small, individual actions all crowding in on each other so that it was impossible to make sense of any of them. She saw a glint of metal, felt the sudden, erratic movement of Philippe beside her, heard his low grunt of rage as he swung the gun towards Olivier.

And she felt as if her heart was being wrenched from inside her as she watched, in slow motion, Olivier lurch towards him, his arm coming out to knock the gun from Philippe's wild, shaking grasp. His face showed no emotion.

There was a noise. Louder than anything Bella had ever heard before. Too loud to be anything other than very, very real.

And then Olivier was falling, and a vivid scarlet stain was spreading on the front of his shirt.

Above his heart.

CHAPTER FIFTEEN

EVERYTHING felt unreal. Like a dream. Or a film.

Before the echo of the single gunshot had died away Bella was dropping to her knees beside Olivier, her fingers fluttering over his neck, searching for a pulse as the crimson stain grew on the white of his shirt like some terrible flower unfurling its petals.

His skin was warm, and bending closer she caught the delicious familiar scent of him above the reek of cordite. She closed her eyes and gave a gasp of relief as she felt the rapid flicker of his pulse.

Opening them again, she glanced up. Philippe was standing motionless, the arm holding the gun held stiffly out at an odd, unnatural angle, almost as if he were trying to pretend it wasn't part of him. His face, she dimly registered, was grey and crumpled with shock, but there was no space in her head for him now.

It was too full of Olivier.

Olivier, Olivier, Olivier, whose exceptional face was now an unearthly chalk-white in the dying light. Olivier, whose blood was warm on her hands. Olivier, who didn't love her.

Who had used her.

And in the whole nightmarish scene this was the only thing that seemed real, the only fact her frozen brain could fix on with any certainty.

She bent over him, her numb fingers clumsily searching for his mobile phone in the inside pocket of his jacket. Finding it, she took it out and looked at it in blank panic, not knowing how to make it work.

'Here…'

Olivier's eyes were open. His voice was just a cracked whisper, but it had lost none of its force. Even lying bleeding on the floor he was still powerful, still somehow in command. With mammoth effort his hand came up and she put the phone into it, and then, his jaw clenching with pain, he raised his head. Mutely Bella cradled him on her knees as he pressed buttons, then held the phone out for her to take.

For the second time in as many days Bella found herself requesting an ambulance. She only hoped this one would arrive more quickly, and anguish swelled inside her as she watched Olivier's eyes flicker closed again. She didn't know how long he could hold on.

Philippe had vanished, she wasn't sure when, and now the only noise in the huge room was the unnatural sucking rasp of Olivier's breathing. She had to do something, but she felt completely powerless. As if she'd been drugged, or was being slowly pulled down by quicksand.

He didn't love her. He'd used her. It was what she'd been afraid of all along, and what she'd tried to block out, but it made perfect sense. He must have known who she was from the start. And hated her for it.

'Bella…'

He was looking up at her, his eyes burning into hers, his face filled with pain and ferocious determination. 'What—I—s-s-said…' He stopped, closing his eyes and swallowing convulsively. Every word was edged with agony, as if he had razor wire wrapped around his throat.

Instinctively she held her hand to his cheek, feeling the tense muscles beneath his stubble-roughened jaw. 'Shhh…' she murmured automatically, shaking her head. 'Don't speak.'

Panic was beginning to break through the anaesthetizing shock. She could feel his chest heaving with the effort of forcing the air in and out of his lungs. Not knowing what else to do, she hurriedly undid the buttons of his shirt, peeling it back from the torn and bloodied flesh beneath.

For the briefest fraction of a second she was struck by how beautiful he was. His skin was bleached of all colour—even his lovely mouth was pale—so that he looked like a marble effigy of some knight crusader. The splash of scarlet on the white of his skin was strangely lovely.

Almost instantly the reality of the situation assailed her. She bent over him in the gathering dusk and focused all her energy on biting back the whimper of distress that threatened to escape her. She kept her face expressionless as she looked at the wound, but behind her impassive mask she raged with panic and terror. *God, oh, please, God—what should I do…?*

'Stop the—blood.'

It was as if she'd spoken out loud. Olivier's voice was like sandpaper, and his eyes stayed closed. But he was still with her. He was still there. And he was still strong.

'Tell me what to do,' she said through frozen lips. 'Tell me, Olivier.'

'Press—hard.'

She felt his icy-cold fingers close around her hand and, lifting it, he placed it over his heart.

Pure astringent agony sliced into her, scalpel-sharp, making her gasp.

It didn't matter if he loved her or not. The fact was she loved him, and she was as helpless to stop that as she was to stop the blood that was seeping through her fingers. And it hurt just as much.

Gradually his face relaxed, and the lines of pain between his brows slowly faded. As minutes passed and the corners of the room were lost in the gathering twilight, Bella's hand grew numb with pressing, and her world shrank to nothing but the rapid beat of his heart and the hoarse suck of his breath.

When she saw the neon blue light of the approaching ambulance flickering over the bare walls there was a tiny, shameful corner of her mind that was disappointed. Because now she'd have to let him go.

Olivier drifted in and out of a place where everything was dark and there was nothing but physical sensation. He felt the hard floor against his back, the cold stealing into his bones, Bella's hand, warm and soft as angel's wings, against his cheek.

And the pain, of course. He felt that. The pain suffused everything, like smoke. It curled around him until he could no longer separate anything out from it. Breathing. Moving. Speaking.

He needed to speak. He had to make sure that Bella knew what he'd said to Delacroix wasn't true. But it was hard to breathe, very hard, and he knew that he needed to keep as still as possible and use his oxygen wisely if he was to stand a chance of surviving until help arrived.

He had to survive, because there was so much he still wanted to do. And say.

I love you.

Summoning all his strength, he opened his eyes a little. Blue lights sliced crazily through the dark fog around him and there was noise. Voices. Footsteps vibrating on the floorboards. Bella's face swam above him. It was pale and perfectly beautiful, and it glistened with tears.

He frowned.

'Don't—cry…' His chest felt as if it was on fire, and the words seemed to scour the raw flesh like acid, but he had to say them. He gathered his failing strength. 'I—'

But she was pulling away from him. 'It's time,' she whispered. 'They're here, Olivier.'

He felt a shot of heat in his arm, and the darkness came back.

Time did strange things in situations of great awfulness, Bella decided as she watched another grey dawn break. The night she had spent in the waiting room of the Paris hospital had felt like a thousand years, with the hands on the oversized clock on the wall opposite moving so slowly she'd wanted to scream. And yet yesterday morning, waking in the sagging old bed that still bore the scent of their bodies and tiptoeing through the luminescent shadows to find Olivier, seemed to have happened only moments ago.

The words she'd said to him then had echoed round her head through the long silent hours. *It seems we're destined to hurt you.* Now, sitting on a hard plastic chair in the empty waiting room, they seemed like a terrible premonition.

The small hospital in Rouen had not been able to deal with Olivier's injuries. The bullet had shattered his ribs and punctured a lung and, although they could stabilise him in the ambulance, he needed surgery immediately. Bella had followed behind the ambulance in a police car, and throughout the dark journey the only emotion to penetrate the thick blanket of numbness in her head had been guilt.

The *gendarmes* were being so kind—what would they say if they found out that she was being ushered to Olivier's bedside under false pretences? He wouldn't want her to be there because he didn't love her. It was just her own selfishness, her desperate, hopeless longing to be with him for as long as possible that compelled her to follow.

A nurse with a plump, concerned face appeared in front of her now, smiling kindly. Bella kept her eyes fixed to the blank face of the clock over her shoulder, afraid that even the smallest gesture of warmth would cause the dam on her emotions to burst and the tidal wave of grief it unleashed to wash her away.

Monsieur Moreau had come round from the surgery a little while ago, the nurse explained in a slow and disjointed mixture of French and English. His injuries, though severe, were no longer life threatening, and it was a miracle that his heart had escaped completely unscathed.

Bella nodded earnestly. She had known that already, of course. It was only *her* heart that was shattered.

'He has been asking for you, *cherie*,' the nurse said gently.

Bella let her eyes flicker briefly from the hard white disc of the clock face. The nurse was looking at her with infinite compassion. 'Really?' she whispered.

The nurse's smile broadened to a beam. 'He would not lie still. When he come round from the anaesthetic, straight away he try to take out his drip and get up to see you.' She shook her head fondly. 'He keep saying he need to speak with you. He is not an easy patient, but he has the strength of ten men. He's a survivor, *c'est vrai.*'

As she hurried along the corridor to Olivier's room Bella was horribly aware of her unwashed face and creased, day-old clothes, and also of the fragile spark of hope that the nurse's words had ignited. Tethered to machines and tubes, Olivier lay sleeping again, and she felt scoured out and weak with love as she looked down into his peaceful face.

Tentatively she reached out her hand and stroked her fingertips along the smooth brown underside of his forearm, beneath the brutal needles that dripped fluid into his veins.

He stirred instantly, as if he had been waiting for her to call him back from whatever unreachable place he was in. Gripped by anguish, Bella watched helplessly as the shadows and pain flooded back into his face and his fingers flexed and clenched.

'Veronique...'

Ice dripped down Bella's spine. Her hand stayed on his arm, her fingers still stroking and caressing, but the rest of her was frozen with shock.

'I need…Veronique…'

Nausea rose up inside her. Of course the nurse had no way of knowing that Veronique wasn't *her* name; that she wasn't the one Olivier wanted to see. Horrorstruck, Bella snatched her hand away as he struggled to sit up, his fingers groping desperately at the narrow tubes, pulling at the tapes that fastened the needle into the crook of his arm. Dumbly she stepped backwards, her hands flying to cover her mouth as the machine beside him began to emit a high-pitched wail. In the bed Olivier thrashed, his face contorted with anguish and pain, the same word coming from his pale lips over and over again.

'*Veronique.*'

From out in the corridor there was the sound of running feet, and Bella shrank back as two nurses burst into the room and bent over Olivier, easing him back against the pillows, soothing, checking the lines and tubes and pressing buttons on the machine. Hovering in the doorway, Bella felt like an impostor.

She should go. Leave. Now. But…

'Bella? Oh, my God, darling, there you are…'

For a moment she thought exhaustion and grief had finally undone her and she was hallucinating, but she found herself being swept into a perfumed, silken embrace.

Ashley.

'Oh, sweetheart, thank goodness I found you. Miles is frantic. I came as soon as we heard about Philippe. You've been through so much, you poor, poor baby.'

As Ashley led her gently out of the room, away from Olivier, the dam inside Bella burst. She wasn't sure how long they stood there in the corridor as she wept and Ashley rocked and soothed and stroked her hair, but when she finally pulled away her eyes were swollen almost shut and Ashley's grey silk jacket was soaked with tears.

'Oh, Ash,' she croaked, 'it's all such a mess. I'm so glad you're here.'

'So am I. Come on, you need a break. I'm taking you back to my hotel for a hot bath and a good sleep. Don't even bother to argue.'

Bella bit her lip against another surge of tears and shook her head wanly.

'I wasn't going to. I'm done here. Let's go.'

'What time is it?'

Ashley smiled down at her. 'Nearly eight o'clock.'

Bella rubbed a hand across her gritty eyes and frowned. 'I've slept all day.'

'And all night, darling, thank goodness. You needed the rest.' Ashley crossed the thickly carpeted floor of the hotel suite and pulled back the curtains, letting thin sunlight flood the room. 'It's nearly eight o'clock on Sunday morning.'

Struggling upright, Bella blinked and pushed the hair back from her face as the real world reassembled itself in her consciousness. She had slept a blank, dreamless sleep, no doubt brought about by the large gin and tonic and the sleeping pill that Ashley had given her, but now the memory of yesterday began to come back to her with the same screaming pain as blood returning to a cramped limb.

'Olivier?' she croaked desperately. 'How is he?'

Perching on the edge of the bed, Ashley placed a steadying hand on Bella's shoulder. 'It's OK. Miles rang about half an hour ago, when he'd spoken to the hospital, and the news is Olivier's doing fine. It's you we're worried about.'

Bella collapsed back against the pillows and turned her face away.

'I'm all right.'

'I'm not so sure about that,' Ashley said gently. 'Bella—what happened…what you've been through…it must have been so terrible, and I know it's difficult, but it would be so much better if you could talk about it.'

'There's nothing to say except that I did it again.' Bella turned to look up at Ashley as tears slid down her face and into her hair. 'I fell for someone who was just using me. Only this time it's a thousand times worse because now I know he was in love with someone else all along. Veronique.'

Ashley frowned and shook her head in confusion. 'Darling, I don't understand. I was talking about what happened with Philippe, and the shooting…' She paused, then smoothed Bella's hair back from her damp forehead and stood up, her eyes full of concern. 'I'm going to make you a coffee, and then I think you'd better tell me everything. From the beginning.'

And so, clutching the gold-rimmed cup between her frozen hands, Bella began with that first evening in London, when Olivier had deliberately, single-mindedly, unravelled her from her cotton-wool numbness and brought her back to life, and went right up to night at the mill, where he'd held her in the firelight and listened to her as she'd bared her soul. Ashley listened without interrupting.

'It was so sudden and intense,' Bella whispered tonelessly, as Ashley gently took the now-cold coffee cup from her grasp and put it on the bedside table. 'But so right…so *perfect* that I thought it must be meant to be.' She looked up with a smile of infinite sadness. 'How ridiculous that sounds now, when I know he was putting it on the whole time. He set out deliberately to seduce me. As revenge for what my family had done to his father.'

Ashley shook her head decisively. 'I don't think so. If that was the case you would have sensed it. You would have known.'

Bella's eyes were black holes of despair. 'Why? I didn't last time, with Dan Nightingale. And Olivier *said* it, Ashley—I heard him, remember, at Le Manoir?'

For the first time a note of impatience crept into Ashley's tone. 'Give the guy a break, Bella! He was dealing with a gun-toting psycho at the time. I think that can make you say things you don't mean.'

Beneath the covers Bella drew her knees more tightly up to her body, bringing her head down onto them and squeezing her eyes closed. 'I *know*. I've thought about that,' she moaned. 'I thought that maybe it could have been part of some plan to divert Philippe's attention or something, but if it was, it was the most insane thing to do. Why would he deliberately provoke a man with a gun?'

Ashley's voice was very tender. 'Because he loves you, of course.'

For a moment Bella didn't move, or lift her head. Her hair fell forward, completely obscuring her face, and in the dark cave it created she explored what Ashley had just said. Hesitantly she looked up, trying to keep the tremulous hope from her voice.

'But Veronique… He was asking for Veronique.'

'You're jumping to conclusions, honey. She could be his sister for all you know.'

'He doesn't have a sister.'

There was a knock at the door and Ashley got up. 'OK, his secretary, then. But from what you've just told me he's worth a little faith. You at least owe him that.' She smiled, going towards the door. 'Now, here's breakfast.'

While she was gone Bella tried to make her brain accommodate this new, tempting perspective. There was a wonderful logic to Ashley's theory, but could she really allow herself to hope that—

'Bella, love? Some gentlemen to see you.'

Surprised, she looked up as Ashley ushered the two *gendarmes* who had taken Bella to the hospital the other night into the room. Seeing them in daylight, in the orderly opulence of the hotel, was seriously bizarre—like characters from a film, they belonged to a world of chaos and mess.

They had come to give Bella the news that Philippe Delacroix's body had been discovered in a disused farm building on the St Laurien estate. He had shot himself, they explained gently, and this time the bullet had been fatal.

Bella felt nothing but relief.

They had also come to give her back the keys to the MG, which had been returned to the mill, and to inform her that Olivier's Aston Martin had been collected by the hire company. Then, blushing furiously, the shorter of the two men stepped forward and held out a stiff peppermint-green carrier bag, of the kind used by extremely exclusive boutiques. Pink tissue paper frothed from the top.

'The car hire firm found this in Monsieur Moreau's car, *mademoiselle*. They asked that it be passed on to him.'

The moment they'd gone, Ashley rushed forward. 'Well, what are you waiting for? See what's in it!'

As if she'd been hypnotised Bella looked into the bag. Her face bore an expression of trepidation that suggested she was expecting to find a live snake coiled in the crisp layers of tissue. Slowly she put her hand in and drew out a delicate pink-wrapped package, as light as air.

Inside lay a pair of silk knickers in a delicious, stinging chartreuse-green. They were edged with satin ribbon the colour of kingfisher wings, and against the bright pink tissue they looked so incredibly beautiful that for a moment all either of them could do was stare.

'Oh, wow, Bella…' Ashley's voice was a wistful moan that said very clearly that Miles had never bought anything as wildly lovely as this for her. She looked at Bella in open admiration. 'This man has seriously good taste.'

One by one the packages were pulled out, and the tissue stripped back to reveal bras and knickers in Parma violet and strawberry-pink and aquamarine. Nothing matched, every silken whisper was different, and by the time they'd finished, the bed was like a molten rainbow.

'So,' said Ashley in quiet triumph, 'what does this tell you?'

Before Bella could make her dazzled brain conjure up the words to answer, they were interrupted by another knock on the door as Room Service arrived with breakfast. On the trolley with the warm croissants and fragrant coffee lay a selection of the Sunday newspapers, which Ashley tossed onto the bed, sending pieces of pink tissue fluttering in all directions, like flamingos taking flight.

'Coffee or tea?' she asked happily, and when Bella didn't answer she laughed and went on, 'Or, if you're too stunned with love to choose, would you like me to decide for you?' She poured coffee into two cups and turned round.

The smile died on her lips.

Afterwards, she described to Miles the look on Bella's face as that of someone who had just been diagnosed with a terminal illness. All the life, all the hope had been brutally extinguished, leaving her gaunt and ashen.

Instantly Ashley was beside her, following her agonised, beseeching gaze to the newspaper that lay face-up on the bed. For a moment they both just stared, transfixed with shock, at the picture that covered most of the front page. *La Dame de la Croix,* her luminous glory only slightly dimmed in newsprint, stared serenely up at them, almost mocking them with her composure.

'How did they…? Who could have…?'

Ashley's incredulous question died on her lips as she noticed what Bella had seen already: the name beneath the headline.

Veronique Lemercier.

With a succinct curse Ashley made a grab for the paper, but Bella was too quick for her. Snatching it up, she clutched it to her with the sadistic ferocity of an alcoholic seizing the last bottle of gin in the shop.

'Bella, don't read it—please. Let me…'

'No!' Bella spat. She was white and shaking, but her eyes burned with a forceful intensity. Ashley knew there was no point in arguing. She watched helplessly as Bella spread out the paper with trembling hands and began to read. With a terrible sense of foreboding she moved closer and scanned the print from above Bella's bent head.

Veronique Lemercier was 'a long-standing intimate acquaintance' of Olivier Moreau, the introduction to the article stated. Ashley heard Bella's ragged gasp of pain as she read this, and her heart bled for her. She wanted to pick up the paper and tear it into a thousand pieces, but she knew that wouldn't help. It was too late to take refuge in ignorance now. Taking a deep breath, she forced herself to read on.

It was all exactly as Bella had feared. Veronique's article described in moving detail how she had helped Olivier Moreau in his single-minded quest to find the only painting to survive the fire that had destroyed his father's career and prevented him from achieving the greatness and recognition he so deserved.

Halfway down the page, Ashley stopped reading and swore quietly. She realised, distantly, that her hands were clenched into fists and the nails were digging into her palms. Beside her, Bella gave a whimper of anguish as she reached the same line.

I was due to meet Olivier for lunch in Paris on the day he was shot. In the whole of our relationship I had never known him to be late…

Ashley put out her hand. Bella flinched as it touched her hair, and looked up at Ashley with dead eyes.

'So that's it. He was on his way to meet her. In Paris.' Her gaze moved slowly over the bed, where the scraps of iridescent silk lay like drifts of exotic blossom. 'All this was for her.' She slid stiffly from beneath the covers and shrank back from the bed as if it would contaminate her. 'It's her he loves. Not me.'

Ashley opened her mouth to argue, but closed it again. She had been wrong to give Bella false hope before. The writing wasn't just on the wall—it was in a feature-length article in a national newspaper. All she could do now was deal with the fallout.

CHAPTER SIXTEEN

WHILST the inside of the parish church of St Saviour in the rural heart of Miles's constituency was bathed in beautiful flickering candlelight, the outside was exposed to the full glare of the media spotlight. The marriage of a political figure would usually command a fairly modest level of press interest, but, thanks to recent events, Miles Lawrence's wedding was on a par with that of any minor royal or premiership footballer.

Ashley had played a masterful PR game. From the moment she had emerged with a white-faced and silent Bella from the Paris hotel on the morning the story broke she had faced the press with gratifying openness and brought a touch of vulnerability and humanity to the Delacroix-Lawrence camp. She expressed the family's sincere regret for Olivier Moreau's injury, and said that she hoped that the death of Philippe Delacroix, who it was now believed had been suffering from mental health problems for some time, would mark an end to the long-standing disagreement between the two families.

By the following day the photograph of *La Dame de la Croix,* originally only carried by Veronique Lemercier's article, had been picked up by all the newspapers, and Genevieve Delacroix was an instant celebrity. Her continued elusive silence fanned the flames of media interest to a white-hot firestorm, which was further nourished by Ashley's very discreet drip-feed of information about the picture and the passionate, tragic, *Romeo and Juliet* story behind it. The transformation of the Lawrences in the eyes of the world from dry pillars of the establishment to glamorous, intriguing Euro-aristocrats was swift and complete.

There was an explosion of flashbulbs as the vintage Rolls Royce carrying the bride and her father pulled into the gates of the church and Ashley emerged.

Bella watched her turn briefly to the cameras—enough time for them to get a chance of a good shot but not long enough for it to look tacky—before taking her father's arm and walking towards where Bella stood, shivering in her black silk bridesmaid's dress near the church door.

She smiled. 'You look so beautiful, Ashley.'

It was true. In the dull November afternoon Ashley was radiant. The black and white theme of the wedding, initially inspired by the elegant chequered flooring of the ancient church, provided the perfect foil for the rich colours of the Delacroix cross, which gleamed at her throat.

'Thanks, honey.' Taking care not to damage either of their bouquets, Ashley gave her an awkward squeeze. 'So do you.'

As Bella disentangled herself from the froth of Ashley's veil she gave a bleak laugh. She looked like a train wreck, and they both knew that, although the team of professionals Ashley had hired for the day had brought about some improvement. They had at least put colour in her hollow cheeks and added some sparkle—albeit artificial—to eyes that were dull and lustreless. But they were make-up artists, not miracle workers.

'As it's your wedding day I'll refrain from calling you a big fat liar,' Bella said ruefully, 'but just watch that your pants don't burst into flame.'

Ashley caught her hand. 'You're doing fine, sweetie,' she said fiercely. 'And I wouldn't care if you'd turned up with your head shaved and a tattoo saying "anarchy rules" across your shoulders. I'm just glad you're here. I know that all this—' she waved her heavy bouquet in the direction of the packed church '—was the last thing you needed at the moment, and I appreciate that you're doing it.'

'I'm not sure Miles would take the same view about the tattoo,' Bella said with a weak smile. 'Very bad for his political image.'

'You're far more important to him. You know very well that underneath all that political starch he loves you like mad.'

Bella winced. 'I think we should try and avoid all references to madness in the family, under the circumstances. Come on. Let's get you married off to my overbearing brother, and then we can start on the champagne.'

As the organ launched into the first poignant notes of Pachelbel's *Canon,* Bella took a deep breath and clutched her bouquet of scarlet roses very tightly. The scent of incense and polish mixed with the heady perfume of the flowers as they stepped forward to begin their slow and solemn progress down the candlelit aisle—Ashley on the arm of her father, Bella behind them alone.

Profoundly alone.

Fortunately most of the congregation were too busy looking at the radiant bride and the now-legendary piece of jewellery she wore to notice that the lone bridesmaid, following in her wake like a shadow, had tears spilling down her cheeks.

Walking quickly between the graves behind the church, hidden from the media scrum around the other side, Olivier paused to lean for a moment against a headstone.

With every movement he could feel the bones of his shattered ribs grating together, and even after three weeks the slightest exertion made breathing feel as if he was swallowing fire. When he had discharged himself from the hospital two days ago it had been against the strongest advice of his doctors, but he knew that if he didn't talk to Bella here, today, he might never find her again.

From the moment he had been sufficiently coherent to understand that she had left the hospital, he had ordered Alicia to do everything she could to find her again. Throughout the morphine-drenched days after the shooting a part of his brain had remained perfectly awake, perfectly aware of what had happened and what he'd said, and his physical suffering had paled into insignificance beside his mental torment. He needed to see her so badly.

But the Lawrence ranks had closed round her completely, placing her beyond his reach, and letters and telephone calls to the house in Wilton Square and the shop in Notting Hill had yielded nothing. He'd had no choice but to come and find her himself.

So yesterday, still frighteningly weak, he had gone to the shop, and Celia—visibly shocked by his obvious despair—had eventually relented and passed on the details he needed to get to the wedding. This was his only chance to see her, the only place he knew he could find her, and just the thought that she was so near filled him with fierce determination. Taking a searing breath and ignoring the flare of pain in his chest, he straightened up and carried on towards an arched doorway in the side of the church.

The service was well under way. Music and candlelight enfolded him as he opened the door a crack and slipped through.

He had timed it perfectly. A hymn was just coming to an end. With much shuffling of feet and rustling of service sheets the congregation was sitting down, adjusting cumbersome wedding hats and making themselves comfortable for the reading, meaning that Olivier was able to walk quietly along the back of the church and down a side aisle, unnoticed.

Bella was standing behind the bride and groom, a little to the side. Her head was bent, and candlelight shone on her hair and gleamed from her bare shoulders. In the midst of the quiet jubilation of the wedding service her face wore an expression of unbearable sorrow.

Olivier stopped, leaning against a pillar for support. The

sudden tightening of his chest had nothing to do with cracked ribs or punctured lungs, and everything to do with the girl standing a few feet away in the black dress.

The girl with the trembling mouth and the tear falling slowly down her face.

The girl who at that moment slowly lifted her head and looked straight at him.

'*Love is patient, love is kind…*' the vicar read in solemn tones from the pulpit.

Helplessly, impaled on spears of silent torment, they looked at each other across the candlelit space, separated by a hundred yards of chilly marble and a continent of misery and incomprehension. Olivier's fists were clenched with the superhuman effort of not striding to the front of the church and snatching her into his arms and holding her and kissing her until the shadows had left her face.

'*Love bears all things, believes all things…*'

Bella's eyes flickered closed for a second, as if she'd been hurt. Olivier had to look away then, tipping his head back against the cool stone of the pillar as the words fell between them, taunting and cruel. Gazing up into the majestic sweep of the arched ceiling high above, Olivier Moreau knew that everything he had ever believed in or wanted in his life before this point was nothing.

Money. Respect. Revenge…

Nothing.

The reading ended. There was a pause as the vicar came down the steps from the pulpit, and a murmur of conversation broke out amongst the congregation as the wedding party gathered themselves to go and sign the register. As if from a great distance Bella saw Ashley glance round at her, checking that she was all right, indicating for her to follow them. They were walking across the front of the church towards the vestry.

Towards Olivier.

Bella kept her eyes downcast as they got closer to him. She had gone back to that safe place of numb unreality, removed from the tornado of emotions that raged inside her and battered against the invisible walls of her hiding place. She couldn't think, couldn't comprehend... Couldn't allow herself to hope.

He was leaning back against the pillar. It was useless trying to stop herself looking at him, as pointless as trying to stop herself from loving him. Her mouth went dry and her heart cracked wide open as she saw that his still, impassive face was lined with suffering.

He levered himself up as the bride and groom passed. Bella saw Miles's head whip round, but Ashley steered him into the vestry with steely determination, saying something very quietly into his ear and leaving nothing between Bella and Olivier.

Her footsteps slowed. Neither of them spoke for a moment as their eyes devoured each other, then stiffly he motioned for her to follow Miles and Ashley into the small, cluttered vestry. But while the rest of the wedding group arranged themselves around the registry table, Bella and Olivier stayed separate, instinctively drifting into the shadows at the far end of the room.

He made no attempt to touch her. Part of her was glad—the defences she had built around herself were as fine as spun glass and one brush of his fingertip would shatter them completely. But her own hands shook with longing to reach out to him. Instead she stroked her fingers over the blood-red petals of her roses and looked down.

'You have a habit of appearing when I least expect it,' she said quietly.

'And you have a habit of *disappearing* when I least expect it.'

Bella took a sharp breath in. The coldness of his tone, the cruelty of his words made her want to retreat into the safe place again, away from the welling hurt. She frowned, keeping her eyes fixed on the furled blood-red hearts of her flowers. 'I don't think I can handle any word games right now, Olivier.'

Or any reminders of what happened between us. 'What did you come for?'

He thrust his hands into his pockets and gave a small shrug, as if he was at a loss to know where to begin to answer. 'To say thank you,' he said abruptly, and then gave a short, bitter laugh. 'Some of your perfect manners must have rubbed off on me a little.'

At the other end of the room Ashley and Miles smiled serenely into each other's eyes and there was a flash of white light. The perfection of the tableau they presented provided a cruel contrast with the desolate wasteland that lay between Bella and Olivier. 'Thank you? Thank you for what?'

His voice was like tautly stretched wire. 'For saving my life.'

Unconsciously, her fingers had tightened around a rose petal and she felt it break off, fleshy and fragrant. Instantly she was back in that empty room with her hand on Olivier's heart, his bleeding heart, as the darkness closed around them.

'I just did what you told me to do,' she said hollowly, looking down at the vivid splash of red in her hand. 'You were in control even then. I would have been useless if you hadn't told me what to do.'

'You did it. That's what matters.'

She shook her head, managing a broken, painful smile. 'It was the least I could do under the circumstances. After all, it was my psychotic relative who nearly killed you, and it was me who told him about the painting, so it was pretty much my fault.'

'No, it wasn't. It was *my* fault,' he said through gritted teeth. 'What happened…was no more than I deserved.'

Finally Bella raised her eyes to his then. His expression was devoid of emotion, and in that moment she almost hated him for the pain he had deliberately, ruthlessly caused her. 'Actually, yes,' she said slowly. 'Yes, you're right, you did deserve it, and I can't pretend that if the gun had been in my hand at that moment I wouldn't have done the same thing. You *used* me, Olivier!'

The last words came out on a low note of anguish. His head went back an inch, and he looked more distant than ever. 'Yes. Yes, that's how it started. You were a Delacroix, and I wanted to hurt you—all of you. I wanted to make you feel as worthless as I'd felt, and I wanted the world to know what you'd done. I deliberately seduced you.' He rubbed a hand suddenly over his face, hiding the emotion that flared there for a second, and gave a bleak laugh. 'But I certainly ended up being punished for it.'

'Yes,' said Bella savagely. 'I'd say that a bullet in the chest just about levels the score.'

He shook his head. 'That wasn't the punishment. That was nothing—an accident, that's all. No, my punishment was falling in love with you,' he said bleakly. 'Falling in love with you and knowing beyond a shadow of a doubt that I'm completely unworthy of you.'

At that moment there was a scraping of chairs and the bride and groom got up from the little table where they had signed their names, ready to go back for the last part of the service. As he left, Miles shot Olivier a brief, suspicious glance, but Ashley ushered him forward, telegraphing Bella a look of silent support behind his back.

She stood, completely motionless. And then, very slowly, she began to move away from him towards the door back into the church, shaking her head as if she was trying to remember something important. There was a frown of deep concentration on her face.

'But you were in love with Veronique…' she said painfully. 'I know you were…'

Instantly Olivier moved in front of her, blocking her path, taking her by the shoulders. His eyes blazed.

'*What?* What makes you think that?'

She forced herself to look up at him, holding herself very stiffly. She was focusing all her effort on blocking out the feel of his hands on her bare shoulders, because if she let herself think about how good it was she would never be able to say this, or be strong enough to face the hurt.

'It was *her* name you were saying in the hospital, Olivier. Not mine. It was *her* you were desperate to see, not me. And then I found out that you were going to meet her in Paris that day… You were on your way to meet her, and you had bought beautiful underwear…'

He gripped her shoulders, shaking her very gently. '*Mon Dieu*… For you!' he moaned. 'The underwear was for *you,* because yours all seems to be black…' He looked down at the bridesmaid's dress which hung from her thin frame. 'Black means unhappy. Unloved. And I *never* want you to feel either of those things again.'

Bella put her hands over her ears to muffle the terrifying, wonderful words, because she knew that if she didn't all sense and reason would be lost. 'But the article!' She was almost shouting, past caring about the wedding service that was continuing without her on the other side of the low door. 'All the time you were collaborating with her on an article to ruin us!'

'That's why I had to meet her that day.' He spoke very slowly and deliberately. His hands moved from her shoulders up to her head, and he was holding her face and forcing her to look up at him as he spoke. 'Bella, I'm sorry. I'm so *sorry.* I was on my way to meet her that day to *stop* the article…' His fingers were twining into her hair as he tilted her head up. 'I had to tell her to pull it because I had no interest in damaging the family that I want to make my own.'

Two tears slid down Bella's cheeks, and from beyond the door there was a triumphant blast of Beethoven as the organ started the recessional.

'What?' she whispered, so softly that it was inaudible. Only the movement of her lips, like a kiss, told him she'd spoken at all.

'I love you,' he said ferociously. 'I want to marry you. *Please.*'

She didn't answer. She couldn't, because her mouth, too close to his to resist any more, had found his, and it was a long, long time before she could say anything again.

When they broke apart her bouquet lay bruised on the floor and all trace of the lipstick so carefully applied by Ashley's make-up artists had completely vanished. But, just as it had been that first night at the Tate, her mouth wore the glow of his touch. She pulled back from him, smiling through the tears.

'Hold on. I think that was a thank you, a sorry *and* a please... all in the space of a few minutes.'

His slow smile made her heart turn over. 'You're a very good influence on me,' he said hoarsely. 'I need you. Without you I'm uncivilised and unfeeling and not very likeable. Say you'll marry me or I'm doomed.'

She looked at him from under her hair. 'That's blackmail...'

He shrugged, flinching slightly he pulled her against his broken ribs, and kissed her hair. 'So what?' he said gruffly. 'It's the way our families have always done it.'

The organist was finishing and the church had emptied when they re-emerged. Beyond the doorway in the frosty afternoon the November darkness was lit up by the glitter of camera flashes and filled with the exuberant peal of bells and the frantic clamour of the press. The church was quiet and still.

They stood together in the middle of the aisle. Bella shivered in the ice-spiked air from the open doorway, and held tightly to the lapels of Olivier's jacket. They looked out into the crush of people, isolated by their raw, selfish need to be alone.

'I should be out there,' Bella murmured. She didn't move.

'You'll freeze,' he growled, kissing the angle of her jaw. 'That dress is completely inadequate for this time of year.' His lips brushed her earlobe, her throat. 'And it's black. I don't ever want to see you in black again.'

His mouth was still on hers as he reached inside his jacket and drew something out, and then in the warm candle glow there was a flash of crimson and emerald as folds of papery silk billowed on the chill air. Bella felt him wrapping the shawl tightly around her trembling shoulders and drawing her into him as the tears rained down her cheeks.

'Where did you find it?' she breathed in awe and love.

'Celia's shop. She wouldn't take my calls, so I had to go and see her to try to find out where you were, and that's when I saw it. It made me think of…'

'*Olympia.* I know. I bought it that morning when you left for Paris. And then…' For a second the anguish crept back into her eyes. 'And then when I got back here I couldn't bear to keep it, so I let it go.'

He folded her into his arms with infinite tenderness. 'You have it back now.'

Bella rested against him for a second, closing her eyes and listening to the strong, steady beat of his heart. 'And you. I have you…' She pulled away from him. 'Did you really just ask me to marry you in there?'

'Yes, but I notice you haven't answered,' he said soberly. 'Does that mean no?'

Joy flooded her, sudden and exhilarating, and she threw her arms out and twirled around in the candlelit church so the silken tassels of the shawl fluttered and the colours swirled and blurred. 'Are you *kidding*? Like I'm going to pass up an opportunity for all of this! I want roses and candles and…and three hundred guests…and a *fabulous* dress, and of course the Delacroix diamonds…'

Olivier leaned back against a pew, watching her steadily. His dark, delicious eyes gleamed. 'Great. Whatever you want.'

She stopped and came back to stand before him. 'Olivier! I'm joking…'

'That's a shame,' he said dryly, brushing her hair back from her face with a fingertip as his lips twitched into a wicked smile. 'I was starting to quite like the idea. That necklace did look very good on you…'

From beneath her eyelashes Bella gave him a look that made his blood sing. 'OK, we'll keep the necklace, then…' Her voice echoed with love. 'But could we possibly leave out all the guests?'

'Deal,' he said gravely. 'And the dress. Could we leave that out too?'

'Oh, yes,' she sighed, reaching up to kiss him gently. 'Yes, please. It's beginning to sound like my idea of a perfect wedding…'

Happy ever after is only the beginning!

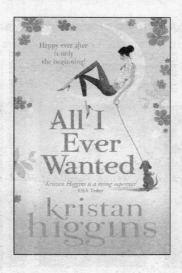

Callie Grey has got a great job, a great man and, fingers crossed, a whopping great diamond—then her boss/boyfriend gives her dream and her sparkly ring to someone else...

She's spent her life reaching for the moon.
Now Callie's let go and, falling among the stars, who will be there to catch her?

www.millsandboon.co.uk

The World of Mills & Boon®

There's a Mills & Boon® series that's perfect for you. We publish ten series and with new titles every month, you never have to wait long for your favourite to come along.

Blaze®
Scorching hot, sexy reads

By Request
Relive the romance with the best of the best

Cherish™
Romance to melt the heart every time

Desire™
Passionate and dramatic love stories